TITLE:	We Are the Perfect Girl
AUTHOR:	Ariel Kaplan
IMPRINT:	Alfred A. Knopf Books for Young Readers
PUBLICATION DATE:	May 21, 2019
ISBN:	978-0-525-64710-2
TENTATIVE PRICE:	$17.99 U.S./$23.99 CAN.
GLB ISBN:	978-0-525-64711-9
GLB TENTATIVE PRICE:	$20.99 U.S./$27.99 CAN.
EBOOK ISBN:	978-0-525-64712-6
PAGES:	384
TRIM SIZE:	5-1/2" x 8-1/4"
AGES:	12 and up

Please send any review or mention of this book to:
Random House Children's Books Publicity Department
1745 Broadway, Mail Drop 9-1
New York, NY 10019

rhkidspublicity@penguinrandomhouse.com

TITLE:	We Are the Perfect Girl
AUTHOR:	Ariel Kaplan
IMPRINT:	Alfred A. Knopf Books for Young Readers
PUBLICATION DATE:	May 21, 2019
ISBN:	978-0-525-64710-2
TENTATIVE PRICE:	$17.99 U.S./$22.99 CAN.
GLB ISBN:	978-0-525-64711-9
GLB TENTATIVE PRICE:	$20.99 U.S./$27.99 CAN.
EBOOK ISBN:	978-0-525-64712-6
PAGES:	384
TRIM SIZE:	5-1/2" x 8-1/4"
AGES:	12 and up

ATTENTION, READER: THESE ARE UNCORRECTED ADVANCE PROOFS BOUND FOR REVIEW PURPOSES. All trim sizes, page counts, months of publication, and prices should be considered tentative and subject to change without notice. Please check publication information and any quotations against the bound copy of the book. We urge this for the sake of editorial accuracy as well as for your legal protection and ours.

Please send any review or mention of this book to:
Random House Children's Books Publicity Department
1745 Broadway, Mail Drop 9-1
New York, NY 10019

rhkidspublicity@penguinrandomhouse.com

WE ARE THE *Perfect* GIRL

WE ARE THE Perfect GIRL

ARIEL KAPLAN

ALFRED A. KNOPF

New York

THIS IS A BORZOI BOOK PUBLISHED BY ALFRED A. KNOPF

Visit us on the Web! GetUnderlined.com

Educators and librarians, for a variety of teaching tools, visit us at
RHTeachersLibrarians.com

Library of Congress Cataloging-in-Publication Data is available upon request.
ISBN 978-0-525-64710-2 (trade) — ISBN 978-0-525-64711-9 (lib. bdg.) —
ISBN 978-0-525-64712-6 (ebook)

The text of this book is set in 11-point Minion.

Printed in the United States of America
May 2019
10 9 8 7 6 5 4 3 2 1
First Edition

Random House Children's Books
supports the First Amendment and celebrates the right to read.

dedication

My heart always timidly hides itself behind my mind. I set out to bring down stars from the sky; then, for fear of ridicule, I stop and pick little flowers of eloquence.

—Edmund Rostand, *Cyrano de Bergerac*

Chapter One

Sometimes, when I'm lying in my bed at night, staring up at the darkened ceiling, I think that the greatest problem in the English-speaking world is that we don't understand love.

It's a lack of vocabulary, that's what I've decided. We have one word: *love.* And we expect it to mean everything, only it's clunky and imprecise and leads to misunderstandings and anger and frustration and tears.

The ancient Greeks, I think, had a better system; multiple love words, a love word for every possible occasion. If you love your friend, you've got *philia.* If you love your mom, you've got *storge.* If you love the sexy, sexy guy who sits across from you in biology, you have *eros.* And if you feel some great, cosmic, unconditional love for God or the Universe or your Fellow Man, you have *agape.*

There are others, actually, but those are the mains. So while in English we may have beautiful sentiments like "Love is love," clearly eros is not storge, unless you are Oedipus and then you have a problem. Anyway, the specificity of the Greek system has always appealed to me.

I guess philia is probably my favorite. I don't exactly understand agape, and eros is not something I ever expect to experience myself. But philia is love for the masses. Everyone has a friend. At least, I hope they do.

My greatest source of philia is Bethany Newman, who has been my best friend since we were eight. I have other friends, of course, but Bethany is special because she looks at me and sees me exactly as I am. I really philia her for that.

I was philia-ing her a little less this morning, though, when I woke up to find her sitting on my kneecaps. She was smiling at me with a smile that was too wide to look at first thing upon waking. It was more like a midafternoon smile. An "I've already had two cups of coffee" smile.

"Ow," I said.

"The pool opens today," she replied. She bounced a little. "Did you forget?"

I kind of had, being asleep and all. Our town had splurged and installed a heating system in one of our outdoor pools, which meant it opened on the first of May instead of over Memorial Day like the rest of the pools in the area. I remembered that we'd talked about going last night, but I didn't remember agreeing to wake up at the crack of dawn for it.

"My knees don't bend that way," I said, shoving her off. "Why are you waking me up to tell me about the pool?"

"We were supposed to go shopping!" she said. "Half an hour ago! It's 11:30."

"It is not," I said, but it did seem kind of bright out. I'd set my alarm for ten. Hadn't I? I was pretty sure I had. I felt around on the bedside table for my glasses and then for my phone. "Where's my phone?"

"I have no idea. Come on, Aphra, get up."

I sat up slowly. It wasn't regular shopping Bethany wanted to do; it was *bathing suit* shopping, which is the worst kind of shopping. Bright lights. Spandex. Those hygienic liners that don't make me feel any better about trying on a suit 50 other people have already tried on, even with underwear.

I had agreed to go, though, because Bethany came to me last week with a Plan, and Bethany so seldom has Plans that I felt like I had to go along with it.

The Plan was agreed upon the night of junior prom. Bethany and I went together with a bunch of other girls, and while we were there, we saw Greg D'Agostino with a bunch of his friends from the swim team. He was in a tux, and he looked, possibly, even hotter than usual.

Bethany really wanted to ask him to dance and spent nearly the whole night trying to work up the nerve. Around 10:30, she decided to walk by him during a slow song and hope he'd take the hint.

Except by then, he'd already left.

So now we had a plan to throw Bethany's bikini-clad body in front of Greg D'Agostino until he magically notices her, falls in love (technically, in eros, but Bethany doesn't appreciate the Greek system like I do), and then . . . I'm not really sure what happens after that. I guess maybe he'll ask her out? And then they'll go out. And then Bethany will, with any luck, be able to speak more than four words to him.

This seems a little unlikely to me, but I haven't said anything because I'm sure Bethany already knows that.

I pried myself out of bed, jammed my contacts into my eyes—I swear, this is not vanity, glasses just annoy me—put on some clothes, and went off in search of my phone, which was in the hands of my little brother, who was using it to play Minecraft. Walnut the cat was curled up on his lap while Kit used him as a furry lap desk.

"Why are you on my phone?" I asked, pointing at the laptop he'd abandoned on the coffee table.

Without looking up, he said, "I hit my time limit."

There are parental controls on the family computer that cut Kit off after an hour so he doesn't rot his little brain. "So do something else," I said. "How did you get my phone?"

"It was by your bed."

"You can't just steal it while I'm sleeping!"

"You weren't using it."

"Did my alarm go off?"

"Oh." He looked up. "I didn't know what that was. I turned it off." He switched off his game and handed the phone to me, looking contrite, because Bethany and I row on the crew team and he knows that we usually have regattas on Saturday mornings. "Sorry. Did I make you late for your boat race?"

"I'm not mad," I said, patting his little head. Kit is only nine, and I think he has the softest hair in the whole world, like the down on a baby duck. Someday he probably won't want me to pat his head anymore, so I'm getting my Kit-hair fix now, while I still can. Plus, he's the only sibling I have that I'm on speaking terms with, and I'm not willing to let a hijacked cell phone get in the way of that. "We didn't race today," I said. "Where's Mom and Dad?"

"Dad's at the store. Mom's asleep."

Both of my parents are professors at George Mason: Mom teaches English, Dad teaches medieval history, and Mom has an evening class on Fridays and likes to sleep in on Saturday mornings. This was a little late, though, even for her.

"You should wake her up," I said. "I'm leaving with Bethany."

"Can I go with you?"

"You'll be super bored," I said. "We're going shopping."

"For candy?" he asked hopefully.

"Could we do candy?" I asked Bethany. "That actually does sound better."

"No candy," Bethany said. "Suits." She leaned down and we gave him the Kit Kiss, which we've been giving him since he was a baby, where I kiss one cheek and Bethany kisses the other. Probably someday he won't let us do that anymore, either. "We're going to the pool later, if you want to come."

"Can I play on your phone there?"

"No," I said. "But you can swim."

He made a face.

"I'll buy you a Fudgsicle," I said.

He made another face.

"I'll let you eat half my cookie-wich, too," I offered.

"If you let me eat the whole thing, I promise not to steal your phone again."

"Sorry," I said. "I don't negotiate with terrorists."

"You're mean."

I ruffled his hair again, saying, "The meanest."

30 minutes later, we were ensconced in a dressing room in the Wet Seal at the mall.

I stood holding an armful of Bethany's discarded bathing

suits while she stuffed herself into a one-piece with these weird spiderweb cutouts in the middle.

"That's going to give you the worst tan lines ever," I said.

She looked in the mirror. Bethany has, like, actual abs, but even she could not make this work. "This is hideous," she said. "Who designed this?"

"It's like the *Charlotte's Web* model," I said. "Only it should give you tan lines that say *Terrific*! Or *Radiant*!"

"Or *Some Pig*," she said, and we both cackled. The woman in the stall next to us made a *hrmph* noise.

"Shhh," I said. "There is no laughing while swimsuit shopping. This is very serious business."

"Serious," she said, dropping her voice.

"The fate of the world may be at stake," I said. "I mean, really. That suit could kill someone."

"The person wearing it, or the person looking at it?"

"Possibly both," I said. She was already peeling the straps over her shoulders, because we've been friends so long that nudity is no longer a thing between us. I handed her the next one, which was a blue bikini with hibiscus flowers on it. She put it on and turned to look in the mirror. "I like this one," she said. "The top's really supportive." She gave an experimental wiggle and nothing fell out.

"Looks good to me," I said.

"Here, they have one in red," she said, taking a suit with white polka dots out of the pile. "You should try it. It's on clearance and everything."

"Oh," I said. "No."

"You always wear red."

This is true. . . . I always buy a red bathing suit. A red one-piece bathing suit. I like a utilitarian approach to swimwear, which means not having to put sunscreen in locations I would prefer not to be seen touching in public.

Unfortunately, they did not have any red one-pieces at the Wet Seal that day. Bethany thrust the bikini at me. "It's your color," she said. "And it's only 12 bucks."

"Fine," I said. I put it on and then stepped out to look in the three-way mirror. There was a salesgirl out there putting discarded suits on hangers; the *hrmph*ing woman seemed to have exited the premises to find a more serious bathing suit store. I stood in front of the mirror and held out my arms to either side for Bethany's inspection.

"Oh," she said.

I poked myself in the rear. The leg holes were so tight and cut so high I looked a little like a segmented insect. "I appear to have grown a second butt," I said. "I don't think it's a good look for me."

"You need a bigger bottom," the salesgirl said. "But the top's fine. I mean, that side's fine." She pointed at my left boob.

I glanced down. Yeah. So the thing is, one of my boobs is a cup size bigger than the other. I've been informed—numerous times!—that this is very common. Very common. Also: annoying. I have discovered that if I tighten the straps on the left side of my bra, it is mostly not noticeable when I have clothes on. But in a bikini? I am exquisitely lopsided. My left boob looked great. My right looked . . . kind of sad.

"I can give you a cookie," the salesgirl said.

"I love cookies," I said. "I'm not sure that would help, though. Unless you can make all the fat from the cookie metabolize into my right boob."

She laughed. "No, I mean, it's a little insert that goes in the bottom of the cup and makes your smaller side a little bigger. It'll just even you out."

"Won't that be noticeable?"

"Nah, it's silicone," she said. "They look super natural."

"Okay," I said. "Let's see the fake boob."

"It's not a fake boob," Bethany whispered as the clerk ducked out. "It's a cookie."

"That is not a real distinction," I said.

The salesgirl reappeared with a little moon-shaped piece of beige silicone, which she directed me to put in the bottom of the bikini cup, plus a bigger-sized bottom.

"Wow," Bethany said. "Look at your rack!"

I looked in the mirror. I had to admit, my torso had never looked this good. There was still an awful lot of my butt on display, though.

"I don't know," I said.

"Get it," she said. "Get it, get it, and we can go to the pool later."

I poked the cookie through my bikini top. "Is this really going to stay put?" I asked. "Like, even if I go swimming?"

"It will," the clerk said. "Promise."

I thought, *Do you work on commission?* But I didn't say it, because it seemed kind of rude, and also because I couldn't imagine what commission she'd get for selling a 12-dollar suit. Instead, I just stared at myself in the three-way mirror, turning right and then left, mostly checking out my chest, which did look amazing. I tried to ignore the other parts of me that looked less good. Of which there were several.

I have never, myself, sat down and catalogued my many

imperfections, but if you are a girl-person and you live in the world, people feel compelled to let you know this stuff. So I am aware that, in addition to the lopsided boobs, my shoulders are too wide (rowing crew has not helped with this) and my eyes are too small; I have a weak chin, no cheekbones, stumpy legs, and, oh yes, a big bump on the bridge of my nose, which itself is not particularly small.

Most days, none of this bothers me. I know that's a radical position, to be a homely girl who does not secretly dream of a makeover, but I truly don't. Of course, part of that is because I can do all the extreme makeovers on earth, but nothing will fundamentally change what I look like. I will look like me, but with extra makeup. Me, but a tiny bit thinner. Me, but with a new haircut.

On the whole, this is not something I mind, because knowing this gives me license not to obsess about it too much. If it's not a thing I can change, then there's no point in worrying about it, and it's not like my self-worth is tied to whether random guys want to hook up with me.

I'm actually a very secure and happy person, and I know this because I tell it to my therapist every Monday for 50 minutes.

I pushed my hair behind my ears and checked out my reflection. It was a radical act, to be the homely girl in the red bikini. It was a giant middle finger to men and the world and my fellow swimmers at the Hidden Oaks community pool.

In my ear, Bethany said, "Get it."

So I bought the bikini. And then I went to the pool with Bethany.

• • •

The cookie in the right side of my bikini top felt kind of nasty and sweaty, but it made my boobs look great, so I tried to ignore it. We gave our passes to Shannon Garcia, who goes to school with us, and went through the locker room.

We walked out onto the pool deck. Kit, who had gone through the men's room, ran off to join some kids from his school who were playing Marco Polo in the shallow end. "Don't forget about my Fudgsicle!" he called.

"Don't run on the deck!" I called back, and we watched as he did a belly flop next to his friends, who screamed at the splash of chilly water. There's something kind of liberating about seeing little kids at the pool; they're just there to have fun and that's it.

Bethany grabbed my arm. "Ohmigod," she said. "Ohmigod."

"What?"

She jerked her head toward the guard chair. I shaded my eyes and looked up at the bronzed body of the lifeguard. I had to squint against the sun to see who it was—he was wearing sunglasses and his face was in profile. Of course, it was Greg D'Agostino, every bit as handsome as he'd been the last time I'd seen him. You know. Yesterday. I'm not sure why Bethany was acting like seeing him was a surprise, since that was literally the entire purpose for our being at the pool: to see Greg, or, more to the point, for Greg to see Bethany.

We were not the only people who had noticed Greg in his half-naked splendor. There was a whole contingent of girls sitting opposite the pool from him, in the best viewing spot. They weren't even trying to pretend not to stare. Greg was trying his best to pretend not to notice. Or maybe he really was watching the pool. Which I guess was his job.

He glanced up as we walked over and took seats to his left.

His eyes barely stopped on me or my perfect, symmetrical chest. But they went to Bethany in her blue bikini and stuck there.

I'd expected that, honestly. Bethany is legitimately the prettiest girl I have ever seen; I suspect she's probably the prettiest girl most people have ever seen. I swear to God I'm not jealous, though. I've seen the way people treat her for it, and in my opinion, it's actually better to be plain.

Bethany noticed him watching and stood up a little straighter. Which basically means she stuck her chest out a little farther.

I rolled my eyes, just a little. I couldn't see Greg's, obviously, because of the sunglasses, but his face was still pointed in our direction. I'd already spread my towel out on one of the deck chairs and sat down, but Bethany was still standing up. She cocked a hip, propped a toe on the chair, and started to spray sunscreen on her leg.

I snorted, because she'd already put on sunscreen before we left the house. I watched as she repeated the process with the other leg.

"He's still looking," she hissed. "Do yours, too."

"He's not looking at *my* legs," I said. I was already sitting on my very exposed butt and I was not getting up for anything. I pulled out my AP Euro reading, which was Dostoyevsky's *Crime and Punishment*, and dropped it on my chair. It was a big book. It went *thunk*.

"Why did you bring that? That isn't a beach book."

"We aren't at the beach, and I have to write an essay on it for next week."

She shoved the book away from me and pulled her bikini straps down her shoulders. "Do my back," she whispered. "And make it look good."

This whole business was shockingly un-Bethany-like.

"Did you get a personality transplant since yesterday?" I asked.

"Shhh. He's still looking."

"Possibly because you woke up this morning and decided to become a complete attention whore."

"Shhh!"

But I was already spraying her back down. "This is ridiculous," I said. "You're going to fall out of your top."

"He stopped looking," she said. "Can you get him to look over here again?"

"Oh, Bethany!" I shouted, making a show of rubbing in the sunscreen. "Your skin is so soft!"

"Not like that," she hissed. I glanced up at Greg, who had just moved to hide a smile behind his hand.

I'd made Greg D'Agostino smile.

I pulled Bethany's straps up and sat back with my book, glancing down toward the shallow end to make sure Kit was still playing with his friends. "I've done my duty," I said. "I'm going to read now."

She took a few deep breaths, like she was psyching herself up for something, and then said, "Let's go off the board."

I blinked at her a few times and shut my book. This was another un-Bethany-like thing to suggest. "What?"

"Come on," she said. "I'll look stupid if I go by myself."

I was about to say *You'll look stupid anyway,* but she was doing pleading Bethany eyes, which work as well on me as on anyone else. Also, it was kind of hot, and I was starting to leave sweat marks on my towel.

"Fine," I said. "I'll go off the board." I got in line behind Bethany and a couple of other girls, who were trying to get Greg's attention with flips and twists. Bethany did an elegant swan dive. I got up on the board.

Greg's eyes were still on Bethany as she climbed the ladder, flipping her shiny black hair over her shoulder.

I felt something weird.

I tried to catalog the feeling. It was definitely not philia. I was jealous. I am never jealous of Bethany, but right then, for some reason, as I stood at the end of the board with my perfect chest in my red twelve-dollar bikini, I wanted, just once, for Greg to look at me. That's it. Just for him to acknowledge that I was even there, that I existed, and that my boobs looked really, really good. I bounced my way down the board. One major jump at the end, and I catapulted myself up in the air for the biggest cannonball Greg would see all summer.

At the last second, I heard Bethany call "Wait!" I twisted around to see what was wrong and ended up landing flat on my back.

Which caused the clasp of my top to pop open.

It occurred to me, belatedly, that there might have been a reason this suit was on clearance.

I managed to clasp it again before I surfaced, and I hoped no one had actually seen anything important. It had been a huge splash—my back still stung from it—so hopefully that had been enough to cover my nakedness.

Bethany was standing at the top of the ladder.

"What is wrong with you?" I asked.

"Nothing," she said. "Uh, are you okay?"

"Yeah." I dog-paddled over to where she was standing and pulled myself out of the water. "What were you screaming about?"

"It's just, I remembered something. Like, a reason you might not want to go off the board."

"You were the one who told me to do it!"

"Yeah, because I forgot. . . ." I pulled myself out of the pool, and she said. "Oh, no."

"What? What?"

She stared pointedly at my chest. I looked down.

I had one full-looking boob and one that looked sadly deflated.

"Oh, no," I said. "Where is it?"

We stood side by side looking down into the water. By now, some little kids had lined up and were splashing in behind me.

"I don't see it," she whispered. "Do you think silicone floats or sinks?"

"I don't know!"

"Well, if it were floating, we'd see it, right? So it must be under there somewhere." She prodded me with her elbow. "Go get it."

"What?"

I had to move out of the way of the ten-year-old boy coming up the ladder behind me. "Would you move?" he said.

"Sorry," I said.

"Just dive in and get it!" Bethany whispered.

"I don't have any goggles! You get it."

"I don't have any goggles, either, and it's your boob!"

"It's not a boob! It's a cookie! And it was your idea! You get it!"

"What am I going to do with it? I'll look pretty suspicious climbing out of the deep end with a fake boob"—I gave her a dirty look—"I mean, a cookie in my hand. Just dive in, find it, put it back in your top, and get out again."

"How long do you think I'm capable of holding my breath?" I asked, but I turned to one of the little kids in line and said, "Can I borrow your goggles?" and someone else in line ahead of me said "OW!" and I looked up and realized one of the other little shits—kids! I mean kids!—had thrown my fake boob in his face.

"What was that for?" he shouted, picking it up and throwing it back.

"OW!" said the first kid. "I found it in the pool! It's a tan jellyfish!"

"It doesn't have any testicles," one of the other kids pointed out.

"You mean *tentacles!*"

"That's what I said!"

He threw it back and it hit the kid next to him in the stomach, who shouted, "You *suck*, Cooper!" and then pelted him back.

"Do something," Bethany whispered. "Do something, do something, do something."

"Boys," I said in my best babysitter voice. "Can I please have the . . . uh . . . jellyfish?"

"We found it!"

"I just want to check something," I said.

"You're gonna steal it!"

"I want to see what brand it is!" I tried grabbing it from the nearest kid, but now the little boys were in full-on keep-away mode, and he threw it over my head to someone else, which was when it hit Greg D'Agostino square in the chest.

And for one long, horrible second, thanks to the viscosity of wet silicone and the terrible luck I was born with, it stuck there.

"Oh God," I said.

"Oh God," Bethany said.

The fake boob dropped to the floor of the guard stand. Greg picked it up between his thumb and forefinger and looked at it.

Greg D'Agostino was touching my boob.

It was a lot less enjoyable than I would have expected.

I tried to decide which was worse: claiming the boob or walking away and hoping that he maybe thought it belonged to someone else. "We'll go sit down," I muttered to Bethany. "And we'll walk slowly. Just pretend it doesn't exist."

"Okay," she said. "I'm walking in front of you. We're walking. . . . We're walking. . . . Hey, do you want a Dr Pepper?"

"Not. Now."

"Right, sorry." She sat in her chair, and I sat next to her. Greg D'Agostino blew the whistle for break and climbed down from the guard stand.

He was yelling at the little boys, who were trying to get my boob back from him. "It's ours! It's ours!" they shouted.

"It's not yours!"

"Yuh-huh!"

"Do you guys want a time-out? It's break. Go sit down."

"We want the jellyfish!"

"Do I need to call your mom again, Cooper?"

"You suck!"

"I told you to sit down!"

Cooper stuck out his tongue, but Greg already had his back

to him, because he was walking around the edge of the pool. Toward us.

"Your book," Bethany whispered. "Get your book."

I grabbed *Crime and Punishment* from the foot of my chair and opened to a random page. As Greg approached, I turned the page and said airily, "I just love Russian novels, don't you?"

"American novels are so short," she agreed nervously.

"I mean, why bother? You might as well read the back of a cereal box."

"I know!"

By now, Greg was standing at the foot of my chair. I swallowed.

He said, "Hi."

"Oh," I said. "Hello. We were just discussing the merits of Russian literature. Thoughts? Opinions?" I glanced up at him. He really was beautiful. Dark wavy hair. Good muscle tone. Excellent teeth. "Revelations?"

He glanced at my book. He said, "Лично, я думаю что работа Чехова немного более актуальна."

I . . . had not seen that coming. I glanced at Bethany, who I knew did not speak Russian any better than I did, and she raised her eyebrows fractionally.

He still had my boob in his hand, this beautiful, barechested, Russian-speaking boy. I wasn't sure whether this was extremely funny or extremely sad, but I guess my better nature won out, because I started laughing. I hoped Greg didn't think I was laughing at him. Bethany shot me a horrified look.

I only know one Russian phrase; my father went to St. Petersburg for a history conference a few years ago, and I convinced him that this was the only thing he really needed to learn out of his phrasebook. I asked, maybe a little suggestively, "Скажите пожалуйста, где туалет?"

He laughed.

He tossed my fake boob to me. It landed on page 327 with a splat. I stared at it. He said, "Nice cannonball. By the way." He smiled. Such good teeth.

And then he walked away.

"What did you say to him?" Bethany asked out of the side of her mouth. "It sounded hot."

I put my sunglasses on and tried to look as cool as a lopsided girl in a discount-bin bikini can look. "I asked him where the bathroom is."

She looked momentarily stricken, and then she laughed and so did I. I said, "You're lucky I philia you so much."

"I philia you too," Bethany said. Then, pointing at the cookie, she added, "So are you going to put it back in or what?"

I picked it up, letting it dangle between my thumb and forefinger as if it really were a jellyfish I'd found in the pool. It was kind of gummy and awful. I looked down at my chest. I said, "Sorry, girls." And then I shouted, "HEY, COOPER!" and when he looked up, I thwacked him in the nose with my boob. He grabbed it, whooped, and went off to play catch with his friends.

Chapter Two

I first met Bethany back in second grade; she was the shiest kid in the class and I was the loudest, so Mrs. White stuck us next to each other in hopes that we'd rub off on each other.

I didn't really have any other friends then. The other girls in our class called me obnoxious. I talked too loud, I told too many jokes, I was too sarcastic, and the Future Pearl Clutchers of America were not having it.

I remember the day Mrs. White moved our seats. I'd gotten in trouble three times in the last hour for talking without raising my hand (she called me Aphra the Gabber because I would not shut up). So she moved me up to the front of the room to sit next to the girl the other kids called Bethany Boring because she never talked at all. "Maybe you two can find a happy medium," she'd said.

I'd leaned over to Bethany and stage-whispered, "Mrs. White has chalk on her butt, pass it on."

Bethany hadn't answered. But she'd smiled. She'd told me later that I'd been the first kid to talk to her in weeks.

So we'd sat together at lunch that day and just clicked, because she didn't mind if I talked too much, and I didn't mind if she was too nervous to talk back. I'd maintained both sides of a conversation about *My Little Pony*, until the very end, she'd whispered, "I'm a Fluttershy and you're a Rainbow Dash."

I'd liked that, even though I'd always thought of myself more as a Twilight Sparkle. So we sat together again the next day, and the next. My mom once said I had to grow into my personality, and I guess she was right; no one appreciates a smart mouth on a seven-year-old, but at 17 it's kind of an asset. But Bethany liked me just the way I was, right from the beginning, which is probably why I never had the loud beaten out of me. She gave me permission to be myself. And since I was never jealous of how pretty she was or put off by how quiet she was (the other girls used to call her a snob, which was just plain stupid), I hoped I did the same thing for her.

After we got back from the pool, we made Kit wash the Fudgsicle off his face and the three of us lay down on the couch to watch some cartoons. We were two episodes into *Steven Universe* when my phone pinged with an alert that meant someone had used the app I was designing for my computer science class.

Kit had fallen asleep and Bethany was dozing, too—I guess being ogled by Greg D'Agostino is pretty tiring—so I extracted myself from their tangle of legs and went to my room to use my laptop.

The class is called Basic App Design, and I've been working on the final project for the last month or so. It's due in two weeks, and it's worth 35% of my grade, and it is totally not working.

The premise of my project is this: last year, some kids in the computer science department at GMU created an open-source chatbot program and gave it a twitter account. It was called Lola, and it was supposed to learn language the more you talked to it. It's a simple enough algorithm, and I had an idea to use their base code and turn it into an app. Essentially, it's an advice app.

Basically, it scans for keywords, and then it replies with customized advice. So, like, if you tell it something with the words "cheating" and "boyfriend" in it, it tells you to break up with him (which is generally the best course no matter who's the one cheating). If you tell it something with the word "grade," it tells you to study harder. The trick is that it's supposed to remember what you asked, so that the next time you log in it asks you a follow-up question, and over time it's supposed to learn patterns and anticipate issues that tend to go together, like poor self-esteem and anxiety. It's not like it's a substitute for a real therapist, but I know firsthand how hard it can be to find one of those.

My chatbot is called Deanna, after the counselor from *Star Trek*. She was supposed to talk, but I ran out of time, and the text-to-speech software was making the app take too long to download, so now she just types at you. What you see, if you download it, is a cartoon picture of Deanna Troi, in her blue officer's uniform, and then her advice appears in a dialogue bubble.

In a few weeks, I'm supposed to turn in a copy of the app, along with copies of the advice Deanna has given to at least ten people. The app is anonymous, because no one will ask for advice if they know the person at the other end, and last Friday I'd put flyers up at school, advertising the program.

I sat down and pulled up Deanna's stats on my computer.

I jumped a little. 46 people had downloaded the app, and

five of them had actually used it. I went to check the logs, to see if she'd actually learned anything yet.

The first person had written, *I hate my mom.*

Deanna had written back, *Relationships with parental figures can be very important, especially to the bourgeoning adolescent. Have you tried telling your mom how you feel?*

No, stupid. She's a total skank who left my dad for her personal trainer.

For example, Deanna continued blithely, *you might say, "I am having difficult feelings right now. Is this a good time for us to talk?"*

No response.

The next person had written, *Your a stupid stupid stupid stupid stupid stupid stupid stupid ho.*

Deanna had written, *Intelligence comes in many forms. Einstein once said, "If you judge a fish by its ability to climb a tree, it will live its whole life believing that it is stupid."*

Stupid beyotch.

This was a problem. And not just because it should have been "You're."

The way the original programming—a two-way AI—works is that it learns by talking to people. She learns how to map questions onto different responses. So, for example, over time she learns that *Hi, Hello, Hola,* and *Good afternoon* are all greetings and answers appropriately. Basically, she is supposed to determine a user's intent and then find a way to respond.

But if her users are teaching her that "Your a stupid stupid stupid stupid stupid stupid stupid stupid ho" is a greeting . . . that's not good. I'd already blacklisted every four-letter word I could think of to keep her from developing a potty mouth, but

I couldn't blacklist *stupid,* because that was something Deanna might need to talk about at some point, like if someone was feeling bad because they flunked a test or whatever. I made a note to blacklist *beyotch, ho,* and *skank,* since those words, at least, she wouldn't need.

The next message said: *I think I have herpes.*

Deanna said, *An STD is a communicable illness like any other. It's important, though, to get immediate treatment and notify your current and former sex partners.* And then she gave the number for the closest Planned Parenthood.

The response was, *K thanks.*

Well, at least she helped someone.

I got the ping of an email and saw that it was from Delia, who is my older sister. She's a freshman at the University of Virginia. The subject line said, *Hi.*

Here is the story of Delia Brown, the abridged version:

Delia is barely two years older than me. We looked so much alike as babies that in our old photos, no one can tell which of us is which. And we looked alike until high school, when Delia did some weird business with her eyebrows and started going in for Brazilian blowouts every three weeks. She still looked like me, mostly, but with overly groomed eyebrows and shinier hair.

"Why are you doing that?" I'd asked her.

"I like it better," she'd said. "You'll understand when you're older."

And then, the summer after she graduated from high school, she informed my parents that she'd been saving all her birthday and babysitting and summer job money for the last four years, and she was getting a nose job.

"What?" they'd said.

"What?" I'd said.

But she was 18 and it was her money, so one Tuesday in June my sister went into one of those outpatient surgery centers looking just like me, and a few hours later she came out looking like we were unrelated.

I have not spoken to her since.

I mean, it's not like it's been that hard to avoid her. Two months later she went off to college with three boxes of clothes, a new laptop, and a nose that looked like a stupid ski slope.

The worst thing is, before this happened, I never really hated my nose. It has a bump on the bridge, and it's definitely bigger than average, but so what? It's a nose. I use it to breathe in and out, and it generally works pretty well for that unless I have a cold. It's also useful for holding up my sunglasses. When I was little, my father always said it looked aristocratic, and in my small-child brain, it must have been true because Dad wouldn't lie about something like that.

I mean, I didn't think it was perfect or anything. But among my litany of less-than-attractive features, it didn't stand out as anything awful.

But now, every time I look at my nose in the mirror, I think, *Delia thinks you are so ugly she paid $4,000 to some guy to break you with a hammer and cut you up.* That's what they do, you know. They pump you full of anesthesia, they break your nose with a hammer, and then they go at you with sharp objects. I looked it up before Delia had it done, when I was trying to talk her out of it.

"Do you know what they're going to do to you?" I'd asked.

"Of course I know. But it's worth it."

"How is it worth it?"

But Delia couldn't answer, because the truth was she thought it was worth it to get bashed in the face and cut up so that she wouldn't have to look like me anymore.

And now she had the unmitigated gall to say hi to me on email.

I deleted the message without reading it and went back to Deanna's source code. When someone typed the keyword "sister," I programmed her to respond: *Genetic relationships aren't everything.*

Chapter Three

On Monday afternoon, I was in Latin staring at Greg D'Agostino, who sits toward the front of the room, wondering when he'd learned Russian. Our school doesn't teach it, and I didn't think he'd learned it at home. We were translating Ovid in pairs; he was working with Mitzi Schwartz, who seemed to be getting distracted staring at his face. I was working with John O'Malley, who is the coxswain for the boys' eight and who was definitely *not* getting distracted staring at *my* face.

Bethany has had a thing for Greg for a few months now, and, I mean, it's not for nothing. He's hot. He's athletic. And besides that, he's actually nice. I don't think I've ever heard him say a mean word to anyone, ever. Except one time.

That one time.

I'm sure he doesn't remember it, but it will stay with me until I'm an old lady drowning in half-done knitting projects and a dozen mismatched cats.

It was eighth grade. We were in the health unit of PE, and our teacher, Mr. Fordham, put us in pairs to practice doing the

Heimlich. We were supposed to pair up by gender, but we had an odd number and I'd come to class late—I can't remember why; doctor's appointment, maybe—so I'd been the odd duck. I'd ended up paired with Kieran Thompson. He looked at me. I looked at him. I was taller than he was, and probably stronger, too, and when he looked at me and said, "Ugh," I briefly thought about slugging him. But I pretended I didn't hear him, until he went to put his arms around me and said, to Nick Tanner, who was next to us, "At least I don't have to worry about getting a boner, right?"

I yanked away from him, and then I really did think about punching him. The thing is, I wasn't even sure which was worse: the idea of Kieran Thompson getting a boner (ugh) or the idea that his *not* having one was some kind of an insult. I was ready with about five quips concerning the inconsequentialness of the state of his dick, or the inconsequentialness of his dick itself, or why he thought anyone needed to hear about it when clearly no one was asking to see it. Before I could pick a comeback, though, Greg D'Agostino, who was Nick Tanner's partner, said, "You're such a dumbass." Then, to Nick, he said, "Dude, go switch with Aphra so she doesn't have to worry about Kieran's boner."

Nick made a face. "I don't want to have to worry about Kieran's boner, either," he said, but since he was actually a pretty decent guy, he went over and stood next to Kieran, saying, "Keep your dick away from me, please."

Greg walked up to me. I felt . . . weird. On the one hand, I was grateful. On the other, I felt kind of pathetic.

"I could have handled that," I said.

"Of course you could," he said. "He's a dipshit." Then he shrugged and said, "Can you speak? Can you breathe?"

I stared at him for a second before I realized this was the script for the Heimlich. I bugged my eyes, stuck out my tongue, and put my hands around my own throat. He laughed.

He had, I thought, a really nice laugh.

And then he wrapped his arms around me from behind, put his fist in my diaphragm, and pumped three times.

It was, to date, the most erotically charged moment of my life.

I'm sure I must have Heimliched him next, but I don't remember it all that well because of the searing feeling of Greg D'Agostino's chest against my back. There is some part of me that's still back in that health room, with the posters that say HUGS, NOT DRUGS! and CHLAMYDIA IS NOT A FLOWER! feeling Greg's arms around me and his breath on my neck.

After that, whenever Bethany mentioned Greg, I went kind of quiet. I started to notice things about him I hadn't before, like the way he sometimes smiled with one side of his mouth when he was alone, as if he was thinking of some private joke. Or how he came to school with his hair still wet from the pool because he swam on some year-round club team. That day in the health room, he'd smelled like chlorine, and ever since then, the smell of swimming pools has always made me a little giddy. Which is stupid. It's stupid. But there you are.

I remembered, after a moment of staring too long, that I was supposed to be translating Ovid, not waxing poetic about having once received the Heimlich from Greg. Next to me, John was saying, "Okay—Miratur et haurit pectore Pygmalion simulati corporis ignes. What do you think?"

I said, "Yes. Please."

John snorted a little. "Take a picture," he said. "It'll last longer."

"What?" I asked. He nodded in Greg's direction. "I wasn't looking at Greg."

"Oh, of course you weren't. You were watching Mitzi sweat through her shirt."

"She's not—" I started, but then I stopped talking because I looked, and she was. I felt legitimately sorry for her. If I'd been partnered with Greg, I might have sweat through my shirt, too, especially since we'd been working on the part of *Metamorphoses* that talks about Pygmalion feeling up his statue of the ideal woman, which he apparently did repeatedly and, like, with vigor.

"Should we get her some water?" I asked.

Mitzi looked up and saw John and me looking at her and mouthed "Help."

I shouted, "Hey, Mitzi, can you help us out with this noun? John thinks it's *potato,* he's so dumb."

"I know the Romans didn't have potatoes!" he protested, but Mitzi was already bolting from her desk. Ms. Wright, the teacher, ignored us, because she was grading Friday's quizzes at the front of the room.

Mitzi skidded into an empty chair next to us. "I'm not sure how much more of that I can stand," she said. "I don't want to objectify him, but I can't even help it. I'm just, like, flop sweat all the way down."

"At least you're good at Latin," John said. "Just dazzle him with your declension skills."

"Oh," she said. "No. That's the worst part. He's, like, fluent. He already did the whole thing. I just sat there like a sweaty statue." She winced. "I mean, not like the statue in the story. The sex statue. I mean, Pygmalion's basically a misogynistic creeper who made a sex statue, right? That is what's going on here?"

Mitzi was saying *sex statue* way too loud, and people were starting to stare, although we were all reading the same poem, so I'm not sure why anyone was surprised. Pygmalion *was* a misogynistic creeper, and he totally did make a sex statue.

"Fluent?" I asked. "In Latin?"

"Yeah. I don't even know why he's in this class."

"Hang on," I said, and took my notebook up to Mitzi's empty desk.

"Salve," I said to Greg.

"Salve," he said. I wondered if he was remembering my fake boob incident. Probably. I fiddled a little with my bra strap. "So how is it that you speak Russian *and* Latin?"

"Lots of people speak more than one language," he said.

"Actually, you speak three. By my count. Because of the English."

"Actually, it's more like six."

"Six!"

He shrugged. "Everybody has a hobby."

"So, what, you take classes?"

"Well, I've always known Spanish, because of my mom." I remembered that Greg's mom is from Buenos Aires. I've seen her a couple of times at Back to School night. She's tall and beautiful, which is probably where Greg gets it from. "Plus, I take some classes at NVCC, and I did a little studying on my own."

NVCC is Northern Virginia Community College. "You take classes at NVCC?"

"Yeah, two. I'm dual enrolled."

"Huh. So what other languages do you know? Besides the Spanish and the Russian."

"Oh. Uh, well, Latin, obviously, plus Italian, and I guess Mandarin, but I'm not very good at that yet."

"Holy shit."

"Well, the romance languages are all pretty easy once you know the first one, so I mostly learned those on my own."

"Obviously," I said, a little incredulously. He'd taught himself all those languages? Did people know this about him?

Just then, the alarm went off on my phone. I leave school 15 minutes early on Mondays because I have therapy. I thought about ignoring the alarm, but Greg had already heard it.

"Time to turn back into a pumpkin?" he asked.

I shut it off in my pocket. *Sextilingual.* That was the word. And here I thought I was some kind of prodigy for taking AP Latin as a junior.

"I am always a pumpkin," I said. I grabbed my bag and waved at Ms. Wright, who barely acknowledged me as I left the room.

On my way out, Greg called, "Hey!" and when I turned around, he said, "До свидания." *Do svidaniya. See you later.*

"До свидания," I said, and shut the door behind me. In my dad's 20-year-old Honda—he and my mother drive to work together most days—I took out a pen and wrote *Russian, Latin, Spanish, Italian, Mandarin* on my left palm. I'd mention it to Bethany. Bethany took Spanish. That was something she and Greg had in common.

• • •

I started therapy last summer after the whole Delia situation went down. I became kind of an angry person for a while, partly because I was mad at Delia and partly because I had to live with the person I was mad at, but yelling at her about it would have meant talking to her, and I really just didn't want anything to do with her. So one day I bumped into my baby brother and made him drop a glass of milk, and he called me a poopoohead and I blew up and called him a rotten little asshole.

I still feel bad about that. I remember him crying, because no one in our family ever yells at Kit; he's the baby, and he's actually a pretty nice kid. And no amount of saying I'm sorry can ever make up for the fact that I called an eight-year-old an asshole.

My parents stuck me in therapy a few weeks later. "You need a release valve," my mom said, and I didn't really want to go, but if talking to a therapist meant I wouldn't blow up at Kit anymore, it was the least I could do.

Dr. Pascal works at the Jewish Community Center, which offers mental health services and is one of the few places that has therapists who take insurance. I remember my mom calling around and around, but everyone she talked to charged like $180 an hour, all out of pocket. I told my mom if she paid me $700 a month, I could buy a red convertible and that would probably fix my mental health by itself.

Instead, I'd started with this little redheaded woman named Lisa Fagan, but that had only lasted about a month before we realized we were a bad fit, which I think means, like, I was too much woman for Dr. Fagan, who was used to kids who didn't talk back. She'd sent me off to Marc Eberhardt, who, after one session, had referred me back to the front office because I needed someone with a strong personality to "handle" me (and way to go with that weak personality, Marc), and they'd sent me to Dr. Pascal, who normally only works with little kids but took me on out of pity. Whether it was pity for me or for her coworkers I was never entirely sure, especially because I saw Dr. Fagan in the ladies' room once, and she hid in her stall until after I left.

Sometimes, when I really don't want to talk about my own stuff, I flip the script and get Dr. Pascal to talk about herself instead, which is actually fun because she's pretty cool. Like, if I were 50 years old and not her client, we would probably be friends. At least, I like to think so. We'd go antiquing on the weekends and then go drink sherry, or whatever middle-aged therapists do for kicks.

Here's what I know about her so far: she's half Ashkenazi Jewish and half Indian, she was born in Bethesda, she has two kids, and her husband doesn't like cats. She's been trying to talk him into getting one for the past few months, but so far, no luck. When I was in her office a few weeks ago, I gave her some printouts describing how cats lower your blood pressure, but he doesn't seem to be buying it.

I sat down on the couch and grabbed three peppermint Life Savers out of the bowl she always keeps on the coffee table.

"Aphra." She put on a fake German accent. "Tell me about your mother."

This is a Sigmund Freud joke we frequently start off with. I laughed, but I said, "Mom's fine. She said she's sending me with cookies for you next week."

"Ooh. Chocolate chip, please."

"I'll let her know," I said.

"So what's new? Last I heard, you were working on a new app for your computer class."

I chomped into my mint. I guess you're supposed to suck them or let them dissolve, but I can never seem to manage it. "It's okay. I think I'm almost done."

"And how's Bethany?"

"Bethany's good. Also, Dad's good, Kit's good, and Walnut's good."

She raised a single eyebrow. I wonder if that's a thing they teach you in therapist school, the single eyebrow raise.

"And Delia?" she asked.

I cut my eyes toward the clock. I'd been there about three minutes.

"Did you show your husband the thing about the blood pressure?" I asked.

"Aphra," she said, which meant she was not having my deflection today.

"She's fine," I said. "I mean, someone would have told me if she wasn't."

"You told me last week you were going to send her an email."

"Yeah," I said. "I didn't actually get around to that."

"When is she coming home, again?" she asked.

"Next week," I said. "She's coming home a week from Sunday."

"I thought we agreed it would be better if you cleared the air before you guys have to share a bathroom again."

I sighed. "Here's the thing—" I said.

"No," she said, cutting me off. I don't think therapists are supposed to do that, but Dr. Pascal is not about wasting time.

"You've been telling me about the thing for the last ten months. I know you're mad at Delia. You feel like she insulted you. You're mad that she hasn't apologized. But you don't get to control Delia. You only control Aphra. So what are *you* going to do?"

I fiddled with a hangnail.

"Have you reconsidered bringing her in for a few joint sessions with me once she gets back?"

"No," I said. "I mean, I've thought about it, but I don't want to."

She nodded. "Okay. Well, I seem to remember you saying that you wanted this summer to be better than last year. You said the tension was really bad for your brother."

That was true. Kit doesn't like it when people fight; it makes him super anxious. "He's just a little kid."

"He is. And you also said there were five people in your house who deserved to have some peace. Including you."

"You said that," I said. "Not me."

"Pretty sure it was you."

"I don't think so." I tapped my temple. "Photographic memory. You said it."

She held up her notepad. "I take notes. It was you. And you were right. You also said you thought this had gone on long enough."

Shoot, I had said that. Maybe I'd come to therapy hungry last week. That was always a bad idea. "Fine. I'll say something to Delia."

"Do you want to work out a script? Sometimes that can be helpful."

"Nah," I said. "I've got this."

"Aphra . . ."

"So did I tell you I got a fake boob?"

• • •

Back in my car, I opened up my email and sent my sister a note that said, *Mom's roses are blooming. Too bad you can't smell anymore.*

There. I'd said something.

I put my phone away and pulled out of my parking space, and then I stopped and pulled back in. There's a bookstore across the street from the JCC. I walked over there and found myself standing in the Modern Languages section. I picked up a copy of *Learn Russian the Fast and Easy Way.* And then I bought it.

I'm not really sure why.

Chapter Four

The pit stop at the bookstore made me late for crew, and everyone was halfway through their warm-up run by the time I got there. I sprinted like crazy and managed to catch up to them just as they got to the boathouse.

"You're late," Sophie said. Sophie is our coxswain, and she's tiny but not to be trifled with. You might think she'd cut me some slack since I was the one who recruited her in the first place, but you'd be wrong.

I used to be the coxswain, but by the end of freshman year, it became clear that I was better off as a rower; I'd started working out with the rest of the team, and I was going harder on the erg than most of them, probably because I had a little brother who still insisted on daily piggyback rides despite being well over 50 pounds, which meant that about four times a day I was doing squats with a wriggling kettlebell strapped to my back. Coach Kim wanted to move me into the four-seat, which meant we needed a new coxswain: someone small, loud, and enthusiastic. Where does one find such a person? I should think the answer is obvious. I told Coach Kim I had the perfect person in mind.

So that fall, I'd sat in the front row of a football game against Audubon, watching the halftime show, where Sophie Bell was being tossed repeatedly in the air like she weighed nothing, her braids—black but spray-dyed at the ends with our school colors—were tied into a ponytail that flew over her head every time her team threw her upward. Sophie was only 4'11" and probably weighed 90 pounds soaking wet, but she shouted louder than any of the others. I wondered where she got the lung capacity. After the halftime show, she'd sat down in the row in front of me.

"Hey," I said. We didn't know each other, really, despite having been in algebra together in seventh grade.

"Hey, Aphra," she said brightly, because among other things, Sophie is very nice.

"Do you have a minute?" I asked.

The other cheerleaders were drinking Gatorade and putting on sweatpants since it was still cold out, but she said, "Sure," and climbed over the bleachers to sit next to me. Everything about her was so put together . . . the dyed braids, the sparkly eye shadow, the bubble-gum-pink nails that popped against her black skin. I wondered how much of that was required for cheerleading and how much of it was her own style.

"So here's the thing: you look like you're having an awesome time out there, and you're obviously really good at this, but how would you like to add a second sport to your résumé?"

"A second sport?"

"Mmm-hmm. Picture this: literally all you have to do is order people around, and they have to do exactly what you say without talking back." I pointed a finger at her. "In a boat."

From the bench, Sigrid Dupain called, "Sophie, get back down here!"

"One sec!" she called back.

"I said now!"

"We're not even doing anything now!"

"You're supposed to be on the field until the end of the game!"

Under her breath, Sophie muttered, "Please." To me, she said, "So I tell people what to do."

From the stands, a cheer went up. I guessed we'd scored or something. I said, "Loudly, yes."

"And they have to do it?"

"Unquestioningly. You're the boss. I mean, except for the coach, but apart from her, yeah, you're running the show."

"And what's the time commitment?"

"Practices five afternoons a week in the spring, regattas on Saturdays."

Down on the field, someone tackled someone else and there was a lot of grunting. Around us, people shouted "DE-FENSE! DE-FENSE!" Sigrid screamed, "SOPHIE, GET YOUR BUTT DOWN HERE!"

"Are you for real right now?" Sophie shouted back. "YOU'RE EATING PRETZELS." Behind her pompon, she flipped Sigrid off. Sigrid scowled and turned back around, her hair ribbons spinning with the speed of her flounce.

"I swear to God," she said. "So who else is on the team?"

"Oh. Well, right now from our school it's just me and Bethany Newman—"

"The girl who doesn't talk?"

I bristled. "She talks."

"Like every other Tuesday?"

I got up. "You know, if you're going to be like that, never mind."

"Wait," she said.

I turned back around.

"I'm sorry. You know what? I'll try it. Can I bring some people?"

"Yeah, absolutely."

Sigrid bellowed, "SOPHIE!" and Sophie muttered, "Might as well get to scream at someone else for a change."

She'd showed up at our preseason practice the next week, and she'd brought Claire Okeke and Talia Reyes with her.

We have about 20 girls on our team, which is unusually small, and we're not actually affiliated with a high school. Our team—the junior division of the Occoquan Rowing Club—is made up of all the kids whose high schools don't have their own teams, so right now we have kids rowing from Middleridge, South County, and Fair Lakes High.

We're a small but scrappy bunch. This year, we have two standard eights—one varsity and one JV—plus a varsity four, and this season we also have a coxless pair, which sounds dirty but isn't. I row with the varsity eight on *Dullahan*, which consists of eight rowers, plus the coxswain. Bethany is the stroke, which means she sits in the stern opposite Sophie because she's the best technical rower. I sit in the middle because I am strong like bull.

I clipped my feet into the stretchers and waited while Sophie adjusted her headset. "WHO IS READY TO DIE?" she called. I grabbed my oar and we started out into the river. "Hard ten in two!" she called, and we leaned into our strokes.

I like the focus of rowing, but that day I was having trouble keeping my head in it because my brain wanted to think about Greg. Mostly, I was wondering how I'd managed to know him for five years and never learn anything about him besides the fact that he's cute.

It was kind of a problem. It was, I knew, the exact way people treat Bethany, like she's pretty and that's enough. I felt kind of gross for having thought about Greg the same way. I mean, I knew he wasn't stupid; he takes all the honors classes and he does well. But I never bothered to find out anything else about him.

So I was pretty surprised when we got back to the dock and he was standing there with the boys' team.

We got out and got *Dullahan* back in the boathouse. I was very sweaty. I mean, we were all sweaty, but somehow I seemed sweatier than everyone else. I ran my finger across the bridge of my nose.

Bethany hung back next to me. "Ohmigod," she said.

"Go talk to him!"

"I can't!"

Because I'm a good friend—and not at all because I wanted to—I took Bethany's hand in mine and walked up to Greg. "Здравствуйте," I said, because I'd taken a minute to skim the Easy Russian book while standing in the checkout line at the bookstore. I had no idea whether I was saying it right, but what I lacked in an acceptable accent I made up for with panache. In other words, I rolled the *r*. I don't actually know if Russian has rolled *r*'s.

He smiled. "Здравствуйте."

Rolled *r*. I smiled back. "Are you rowing these days?" The season was nearly over; it was a strange time to be starting out.

"Coach Allen's my next-door neighbor. I told him I was thinking about doing it next year, and he said I could try a couple of practices and see what I think."

"Oh," I said. "Well, good. I'm sure you'll be good at it. Don't you think? Bethany?"

Bethany said, "So good."

"I mean, I imagine rowing uses a lot of the same muscle groups as swimming, you know. Like, you need a really strong set of delts."

I elbowed Bethany. She said, "Delts."

We both stared at Greg's delts.

We were so, so gross. And I think Bethany maybe was suffering some kind of Greg-induced breakdown.

"I think Bethany needs water," I said.

"Water," she repeated, nodding vigorously. I shrugged at Greg and dragged her back in the direction of the cooler.

"What is wrong with me?" she asked once Greg was too far away to hear. She poured part of her water over her head before drinking the rest.

"I don't even think he noticed," I said. It was probably true. He probably thought she was silly and adorable.

"Literally all I did was repeat the last word you said. Three times. I did it three times."

I glanced over to where Greg was climbing into the middle of the boat. He glanced at us and waved.

Bethany waved back. "I think I've decided to give up."

"Give up? You've been trying to talk to him for, like, three days, and you haven't actually had a conversation yet. That's not even trying. That's just . . . I don't know. Aborting the mission before you even start."

We sat on the grass and stretched; Bethany and I did a v-sit foot to foot and took turns pulling each other forward to get the kinks out of our backs. We watched the boys' team; Coach Allen looked to be explaining boat terms to Greg and was giving him a brief demonstration of what to do with his oar.

I wondered why Greg was interested in rowing next year. He still swam on his year-round team, so I was a little surprised he had time.

We watched the boys working their way across the lake in *Bucephalus;* John O'Malley's super loud once he gets in a boat, and we could hear him from several hundred yards off.

"Go!" he said. "Go, go!"

We watched them go a few hundred feet. They looked all right, I guess. Greg wasn't feathering his strokes right, but it was his first day. And then he lost control of his oar, which snapped back at him, catching him across the chest.

"Ouch," I said.

"Do you think he's okay?" Bethany asked.

The rest of the guys in the boat were laughing while Greg rubbed his sternum. He said something to them that we couldn't hear. If it had been me, I would have told them off for laughing, but apparently he's a little nicer than I am, because they just laughed some more and started rowing again. Two minutes later, he did it again.

Bethany said. "What is he even doing wrong?"

It was hard to see from where we were sitting, but it looked like he was probably just rowing too deep. We watched them for a few more minutes; John appeared to be calling directions to Greg, but it didn't seem to be helping. Most guys, I think, would be planning on giving up now. I figured he'd be back in the pool by tomorrow morning and that was the last we'd see of him.

When they got back to the shore, their coach beckoned me over. "Aphra," he said. "Would you take Greg out in *Selkie*? Just give him the lay of the land for a bit."

I looked at him a little dubiously, because *Selkie* is one of our pairs and rowing a pair is *hard*. I'd done it in practice only enough times to know that it's not really my thing; if both people don't know what they're doing, it's just a hot mess of swearing and rowing in circles, and I'd already watched Greg eat his oar twice. It would have made more sense to take him out in one of the fours if he didn't want the whole team out there.

"Just for ten minutes," he said. "I just want him to concentrate on what the oar is supposed to do without worrying about keeping up a stroke rhythm."

"O-okay," I said. Greg looked a little guilty. "But you know, Bethany's a better technical rower." I gave her a little push forward with my shoulder.

Coach Allen looked at Bethany, frowning just a little. I willed her to speak, take control of the situation, and spend ten minutes in a boat with the boy she liked. Instead, she looked a little like she might barf.

"You've got the coxing experience," he said. "Just take him for a spin for a few minutes."

I guess I should have been flattered that he thought I was a better teacher, but it irked me. Bethany was always being overlooked, and in this particular case, she really was a better rower than me. But people see a pretty girl who doesn't want to talk and they think she's either a snob or she's stupid. I'm not sure which one Coach Allen was assuming right then. "I really think Bethany—"

But Bethany just whispered to me, "It's okay, Aphra. You go."

I said, "But—"

Allen slapped me on the shoulder. "Great! Don't go easy on him." He walked away.

"Right," I said. "Well, let's go see what those delts have got going on."

In *Selkie,* I sat in the stroke and put Greg in the bow so that he could copy my movements. "Okay," I said. "We're going to do a little drill. Check your oar."

"What?"

"Put the blade in, but flat side out. You're going to hold us still, and I'm going to row us around in a circle so you can see what a good catch looks like. Watch the end of my oar." I demonstrated for a few minutes. "Now you," I said, looking over my left shoulder to watch the end of his oar. "Yeah, that's what I thought. You're digging too deep. Hence the crab-catching."

"Crab-catching?"

"Catching a crab is when you lose control of your oar. It's like Goldilocks: It has to be just right. If you go in too deep, you'll catch a crab. Too shallow and you're skimming, and then the boat won't go straight. Try it again."

He did, a little better. I held us steady while he went around in another circle. I was actually starting to enjoy myself—late afternoon was my favorite time to be out on the water. The sun was starting to sink overhead, and Greg's oars cast a series of ripples across the water.

He grunted. "You okay?" I asked. "We should probably head back in a minute."

"You don't have to go easy on me," he said.

"I'm not. I already rowed for two hours and I'm tired."

It was strange talking to him, being just a few feet from him, but not being able to see him. But I guess that meant he couldn't see my face, either. I wondered what the back of my neck looks like. Probably like the back of everyone else's neck.

He was quiet for a few minutes. I called out a few rowing terms so he'd get used to hearing them. He was a pretty quick study. Of course. What are a couple of boat words to someone who speaks six languages?

"If you don't mind my asking," I said, "how exactly do you have time for this? Don't you swim year-round?"

He let out a sigh. "That's a little complicated right now. But swim practice is in the morning, anyway."

"Still," I said. "That's a lot of practice time, two hours in the morning and then two hours with us after school. You must be pretty tired right now."

"I didn't actually swim this morning."

I waited to see if he would follow that up. He did not. So I said, "Oh. Well, I think you've got the hang of it. Let's head back."

I glanced over my shoulder to judge the distance to the dock and saw Bethany sitting there with her knees to her chest. The rest of the girls were gone. Behind me, I felt Greg bobble in the boat.

Right. I was supposed to be talking up Bethany. I said, "You know Bethany, right?"

"Sure," he said. "I mean, I don't think I've ever actually talked to her."

“She’s . . . ,” I said. “She’s shy. But she’s great, though.” I chewed on my lip. “She’s really good at Spanish.”

That last part was a total lie; it’s hard to be good at a foreign language if you won’t practice out loud because you’re scared of screwing up. But Greg didn’t have to know that. He said, “Really?”

“Let’s head to starboard,” I said.

“How do I do that?”

“Maybe let me do it this time,” I said. “Just go easy and let me pull us around.”

We straightened out and started rowing toward Bethany.

Chapter Five

A few days later, I was sitting in my app design class with Bethany, supposedly fine-tuning the Deanna app but really finishing the Dostoyevsky essay I had open in a second tab. Mr. Positano was in the back of the room helping a couple of seniors who had teamed up to write a game that was exactly like *Fruit Ninja* except with cows—creatively titled *Steak Ninja*—which managed to crash every time somebody started it up.

I scowled at my word processor and listened to Mr. Positano saying, "No, not like— No. No. No. Not that, either." Then: "Have you thought about starting over?"

I jumped when Bethany popped up next to my chair.

"Sheesh," I said. "Give me a heart attack. What's another word for *redundant*?"

She frowned. "*Repetitive?*"

"Besides that."

"Um, I can't think of one. Hey. Have you checked on Deanna lately?"

"*Superfluous!* I already used *redundant* twice." I typed *su-*

perfluous into my sentence and then retyped it when the spell-checker told me I had messed up. Too many *us*. Talk about superfluous. Or redundant. "I'm just letting her run, that's kind of the point. I'll check her responses at the end of the week."

I ran the word count. I was 50 short. I thought about altering the margins. Mr. Edwards would probably notice that. I changed the font to Courier. Way too obvious.

Bethany said, "I think you should check her."

"Maybe I need a longer title," I said. "Wait, why should I check Deanna?"

"Well, I was sitting back there finishing my calculus and I was bored, so I decided to ask her what I should have for dinner, and she got kind of vulgar."

"Vulgar? I didn't program her to be vulgar."

"Yeah, but if she's picking up stuff from the people who downloaded the app . . ."

"No," I said. "I accounted for that." I had been, in fact, very careful, having anticipated that some of my classmates might try something like this. I specifically blocked every four-letter word I could think of. The point of Deanna's algorithm was that she was supposed to learn to anticipate follow-up issues. She wasn't supposed to be a dirty-word lexicon.

"There's no way," I said. "I made sure she was bulletproof." But I minimized my essay and pulled up the tab with Deanna's program. I typed, *Should I eat a burger or a peanut butter sandwich?*

Deanna said *Check this out!* And then there was a link to one of those tiny URLs.

I'd programmed her with some links to various mental health sites. Maybe she was being oversensitive and sending me to the National Eating Disorders Association site? But asking about sandwiches shouldn't have triggered that. I clicked on the link.

I let out an involuntary shriek and closed the browser before anyone else could see the images of people doing unspeakable things with peanut butter. From the back of the room, Mr. Positano called, "Aphra?"

"Nothing!" I said. "I, uh, thought I deleted something, but it's fine."

"Control Z for the win!" he called back.

"Woo!" I said, clearing my browser history and making a mental note that the campus porn blocker was even weaker than I'd thought. "Holy shit. Where did she pick that up?"

Ugh. If people were sending in porn links, she might have decided those were greetings, or conversational filler when talking about food. Or maybe she was just pulling them off Google somehow? I wasn't even sure. And that was an even bigger problem, because if I didn't know how this was going wrong, there was no way for me to fix it.

Bethany said, "You programmed her to give out links, right?"

"Links to mental health sites! Not naked people!"

"I guess people were inputting those, and she kept them?"

"I guess so. Well, at least it's food-specific. It could be worse."

She sighed.

"What?" I asked.

"It's worse," she said. "Type anything."

I typed, *Hi, Deanna.*

Deanna said, *Tell me what you're wearing.*

"Oh," I said. "No." But just to make sure, I typed, *I am in my favorite shirt, which I also wore yesterday.*

She replied, *That sounds hot, big boy.*

"Like, not to freak you out or anything," Bethany said, "but you realize that if she's sending porn links to the kids at Middleridge who downloaded your app, they're probably all minors?"

That actually hadn't occurred to me. Was that a misdemeanor or a felony? I wasn't even sure.

I lowered my forehead to my keyboard as I contemplated turning in ten pages of Deanna the Phone Sex Operator to Mr. Positano. Not only would I fail, I would probably get suspended.

"Oh, God," I said. "I can't turn this in."

"You really can't."

"Shit," I said. "Shit, shit. I'm going to flunk."

"Can't you just put her back the way she was? Take out the learning algorithm?"

"I can't," I said. "The learning algorithm was my whole project. Without that, she's just an open-source chatbot written by someone else. I can't get credit for that."

"Look, I'm still doing that weather program," she said. "Mr. Positano said people could pair up."

"But you already finished!"

"Well, you can't turn this in. All she does now is show you naked people and give you 15 euphemisms for *penis.*"

"There aren't 15 euphemisms for *penis*!" I said. "Wait, are there 15 euphemisms for *penis*?"

"I think some of them might be made up," she said.

At that, the bell rang. "Crap," I muttered, logging out of the computer.

"Remember!" Mr. Positano called. "These are due *Friday*!"

The seniors in the back groaned.

"What are you going to do?" Bethany asked as we walked out the door.

"Not sure yet," I said.

As soon as I got home that afternoon, I opened the program I'd used to create Deanna and reset it to the original vanilla chatbot. I'd spent weeks writing that algorithm. I thought I'd made it vandal-proof, too, but I guess I underestimated how much people would want to mess with it and how gross they'd be.

So where did that leave me? The project was worth a third of my grade. I couldn't turn in what I'd done. I couldn't turn in the original program the kids at GMU had made. I didn't have enough time to come up with another project. I could piggyback on Bethany, but that seemed wrong, too, since I hadn't done any of the actual work and it amounted to cheating off my best friend.

An alert beeped on my phone. . . . It was Bethany's app. Essentially, what it did was link up with the AccuWeather website, and based on the next day's temperature and precipitation, it told you what you should wear.

Tomorrow will be drizzly with a daytime high of 62. You will be comfortable in layers—wear a sweater or jacket. Wear closed-toe shoes with a good tread so you won't slip. Remember your umbrella!

I smiled. It was a pretty clever app, actually. She'd written it with Kit in mind, since he always refuses to wear a jacket when it's cold out and then freezes at recess.

I started a text to tell Bethany that her app, at least, was working. Our text logs are long, stretching back since I bought the phone last year. My mom is always on us for texting too much ("You just saw each other an hour ago! You don't need to text her at dinner!"). But there's a certain kind of comfort to knowing someone is always there, waiting to hear from you, like you're never a 100% alone.

Then it occurred to me that basically, Deanna was also kind of a chat app. The person on the other end was talking to my AI, but only because I'd routed it that way. There was no reason *I* couldn't be the person on the other end; the person using the app would never know it wasn't really Deanna. I just had to sound like a computer, that was all.

It would be like a reverse Turing test—instead of trying to convince someone that a computer was a person, I'd be trying to convince people that I was a computer.

I deactivated Deanna and updated the app so the interface would look the same from the user's end, but instead of talking to the chatbot, the app initiated a chat session with my phone. I would just write in her place. I could turn in the algorithm I'd written—which would have worked, if everyone who downloaded it wasn't such an asshole—and for sample replies, I'd write them myself. Was that completely honest? Well, no. But otherwise I was going to fail, and that wasn't fair. I'd worked way too hard on this project to turn in Deanna the Sexbot.

I'd already set the app to automatically update, so as long as everyone using it was hooked up to Wi-Fi or mobile data, I'd be good to go. It would be a lot slower than it should be with me typing, but hopefully people would assume it was glitchy or something. I would just have to hope that 50 people didn't log in at once.

I printed out my Dostoyevsky essay and got up to get some

cookies, when my phone pinged. Someone was using the Deanna app.

Grabbing the phone off my bed, I went into the kitchen and got some of the chocolate chip cookies my mom and Kit had made after school. I sat down at the counter. The Deanna user had typed: *Pancakes or french toast?*

I wondered why everyone kept asking my advice app about food. I guess those are easy choices. Low-risk. I took a bite of my cookie. The chocolate was still a little soft. From down the hall, I could hear my mom reading Kit his nightly chapter of Harry Potter.

Because I was a little cranky, I typed back, *The overconsumption of carbohydrates can lead to insulin resistance.*

You sound like my mom.

Always listen to your mother.

But I want french toast.

I rolled my eyes. *So eat the french toast.*

I knew I liked you.

I smiled at my phone. I typed, *I like you too.*

Careful, Deanna. Getting unprofessional.

Empathy is always professional.

I realized I was sounding a little too slick for a chatbot, so I decided to throw in something random. I typed: *Where does the blue sky go at night?*

Oh. Getting philosophical on me now.

Philosophy is the study of wisdom.

Yeah, I knew that.

Did you eat your french toast?

Yeah, I'm eating it now. You'll be happy to know I left off the syrup.

I typed, *Canada produces 73 million liters of maple syrup every year, much of it for the export market.*

I waited a few minutes, but there was no response. There's really no reason to formally end a conversation with a piece of technology, so I wasn't exactly offended. I put my plate away and went back to my room, where I found Kit curled up in my bed with Walnut under his arm.

"Didn't Mom already tuck you in?" I asked.

"Yeah, but I'm not tired." I looked at Kit a little more carefully. He's had this sandpapery rash on the left side of his face for a month or so; sometimes it's just like really dry skin and sometimes it's worse than that. Mom is always putting lotion on him and telling him to stop scratching. The pediatrician thought it might be a milk allergy, but Kit had been off dairy for two weeks and it didn't seem to make any difference. I could see that his skin was shiny from whatever Mom was putting on it, but it looked a little redder than usual.

"I'm tired," I said, climbing in next to him so that Walnut was sandwiched between us. I scratched between Walnut's ears. He purred. "Maybe you could sleep for both of us."

"If you're tired, why aren't you going to bed?"

"Not done with my homework," I said. It had occurred to me that people might be trying to use Deanna in the middle of the night. I needed to program it with a backup so if I wasn't around it would go back to the original open-source programming. I just wouldn't turn that part in.

"I hate homework," he said, even though I know he barely has any.

"Yeah. It's no fun," I said. "Something on your mind? Afraid something bad's going to happen to Harry?"

He shrugged.

"What, then?"

"I called Delia today."

I sat down. "Did you?"

"Yeah."

"What did she say?"

"Nothing. She's coming home next weekend."

"Yeah, I knew that."

"Are you still mad at her?"

I swallowed. "No."

"Liar."

"Yeah. Sorry."

"Can't you just *not* be mad at her?"

"It's complicated, buddy," I said, ruffling his hair. He batted my hand away.

"No it's not," he said. "You just decide not to be mad, and then you're not mad."

I didn't say anything. He said, "Do you like being mad?"

"No, of course not."

"You do. I think you do."

"Why would I like being mad?"

"I don't know. I just think if you didn't, you'd stop."

Mom stopped in my doorway. "I thought you were in bed," she said to Kit.

"I am in bed," he said.

"Your own bed," she said. "In your room. With the lights out."

"Aphra's bed's more comfortable," he said.

"Go," Mom said. "Sleep."

"Fine," he grumbled, stumbling from the room with Walnut following him.

"Hey," Mom said once he was gone.

"Hey."

"So," she said, sitting down in Kit's place. "Delia."

I wished I'd gone to sleep when I'd had the chance. "I have a sister named Delia," I said, sounding a little too much like a chatbot. At least chatbots don't get talkings-to for being pissed off.

"Isn't this something you've been working through with Dr. Pascal?"

I angled my face toward the ceiling. "You aren't supposed to ask about what I discuss with Dr. Pascal."

"Right. Right. Sorry. It's just . . . ," she said. "Well."

It was just that I'd been in therapy for the last ten months, and had not, as yet, made any headway in dealing with my feelings about my sister. In terms of investments, Dr. Pascal was turning out to be a bad one, as far as my parents were concerned.

"You know, your father and I will be dead someday," she said. "And you might wish you hadn't torched your relationship with your sister."

"Nice emotional manipulation, Mom," I said. "And I didn't torch it. Delia did."

"You know she didn't hurt you on purpose."

"That has nothing to do with it! Look, I know everybody wants me to just forget about it, but I can't. It's not like she shrank my favorite sweater."

"No. She shrank her nose."

I made a face.

Mom doesn't exactly understand, because she doesn't have the Nose. The Nose is an inheritance from our father, and everyone considers it to be a perfectly acceptable man nose. It's only on girls that it seems to be a problem.

"Hey," she said. "I wish that if she was bound and determined to do this, she had waited until you weren't at such a vulnerable age. But that wasn't the choice she made."

"You sound like Dr. Pascal."

"She may have recommended some books for me," she admitted. "Look, the point is, Delia did what she did, and we just have to accept it."

"Just because you say I have to accept it doesn't mean I do."

"Aphra," she said.

"Look. Do you just want me to promise that when she gets home I'll pretend everything's fine? Is that it?"

"No, that's not actually what I want."

"It's the best I can do," I said. I rolled over toward the wall. "I'm going to bed now."

"Aphra."

"Good night, Mom."

"Aphra."

I made a few snoring noises. She sighed and patted my shoulder before she left the room, turning off the light on her way out.

I lay there for about five minutes before I remembered that I hadn't finished my Latin homework, so I sat up and turned the lights back on. My phone pinged again with the Deanna app. I was debating letting it go to autopilot, but I took a look at it to see if it was a good question first. According to the IP address, it was the same person I'd been talking to earlier about the french toast. The question was: *How bad is it to disappoint your parents?*

Oof.

I typed, *Disappointment is a part of life. Even for parents.*

Easy for you to say. You're just a computer.

I typed, *Bleep bleep bloop.*

Do you ever feel guilty?

I said, *Guilt is a normal emotion felt by everyone at some point in time.*

Does it do any good?

I typed, *Guilt is useful when it gets you to change your behavior in a positive way.*

What about when you can't help it?

I frowned at my phone.

I mean, what if you feel guilty for something you can't change?

In that case, I typed, *it would be a wasted emotion.*

I rolled my eyes at myself a little, counseling people about wasted emotions.

It would be nice if you could just disconnect those. Wasted emotions, I mean.

Yes, I said. *It would be very useful.*

Okay. I should go to bed now. Say good night, Deanna.

I typed, *Good night, Deanna.*

And then, because I couldn't help it, I typed, *Come back and talk to me tomorrow.*

Okay. I'll talk to you tomorrow.

Chapter Six

Crew practice the next day was brutal. The last regatta of the season was coming up in less than a month, so the coach had us rowing sprints until the entire team was dropping f-bombs under their breath. By the end, even Sophie had lost her luster, drooping like a wilting flower in the stern.

While we cooled down, we watched the boys put their boats away. There's something sort of magnificent about watching them hoist a 62-foot boat out of the water and onto their shoulders. I'd never really noticed that before.

"Hey," I said to Bethany as I pulled my aching arm behind my back, stretching my shoulder and leaning until I felt the pull down my side. There's nothing, I think, as nice as a good stretch after a workout. It's probably the best part of the whole thing. "Greg's about done. You should go talk to him."

Bethany pulled both arms behind her back and bent at the waist, frowning.

"Come on," I said. "He's got to be too tired to run away."

"Gee," she said flatly. "Thanks."

"Not that he *would* run away," I said. "It's just that he would probably be amenable to a distraction." I looked sideways at my friend. "That's you. The distraction."

"I get it," she said. "But . . ." She pulled the front of her tank top a few inches away from her chest. "I'm sweaty."

"We're all sweaty. He's also sweaty."

"Yeah, but I think I smell bad."

"I'm sure he smells worse," I said.

"That's not really the point. I'm just not . . ." She uncorkscrewed her body from her lower-back stretch and moved her gaze toward where the boys were locking their boat up in the boathouse. "I'm not prepared."

I sighed. The boys were finished getting their shell away, but hadn't yet stopped grunting and cursing. Greg looked up from checking out some newly formed blisters, saw us watching, and raised a hand. I waved back and then nudged Bethany with my foot because she wasn't doing the same.

"Why is this so hard for you?" I asked. "He's nice! Just talk to him."

"I want to," she said. "I have this whole script in my head, but when he's there, it's like I just can't talk. My voice stops working."

I didn't know how to answer that, because really, my voice is most of what I have going for me.

Fortunately, Greg seemed to be oblivious to Bethany's inability to speak and was ambling over to us.

"Hey," I called to him. "You did great today."

He smiled at my words and Bethany's face. "Well, I didn't eat the oar this time."

"That is a marked improvement from yesterday." I turned to Bethany, who nodded enthusiastically and said nothing.

"So," he said, and this was addressed to Bethany, "you ready for your chem presentation?"

I . . . could not help with this answer.

Bethany said, "Uh . . . that's next week," and looked a little panicked. I smiled encouragingly at her. Bethany likes chem. Bethany likes talking about chem.

Greg waited for her to go on. She did not.

"Nothing better than a group presentation, right?" I chimed in. "What are you doing, polyatomic ions or something?"

"Yes! Yes. Polyatomic ions. I'm doing the part about coordination complexes. You know, metals, and I—I—I—have some PowerPoint slides with diagrams about isometrism." She blinked rapidly. "I'm . . . I'm almost ready, I think. I just need to read my cards through a few more times."

This may have been the most Bethany had ever said to Greg, and he looked delighted. I tried to remember what isometrism was. I didn't think we'd covered it in class.

"I'm sure you'll do great," he said. And they smiled at each other, this wonderful, private, delicious smile—an eros smile, if there ever was one—until someone called, "Greg! We're leaving!"

"That's my ride," he said. "See you tomorrow." And he jogged after a group of boys heading toward the parking lot.

Bethany smiled that same smile, not at Greg's retreating back, but at the spot where he'd been standing.

"You really ready for that presentation?" I asked.

She just said, "Help."

• • •

Sophie dropped us off at Bethany's house, where she took a shower in her mom's bathroom and I took one in the hall bathroom until we smelled a little less like we'd been goat wrestling, and then, after we changed into our regular clothes, we went down to the kitchen because we were starving.

Bethany started boiling a pot of water to make ramen (the instant kind, because it's all we can manage on our own), and I sat down at the table to drink a second glass of water while Bethany got the soy sauce out of the pantry, saying, "This is for us. You can make your own damn ramen."

This statement was arrowed at her brother, who had wandered up from the basement and looked like he'd just woken up, despite its being five in the afternoon.

Colin ran a hand through his unbrushed hair and slumped into the chair next to mine, sorting through the pile of mail before concluding there was nothing of interest. What would have been of interest to Colin was something of a mystery. A video game catalog, maybe, or a magazine with pictures of naked women posed on aspirational vehicles.

"You need a shower," he grunted in my direction.

"Already had one. That's the smell of ambition, I wouldn't expect you to recognize it."

From the sink, where she was draining the ramen in a colander, Bethany snorted. Colin was 20 and a professional basement troll, a label that didn't speak so much to his unemployed status as to his utter lack of desire to do anything aside from play video games and treat his mother like the maid.

He gave me a lazy glare before grabbing a single-serve package of cookies out of the pantry and tearing it open. "What's for dinner?" he asked Bethany.

"How should I know?"

This was our usual pattern. Bethany and I would come home, Colin would come up from the basement, eat something, say something rude, and then retreat downstairs. He is the reason that, for the most part, we do most of our hanging out at my house. Also, my brother is little and cute and my parents buy good snacks.

But today we were there because I was supposed to help Bethany go through her closet and pick something to wear for her chem presentation, which she was panicking over now that she knew Greg was going to be paying extra-special attention, even though it wasn't for days.

She was already pretty miserable about having to speak in front of the class, but I kept reminding her she was allowed to use notecards. "Just read them," I told her. "Pretend no one's even there." Her group had strategically given her the second spot—not as much pressure as going first, but less agonizing than going last. So after we finished our noodles, we went upstairs. Bethany threw open her closet door and then flopped belly-first onto her bed.

"Ugh," she said. "I can't believe I have to do this."

"You'll be fine," I said. "Just remember the number one rule of giving a class presentation."

"Picture them in their underwear?"

"Nope. Remember that no one's listening to you."

Into her pillow, she said, "You're probably right."

"I'm totally right. I'm sure you're the only one in there who gives two shits about isometric ions or whatever."

I pulled out a tomato-red T-shirt dress that was actually mine. I'd lent it to her for some dinner out with her grandparents a few weeks earlier. "I forgot you still had this," I said.

"Oh," she said, sitting up, "sorry. Go ahead and take it."

I held it out to her. "No, you should wear it for your presentation."

"Oh, Aphra, no way. Not to school."

"Why?"

"My grandmother said it made me look like a cheap tart."

"Well," I said. "Takes one to know one, Grandma. You should wear it. You want Greg to look at you, right?"

"Maybe not that much."

"Yes that much. Come on." I held the dress out and she took it.

"I'll think about it."

We heard the front door close, which was the sound of Bethany's mom coming home from work, and then the sound of Colin bellowing up the stairs, "What's for dinner?"

"If your mom just never came home again," I asked, "would he starve? Like, would we find his desiccated corpse on the couch in the basement?"

Nodding thoughtfully, Bethany said, "It's possible."

From the kitchen, Bethany's mom called, "Leftover chicken."

And her brother called back, "*UGH*."

Bethany said, "Let's go to your house tomorrow."

After dinner, I helped Kit with his Mali project, finished my own homework, and fell into bed just as my phone rang with the opening from the *Star Trek* theme song.

I'd set it as a ringtone for when someone was trying to use the Deanna app, which no one had done anything with since last night. I wondered if it was French Toast Person again. I kind of hoped so.

The incoming message read, *Hey Deanna.* I checked the IP address. . . . It was the person from last night. I smiled at my phone.

Hello, I typed. *I hope you are having a lovely evening.*

Do you remember what I type from one session to the next?

She was programmed to do that, so I typed, *Yes.* Then: *Are you eating breakfast again?*

Not tonight, he wrote. *I used up all the syrup yesterday.*

Butter is a better condiment than syrup, because its fat content slows digestion and prevents blood sugar crashes.

Thanks for the tip. So I was thinking about what you were saying last night, about guilt being a wasted emotion if it doesn't get you to change your behavior.

Had I said that? Huh. I guess Dr. Pascal must be getting to me. *Why were you thinking about that?*

I guess I was just thinking it's easier said than done.

Most things are.

Yeah, but I keep thinking, what if I'm feeling guilty because I know they're right?

I frowned. This conversation seemed like some kind of a journaling exercise for this person, because he/she couldn't really expect a response to that. But I was kind of curious, so I typed, *I don't have enough information to hazard an opinion.* Which was computer for *What are you talking about?*

There was no forthcoming answer, so I typed, *You mentioned your parents earlier. How are they?*

Angry, came the answer.

Why are they angry?

I'm not doing what they want me to do. Well, it's more that I can't do what they want me to do.

I resisted the urge to type a joke, because this sounded like it was more serious than pancakes. *It is a parent's job to provide emotional and material support to their children.* I thought about Colin. *Up to a point, anyway.*

Ha, came the answer. *Ha ha. But what if that's the problem? What if my shortcomings lead to me require more support than they are prepared to offer? Material support, I mean.*

I am hearing that you are planning to become an expensive child.

Something like that.

From the room next door, I heard Kit's soprano as he sang some made-up song to Walnut. I wondered how Walnut felt about this. Good, probably. My life's goal was to meet someone who looked at me the way that damn cat looked at my brother.

From the hallway, I heard my father urging Kit to go to sleep, which was when I realized it was past ten o'clock and I really needed to go to bed, too.

There was a long pause, and I thought my partner in chat had put the phone down, but then they typed, *Sorry, falling asleep. So what do you know about NCAA sports?*

I likely know more than the average person because of crew. There isn't a ton of scholarship money for rowers, but I think I'm good enough to row in college if I want to, depending on where I end up. I mean, I probably couldn't row at Princeton, but at most schools I'd say I'm pretty solid. I typed, *I am programmed with an adequate knowledge of collegiate athletics.*

I racked my brain, trying to figure out who this was. It was someone who played an NCAA sport, which didn't narrow it down much. And it sounded like they—*they*?—I'm going with *they*—weren't very good at whatever sport it was. Which also didn't narrow it down very much.

I typed, *Some typical Division I college sports include football, basketball, soccer, and lacrosse. Do you enjoy one of those?*

The reply came: *Ижм реаллы стартинг то чате сшиммминг.*

I started at that line for a minute, not understanding what I was seeing, and then a second line appeared: *Чеадинг то бед нош. Гооднигчт.* And then the app disconnected from the other end.

"Oh, my God," I said out loud, because I was beginning to have a pretty good idea who I was talking to. I got out of my bed and went to my desk, where I opened a browser and searched for a Cyrillic keyboard. As I'd suspected, the words were in English, just typed in the wrong alphabet, like he'd accidentally toggled to his Russian keyboard instead of the regular Latin one. And I say *he*, because as I picked out what he'd typed, letter by letter, it only confirmed what I'd already guessed.

The message said, *I'm really starting to hate swimming.* And then: *Going to bed, good night.*

Probably he didn't even realize he'd switched, because he was typing fast and tired. But there was only one person I knew of who swam at our high school and spoke Russian, and that was Greg D'Agostino.

Chapter Seven

I'd been talking to Greg D'Agostino online. Late at night. In my bed. While he was falling asleep. In his bed. And he seemed to actually like me, and talking to me, in his bed.

Only, he thought I was a chatbot.

On the one hand, I thought, I should probably let him know that I was actually not a bot, before he told me anything really personal. On the other hand, he hadn't told me anything really personal so far, and I did seem to be helping him in my roundabout way. And if I told him, it was bound to be super awkward, and it could also get me in trouble with Mr. Positano, since what I was doing was not entirely honest academically.

It seemed like my best bet was to keep going with my original plan. . . . I still needed a few more days' worth of responses to hand in along with my source code. I would just keep things with Greg strictly patient-chatbot. Nothing personal. I would not abuse my power as a fake cybertherapist.

This was fine, really. It was totally okay.

I got last year's yearbook out of my bookcase and cracked it to Greg's headshot, smiling at me from a sea of sophomores.

It was not totally okay.

Maybe it would have been okay had Greg been someone else. But it was Greg.

I felt his phantom arms around me, my most precious middle school memory. How could I keep forgetting the charges on polyatomic ions but remember Greg giving me the Heimlich as if it had happened five minutes ago? His breath on my neck. *Can you speak? Can you breathe?*

No, Greg. No, I can't.

The next Tuesday, after last period, I stood in the hall by the soda machine waiting for Bethany. I was starting to stress a little about the fate of the Deanna app, because I didn't really have enough to turn in (despite that morning's argument with some random user about whether skinny jeans were over) and what I did have consisted mostly of me talking to Greg in ways that didn't look too authentically computerish. I needed to sound a lot stupider and a lot more stilted. Maybe intersperse my real answers with some facts I'd preassembled from Google that I could toss out at random intervals. I made a mental note to look up how many delegates are in the Virginia General Assembly and what the wave frequency of yellow light is. Across the hall, Officer Barry, the narc, was breaking up a heated argument between two girls about one having sent a questionable selfie to the other's boyfriend. One of them kept saying, "It was the wrong number!" and the other one kept saying, "How stupid do you think I am?" and Officer Barry kept saying, "Just go home!"

After they left, he shot me a look and shook his head. I smiled and gave him a big thumbs-up, because I'd learned long ago that the best way through high school is to keep your friends close and your school resource officer closer.

I'd developed this maxim last year, after some stoners in my gym class explained to me that the path to Officer Barry's heart—and out of the school building at lunchtime—is indeed through his stomach.

"Dude," Jake Ellerson had said to me as we stretched after our quarter-mile run, "all you have to do is bring him a burger. He really doesn't care if you leave."

Barry generally spent lunchtime hovering in front of the back doors to keep people from leaving, when he wasn't half-heartedly busting kids for smoking weed at the far end of the parking lot, which he only did when one of the vice principals forced the issue.

"Won't he get in trouble for that?"

"With who?"

I paused, one foot propped on the opposite thigh as I stretched my hamstring. "The principal?"

"He never comes out of his office. How's he going to know?"

I'd been intrigued by the idea that the price of my freedom was a 99-cent Big Mac. So the next week, while Bethany was home with a cold, I'd decided to ride my bike three blocks to Taco Bell for lunch, just to see what would happen. It was an experiment; it was less that I really wanted a seven-layer burrito and more that I wanted to see if I could sweet-talk Officer Barry into letting me out. Because if I could get out for a burrito, someday I might be able to get out for something more important.

Officer Barry stopped me at the door. "Where do you think

you're going?" he'd said. He was very big and very gruff; I'd deliberately attempted my escape without Bethany because I'd known she would fall apart at this moment.

"Hello," I said. "I have lunch now, and I'm not exactly enjoying the food selections today."

He pointed back down the hallway, toward the cafeteria. "Go back to lunch," he said.

"Well, I was thinking," I said. "See, they have that new burrito with the rice and the guacamole? And I was thinking that sounds better than the sloppy joes in there, right? And what I was thinking is that you've been standing here at this door an awfully long time, and I'm sure you're very hungry, since you've been standing there smelling the sloppy joes since 10:30. So I was thinking that if I take my bike and go very fast, I could get to Taco Bell in five minutes and be back with a second guacamole burrito for you, and it would even still be hot by the time you got it."

He narrowed his eyes at me. I did my best to look innocent and winsome.

"20 minutes," I said. "I'm very fast. My name's Aphra, by the way; we've never met because I am never in trouble."

"Why do I find that hard to believe?"

"Oh, it's true," I said. "I have very good grades and everyone likes me, I swear."

He scowled, but he didn't look like he meant it. I gave him my best smile and bounced on my toes. "20 minutes?" he said.

"19, if the line's short."

And then—and I'll never forget this—he took a step to the side and turned his back to me. I slipped out the door.

I ran all the way to the bike rack, not really believing how easy it had been. It seemed to me at that moment that the entire world was full of people like Jake Ellerson, people who knew stuff, if you were just clever enough to ask.

I decided not to push my luck that day, I got back in 17 minutes, and I brought Barry an order of churros to go with his burrito. When I got back to the building, he moved aside to let me in, never making eye contact, and I slipped the handle of the Taco Bell bag into his hand as I walked by.

"Thank you very much," I said. "I got you two kinds of salsa."

So when Barry walked by me in front of the vending machine, muttering, "Six more years," I knew he meant "until retirement," and I said, "I believe in you, sir." He smiled, just a little, and kept going, off to make sure no one killed anyone else on their way to the buses.

Bethany ambled up to me a minute later. She was not wearing my tomato-red dress.

What she was wearing was my old GMU hoodie and a pair of leggings. "What do you have on?" I asked. "That's not your presentation outfit."

She picked at the kangaroo pocket of the hoodie, which I'd forgotten I'd loaned to her. I have no idea why all my clothes end up with Bethany, but it seems to happen a lot.

"It was cold this morning," she said.

"It was not cold." I held up my phone and played the Bethany app for her. It said, *Today's going to be a warm one, a high of 78 with a 30% chance of afternoon drizzle. You'll be fine in a T-shirt, but take your umbrella.*

"Well," she said. "*I* was cold."

I rolled my eyes. I kind of wanted a soda, but the machine was turned off, so we headed out to the parking lot, where we were carpooling to crew practice. "You put on a bikini for him, but you couldn't manage a midthigh dress?"

"That . . . that was different."

I wasn't sure how, but I said, "Whatever. How was the presentation?"

"He was there," she said.

"Of course he was there," I said. "He's been there since September."

"Yeah, I know." We moved out of the way of the basketball team coming in the other direction. "I dropped all my cards on the floor. It was super embarrassing."

"That's not super embarrassing. Unless your pants split when you went to pick them up. Did they split when you went to pick up the cards?"

"What? No. My pants are fine. It was okay, I got through it. I was fine as long as I was reading something I'd written down, so I just did that."

She wasn't looking quite at me, and her face was flushed.

"So if it was fine, why are you all red in the face?"

She said, "Greg tried to talk to me afterward."

"Define *tried to.* He tried to talk to you and fell down a manhole?"

"No. He did talk to me. I just didn't talk back."

"Oh. Bethany."

"I know! He's was just so . . . right there in front of my face, and he asked me this question about isometry, right? He said, 'I don't really get the difference between chain isomers and position isomers.' "

I stared at her blankly.

"I know! And even though I know the answer, I just sort of went *gaaaah*, and then I ran away."

"You *ran away*?"

"I told him I was late to Spanish."

"That was last period!"

"I know! You think he realized?"

"That you don't have a class after school lets out? Yes, I think he realized."

"Aphra, you have to help me, here."

"I'm trying. You wouldn't even wear the red dress." Though I guess she hadn't needed it. "You just have to talk to him. You know, use your words?"

"If I could do that, I would."

"You're talking to me right now!"

A couple of girls from crew joined up with us.

"It's raining," Sophie whined. "I hate rowing in the rain."

"You don't row in the rain," I pointed out. "You yell in the rain."

"It still sucks," she said.

"Hey," Jenna said. "We're having a study group at Sophie's after practice, if you want to come. I brought a box of brownie mix."

"Can't," I said. "I promised my brother I'd help him with his homework after dinner."

"He's so cute," Sophie said. "I wish I had a cute little brother."

"My brother can't get his pee in the toilet," Claire lamented. "Like, there's this buildup of pee scum everywhere. It's disgusting."

"Ew," Sophie said. "Tell me Kit doesn't do that. It will shatter my whole little-brother fantasy."

“We got him pretty well potty-trained,” I said.

“Maybe we need to go back to that with Serge,” she said. “What did you do with Kit?”

“Cattle prod,” I said.

“Really?”

“No, we just told him not to pee on the damn floor,” I said. “Only he was three, so we said it nicer.”

By then we were at Sophie’s car, so I climbed into the back next to Bethany, her by the window, me in the middle, as per usual. It was only later that I realized Jenna and the others hadn’t asked Bethany if she wanted to go to the study group, and that she might have actually wanted to go.

Chapter Eight

Kit was on the floor of the kitchen when I got home, sobbing loudly with his face mashed into his knees.

Kit was my parents' "Whoops, we thought your mom was menopausal" baby, born when I was eight and Delia was ten. I'm pretty much 100% sure my parents didn't plan to have a third kid; they were kind of crazy-eyed when they told us Mom was pregnant, and it was an expression that didn't fade until Kit went off to preschool, a "Ha ha ha, what have we done to ourselves" kind of expression.

Fortunately for them (and Kit), Delia and I didn't mind the intrusion of a new family member. I overheard Dad tell Mom once, "Just wait until the novelty wears off," but he's nine now, and so far it hasn't, maybe because Delia and I were so entrenched in our own lives by then that the loss of parental attention didn't really register.

Right after my brother was born, Delia and I used to sneak into his room at night to watch him sleep.

Our house only has three bedrooms, so when my parents

found out they were having their oops, they transformed the basement into a bedroom for Delia and turned her old room into a nursery. There was never a conversation about having us share a room, because it was understood that we would have killed each other.

The first time we ended up in Kit's room was about a week after he was born. I'd been reading some baby book my mom had left lying around, and there'd been a chapter on SIDS and I was kind of freaked out by the whole thing, so I decided that maybe I'd really better make sure he was still, you know, breathing. I waited until my parents were in bed, snuck down the hall, and tiptoed into his room.

Delia's old *Death Note* posters were still up, since the conversion of the bedroom had entailed swapping Delia's bed for a crib and that was pretty much it. I didn't think they were exactly appropriate nursery decor, but, you know. Whatever. So the first thing I saw when I went into the room was a Shinigami with pointy teeth eating an apple, and the second was Delia herself, sitting on the floor next to the crib.

I squatted down next to her and she whispered, "What are you doing here?"

I shrugged.

"You read the SIDS thing?" she asked.

"Yeah," I said.

"Yeah, me too."

"Why aren't Mom and Dad in here?"

"I don't know. Maybe they figure *we* survived."

Kit opened his mouth and yawned and the two of us held our breath until he settled back to sleep.

"Were you going to stay here all night?" I asked.

"Were you?"

I shrugged again, because I hadn't really gone in with a plan beyond making sure Kit didn't asphyxiate. "There's sleeping bags in my closet," I said, because those were the ones Bethany and I used when she slept over.

"But if we go to sleep, how are we going to know if he stops breathing and wake him up?"

This was a good point, but neither of us thought we'd be able to stay up the entire night every night. We got the sleeping bags anyway and stationed ourselves next to the crib. Then we proceeded to lie there and not sleep.

"Are you awake?" I asked after an hour had gone by.

"Yeah."

"Doesn't he need to eat soon or something?"

"Maybe, I don't know. Does he wake up on his own, or do they get him up for that?"

"I think usually he cries," I said. Delia, banished to the basement, would not know this.

"Is he still breathing?"

I checked. "Yeah."

Just then, Kit started to stir; whether we'd woken him up or it was his empty stomach I'm not sure. Then he cried, softly at first and then full-throated.

"Should we get Mom?" I asked just as Dad threw open the door, staggered into the room, and tripped over Delia's legs.

"Jesus Christ," he muttered, picking himself up off the floor. "What're you guys doing in here?"

"We thought Kit might die," I said. And then I started

bawling, because it was too horrible a thing even to say out loud.

Dad looked rather alarmed. "Kit's not going to die!" he said. "Where are you getting that from?"

"We read the book," Delia said. "About SIDS."

"Oh," he said, scooping the baby out of the crib. "I see. But guys, that's not going to happen."

"You don't know that," I insisted.

"He's big and healthy and no one smokes in the house. Plus, we always put him down on his back; he'll be fine."

"But," I said. "But the book says sometimes it happens anyway. And nobody knows why."

Dad didn't answer right away; Kit was starting to fuss again, and he bounced him around to distract him. "It's very unlikely," he said.

"But can you promise it won't happen to him?" Delia asked.

There was a moment's hesitation, and then he said, "Yes, I promise," and took the baby to Mom to be fed. Delia and I stayed in the room, our eyes meeting in the semidarkness, because we'd both taken note of that pause. Dad couldn't promise that. Not really.

I think it was the first time I realized that bad things can happen for no reason, and I could not count on my parents to be able to fix them.

"What the hell happened?" I said to my mother, who was putting a lasagna into the oven.

Kit let out a particularly loud bellow. My mother said, "We saw the allergist after school today about that rash."

"Oh," I said, petting his little head. "Did they poke you a bunch of times? That sucks. Are you still itchy?" I'd had allergy testing when I was around Kit's age, and they'd stuck me about 20 times up and down each arm with a little pin covered in various allergens. I am, it turns out, very allergic to ragweed and oak pollen. "So what's he allergic to?"

"Walnut!" he sobbed.

"Walnuts?" I asked my mother.

He wailed again. "No," Mom said. "Not *walnuts,* Walnut, and not just Walnut." She shut the oven. "Cats in general."

"He said we have to give Walnut away!" Kit cried.

"What?" I said. "What do you mean?"

"The doctor said," she said, with a pained expression, "that the best course of action would be to find Walnut a new home."

I looked down to where Kit was hiccupping on the floor. "Or," I said, "the alternative course of action would be . . ."

"He was pretty emphatic," she said. "He said your brother could develop asthma."

"But the alternative would be . . ."

"Aphra," she said.

It kind of made sense: Kit's always mashing his face into the cat. It's like a leftover thing from when he was a baby, his need to mash his face into things if he likes them, and I'm pretty sure he'll get over it eventually, or at least I hope he will, because he does it to me, too. It's not so bad except when his nose is runny and he leaves snot prints on my shoulders. But the reason he face-mashes Walnut is because he loves him so much. He'd been begging for a pet since preschool, and my parents finally gave in this year, figuring that an adult cat wouldn't be too much work. The cat had taken one look at Kit in the shelter and that had been the end for both of them: it was true love. I'm not sure if the Greeks have a name for the love between a small child and a domestic animal, but it was definitely a real thing.

I grabbed a juice box from the fridge and jammed the straw in it, then handed it to Kit. "Drink this," I said, and to Mom I said, "Mom. Walk with me," and pulled her out of the kitchen into the laundry room and shut the door.

"You can't make him give up his cat," I said. "Just how many therapists do you want to shell out for?"

"You are not helping."

"Did you even discuss alternatives? You can't do this," I said. "He loves that stupid cat."

"I know that! But this is his health!"

I moved a box of laundry detergent out of the way and hopped up to sit on the dryer. "What about shots?"

She shook her head. "He hates shots."

"He'd get the shots if it was for Walnut."

"But they don't work right away, and sometimes they don't work at all. Plus, I think at the beginning it's like once or twice a week. Your dad and I don't have time to run him over there that often."

I bent forward until my forehead hit my knees. "Please don't do this to him."

The door opened and in walked my father. "Why are you guys in here with the door shut while Kit's crying in the kitchen?"

Mom briefly caught him up. Dad said, "Shit."

I said, "Shots."

Dad said, "Shots?"

"That's kind of a logistical problem," Mom said.

"I could take him sometimes," I said. "For his shots. On the days you guys can't go, you could leave me the car and I'll drive him."

"How?" Mom said. "You have practice after school every day."

"I'd . . . I'd just have to take him at lunch."

"They don't let you guys leave at lunch," Mom said. "I'm pretty sure."

"Please. That place can't hold me."

My mother said, "Wait a minute. You leave school? In the middle of the day?"

"Hang on, it's not like I'm robbing banks," I said. "I just . . . very occasionally . . . run out for a sandwich. Or something."

"Did you know about this?" my mom asked my father, who shrugged and tried to hide his smile.

"It's not prison," I told my parents. "It's school. The point is, I can duck out long enough to take Kit to the allergist for a shot once in a while, It's not like it'd be every day."

Mom sighed. Dad said, "Hmmm."

I said, "He'll never forgive you if you make him give up that cat without at least trying the shots first."

"This is Kit we're talking about. Not you."

I rolled my eyes, but I knew I already had her. It was the only logical course of action. When plan A sucks, you try plan B first. She said, "I'll call the doctor and see what he says."

Back in the kitchen, I pressed a cookie into Kit's hand. "Okay, mon frère," I said as Kit lifted his head and looked at me through swollen eyes. "Here is what I got you."

"We can keep Walnut?"

"Maybe," I said. "We're going to try, but Walnut can't sleep in your room anymore, and you're going to have to do allergy shots."

"I have to get shots?"

"Kid," I said, "I told them you'd do it."

"Shots? Like a lot of shots?"

"Twice a week," I said. "For the first few months. Then you don't have to go as often."

He snuffled. "I hate shots."

"I know you do."

"And I can't sleep with Walnut anymore?"

"Sorry, buddy."

"He'll be sad. He doesn't like to sleep by himself."

I suspected what he really meant was that *he* didn't like to sleep by himself. I said, "He can sleep with me if he wants."

"Really? Because he likes to be on the pillow. That's his favorite."

"All right," I said. "He can have the pillow."

Chapter Nine

I had just turned off my light when I heard the *Star Trek* theme coming from the bottom of my backpack, where I'd left my phone.

Walnut was glaring at me; he'd been howling outside Kit's door while, from inside, I could hear Kit screaming, "I LOVE YOU, WALNUT!" so I'd scooped up the miserable fur ball and deposited him on my bed, shutting the door so he couldn't get back out. "You'd better not pee in here," I'd said, but he'd already jumped down and was scratching at the door.

I grabbed a paper shopping bag out of the bottom of my closet and put it sideways on the floor, hoping Walnut would climb into it and forget his troubles for a while, which he did, and then I picked up my phone.

I felt a tiny thrill. It was Greg. He'd texted me at the same time three nights in a row. I'd become part of his nightly routine, I guessed. Well, not me, exactly. But Deanna had. By the time I got my phone, Deanna's autopilot had engaged and she'd already said, *Adolescents require approximately nine hours of sleep and it is presently 10:37.*

Damn it. I took over and typed, *However, unburdening yourself of your troubles before bed can reduce cortisol levels and increase sleep value.*

Sleep value? What the hell is sleep value?

I winced, but he must have attributed that statement to Deanna's programming, since he said, *I don't have to be up until 8 tomorrow, anyway.*

Without thinking, I typed, *Don't you have school?*

I don't go to first period. I take two classes at the community college.

He'd mentioned something like that to me in Latin, but I hadn't really thought about what it meant. *What classes do you take at the community college?*

Russian and Mandarin.

I knew there were people at Middleridge who were dual enrolled—taking high school and college classes at the same time—but I didn't know any of them personally. It did sound pretty cool not to be limited by our tiny course catalog. I wanted to ask what it took to sign up, but I was aware this conversation already sounded extremely un-chatbot-y, so I'd just have to look it up later.

I said, *Russian is the native language of approximately 153 million people.*

Yeah, that sounds about right.

I wanted to bring up swimming, but since he'd only mentioned it using Cyrillic characters, I wasn't sure I could get away with it. I said, *Learning multiple languages is beneficial for brain development and good for your employment prospects.*

Unfortunately it does not also pay for college, he said.

Ah, now we were getting to it. I typed *NCAA sports occasionally provide scholarship opportunities, particularly at the Division I level.*

Yes. Except when they don't.

I was starting to get the picture here . . . Greg said he hated swimming, was skipping practice, and worried about his parents paying for college. I said, *However, there are other ways to pay for college tuition.*

Yeah, and they're called loans. Expensive loans.

The size of a loan is dependent on a parent's estimated financial contribution.

It sure is. But what if your parents feel like they already spent that money putting you in a sport because they thought you'd get a scholarship, and you aren't good enough?

Oh.

Parents should be aware that children are humans and not commodities that can be manipulated at will, I said.

I don't think they see it as manipulation.

I didn't mean manipulated that way, but I tried again: *Put another way: a child is not something one creates with a specific vision in mind. He is an independent being, not a sculpture you make and then love because it turned out just as you planned.*

A sculpture, huh? Like in Pygmalion?

I realized I might be tipping my hand, since we'd just been reading it in class. I said, *Pygmalion is a very famous story from Ovid's Metamorphoses.*

I always thought it was kind of gross, he said. *Like, if you fall in love with something you made, aren't you just falling in love with yourself?*

I'd never thought about it that way. I didn't exactly know how to respond, so I said, with the help of some quick googling, *Pygmalion has been reinterpreted several times in modern times, as in the film My Fair Lady. The Japanese novel Naomi, written by Jun'ichirō Tanizaki, is often considered a related work, although in that version the protagonist is ultimately rejected by the woman he creates.*

I then added, *In a modern rendition, Pygmalion might be interpreted as the villain.*

I imagined him smiling. That was the downside of this: I could imagine Greg sitting in front of his phone, typing to me, but I couldn't see how he was reacting. Did he think I was clever? I'd never be sure. He hadn't hung up yet, though. He said, *Too bad you aren't real. You could talk to my parents for me.*

You seem to be articulate enough to speak to them yourself. In several languages, even.

It's very hard to deliver a message no one wants to hear, he said.

People don't always want to know what they need to know, I replied. *Be bold.*

Be bold, he repeated. *All right. Say good night, Deanna.*

Good night, Deanna.

We ended up going back to Bethany's after crew the next day, because I'd left my Latin books there and needed them for class tomorrow. I went up to her room to get them and came down to find Bethany standing in the kitchen with a pamphlet in either hand. "What are those?" I asked.

Bethany's eyes were a little glassy. "I found these in the dining room, mixed in with the mail."

I took one of the brochures from her and read the front page. "'Shady Pines Adult Living.'" I flipped it open to see pictures of smiling old people playing golf and doing water aerobics. "I don't understand. Is it like assisted living?" I couldn't figure out who it might be for. . . . Bethany's maternal grandmother already lives in assisted living, and as far as I know, they never hear from her dad's parents at all.

"It's an over-55 community," she said. She handed me the second brochure, which was for the Windy Oaks Adult Living Community.

"So . . . she's on a mailing list? I don't get it."

"No! She requested these. They aren't junk mail." She flipped over the first one and pointed out the first-class stamp.

"But why would your mom want to live in an . . . Oh." My eyes went to the pile of Colin's dirty laundry, which he'd left next to the stove for some inexplicable reason, and back to Bethany, who was looking at me like I was a little slow on the uptake.

"It gets him out of the house," she said. "They won't let him live there since he's under 55."

"I guess that's one way of solving the problem," I said. "The passive-aggressive way."

"There's just one thing, though," she said.

I turned to the back of the Shady Pines brochure, where two old people were walking into the sunset. It was creepy. Like looking at a brochure for heaven's waiting room, and here were two people making their final exit. "What's that?" I asked.

She gave a little huff of exasperation. "*I'm* under 55, too!"

I dropped the brochure on the table. "Oh," I said. "Crap."

"Yeah, crap."

"Well, wait. Maybe this isn't going to happen until after you go to college."

"Yeah, *or* maybe she's just going to put all my stuff out on the lawn once I turn 18!"

"She wouldn't . . . she wouldn't do that. Would she do that?"

She gestured at the giant pile of laundry. "Are you kidding? I'd go there tomorrow if I were her."

"Maybe you should talk to her," I said. "I mean, this is probably just a misunderstanding."

"I'm not sure," she said. "I think she really wants him out."

"Yeah, but wanting *him* out is not wanting *you* out."

"Maybe it is," she said. "I mean, maybe she thinks I'm going to end up like that, too."

On cue, Colin appeared from the basement. He said, "Do you guys have to be so loud? I was trying to sleep."

Bethany sort of made a strangled cry of either rage or despair. I said, "I've got to get home anyway, B. I'm watching Kit tonight."

"Babysitting?" Colin said. "For your mommy?"

"That's the plan," I said.

"Three kids in ten years? Is she even done yet?" I felt my ire begin to rise. "I mean, that's too many kids, I'm just saying."

"When are you going to stop making your mommy wash your socks?" I said acidly. *"I'm just saying."*

"You know," he said, "our planet has a carrying capacity."

"If you're worried about overpopulation," I said, "I'd be happy to step outside with you and even things out."

He stared at me for a long minute and then disappeared back into the basement.

"There but for the grace of God," Bethany said.

"No," I said. "Come on, you're not anything like that. Colin's not shy, he's a lazy little twit who thinks his mom should still be buying his underpants. You're not going to end up like that."

"Are you kidding? Do you know how many days I would like to just lock myself in my room and never talk to anybody? All the time. All the time. It's like, every day when I go out of the house I feel like I'm holding my breath. I hate it." She collapsed into the nearest chair, pulling a canvas grocery bag out from under her butt and kneading it between her hands.

I frowned. "You feel like that when you're talking to me?"

"No. But you're different."

"I'm not different."

"You are, though."

"You're just used to me."

"I guess," she said. She tossed the grocery bag across the room. "Are you really babysitting tonight?"

"Yeah, Mom has some birthday party and Dad's teaching."

"Can I come over? I might as well have fun before Mom throws me out on my butt."

"Sure, if you want. It's just going to be cartoons and homework."

"That sounds really good, actually. Well, not the homework, I guess. Are you done fixing the Deanna app?"

I hesitated before saying, "Almost."

"You want me to log in some?" she asked. "I can ask her some questions for you."

"No, no," I said. "It's fine."

We sat on my living room floor with our stuff spread out on the coffee table while Kit and Walnut took over the couch; me with my Latin, Bethany with her Spanish, and Kit with some T-rated anime that was probably not strictly age appropriate, but when you're the third child no one cares about that stuff anymore. On the screen, some guy produced a sword from inside his own throat and started hacking at people with it while it was still sticking out of his mouth.

"That's disturbing," Bethany said.

"But handy," I replied. "I mean, I often wish I had a sword I could pull out of my own throat and use to attack people."

"Do you think he sets off metal detectors?" There was a lot of blood, and Bethany flinched. "Could we watch *My Little Pony* instead?"

Kit cried, "NO, DON'T SUMMON GAMAKATSU!"

"What does that mean?" Bethany asked.

"I have no idea," I said, hoping we weren't scarring him too badly. I went back to my *Metamorphoses* translation, which was due tomorrow. I'd gotten to the part toward the end where Pygmalion goes to cop a feel on this poor statue and he's like, "A REAL BOOB!" so he pokes it a couple of more times to be sure, and somehow, miraculously, the come-to-life statue does not murder him right there. "I hate this story." I put my pencil down. "This guy sucks."

Bethany glanced over my shoulder at my translation. "Does he really poke her in the boob?"

"Well, I'm taking some artistic license translating *temptat* as 'poke,' but the rest of it's spot-on."

"I think I'd rather end up with the guy with the throat sword. What a douche."

"Douchecanoe," I suggested.

"Douchenozzle?"

"Douche*cannon.*" That made Bethany laugh until she doubled over.

"What's a douche?" Kit asked from the couch. Bethany looked aghast, but I said, "Something the patriarchy told women they needed but it turned out they didn't."

"What's the patriarchy?"

"That thing that says you can't cry or wear purple."

At that, Mom came out of her room. "I'm heading out," she said, blatantly ignoring the gore on the television. "Don't let him stay up too late."

"Aphra said I can stay up till ten," he piped up.

"I did not say that," I said. "But you can stay up till 9:15 if you let Bethany watch her ponies."

"Ugh," he said. "The ponies."

"You love the ponies!" Bethany protested.

"Not anymore. That's a baby show."

"I'm not a baby, and I like it."

"You're a girl."

I pointed my finger at him and exclaimed, "Patriarchy!" even though, truth be told, I was also sick of the ponies. He glumly handed Bethany the remote, we gave him the Kit Kiss, which he promptly wiped off, and then Bethany scrolled through Crunchyroll until she found her favorite episode with Rainbow Dash and Daring Do. Honestly, I kind of preferred the show with throat-sword guy, but I'm a good friend, and anyway, it's easier to do homework when the show in the background is something you've seen 500 times.

Mom leaned in for a hug and I batted her away. "Stop," I said. "You smell like the white death."

Bethany said, "What?"

"It's the coconut in my shampoo," Mom said. "She's being dramatic."

"Oh, right," Bethany said. "The Girl Scout cookie incident."

"We don't talk about that," I said.

"How many had you eaten?"

"We don't talk about that."

"I think it was eight," Mom said, tying her hair in a ponytail. "I counted when I had to clean them out of the carpet."

"Unless you want to clean tonight's dinner out of the carpet, you really need to stop," I said, because while Superman has kryptonite and the Green Lantern has literally anything yellow (and, like, how does he even pee?), I have . . . coconut. When I was eight, I'd come down with the stomach flu an hour after eating half a box of Samoas, and let me tell you, they don't taste as good coming up as they do going down, and no matter how many times Mom told me it was the norovirus that made me puke, not the cookies, the reptilian part of my brain can never quite believe it. Ever since then, the taste, the smell, even the sight of coconut makes the back of my throat close up. . . . Even the piña colada song is enough to send me running to the bathroom. So of course, when Mom's department secretary starting hawking essential oils, Mom caved and bought two bottles of this coconut-scented shampoo, which in theory is supposed to "dispel stress" but in practice makes me gag.

Mom kissed Kit on the cheek and blew a raspberry on his neck. "I'm going," she said. "Be good." She pointed at me. "9:15."

"Yes'm," I said.

But at 9:30, Bethany had fallen asleep on top of her Spanish and Kit and I were back to gory anime.

"You should go to bed," I said.

"What about Bethany?"

I nudged her shoulder. "B," I said. "B, throat-sword guy got the ponies."

She blinked at me a few times. "Really?"

"Yeah, it was horrible. C'mon, I'll walk you back."

She sat up and rubbed her face. "Crap, I didn't even finish this."

"Get up early and do it tomorrow," I said.

"I hate this," she said, closing her notebook. "Like, there's not that much to remember. How am I so bad at it?" I was putting my shoes on, but she said, "Don't walk me back, that's dumb."

"But it's dark."

"Yeah, but then *you* have to walk home alone in the dark."

"Yeah, but . . ."

"I'll text you when I get there," she said. "In about two minutes."

"Fine," I said. "Don't forget, though, or I'm calling someone."

Two minutes later, I got a proof-of-life text from Bethany, along with a photo. I zoomed in; it was another brochure. This one was titled *Sunset Hills Adult Living,* and the photo was captioned, *I'm so screwed.*

Chapter Ten

That night, at precisely ten o'clock, I heard the strains of *Star Trek* coming from my phone.

This time, I was actually prepared, which meant my phone was by my bed instead of at the bottom of my bag, and I was able to answer it before the autopilot turned on.

Hi, Deanna, he'd written. *So I was wondering, do you speak any languages besides English?*

I have been programmed with a natural language processor, I typed. I didn't think I could play it off that Deanna was programmed to answer questions in Latin, and I was pretty sure Google Translate wasn't going to get me through this. So I said, *I don't speak any languages but English at this time.*

But because I couldn't help myself, I typed. *My programmer is linguistically deficient.*

He typed back, *Perhaps you need a better programmer.*

I laughed. *Perhaps.*

So who is your programmer?

Damn. Damn damn damn. *I am an anonymously authored app, due to privacy concerns.*

Right, he said. *But it was someone at Middleridge. In the app design class. Who likes Star Trek.*

I breathed out. That didn't actually narrow it down all that much. I typed back, *I am a character from Star Trek: The Next Generation. I also appeared in six Star Trek films, and occasionally on Star Trek: Voyager. I like big hair and chocolate.*

Right, right. You boldly go where no one has gone before.

I try. What about you? Have you been bold since the last time we spoke?

Well, I tried to take your advice.

And how did that work out?

I couldn't go through with it. I guess I am not the bold type.

Perhaps you need to work up to it, I said.

Maybe. I don't know. It's hard to be around people who wish you were someone else. You know?

I ran a finger across the bridge of my nose. *That is very true,* I said.

It's like, they say they love you, but what they love is some fantasy version of you. It has nothing to do with you at all. Like we were talking about yesterday, with Pygmalion, right?

It was hard to imagine anyone having a fantasy version of Greg that was better than the reality, but I realized that was kind of a hypocritical thing of me to think. Up until a few weeks ago, I hadn't known anything about him at all, except that he was nice and nice to look at. And still, I'd barely scratched the surface of what Greg was actually like.

But when you try to tell them this, he went on, *they just deny it. So there's no point in even talking about it. And then pretty soon you can't even talk about the fact that you aren't talking. It's just, I don't know.*

Lonely, I typed.

Yeah. I guess. Which is why I'm talking to a chatbot instead of a real person.

I typed, *Bleep bleep bloop.*

Thanks for that. So what do you think I should do?

I think you should be straightforward and tell them everything you told me.

Right, be bold. Easy for you to say. You don't have to live with them.

This is true, I said. *However, you have to ask yourself: Who benefits if you don't tell them how you feel? Them, or you?*

Well, them, because they won't be mad. And me, because it makes my life easier if they aren't mad.

Don't sacrifice long-term happiness for short-term convenience.

You sound like a fortune cookie.

Sometimes fortune cookies are wise beyond the limits of their size and physical appeal.

Like Yoda.

Yes, like Yoda.

. . .

. . .

I was about to turn off my phone, figuring he was done for the night, when he typed, *So there's this girl. Sometimes I think she likes me, but other times she acts like she's totally not interested.*

No. No, no, no, this was definitely veering into TMI, and I'd promised myself I wouldn't let him tell me anything really personal or embarrassing. So I typed: *Gender is a social construct. Have you eaten any waffles lately?*

If I didn't know better, I'd think you were changing the subject.

The subject is the main noun of a sentence, which is minimally constructed of a subject, which may be implied, and a verb.

Oh, now you're definitely changing the subject. Aren't you programmed to give relationship advice?

I rubbed my forehead. *Please,* I thought, *do not tell me who you are into. It will ruin everything.*

I guess it doesn't matter. You'll just tell me to be bold again.

That is very good advice for most situations.

All right, all right. I'm going to bed now. Good night, Deanna.

Good night, Friend.

At lunch, I really wanted to slip out, but Sophie wanted me to look at her English paper, so I sat in the cafeteria between her and Bethany reading her essay about the importance of names in *Sula.*

"Well?" she said.

"It's good," I offered. "I think it's too long, though."

"It's supposed to be 500 words, and it's only 55."

"Yeah, but you could cut a third of it and it would say the same thing."

"Gah," she said. "Why did I even ask you." She slipped the paper back toward her side of the table and went back to eating her fries.

Bethany, who was sitting next to me, finished the last of her bottle of iced tea and said, "Are you wearing perfume?"

"I ran out of deodorant, so I swiped my dad's Old Spice." I

raised my arms. "I smell like Swagger now." I lifted my arms and she took a whiff.

"That's amazing," she said. "Like, I totally want to make out with your armpit right now."

"I know, right?"

Sophie said, "Really?"

I said, "Smell me."

She did. "That's not bad."

Of course, that was the moment that Greg walked by with a bunch of his swim team buddies, getting an eyeful of my friends smelling my pits, because that was the exact impression I wanted to make. He waved. Of the three of us, Sophie was the only one with the intestinal fortitude to wave back.

Bethany lowered her forehead to the table.

Over the top of her head, Talia said, "Do you guys want to do cupcakes or pizza after the next regatta?"

"Pizza," Sophie said. "We did cupcakes last time. Aphra?"

"Huh? Oh. Pizza's fine, I don't really care."

Bethany looked up from the table. "Could we . . . could we maybe get both?"

"Do we want Pizza Trevi or Pizza Firenze?"

"Trevi has the gluten-free crust," Sophie pointed out.

"Ew."

Bethany said, "But if we—"

"Then don't eat it, but Divya can't have the regular kind."

"I have a coupon for Trevi," Divya called from a little farther down the table.

Bethany was looking down at her lap. I elbowed her. When she didn't respond, I said, "We're getting cupcakes after, though, right?"

"What?" Divya called.

"Aphra wants cupcakes!" Sophie called back.

"Fine," Talia said. "We'll do Trevi and cupcakes after." Under the table, I flashed Bethany a little thumbs-up. She smiled a little and gave me one back.

After Latin, Greg tapped my elbow. "Hey," he said. "So I was thinking about coming to crew today. Any chance you could take me out in the pair again after?"

"Really?" I asked.

"Yeah. I mean, I went out with the JV boat for a few minutes on Monday, and I think I'm still doing something wrong. I feel like I'm having trouble keeping up, and my arms hurt like hell after practice."

"Everyone's sore after practice," I pointed out.

"I couldn't lift my arms over my head yesterday. I had to wear a button-down."

"Maybe not that sore. Sure, I'll take you out for a few minutes, if you want."

So after we'd finished practice, while the rest of the team was drinking their Gatorade and stretching, Greg and I pulled *Selkie* up to our shoulders, schlepped her down to the water, and put her in. Before we climbed in, I said, "I think I should sit in the bow today."

"But I won't be able to see what you're doing."

"Yeah, but this time I'd like to check you out." I winced. "I mean, I want to look at your stroke."

"You think I'm rowing wrong?"

"If your arms are that sore, yeah. You should be mostly using your lower body. If you're doing it right, you should be feeling it in your core. Did you have blisters, too?"

"A couple, yeah."

"Try not holding on so tight, and use your core."

"I'll try."

I watched Greg's muscles tense and relax as he rowed in front of me. He was too close. So close, in fact, that I could smell *his* Swagger-scented deodorant. I stifled a laugh.

"What?" he said.

"Nothing," I said, because I didn't want to explain that we were wearing the same deodorant, which was probably the most physically intimate thing Greg D'Agostino and I would ever share, which was simultaneously very funny and very, very sad. "Are you ready to speed it up?"

"I'm ready," he said, and I had him bring the stroke rate up to a 26 for the next three minutes before I could tell he was starting to falter.

"Weigh enough," I said, and he kind of collapsed.

"How is it," he panted out, "that I'm falling over right now and you're fine?"

I wasn't fine, not by a long shot, but I'd seen the problem, so I said, "Your stroke is still too deep. That's what's wearing you out."

"But isn't that what moves the boat forward?"

"Yeah, but you're sacrificing speed for power. It's just like swimming; you don't run your arms like a windmill. Look." He did his best to look over his shoulder, and I bobbled my oar in the water and pointed to the end. "Imagine a line here. That's all you want to submerge. You're putting in way too much."

"Okay," he said. "Okay, I think I get it."

You ready to try again?"

"Yeah, I think so."

"Sit ready," I said, "and go. . . ." I watched his stroke as we made our way back across. "Less," I called. "Even less." He raised his oar just a hair, and I said, "That's perfect."

After five minutes, we paused again. He was still panting, but he'd made it the whole way without collapsing this time.

"That felt better," he said.

"It was better. Just remember, you're not rowing the boat by yourself. Rowing's not like swimming. It's 100% a team sport."

"No *I* in *boat*, huh?"

"Nope," I said. "You're just one leg on a millipede."

He laughed.

"So," I said, trying to figure out how to frame this. "I gather swimming isn't going too well."

His head popped up in surprise, and I quickly added, "You said you've been skipping practice a lot. That's all I meant."

"Oh," he said. "Yeah, I have."

I looked down at my feet. I was wearing the Rainbow Dash socks Bethany had given me.

Greg said, "I kind of want to quit, actually."

This much I knew. "Tired of the early mornings?"

"No. Well, yeah, there's that, but also I'm just super burned out." He exhaled a stream of air. "I've been burned out for a while, actually. I wanted to quit last year."

"So why didn't you?"

"My parents kind of flipped. They were hoping I'd be going to college on a swim scholarship."

"That . . . that sounds tough. But . . . but you talked to them, right?"

"I don't know." I felt a little wobble in the boat. He had a hard time sitting still in general, which was a problem. "It's hard."

"Not for you, though. You could tell them in six different languages."

"Probably only four," he said. "But that's not the point."

"The point is . . ."

He made sort of a choking noise. "Why do you care so much?"

"It's not . . . I don't . . . I just think you'd be happier. Like, you're dreading this conversation, so just have it already, right?"

He shrugged.

"Are your parents as conflict-avoidant as you are?"

He laughed.

"Right. Okay. Got it."

We rowed a few more strokes. Finally, he said, "It's not that I don't know what to say. It's that I can see the entire conversation playing out in my head, and I know exactly, line by line, how it's going to go and where it'll end up, and I really don't want to go there. It's like . . . like every conversation I have with my parents is a script that's already written. All I get to decide is whether to have the conversation or not."

I nodded thoughtfully, because I kind of knew what he meant. Sometimes I'll work out a whole dialogue in my head and then when the actual conversation happens it seems anticlimactic. I smiled. "Did you script this conversation, too?"

"Well, no."

I found that oddly satisfying.

"You're right, though. I should get it over with. Fortuna audaces iuvat, right?"

Fortune favors the bold. "There you go. Sounds like you've got it all figured out."

• • •

That night, when Greg messaged me, I decided to cut to the chase. *Were you bold yet?*

Actually, he typed, *I was.*

I was sore from the extra rowing with Greg, and I had a hot pack wedged behind my lower back. I typed, *Excellent!*

And now my parents hate me.

I put my hand over my mouth.

I'm sure that's not true. What did you tell them?

I told them I wasn't as good a swimmer as they thought, I'd never get money to swim at a Division I school, and I want to quit. In return, they called me an ungrateful brat and yelled about all the money they'd spent for me to swim for the last nine years. It turns out I was a really bad investment.

I felt myself seething at Greg's parents. They had a kind, smart kid who spoke six languages, and all they could see was the money they'd poured down the drain for sports? *You are a great person! So what if you aren't some swimming robot? You are more than just some commodity. You're worth more than the size of your financial aid package.*

The was a very long pause, and I realized I was sounding even less like a computer than usual. I was trying to think of something to save it when he typed, *What is the value of 2462/452?*

I stared at the figure for a minute. Why is he asking . . .

Oh, shit.

I pulled my calculator out from under my notebook and started frantically typing in numbers.

427, I replied.

Too late, he said. *No computer would have been that slow.*

I am programmed for dialogue, not mathematical reason—

Bull. Shit. Who is this?

I am an application programmed by a student at

BULLSHIT. Who is this?

Bleep bleep bloop.

Don't give me that crap. I've been telling you my life story for days. Who is this? I'm sure you know exactly who I am.

I sat back and ran my palms down my face. This was bad. The whole point of the app was that it was supposed to be anonymous. I'd been so, so careless. Of course he knew I wasn't a computer.

So here's what I've figured out: You're in the app design class at Middleridge.

That didn't narrow it down too much; of course he'd know that.

And you knew all about Division I sports being the ones with the scholarship money, so you're an athlete.

I sat up. Oh, shit.

And you're a girl.

There's no way he could have known that.

Women use language differently than men. You have feminine speech patterns.

That may have been the first time anyone said that to me. *I do not!* I typed.

The exclamation point gives it away, he said. *So how many female athletes are there in Mr. Positano's app design class?*

Answer: not many. Aside from me, Amy Berger played field hockey, Mitzi Schwartz was on the swim team with Greg, and then there was Bethany.

Probably he wouldn't have figured that out yet.

I just texted Matt Williams for a class roster, so it's really only a process of elimination.

Ugh. Matt Williams was one of the seniors with the non-functioning *Steak Ninja* game, and he swam with Greg. I closed out of the app and threw my phone to the far end of my bed, where it landed next to Walnut, who promptly sat on it. Then I sat up, curling my knees into my chest.

I heard the *Star Trek* theme from underneath the cat, but no way was I picking up. Let him talk to the Deanna autopilot for a while. I needed to figure out what to do.

What was I going to do?

I needed to turn in the source code and my sample pages tomorrow, so at least I had an excuse not to run the app anymore. I could take the entire thing down and just hope he never figured it out. That sounded like a good plan to me.

I also wouldn't get to talk to him anymore, but that seemed like a small price to pay for not flunking my class.

I fished my phone out from under the cat, not because I wanted to reply, but because I wanted to know what he'd said.

He'd typed, *Please just tell me who you are. I promise I won't get mad. I just want to know who I've been talking to this whole time. Be bold, right? Who are you?*

I touched the screen. *Who are you?*

I imagined a world where I could tell him. Where he'd actually want to know who I was, where I would tell him and he'd drive to my house and climb up to my window. I'd open the glass—in my fantasy, there's no screen—and he'd lean inside, his face flushed with longing, and he'd tell me he'd been hoping, all this time, that it was really me. He'd touch my face and tell me I had the prettiest eyes in the world, and then he'd kiss me, and

I'd kiss him, and it would be the most perfect moment that ever existed.

My heart was racing with imagining it. I tried not to think of what people would say if they saw us together, or how we'd look in pictures, or how it would hurt when he realized that my face was not something he could overlook.

It was so stupid to even think that far ahead, because I knew we would never get that far. I could tell him, sure, and then there'd be some banter, and maybe we'd go on being friends, but I couldn't pretend not to be disappointed.

On the other hand, being friends wasn't nothing, either.

I rolled over in my bed, the phone still clutched in my hand. I would tell him, I decided. When I saw him tomorrow, I would tell him. There wouldn't be any declarations of love or midnight kisses at my window, but I knew him and he knew me and we were friends and that wasn't nothing. Maybe I'd even take him some french toast. He'd like that, probably.

I'd tell him tomorrow, and I would not, *would not* let myself hope for anything more.

Chapter Eleven

I was off-kilter the next morning, probably because I'd woken up half an hour earlier than normal after a weird dream. Well, not weird so much as bad. Actually, it was both weird and bad.

I was sitting by my window, watching Delia come home from college. She pulled up in a yellow taxi, like they have in New York, and she got out and came inside, where I was waiting for her in the kitchen. I went to hug her, but then at that point I realized I was wearing a porcelain mask— like, a mask of my face on top of my real face—so I looked exactly the same, only it was pretty clear my skin wasn't real. Before I could hug her, she stiff-armed me, holding me back, and said, "You know, we can fix that." And before I could answer, she pulled out this giant ball-peen hammer and smashed it into my left cheek. I expected it to hurt, and it did, but I didn't scream because that seemed embarrassing, as if Delia didn't already know that it hurt to get hit in the face with a hammer. Anyway, then she picked off the remaining pieces of porcelain until my true face was revealed—exactly the same as the mask.

"Well, that's disappointing," she said, and then hit me with the hammer again, right between the eyes.

So anyway, I got up and ate two bowls of Kit's frosted wheats, which I have promised never to eat since I accidentally finished the box before he got breakfast one time, but it seemed like I needed some sugar that morning. Probably that was a low-blood-sugar dream. Also, I had a little bit of a sinus headache on the left side, which might explain the hit-in-the-face-with-a-hammer part. I took an ibuprofen and went out to get the bus.

At lunch, I still felt a little sick, maybe from my weird dream or my weird breakfast or from knowing I was going to see Greg in the not-too-distant future, and I was having major second thoughts about this entire operation. I ate one of Bethany's Oreos, telling myself *I'll tell him, I won't tell him* with alternate bites. I ended on *I'll tell him,* but this really didn't seem to be the best way to make a decision.

Bethany, for her part, was also kind of upset, to the point of not being able to finish the Twinkie I'd packed, which she usually would have been the first thing she ate. After staring at it for a minute, she said, "She's buying a house there."

"Who?" I said with a mouthful of cookie. "Whoa. Wait. Are we talking about your mom?"

"Yeah. I asked her about the Shady Pines thing. She's buying a house there. After I graduate from high school, she's selling our house and moving."

"Oh," I said.

"She said I can live at home for the summer, but that's it.

Once I graduate, I'm out. I can't move back after college, or live at home and go to school at the same time." She flattened her Twinkie until the filling squished out.

"Wow," I said.

"Yeah. I mean, it's not like I wanted to live at home forever, but now . . . I don't know. It's like—it's like there's no more margin for error. You know? What if I hate the dorm, or I can't get a job right away when I graduate? Or—or—or I don't know."

It did sound a little like doing the flying trapeze and realizing that someone had just pulled your safety net back. I sure don't want to live with my parents forever, either, but it's nice knowing I have someplace to go if, like, I get a brain tumor or something. "Are you okay?"

"I mean, no? I'm just so pissed at Colin. If he was even kind of pleasant to live with, she wouldn't be doing this. It's just, why can't he buy a gallon of milk once in a while? I'm not like that. But I think Mom's kind of done."

"Yeah, well. What's Colin's doing?"

"He's going to have to get a job and some roommates, I guess. And be 20% less of an asshole or they're going to throw him out, too." She sighed. "I feel like I'm being punished and I didn't actually do anything."

"I know."

"I mean, I do my own laundry. I do the dishes every other night. I make dinner once a week."

"I know."

"It's not fair." She rubbed her face. "Don't say 'I know.' "

"You're not horrible to live with like Colin is. She knows that. You're great. He sucks. It's not fair."

She leaned her head on my shoulder and sounded like she

was thinking about crying. "It's like she doesn't even want me around," she said.

"Hey," I said. "I want you around."

We sat and picked at our food, her wondering what it would be like not to be able to go home anymore, me wanting to tell her she could stay with us if she wanted but knowing my parents' house wasn't exactly mine to offer.

I also wondered if Greg was at school yet.

I did realize that one of these things was probably more significant than the other.

My head was killing me again. Probably eating all of Bethany's Oreos hadn't helped with that. After some time, Bethany said, "It's five till," because lunch was nearly over and people were starting to leave. The bell rang, and my head throbbed in time with it.

"I think," I told Bethany, "I'm going to the nurse."

"Are you okay?"

"I'm fine," I said. "I'm just going to take another ibuprofen and maybe lie down for 20 minutes until it kicks in." I have a bottle on file in the clinic that my mom signs off on every September so I can get it at will for cramps or whatever, since they can technically suspend you if they find it in your backpack, which is both puritanical and stupid. "Tell Mr. Positano I'll be there in a couple of minutes, okay?"

Bethany frowned. "The app's due today."

"Yeah, I— Oh." I understood what Bethany had not said, which was that if I was not in class, Mr. Positano would likely think I was someplace finishing the app and could therefore dock me 10% for handing it in late. "Damn it." I got the folder out of my backpack. "Can you give it to him? That way it's not late."

"Yeah, sure," she said.

"Thanks, B." I rubbed my cheekbone. "I'll see you, okay?" We split up, me heading toward the nurse's office, her toward the app design classroom. I got to the nurse's office and found it locked.

The nurse's office is attached to the main office, so I stuck my head in and asked one of the secretaries, "Where's Ms. Dao?"

"Getting lunch," she said. "Didn't she put up a sign? She'll be back in ten minutes. You should go to class and come back with a pass later."

"But," I said.

"Go to class. Come back with a pass."

I didn't much feel like arguing. "Fine," I said. "I'll come back."

"With a pass."

Geez, it was like dealing with a prison guard. Sometimes being 17 and stuck in high school makes me feel like I'm trapped in a straightjacket. "Sure," I said. "With a pass."

When I walked out I saw Bethany at the far end of the hall and started speed-walking over to tell her she didn't need to hand in my project after all. She rounded the corner to the science hall and I heard the sound of a collision . . . body hitting body and papers hitting the floor. I sped up to see if she was okay, only to discover that she'd run face-first into Greg, who was carrying a travel coffee mug, the contents of which were now mostly dribbling down his shirt.

Bethany was down on her butt, looking like she'd hit Greg and bounced off. She was a little dazed, but I couldn't tell if that was because she'd actually gotten hurt or because it was Greg, who looked a little addled himself.

"I'm sorry," he was saying, pulling his wet, hot, coffee-stained shirt away from his chest. "Are you okay?"

Bethany made some noncommittal noise.

"I'll get these," he said, setting his cup down on the floor and gathering the papers that were scattered in front of her. I recognized the printout of Bethany's chemistry lab, and then . . .

I was close enough now that I could have said something, in a normal tone of voice, and been heard. I wasn't on the other side of the hall, even. I was close enough to smell Greg's spilled coffee and tell it had cinnamon in it. That's how close I was. Bethany, if she'd looked up, could have seen me standing there. She didn't look up. Her world had narrowed down to the slice of it occupied by Greg D'Agostino and his eyes and his smile.

Greg stopped picking things up—he was staring at my green app design folder, with the title of my project front and center in fourteen-point Times New Roman. My name, I realized, was not on the cover. I'd written it inside, on the first page, because Mr. Positano was finicky about his formatting, and that was how he liked it done. At that moment, I could have killed him for that. I willed Greg to open the folder. Look at the first page. Instead, what Greg said was this:

"It was you."

Oh, no. No, no. Greg's heart, I swear I could feel it. It was going . . . going . . . "It was you all the time."

Gone.

He put the stack of papers down on the floor; the top one, which read "Counselor Deanna App: Code and Examples," stared at me. I wanted to pick it up. I didn't pick it up.

Everything in my brain tilted sideways. Greg's eyes went to Bethany's, which was when I saw it . . . how happy he was. There was actual joy there, like he'd just walked through some miles-long dark tunnel and had suddenly gotten his first glimpse of the sun.

There was no way, none at all, he would have looked at me like that.

Bethany seemed to have fallen into the depths of Greg's eyes, because she made no reply. How could she? This beautiful boy was looking at her like he was Pygmalion and she was his own personal Galatea come to life. She had no idea what he was even talking about, except that he was clearly having some kind of an eros moment, and then he was touching her, threading his fingers in her hair.

This was, I realized, the last chance I would ever get to clear up the confusion. I could go over there right now and explain everything; how the app was mine, how I was the one he'd actually been talking to all this time. How I was the one who saw beyond the pretty face to who he really was.

I willed my feet to move forward.

Okay, maybe just my left foot.

I stood stock-still.

I couldn't do it.

Not to either of them. Not to Bethany, who had a chance to be with the guy she wanted, and not to Greg, who deserved to be with someone he could actually fall for. If I left things alone, there would be two very happy people. If I told the truth, it would be awkward and uncomfortable and there would be zero happy people. It was simple math, really. Keeping my mouth shut resulted in the greatest amount of general happiness. I'd have to be the biggest asshole in the world to mess that up, and it would be for nothing. It wasn't even like I was giving him to her, because clearly this was what he wanted, too.

Greg leaned forward slowly, slowly, like I'd always imagined he might if he were ever to kiss me, and he kissed Bethany. She reached around his neck and pulled him closer, kissing him back.

Well, good for her.

I turned, my fingers brushing my own bottom lip, and walked back the other way, back to the nurse's office and my ibuprofen and 20 minutes on a paper-wrapped cot. It hadn't been ten minutes, though, so the secretary, as I entered the office, said, "Did you bring a pass?"

I doubled over into the nearest chair.

"Honey," she said. "I can't let you into the clinic without a pass."

Officer Barry, who must have been finished manning the door during lunch, walked past me and smacked something into my hand. It was, I realized, a blank hall pass. I felt a great surge of affection for Barry and his Taco Bell habit. I got up and set the pass on the secretary's desk. Just as she was unlocking the door for me, the nurse came back with her lunch, so I took my pill and lay down on the cot facing the wall, my brain turning and turning the image of Bethany and Greg in the hall, reminding myself that I had no reason to feel bad because I'd been a good person, a good friend. I'd done a good thing, and I'd made two good people happy, and then I thought about how weird the word *good* is, and I wondered about its derivation, since it clearly doesn't come from Latin. It must be Germanic, I guess. Greg would know. I could ask him. Except that we wouldn't be talking online anymore, because that was done with now. But at least I wouldn't be failing my class because of my crappy app, so that part was good, too. Good. What a stupid word. I should get people to start using something better, like bonum, instead. It makes more sense; we already use the root, like for bonus.

Sum amica bona. I am a good friend.

Mihi est vita bona. I have a good life.

It's so much better than *good*, which doesn't work as a prefix, or a suffix, or anything. It just sounds dumb. *Good. Good.* Fuck my life.

I didn't wake up until the nurse was shaking my shoulder and telling me it was time to go home.

Chapter Twelve

Before my sister went to college, when I wasn't rowing or hanging out with Bethany, I was usually with Delia.

Her basement bedroom was kind of dark, but she made it cool, with glow-in-the-dark stars on the ceiling and chalkboard paint on the wall over her bed that she used to leave notes for herself or doodle pictures of anime characters; Sasuke Uchiha, who'd been her crush since she was Kit's age, or L from Death Note, who was mine. Sometimes she'd leave secret messages for me to find, telling me she was sneaking something into my backpack that day, which usually turned out to be some racy book I'd have to hide at school or risk having confiscated. She belonged to an anime club at school, and they used to go to conventions twice a year. I was never invited . . . it was for club members, and I was usually too busy to be gone all day on a weekend anyway. Except one time, when I was in eighth grade and Delia was in tenth, the group was all going as the girls from Sailor Moon and then Sailor Neptune got sick at the last minute.

They already had her ticket and her costume, and while I was sitting on my bed making my way through *The Golden Compass* for the third time, Delia came in and asked me if I wanted to go.

The costume was not particularly my thing. The skirt was super short, even on my little 13-year-old legs, but I'd never been to anything like that before, so I said okay, and I went, not really sure what it was going to be like.

It turns out that anime conventions are basically like Carnival for nerds, like, in the best way possible. Not everybody was dressed up, but lots of people were. Bunches of people asked us for pictures, so we posed, giving the victory sign or an exaggerated wink. We saw panels of voice actors I'd never heard of who looked more like regular people than normal actors. Delia bought me a key chain that's still in a drawer in my room somewhere, and at the end, we had a picture taken of the two of us together, both of us trying to channel the awesomeness of Sailor Moon and sisterhood, our arms around each other. Our wigs were getting a little droopy by then, but the thing about wearing a wig is that the sudden change in hairstyle seems to make your face really stand out. Back then, Delia and I were almost the same height—I didn't get taller until later—so even though my wig was blue and hers was red, we looked like twins. Like, if you didn't know which one was me, if you were a casual observer and not my parents or Bethany, you would not be able to pick me out in the picture. That's how alike we looked. After Delia changed that, I took that picture off my desk and put it downstairs in the bottom of her dresser, where she keeps her sweaters. I couldn't quite bring myself to throw it out. But I didn't want it anymore, either.

• • •

We had a regatta Saturday morning, which meant enduring five hours of Bethany wide-eyed and vibrating all over. Greg wasn't there; he had a Mandarin final or something, and he's still not on the team, anyway. The girls' eight came in third to Great Falls and Madison, which I guess wasn't bad. Afterward, though, I felt like I couldn't catch my breath, and while everyone else was going out for pizza, I just really wanted to go home.

Fortunately, I can always count on Bethany for that. "God," she said, when I suggested it. "Me too. I haven't slept in three days."

We were driving back up from the Occoquan in Bethany's mother's car, as the team bus was full that day. "Are you sure?" I asked. "They were going to Cake Baby later." Cake Baby was Bethany's favorite cupcake place, and as a team, we'd sampled all the ones in the area.

"I just want to go someplace quiet," she said. "I feel like I haven't been able to talk to you for a week."

It was true; I'd managed to be doing homework at lunch yesterday, and I'd been avoiding her texts, too. I felt bad about that, because she was a completely innocent party here. She didn't know I'd been texting with Greg. Still, I didn't apologize. I guess I was too tired.

"I need to tell you something," she said.

Here it came. I waited. I waited. It did not come.

I said, "Greg kissed you."

"What? Who told you?"

"I kind of saw," I said.

"You saw?"

"You were in the middle of the hall, it wasn't super private."

"Oh."

She drove a little farther. I said, "So?"

She blushed. I knew that Bethany had never actually kissed anyone before; there had been a couple of guys who'd tried to mash their face into hers over the years, but she'd always managed to get out of the way at the last minute. I knew she had princess fantasies of the perfect first kiss, which was something so pure it could break a curse or bring a dying prince back to life. She said, "I was late for class."

"Oh—okay."

"I kind of handed your Deanna thing in late. I told Mr. Positano it was my fault, though."

"Oh. I'm sure that's fine." *But the kiss, Bethany. What kind of toothpaste does Greg use?* No, wait. He'd been drinking coffee. Did he taste like that? Does a kiss have a taste?

"We're supposed to go out tomorrow."

"Ah," I said. I wondered what kind of place Greg likes to take girls. Maybe he knows all the good hole-in-the-wall Russian spots. I don't know what cheap Russian food looks like. Borscht? I like borscht. Bethany hates borscht. The only good thing about it, she says, is the color. Probably because it looks like Twilight Sparkle soup. She doesn't really appreciate it, though. She doesn't understand, like, the nuance of borscht.

At this point in my thought process, I realized I had a problem. I was getting jealous over hypothetical consumption of beet soup, which even I know is, like, just beet soup. I looked at Bethany, who was driving, and knew I did not want to be this way. Sum amica bona. I am a good friend. Right?

"Where are you going?" I asked. "With Greg, I mean."

"Oh, God. He wants to go out for Russian food."

I was fine. I was fine. "You don't seem very happy about that."

"I just . . . A restaurant? Alone? With Greg?"

That sounded very good to me. "That's bad?"

"Aphra, it's like 90 minutes of doing nothing but talking to his face."

"And you'd rather be sucking his face?"

"Jeez! No." *Yes, Bethany.* "That's not what I meant. It's just . . . It's a lot. I don't know."

"So did you suggest an alternative? Why don't you go see a movie?"

"A movie." She was stopped at a light and turned toward me. "I could totally do a movie. That's perfect."

"So tell him you want to see a movie. The new Star Wars is out. Tell him you've been dying to see it."

"But what if he doesn't want to?"

"He won't care, he just wants to see you."

She pulled in to the nearest strip mall. "What are you doing?" I asked.

She thrust her phone at me. "Text him," she said.

"What? Why?"

"If I do it, I'll mess it up!"

"There's nothing to mess up! Just tell him you really want to see the thing with the damn porgs!"

"Aphraaaaaaa . . . ," she whined.

I really was tired. I rubbed my eyes. I said, "Fine."

I texted, *Hey, so as much as I am loving the idea of borscht tomorrow, I can't stop thinking about how fun it would be to share my love of porgs with you. Would you be averse to the idea of seeing a movie instead?*

He texted back so fast I think he must have been waiting to hear from her after the regatta. *Porgs, huh? Sure, that sounds good.*

I looked up the movie listings in a second window. *7:15?*

I'll pick you up at 7. Unless you'd rather pick me up at 7.

I eyed Bethany over the phone, who was staring at me while I typed. "Do you have the car tomorrow?" I asked.

"No, my mom has some Toastmasters thing."

Pick me up at 7, I said.

Can't wait.

I texted him a gif of Yoda saying, *Patience, young Padawan.*

Your gif game is 1,000 times better than that movie.

Yes, I said. *But to be fair, the bar is low.*

Too bad you weren't writing the screenplay.

Well, considering that movie came out when I was 5, the dialog would have been like, "Me no like sand."

Pretty sure that line's in the movie. Is it possible you wrote it and don't remember?

I think I'm insulted. Wait. I'm sure of it. Buy me some Junior Mints and I may forgive you.

Bethany was watching this exchange with her brows knitted together. She couldn't actually read what I was typing, but I knew this was going on too long. I typed, *I'll see you tomorrow. At 7.*

Perfect.

I handed Bethany back her phone, and she mouthed the words as she read what I'd written.

"How did you do that?" she asked. "Like, you didn't even think about any of this before you typed it. You weren't even trying."

"Trying to what?"

"To be flirty! It's just like, you open your mouth . . . or your hands or whatever, and this stuff just comes out. It'd take me all day to come up with this, and it wouldn't be as good, either."

I did not love the way this was going. "Yeah, but," I said. "But you know you can't ask me to do this all the time, right? Like, you're the one who's going out with him, not me. You should, you know, be yourself."

"Yeah, I guess you're probably right. Especially since I don't like Junior Mints."

"Everyone likes Junior Mints."

"No, that's you. They get stuck in my teeth. I hate that."

"Oh. Sorry."

I went home after that, skipped my shower, and fell asleep face-down on my bed. I woke up a few hours later to the sounds of my brother shrieking my sister's name downstairs, and I sat up and looked out the window. There was a car I didn't recognize in front of the house.

It couldn't have been Delia, because she wasn't coming home until Sunday and it was Saturday, which is not at all the same thing. I curled my fingers around the windowsill. "Dad?" I shouted. "DAD?"

No answer. He was probably somewhere reading about medieval tax codes; he spends most of his waking hours translating thousand-year-old pipe rolls. Where was Mom? Downstairs with Kit, it sounded like. Damn. Damn. I was still in my singlet from crew. I couldn't believe I actually took a nap in it. I was greasy and smelly and gross and today was definitely not Sunday, because I know how to read a calendar.

I got up and watched through the window as my sister got out the passenger side of an old sable-colored sedan. Out of the driver's side stepped a boy sporting a man bun, wearing a checked button-down with the sleeves rolled to the elbow. A boy? I shouted, "DAD!"

Delia grabbed the boy by the hand, led him to the front door, and put her tongue in his mouth.

Chapter Thirteen

I took a step back from the window as they pried their faces apart for a millisecond and then knocked, my sister and her boyfriend. Then she went back to eating his face.

Her boyfriend. Had someone told me she was bringing one? I guess it could have been in one of her emails, since I never actually read them.

Dad stuck his head in my door. "What?" He looked out the window. "Ah," he said, cutting his eyes away from some very excessive PDA.

"Aphra!" my mother called. "APHRA!"

My father said, "I suppose this means we have to go down."

"She brought *a boy.*"

"Yes, I witnessed the boy."

"Did we know she was bringing a boy?"

"We did."

"Wait. He's not . . . he's not staying here, is he?"

"He is."

"For how long?!"

"Two weeks." Dad rubbed his eyes. "He's got a bunch of friends he's visiting up here before he flies back to Denver."

"Why isn't he staying with *them*?"

Mom called again. "Where are you people?"

Dad said, "We should go." I was marched down the stairs ahead of my father, who seemed to think I might turn around and flee back to my room otherwise. By the time we'd come down the stairs, Delia was sitting on the living room couch next to the man bun, their fingers threaded together and their knees bouncing up and down in unison. Kit was curled up on the far side of the couch around Walnut, whose eyes bulged like maybe Kit was squeezing the life out of him. I wondered if anyone had told Kit about the boyfriend.

"Hey, Aphra," my sister said. I reluctantly met her eyes , trying to look anywhere but at the middle of her face. She was wearing a bunch of makeup, and her hair was sleek from being blown out. I realized with a stab that she looked . . . pretty.

I hated her for looking pretty. "Hey, Delia," I said brightly, faking it where I could not make it. I perched myself on the arm of the chair where my mother was sitting with her hands wrapped viselike around a cup of tea. Dad, left with nowhere to sit except next to the boyfriend, hovered in the doorway and checked the time on his watch.

"This is Sebastian," she said, nudging Man Bun with her shoulder. He smiled and extended his hand, which I shook.

"Nice to meet you," I said. To Kit, I said, "He's going to puke on you, stop."

He relaxed his grip on Walnut and snuffled.

"Mom said you're getting allergy shots twice a week now," Delia said. "That must suck."

"It doesn't suck," I said, because that was not helpful.

"They aren't so bad," Kit said in a small voice. He hugged the cat a little tighter. Walnut's tongue protruded from between his lips.

"Are they helping? The side of your face is still kind of red."

Kit's eyes flicked to me, and he absently scratched his temple. "Aphra says they take like a year to start working."

"A year!" Delia said. "That's crazy."

"It's not crazy," I said. "He just has to take his antihistamines in the meantime."

"He's snuffling," she said. "Is that new?"

"He's getting a cold!"

"You can't possibly know that."

"Well, let's test it," I said. "Kit, cough on Delia."

Mom pinched the back of my leg. I retaliated by leaning across the back of my chair, my arm stretched behind her head, which put my smelly armpit at roughly the same meridian as her face. She looked at me darkly. I smiled.

"Do you do gymnastics?" the boy said, gesturing at my singlet.

I grit my teeth a little, because obviously no girl my size does gymnastics of any kind; like, my feet would drag on the floor under the uneven bars and my vault landings would leave a crater in the mat. I said, "No."

Leaning to the other side of the chair, Mom said, "Aphra's on the crew team." To me, she said, "Why don't you get changed so we can get dinner, Aphra. Our reservation's in half an hour." She got up. "I'm going to go up and wash my face. . . . I'll be down in a minute."

I followed her up. At the top of the stairs, she said, "Please do not do this today."

"Do what? I'm not doing anything."

"You were nasty to everyone in that room!"

"What? I was kidding about the coughing thing. It was a joke!"

"Not. Today."

"What is your problem? Are you afraid Man Bun won't like you?"

"We don't call people names in this house."

"Man Bun is not a name, it's a descriptor."

"Aphra, so help me God—"

"Okay. I get it. I'll be nice, I promise. I'll tell Sebastian all about my illustrious career as the world's most massive gymnast and that time I left a dent in the balance beam."

"He was just trying to make conversation."

Explaining to my mother that this had been a pointed comment would not do any good. On the surface, it was innocent. She probably hadn't even heard the tone that'd gone along with it. It was meant to be ironic. Because of course I was not a delicate pixie gymnast.

"Just forget it," I said. "I said I'd be nice."

"Don't pick a fight with Delia her first day home," she said. "Please."

"I won't," I said. "I will be the picture of familial harmony."

At Yen Cheng, we were seated at one of those giant lazy Susan tables, me between Kit and my dad, with Delia and Man Bun on the other side of him and Mom between Man Bun and Kit.

"It's so hard to find authentic Chinese food," Man Bun remarked, reading his menu. "Nobody eats this stuff in China."

I happen to know that Yen Cheng has two menus—the American-style one and the Chinese one—and I wished Greg was with me, because he could have asked about it and then ordered in Mandarin. I thought about texting him and then realized I didn't have his number and there was no way to get it from Bethany without looking weird.

"American Chinese food is so sweet," Delia said, as if she doesn't order sweet and sour chicken every single time we go out. I considered asking her if that meant she wasn't a regular at the Charlottesville Panda Express like she was at the one at home, but my mother was giving me serious eyeball, so I smiled and went back to my menu.

"And so bland. Nothing's hot enough," Sebastian agreed.

Kit was frowning, because (like Delia) he likes the American-style sweet stuff. I rested my hand on the back of his chair and said, "They have those paper-wrapped chicken wings you like."

"Can I get those?"

"Sure," Dad said, and, since the waiter had arrived, ordered for himself and Kit. Delia got some kind of spicy beef thing I was pretty sure she wouldn't eat.

I said, "Sweet and sour chicken. Please." Delia glared at me. I smiled. I was being very nice.

"So, Sebastian," Dad said. "Delia said you guys met in a biology class. Are you pre-med, too?"

"What?" he said. The waiter had put out some spring rolls, and he put one on his plate with some hot mustard. "Oh, no. I was just taking that for a gen-ed requirement. You know."

"Oh," Mom said. "Sure, gotta get those out of the way. So have you thought about your major yet?"

He stuffed a big bite of spring roll into his mouth. I noticed, with some satisfaction, that he was holding his chopsticks wrong. "Well, not really. Since I'm actually not going back next semester."

"Oh, you're taking time off? That can be a good thing," Dad said. "Are you planning to work or travel?"

He smirked. "I'm actually not taking time off. I'm just leaving. See, I have this YouTube channel that's making bank, and I'm planning to work full-time on my brand."

"Your . . ." Mom said. "Your brand?"

"His videos have been going viral for months," Delia said. "You've probably seen some of them on Facebook."

"Hm," Sebastian said with his mouth full. "See, I take clips of famous movies, pull out the audio, and replace it with this George Michael song."

My father stopped moving with his fork halfway to his mouth and met my mother's eyes.

"So," I said. I was smiling as nicely as possible. "You . . . post videos of movie clips set to old pop songs?"

"Song," he said. "It's just the one song. You know, 'Careless Whisper'? It kills. My *Rogue One* clip got 20,000 hits last month."

"And," my father said, "you've been able to . . . monetize this?"

"I'm making bank, man," he said, punctuating his words by poking his chopstick into the tablecloth. "Academia's a dead end. Colleges charge all this money for a degree you can't get a job with. I need to strike while the iron's hot."

Nice! I was so nice. "You are so right—wow!" I pointed to my mother. "Wasn't I just saying that to you last week?"

"It's just, what they're teaching is not applicable to my life, right? Most of my profs have been teaching the same exact syllabus for the last 20 years. Like, you're dried up, dude, move on. Nobody's listening." He glanced at my mom. "I mean, no offense."

"HA!" I said. "So dried up!"

Delia said, "Hey, I got an A on my organic chemistry final! They just posted it this morning."

The waiter returned with our food and set it out in the middle of the table.

I dumped the entire order of sweet and sour chicken onto my plate. "I'm *starving,*" I told Delia.

Mom said, "Uh. So. You think there are long-term prospects in setting films to torch songs?"

"That's why I'm leaving UVA. I need more time to expand my brand. The way I figure it, if I can maximize my exposure for two, three years, I can live off the profits for ten."

"That is great!" I said. "Maximizing your brand exposure sounds way more important than sitting in class all day." Someone kicked me under the table. Based on the size of the foot, it was either Delia or my mother.

My father set down his drink. "So . . . um . . . not to pick a fight, but how is this not a copyright violation?"

"It's all under fair use," he said. "I cover my ass."

"Look at you! Covering your ass, wow. That's. That's super impressive," I said. I pulled out my phone. "I've really got to look at this, like, right now. What's your YouTube handle?"

"Um. FilmHaxLolz."

"No way. I . . . ha ha . . . I see what you did there. That is so . . . cool. . . ." I pulled it up and clicked on the top video, which was a scene from *Gladiator.* I turned the volume up. Possibly higher than was strictly necessary. Russell Crowe died in the mud to the sound of emotive pop crooning. To be fair, it was actually pretty funny and it had like 35,000 likes. Mostly I was mad that I hadn't thought of it first, even though I still wasn't sure how the clicks turned into actual dollars.

Across the table, Delia was shoveling spicy beef into her mouth as rapidly as possible. Mom's chopsticks had slid off her plate and into her lap, and Kit was laughing at the video with his mouth full of chicken. To the waiter, Dad said, "Can I get another beer?"

Back at home, Kit went up for a bath, Delia and Sebastian went downstairs—I don't like to think why—while Mom and Dad puttered around the kitchen loading the dishes from earlier in the day.

"Academia's dead," Dad said after he finished rinsing the griddle he'd used to make Kit's Saturday grilled cheese sandwich. "I'm so glad someone's around to blow the dust off our moldering corpses and tell us these things."

"I spent eight years in college," Mom said. "All I needed was a YouTube channel."

"And the foresight to knock off George Michael," I added.

"You," she said. "Were not helping."

"You told me to be nice!"

"We may need to discuss what that actually means. Sheesh. I remember before that song was a joke."

"It's not a joke," Dad protested. "Is it a joke?"

I made a so-so motion with my hand "It's okay. Nobody expects you to know this stuff when you're as out of touch with modern life as you are."

Mom put a box of crackers in the pantry, put her hands over her face, and let out a strangled noise. "This is fine," she said. "This is totally fine."

"Do you want me to get you a pillow to scream into?" I asked.

"No, no. I'm good. My daughter's boyfriend is making bank. That's good, right? I mean, you want your kids to have more than you."

I got up and handed her a throw pillow from the couch.

"It's okay, Mom," I said. "Just let it out."

"I don't need to scream into the pillow," she said.

"Do it."

"I'm good."

"Do it. You know you want to."

"I do want to," she said. "Should I?"

"You totally should." She took the pillow from me, pressed it to her face, and screamed. From the kitchen, Dad said, "Feel better?"

Lifting her face, she said, "No."

"It could be worse," I said. "I mean, he could be in jail. As it is, he's only a vacuous douchenozzle."

"I'm not sure that's worse. What's he in jail for? Is it drugs? I think I'd be okay with drugs."

"Mom."

"It's okay," Dad said. "I'm sure she'll dump him as soon as he gets sued by George Michael."

"It's fair use, old man."

Just then, we were disturbed to hear the distinctive sounds of Delia's bed thumping against the wall.

Perhaps, I thought, it was not too late to insist that Man Bun sleep in a tent out in the yard. Or at the local campground. Or in Greenland.

"Oh my God," Mom said, perhaps regretting her choice to be a Cool Parent. I thought about pointing this out before realizing it was not in my best interest to do so.

"Is that . . . is that for real?" I wheezed.

"I'm going out," Dad said, making a beeline for the front door. "I need. Something. I need something."

"I need something, too," Mom said. "Badly. I don't know what it is, but I need it right now." As I started to put on my own shoes, she said, "Stay here with your brother."

"What?"

"He's in the tub."

"But I don't want to—"

"Thanks," she said, following my dad out the door. From the basement, there was an especially loud thunk. I was glad Kit was upstairs, at least. What were they thinking? "For offering to babysit while we get our, uh, our things. I appreciate that."

"Mom!"

"You're so nice," she said. "Don't you think she's nice, Gordon?"

"The nicest," Dad said.

"I hate you both."

They closed the door, and I went upstairs, both to get out of earshot of my sister's sexytimes and to keep my baby brother from coming down in the middle of said sexytimes. My phone buzzed with a text from Bethany. It said, *Can I come over?*

I texted back, *You really, really don't want to.* And then I turned off my phone and went to make sure Kit hadn't drowned.

Chapter Fourteen

The next day, unsurprisingly, my parents came up with excuses to be on campus.

"I have to finish grading my finals," Mom said. "There's no way I can do that with six people in the house."

I knew Dad had already finished grading *his* finals, but he just said, "Those tax records won't decipher themselves," and then they both vanished, leaving me alone with my brother, my sister, and the shining star of FilmHaxLolz.

Delia, at least, had the good grace to sleep in. Kit, on the other hand, flung open the door to my bedroom, to which I'd retreated after my seven o'clock oatmeal. He was carrying a stack of paper and a box of crayons.

"Draw me a mooshroom," he said.

I was typing—working on a history essay—and went back to it. "Are we doing a reenactment of *The Little Prince*?"

"Please," he said flatly.

I pushed away from my desk. "Fine, but I need cookies

for this," I said, and we went into the kitchen and sat down at the table, me with the box of crayons, Kit with a box of Chips Ahoy! for encouragement. "Why am I drawing a mooshroom?" I asked. At least his rash looked a little better today, which was kind of a relief. "Why aren't *you* drawing a mooshroom?"

For the Minecraft uninitiated, a mooshroom is some kind of unholy union between a cow and a mushroom. Instead of milk, it makes mushroom stew. Or mooshroom stew. Or something like that; I'm not really sure. It's either very clever or downright horrifying, depending on how you look at it. Kit said, "I told Kyle P. about mooshrooms on the bus, but his mom won't let him play Minecraft 'cause she says it's too violent, and he said I was making it up, and you draw better than me, so if I show him a really good drawing of a mooshroom he'll know they're real. Well, real in the game."

"Minecraft's too violent?" I asked.

"Because of the mobs."

"Ah." I nodded thoughtfully. "Right." I sketched out a Guernsey cow with red and white mushrooms on its back. Her back, actually, since all mooshrooms appear to be female. There are no bullshrooms. Which is something, actually. Minecraft has no male animals at all. Yet any two of them can reproduce. I wonder sometimes what the developer was trying to say with that.

"Here you are," I said, handing over the drawing. "One mooshroom."

"Thanks," he said, admiring it. It was, I have to admit, pretty good. "Is he really staying two weeks?" he asked, flopping down on the floor. Walnut had wandered over, and Kit mashed his face into his upturned belly.

"Get your face out of the cat. Yeah, that's what Dad said."

"My friends aren't allowed to sleep over for two weeks," he said, sitting up a little.

"No, they sure aren't."

"That's not fair."

"No, not especially."

"Is it 'cause Delia doesn't live here anymore?"

"Yeah, probably. And he lives far away."

"Where's Denver?"

"Jeez, really?"

"You don't have to be mean about it."

I pulled up a map of the United States on my phone and stuck a finger toward the middle. "Denver," I said. "Capital of . . ."

"Uh. Canada?"

I leaned back in my chair just as Delia and Sebastian came up from the basement.

"Who's going to Canada?" Sebastian asked.

"Apparently you are," I said.

"Do they have YouTube in Canada?" Kit asked.

"That's a good question," Sebastian said. "As a matter of fact, fair use laws aren't consistent internationally, so some of my videos aren't available overseas."

"Is Canada overseas, though?" Delia asked. "I mean, there's no sea. It's more like . . ."

"Over-glacier," I said.

"Is there really a glacier?" Kit asked.

"Yes, but it's farther north. Do you have an atlas?"

"I don't think so."

"Do you have one?" I asked Delia.

"I have an old one of Dad's, but it still has the USSR and East Germany in it."

"What's the USSR?" Kit asked.

"Long story," I said. "Communism. Empire. Babushkas. It's mostly Russia now." My phone buzzed with a text from my mother: *I left my Eng203 finals on my desk.*

I said, *Isn't that the whole reason you went to campus?*

Well, I have the others, just not those. Any chance you could run them over?

Fine, I said. *It's not like I have any homework to do.*

Can you ask Delia to do it, then?

I could have, but then I would have been stuck at home with Sebastian. I said, *It's fine, I'll do it.*

"I have to take Mom some exams," I said. "Can you hang with Kit?"

"Of course we can," Delia said.

"You want to watch some of my videos, man?" Sebastian said.

Kit said, "Do you like Minecraft?"

I dropped off the file of exams with my mother half an hour later. It was weird being on campus on a Sunday right after finals; there were still kids around, but they were kind of wandering aimlessly, like gravity had pulled them there even though there really wasn't anything to do. I guess they were there to meet with advisors or drop off overdue term papers, looking, depending on the person, either exhausted or overly buzzed.

I'd practically grown up on the GMU campus; Mom and

Dad had taken the jobs there when I was three. Before that they'd been at the University of Delaware, which I didn't remember. I'd spent plenty of school vacations watching videos in my mom's office, or when I was too little to be left alone, Dad would sometimes stick me in the front of the lecture hall with a stack of picture books. I never read them, though. Listening to Dad was always more fun, even if I didn't know what he was talking about half the time. Once, when I was home with a cold and he was unable to get a babysitter, he took me with him to teach some class on medieval Britain, and I fell asleep during his lecture on the Battle of Hastings. When I woke up and found out that Harold lost, I bawled in front of the entire class. I was kind of famous in the department after that, which was pretty embarrassing, although it's better than Kit, who once peed on the head of the English department.

Afterward, my phone rang while I was in the ladies' room washing my hands. It was Bethany, and she was trying to do a video chat, which was weird because Bethany never uses video chat. Like, she despises it. But I opened it and said, "Hey, there's your face."

She looked like she'd just woken up. "Aphra," she said. "The date."

"The date? I think it's the tenth?"

"No! I have my date with Greg! It's today!"

"Okay?"

"We're going to the movies!"

"Yeah, I'm the one who helped you set it up. Why are you freaking out?"

"I don't know what to wear, or what to put on my face, or what to freaking say to him!"

"Well, talk about crew. I don't know."

"What am I going to say about crew? *Hey, man, how about rowing that boat, did you manage not to eat your oar half a dozen times this week?* There's no conversation there."

"Then talk about chemistry? Aren't you in class together?"

"I can't talk to him about chemistry!"

"Ugh, Bethany, I don't know. Tell him his eyes are pretty."

"I can't tell him that! Do guys even like hearing that?"

The truth was, I had no idea, but I suspected Greg would be happy with any kind of compliment from Bethany. I said, "He'll love it. Tell him his eyes are pretty and you want to kiss his neck."

"His neck?"

"Well, you do, right?"

"Can you come over and help me get ready?" She pointed to some spot on her cheek. "Look. I have a zit, it's horrible, can you see it? You can probably see it from space. Can you see it from space?"

It was barely visible. "You're right! I heard about it on the radio this morning. The guys on the International Space Station wanted to bomb it from orbit."

"Aphra."

"Just don't pop it," I said. "Your head might collapse."

"You suck. Are you coming over later?"

"All right," I said. "I'm on campus, but I'll call you in a little bit." I hung up.

You know that second where your phone goes black, and you're left looking at your reflection in it? That's what happened then. The phone went black, just for a second, before my lock screen came back up, and I was caught off guard by the version of my face that looked back at me. Maybe it was because I'd just been looking at Bethany's face, which was perfect from every angle. I don't know. But at that moment, I looked like some kind of ghoul: pale, with big bags under my eyes, too much nose, and too little mouth. Was that really what I looked like, or was it some trick of technology?

There was no trick. It was a reflection, that was all. Even if the angle was bad and the lighting was not the best, that was a real representation of me. When Greg looked at me, that was what he saw.

I closed my eyes and took several deep breaths, then stood staring at myself in the mirror until my face stopped making sense. Faces are weird in general. Was mine empirically any weirder than anyone else's?

Yes, it was.

A few sinks down from me, two girls were fixing their eyeliner and having an animated conversation about some party and some boys they were so sure would be there, and whose room would be better for the pre-party. I guess the point of the pre-party is to get drunk before the actual party so if it sucks you are unaware of it. Or something.

"Are you going?" one of them asked me, because I was so obviously eavesdropping. "There's going to be a lot of English majors there."

I blinked at her a few times. She looked a little familiar, and for as often as I was in this building visiting Mom, she probably figured I was another student. I was there, I was about the right age, it made sense. I didn't really want to out myself as a faculty kid (ew), so I said, "I don't know."

"You should," she said. "You know Tim Curran?"

I did not. But I nodded anyway.

"He just made high honors on his senior thesis, and he's buying all the top-drawer stuff for the rest of the department. The password at the bar is Zora Neale Hurston."

"Password at the bar?" I said, imagining a world in which incanting the name of ZNH got you good-quality booze at a frat party.

"He's not buying for *everyone,*" she explained.

"Where did you say this was?"

She held her hand out palm up, and I gave her my phone. She put an address in on Maps. It looked like it was about three blocks from campus. "Thanks," I said, though I wasn't really sure why I'd asked. What did I want to go to a party with a bunch of strangers for? A bunch of strange English majors.

"See you later," she said, and then she and her friend left.

I really couldn't go. Anyway, I'd promised Bethany I'd help her get ready, whatever that meant. Probably she'd need help picking out an outfit, and then at the last minute she'd wear something else anyway. Maybe she'd need help doing her eyes. She was really bad at that.

Just then, my phone began playing the theme for *Star Trek.*

Nobody had used it in days, not even Greg, so I'd kind of forgotten the app was still running. I looked at the incoming message. It said, *Hey, counselor, I can't wait to see you.*

I screwed my eyes shut. Why was he even using the damn app? All he had to do was text Bethany directly. I knew he had her number. Was he just trying to be cute?

My thumb hovered over the screen. Finally, I typed, *What's your favorite color?*

I don't know. I like red, I guess.

To Bethany, I typed, *Pick out something red.* And then I turned my phone completely off. What was I doing?

I checked the time; it was still only twelve o'clock. Bethany texted back, *When are you coming?*

He's not picking you up for seven hours!

. . .

. . .

So when are you coming?

I rolled my eyes. *Fine, I'll come now.*

Getting Bethany ready for a date with Greg involved watching three episodes of *MLP,* sitting in the kitchen with Colin while she showered (!!), eating a sandwich, watching her brush her teeth twice, doing her makeup (with extra concealer for the invisible zit), doing her hair, fixing her makeup, and then emptying her closet onto her bed.

By the time she'd demurred on my red dress once again and settled on a black tank top and skinny jeans, I was exhausted, she was quivering, and all I wanted to do was jump out the window and run home to play Minecraft with my brother, who may not be the most self-sufficient nine-year-old on earth, but at least he doesn't need me to check his shirt for deodorant stains or his butt for a VPL.

"You're perfect," I said, sprawled facedown on Bethany's bed. I was thinking about the fairy godmother in Cinderella, and how that chick was the one who did all the work but never managed to get any credit. Or the prince, for that matter.

Just then, the doorbell rang. "Ohmigod," she said.

"It's fine," I said.

"Ohmigod," she said.

"If you don't go down there, Colin's going to answer the door."

"OHMIGOD." She bolted downstairs, where Colin was already en route to the door. Bethany shoulder-checked him out of the way and pulled it open.

I was too far back for Greg to see me in the mostly dark living room, but I could see him on the illuminated porch just fine. I watched him take in Bethany's freshly washed hair, her newly shined mouth, her perfectly-lined-by-me eyes. I watched his smile go from happy to delighted, like Kit's the day we'd brought Walnut home from the shelter and he'd thought he was the most perfect creature on earth. "Are you ready?" he asked.

"Yeah," she said. She glanced back at me, and I motioned for her to go ahead, letting him take her hand as she shut the door behind her.

Colin turned to me. "You're still here?"

"Oh. I guess so." He disappeared back downstairs, and a minute later I could hear his game system turn back on through the closed door.

I sank down into one of the kitchen chairs. Through the window, I could still see Greg's headlights, because he hadn't pulled out of the driveway yet.

Probably he was too busy kissing Bethany to think about moving the car.

I didn't really want to think about that.

I didn't want to think about all the millions of opportunities Bethany would have to put her hands on Greg in a dark movie theater, or what they'd do sitting in his car afterward.

I also didn't want to go home and spend the evening listening to Sebastian talk about his brand while Delia acted like she'd had a lobotomy instead of a nose job. I actually didn't want to be around anybody I knew at all.

All I wanted was to go someplace dark and anonymous, where nothing I said would follow me home later.

Chapter Fifteen

I got to the party around 9:30, which seemed like it might have been too early to arrive at a college party without looking like a high school kid. I hoped I didn't run into anyone who knew who I was; it wasn't like my parents introduced me to their students, but I was in and out of their offices enough that someone could probably put it together. I decided what I needed was a fake name. A good, all-purpose alias.

I walked into the townhouse my bathroom friend had given me the address for, which had been strung with Christmas lights around all the windows and was otherwise about three-quarters dark. The living room was full of people sitting around drinking and talking loud, and about half a dozen people were bobbing up and down in the middle of the room, which had been converted into a makeshift dance floor. More Christmas lights were strung on the banister down to the basement, which sounded like it was full of even more people, and through the bay window I could see that the back deck and tiny yard were similarly occupied. Across the upstairs staircase, someone had put a piece of crime scene tape and a sheet of paper that read *Nice try.*

Someone jostled me to the left, and I realized I was standing in front of the bar. The person who'd bumped me asked for a beer, and the guy behind the bar poured him one from the keg before turning to me.

"Hey," he said. "What's up?" It was so dark I could barely see what he looked like. My height, or maybe a hair taller. Big eyes, wide mouth, curly hair that hung halfway to his shoulders. I couldn't tell what color his skin was exactly, but he was neither particularly pale nor particularly dark. I wondered what I looked like in that light. Probably not pretty, I decided. But I might be able to pass for average. Maybe even a little above that, if I carried myself with enough panache, and I was good at that.

"Hi," I said, finally getting my feet under me. "Hello. You seem to have quite an assortment back there."

"I do, at that. What can I get you?"

"I don't know," I said. "But I've always found myself to be partial to the works of Zora Neal Hurston."

He winked and started mixing things together in a cocktail shaker. "Really," he said. "What was your favorite?"

"Uh, *Their Eyes Were Watching God,* I guess."

He rolled his eyes. "Disappointing."

"What? Why?"

"Every single person I ask gives me the same answer." He poured the contents of the shaker into a plastic cup and handed it to me.

"What's this?"

"A Zora Neale Hurston," he replied. "What else?"

I eyed the drink. It was blue. I sipped it. It tasted . . . also blue. "What's in this?"

"Curaçao, bitters, and ginger ale."

"*This* is the top-shelf drink?" I asked, as if I normally drink a lot of expensive liquor. The truth is I've been drunk exactly twice. The first time was when Delia and I were younger and found an old bottle of kirsch in the kitchen. We were both home from school with a cold and pretended it was cough syrup, giving each other tablespoonful after tablespoonful until Mom walked in on us and poured the rest of the bottle out, shrieking that we were going to end up just like Great-Aunt Leanne, and to this day we have absolutely no idea who that is. The other time was when Bethany and I found a bottle of cheap champagne in her pantry and decided to have mimosas with our oatmeal one morning, which really does not go, and resulted in Bethany falling down the stairs and losing a toenail.

Nevertheless, I eyed the drink like I was Zelda Fitzgerald, a bon vivant of the highest order. "Hey," he said, grinning at me. "The curaçao is expensive. I'm Mark, by the way. I don't think I've seen you before. Are you a freshman?"

I took another sip of the Zora. It seemed to be growing on me. "Sophomore, actually."

"And do you have a name, Sophomore English Major?"

"Um," I said. "Beth. But I'm actually not an English major. I'm still undeclared."

"Oh, undeclared. I should take that drink back."

But I'd already finished it, so I said, "If you wait half an hour and give me an empty cup, I can oblige you."

He laughed, harder than was probably called for, which

likely meant he'd been sampling his own wares. "I'm off bar duty in 15 minutes," he said. "Will you still be here then?"

"I just got here," I said.

"Brilliant," he said, with a smile that matched the word. I smiled back and let the crowd carry me away from the bar. I wondered what time it was. It was probably late enough that Bethany and Greg would be done with their movie. Maybe they were going home. Maybe they were going out for ice cream. Maybe they were making out in his car.

I made a circuit of the room. Mostly people in twos or threes were talking closely about finals or internships or hookups. I heard strains of a conversation about *Infinite Jest* and backed up so quickly I bumped into the person standing behind me.

"Beth," Mark said in my ear, and I really wished I hadn't gone with that name, but it'd been the first one that popped into my head. I felt the phantom impulse to check my phone for a text but resisted it. I didn't need to know how Bethany's date was going. I didn't want to know; it had nothing to do with me. Nothing at all. It was completely none of my business.

"Hey," I said, and Mark passed another Zora into my hand.

"I thought you'd decided I didn't deserve this."

"Mmm. I realized I may have judged you too harshly."

"And why was that?"

"When I asked the next three people their favorite ZNH, they gave me an Alice Walker title."

"Oh, no."

"Oh, no indeed." He brushed a stray lock of hair off my forehead. I hadn't realized we were at the hair-touching stage, but okay. "Hey, come meet some people." He took my hand and led me to the back deck, which smelled faintly of pot and strongly of Axe body spray. On the wraparound bench, two boys sat drinking while a girl sat sideways next to them, her legs draped over their laps, her bare feet dangling off one of their knees.

"Mark!" one of the boys said. "Is off bar duty!"

"I am," he said. "Guys, this is Beth. She's a sophomore."

I stood up straight and did my best to look 19. No, wait. 20. I'd be 20, probably. "Hey," I said.

"You've got a Zora," the guy who'd just spoken said. "You know, I invented that."

"You must be Tim," I said. "Congrats on the honors thesis." I held up my cup, which was about half empty, since it turns out I'm a fan of the Zora. Big, big fan. "Why blue, though?"

He laughed. "No particular reason. My paper was on the evolution of the American novel."

"See, though, if you wanted a blue drink with the name of an American author, you should have called it the Toni Morrison."

"For *The Bluest Eye*? It's a little on the nose, don't you think?"

"But that's what makes it perfect," I said. "It's so unironic it loops back around." That made no sense. None. But everyone around me was either half or three-quarters drunk, which made me sound like some kind of genius. Everyone nodded.

"That is so true," Tim said. "I think I'm renaming it."

"Too late," Mark said. "We're out of curaçao."

"Damn it. Well, next time."

The girl across Mark's lap said, "Did you read *Bluest Eye* in Eliza Brown's class?"

I perked up at my mom's name. I'd read the book last year in English, and I'd rarely identified with a book so strongly. The scene where Claudia talks about her hatred for Shirley Temple and the sickening reaction she provokes in the adults around her was one of the most cathartic things I'd ever read. "Uh, no," I said. "In high school, actually."

"Oh, good. I hated that class." She turned to the boy next to her. "She's so bourgeois, I just wanted to strangle her."

I felt my eyebrows inch up my forehead. For a minute, I wanted to hand Mark my earrings and throw down with this girl, but that would have looked really suspicious, since I just said I hadn't taken the class. "Really," I said.

"I mean, she gave me a C on my paper on the male gaze's encroachment into the feminine novel. A freaking *C*!"

"How," I said, "is that bourgeois?"

She rolled her eyes. "If I have to explain it to you, you wouldn't understand."

"You mean why you got a C, or the fact that you don't know what *bourgeois* means?"

She squawked a little. Well, good. Call *my* mommy bourgeois. My mom. I mean, my mom. Sheesh.

I wondered how much liquor had been in the Zora. I mean, it hadn't tasted particularly alcoholy. Does curaçao taste boozy? I don't even know what it is, except that it's blue.

"Beth," Mark said. "Come dance with me."

"I'm not done with my drink," I said, because I really wanted to trounce this girl a little more. Little poser probably didn't even know what the male gaze was.. But Mark took the cup from me and downed the last half inch of Zora and said, "Now you are. Come on, I'll get you another one."

"I thought you were out of the blue stuff?"

But we didn't make it back to the bar. Back in the living room, the lights seemed to have gotten lower, and the music had dropped, too, probably to keep the neighbors from complaining.

Mark set his hands on my waist and pulled me into a swaying rhythm. "Don't listen to Amy," he said. "She gets bitter when she's drunk."

"Is that what that was?"

"She also hates any prof who gives her less than an A. But I read that paper, and it sucked." He ran a finger across my cheek. "You're pretty defensive about Dr. Brown, though, for someone who's never taken one of her classes."

"She, ah. She was my academic advisor. Freshman year."

"Yeah?"

"Yeah."

In the low light, everything looked kind of dreamy. I leaned into junior English major Mark a little, and he leaned a little back. He was warm, and I liked that. I liked dancing with a boy, a nice boy who read books and smiled when I talked to him. But really, more than anything, I wished he was someone else.

I shouldn't be here.

"Beth," he said, and I tried not to cringe. "Hey."

"Hey," I said back.

He leaned in and I realized he intended to kiss me, and I thought, *Huh, well, okay, I guess this is a thing that's happening and I'm fine with it.* Because why not? Greg wasn't going to kiss me, not ever, and this guy wanted to, so I figured I might as well make the best of it. I let my eyes drift shut and leaned in so he would know I found this turn of events to be acceptable.

Mouths are weird. I mean, you're supposed to feel all kinds of things when somebody kisses you, but you use the same organ for eating and drinking, and nobody thinks you're supposed to have some kind of cosmic experience putting on lip balm or eating a fried egg or—and I really wish this hadn't occurred to me—throwing up your blue-colored cocktail. But I might as well as been kissing the back of my hand, for all I felt.

I mean, it wasn't unpleasant. He was warm and alive and real, which was more than I could say for my fantasies of Greg D'Agostino. But I waited for something to happen to me inwardly speaking, and it didn't. He broke the kiss and leaned back, a little glassy-eyed. He was drunk, I realized; more than halfway. He was drunk and it was dark and this was stupid. In the harsh light of day, he'd never give me a second glance.

"Mind if I cut in?"

I looked and saw that the voice belonged to Delia. "Oh, God," I said.

Mark looked a little confused. "Uh," he said.

Delia put her hands on my shoulders. "Shoo," she told him. "We're dancing."

"Beth?" he said.

Delia's eyes widened. "Holy crap," she said.

"You should probably go," I told Mark. "I'm . . . I'm sorry."

"Is this your girlfriend or something?"

"Mm," Delia said. "Sure, let's just go with that."

Mark hesitated another second, and then he went back out to the yard.

"Ugh," I said. "Are you stalking me? How did you even know I was here?"

She pointed to a spot over my left shoulder. I glanced and saw, in the corner, a girl who looked familiar. Very familiar. Oh, shoot, that was right. Delia's friend Meg Freedman was a freshman at Mason. I hadn't realized she was an English major. Meg waved at me awkwardly. I winced in response.

"She texted me half an hour ago," she said. "She thought I might be here, too."

"So you came to bust me?"

"If I wanted to bust you, I would have told that guy you're 17. You told him you're a freshman?"

"Sophomore. Actually."

"Oooh," she said, poking a finger into my cheek. "Your mouth was writing checks that baby face can't cash. I always hoped I'd be around to see it. You're lucky it's dark in here."

"I don't have a baby face. And it wasn't a check I couldn't cash; he totally bought it."

"You can't pass for 20, even in the dark. Either he's drunker than he looks or he's a total creeper. Anyway, Meg said you were here by yourself. Do you have any idea how fucking stupid that is?"

I shrugged.

"This is basic stuff, Aphra. You never go to a party alone. And you never get drunk unless you have someone with you who has your back. Ever."

"Afraid I'm going to end up like Great-Aunt Leanne?"

She rolled her eyes. "And everyone thinks you're the smart one," she said.

"Nobody thinks that," I said, although really, everyone did. "Can we just go?"

"God, yes," she said.

• • •

In the car, I leaned my head against the seat while Delia muttered to herself and played with the radio buttons, landing first on the piña colada song.

"Turn it off," I said, feeling the Zora creep up my throat. "Turn it off, turn it off."

"Sheesh," she said, flicking the radio to some Top 40 station. I sighed and slumped against the door.

"Where's Sebastian?" I asked, once I no longer smelled coconut inside my brain.

"Out with some friends."

"You didn't want to go with him?"

"Not really. I was tired, and they were going downtown." On the radio, some guy was singing about being in love with someone's shape, like the object of his affection was a really hot piece of trapezoid. It's one of those songs that every station plays at least once an hour. I don't know why they do that; even if you like the song to begin with, by the end it's just painful. Delia flipped off the radio. "I feel personally violated by that song," she said.

"Just imagine he's singing to a bottle of Mrs. Butterworth's," I said. "That's what I do."

Delia laughed. "Don't make fun. I'm sure Mrs. Butterworth is a lot of people's dream woman."

"She's sweet," she said. "She's curvy."

"She doesn't talk back, and she's recyclable in most municipal locations."

"You want to tell me why that guy was calling you Beth?"

"There's a segue."

"I never really believed in those. So why was he?"

I shrugged.

"Where is Bethany, anyway?"

I said, "On a date."

"A date?"

"Yeah."

"I didn't think Bethany went on dates."

"This is actually the first one," I said.

"Ah," she said. "And everything makes sense again."

"What is that supposed to mean?"

"Nothing. Who's the guy?"

"It doesn't matter," I said bitterly. I turned my phone back on, just to see if I'd missed anything important and crew-related.

"Ha," she said. "Nice tone. I'm surprised she didn't make you go over there and help her get dressed."

"Shut up, Delia," I said.

She glanced at me out of the corner of her eye. "Are you mad because she did ask you, or because she didn't?"

"Can we not do this right now?" I asked. My phone took that opportunity to start pinging with missed texts. There were a good dozen of them, all from Bethany, and I stuck my phone back in my purse without reading them because I didn't want to do it sitting next to Delia.

"Lot of messages," she said.

"I did tell you to shut up, right? That did happen?"

She scoffed. "Must be tough being Aphra Brown, patron saint of the codependent."

"What?"

"Oh, please."

"You might as well finish that thought now. You're going to anyway."

She was silent. Finally, she said, "You have a whole lot of

relationships that are based on other people needing you. That's all."

"Really. Do I."

She sighed. "Bethany needs you because she can't talk or whatever. Mom and Dad need you to take care of Kit. Kit needs you to act like a grown-up because Mom and Dad keep forgetting he exists. And according to Mom, some guy needs you to teach him to row a goddamn boat, like it's so hard."

"Those are called relationships, Delia. They're what people have with each other."

"Mmm, no. A relationship implies something two-sided. That's not what you do. You don't want the give-and-take. You want someone who needs you. You're desperate for people to need you, because you can't believe they could ever possibly *want* you."

I gripped my seat belt very hard with both hands.

"Yeah," I said, "well, I'd rather make myself useful than mutilate my face to make people like me. And by the way, do you think Sebastian's going to keep hanging around once he finds out what you really look like?"

In the headlights of the oncoming traffic, I could see her face go tense and very, very red. "My face," she said. "Looks like *this*. And fuck you."

"Truth hurts, doesn't it?"

"You would know."

"What does that mean?"

"Bethany has a boyfriend now. She's gorgeous. What the hell does she need you for? Nothing. Not anymore."

"I'm her friend."

"Are you? Are you really?"

"You were always jealous of her."

"There's only one jealous person in this car. And it's not me."

By then, we were home. I stormed into the house with Delia on my heels; she blew past my parents and down to the basement. I stomped up the stairs.

"What was that?" my mom called from in front of the TV.

"Oh, nothing," I shouted. "I'm *great.*"

"I thought you were at Bethany's?"

"Change of plans!"

I got ready to slam my door a good one, when I remembered Kit was asleep and that was too bratty even for me; plus, Delia was in the basement and wouldn't hear it anyway. So I just collapsed onto my bed and mashed my face into my pillow, quickly becoming aware of the sickly sweet smell of my own breath.

From downstairs, I heard my father say, "Remind me why we've been farming her out to therapy every week for the past nine months?"

"What else are we going to do?"

I couldn't hear what my dad said, but my mom replied, "I don't know. I don't know! It's going to take time—"

"How much time? How much time is it going to take?" There was silence. "Maybe we need to try something else."

"And what would that be?"

But then their voices dropped, and I never did hear what it was.

Chapter Sixteen

I was brushing the Zora residue off my teeth when I remembered that it was Sunday, which meant I had school tomorrow. I hoped blue liquor didn't make you hungover. I'd never had a hangover before, but they sounded unpleasant.

Going back through Bethany's texts, I read an increasingly frantic series of questions sent from the theater bathroom because Greg wanted to go out for ice cream after the movie and she simultaneously did and did not want to go. The last message had been sent about an hour ago and said, *I just got home, where are you?*

It was 11:30, which meant she was probably asleep by now. Plus, I kind of didn't trust myself to talk to her with Delia's words still stuck in my ear. I hated my sister so much. Like, it wasn't enough for her to go after my face; she had to take a swipe at my personality, too.

Of course, that was the exact moment my phone let loose with the *Star Trek* theme song.

I picked it up to put it in airplane mode for the night, but then I saw the message. It said:

I had fun tonight.

Oh, God.

I flipped my phone upside down. I did not need a rehash of Greg's date with Bethany, as delivered by Greg to Bethany, before going to sleep. I knew I should just deactivate the thing.

But if I did that, Greg would ask Bethany why she'd ignored him, and she'd probably freak out and that would be unfair.

I was not going to talk to him and pretend to be Bethany.

I was not.

I picked up the phone.

Are you there? he'd typed. *I really liked the movie. And the other parts, too.*

He thinks you're Bethany, I told myself. He thinks you're Bethany.

I don't know how much of the next decision was because I was upset at Delia, or lonely, or the result of the two Zoras I'd had, but I typed, *Me too.*

I wish we could have talked more, though. I wanted to tell you something.

Yeah?

Yeah. So I was bold. I talked to my parents again.

This was okay. We weren't talking about the date; we were just talking about Greg's parents. I'd just make sure he was okay, and then I'd tell him I was deactivating the app because I was done with the project, and that would be the end of it. If he wanted to text Bethany, he'd have to use her actual number.

They weren't happy. My father got his calculator out and

added up all the money they've spent on swimming for the past nine years. He wrote it down on a piece of paper and everything.

That's not fair.

It kind of is. They thought it was a long-term investment in getting me a scholarship. They think it's my fault that I haven't kept pace.

You're not an investment. You're a person.

Anyway, I told them I'd pay for college myself.

But it isn't your fault!

Maybe it is.

But you're so—wonderful, brilliant, perfect—*good at so many other things!*

I think they think if I'd been more focused, I could have been the next Michael Phelps. They just thought . . . they thought I was going to be a lot better than I am. And I'm so tired of it now. They don't understand that.

I'm sorry.

I'm just so glad I found you, he said. *You're the only person I can talk to about this.*

I screwed my eyes shut.

Are you still there?

Yeah, I'm still here.

Oh, good. I thought maybe I freaked you out or something.

No, I said. *I'm not freaked out at all.*

Are you okay? You seem kind of quiet.

Well, of course. There's no audio on this app.

Ha, ha.

I had a fight with my sister earlier. I guess I'm still thinking about it.

I managed to catch myself before I hit send, deleted *sister,* and retyped *brother.*

Did something happen?

Not really. Just a character assassination on his part. It's kind of his specialty.

Well, your character is unimpugnable, as far as I can tell.

He said to the person with the fake identity. Still, I said, *Thanks for saying so. I think I should probably go sleep it off. See you tomorrow, right?*

Of course, he said. *I miss you already.*

Me too.

I ended the chat. I should have deleted the app. I *really* should have deleted the app.

I didn't delete the app.

The next day was Therapy Day, which was probably a good thing. I wasn't exactly keen on explaining the Greg situation to the good doctor, but there was really no one else I could tell. And because of that whole doctor-patient confidentiality situation, I didn't even have to worry about her passing the story on to someone else.

Still, I knew she wasn't exactly going to approve. She does this thing where she just looks at me and goes, "Hmm," which I know is her being professionally nonjudgmental while thinking, I would like to smack you. Sometimes I think it would be easier if she would just let me have it, but she never does.

I'd gotten the rundown of Bethany's date at lunch and was still trying to block most of it out. She was all hand-fluttery about the whole thing. And then I got to spend an hour in Latin staring at the back of Greg's head, which didn't make me feel any better.

So by the time I got to Dr. Pascal's, my mood was pretty sour and I was feeling attacked on all fronts. She let me into her office and I sat on the couch, pulling my customary three peppermint Life Savers out of the bowl. My goal, always, was not to chew them. If I did it just right, I could have a mint in my mouth for the entire 50-minute session.

Next to the mints there were a couple of Muppets, probably from her last patient. Sometimes I forget that she mostly sees little kids. I guess she probably talks to them differently from how she talks to me. I scooted Elmo and Cookie Monster out of the way and put my water bottle down while she finished whatever paperwork she was doing from the last patient. I wondered if the kid had been more of an Ernie or more of a Bert. Bert, probably. Ernie doesn't seem like he'd need much in the way of psychological help.

Back when I'd started with Dr. Pascal, I'd looked up the theory of how psychology works on Wikipedia (as one does) and started with the old man (as one does). Sigmund Freud believed that the human mind was composed of three main parts: the ego, the superego, and the id. I imagine that the id is the little devil who sits on your shoulder and tells you to take what you want, the superego is the angel on the other side telling you to behave yourself, and your ego is you, the head in the middle,that has to figure out what to do. In terms of Dr. Pascal's Muppets, the id . . . well, it's like Cookie Monster. It wants what it wants when it wants it, and it wants it now. It's like the two-year-old that lives in your brain and never grows up. It wants cookie, damn it. The ego, maybe, is Big Bird, who is pulled in multiple directions and doesn't really know what to do, and the superego . . . I don't know which Muppet is the superego. Grover, maybe. He's got that superhero thing going on.

"Hello, Aphra," said Dr. Pascal, and then, looking up from her paperwork, she added, "Whoa, there's a mood."

"I'm not in a mood. Wait. Yes I am. I am in a mood. Having a mood? Which is it?"

"There's not a significant difference," she said.

"Really? I think there is. If I *have* a mood, it's something I've developed internally, like the flu. If I'm *in* a mood, it's an external thing I'm caught in. Like fog." I adjusted myself and flopped back against her couch with an *oof*. "Or a hurricane."

"Fortunately your mood doesn't seem to have damaged your verbal acuity."

"It never does, Dr. Pascal."

"Well, let's go with that second analogy, then. You're in a mood. What do you think would help?"

"An umbrella. And maybe some boots. Like, those kind that go over your knees and keep all the water out, but I would like a pair that don't make my feet sweat, so if you could make that happen that would be great."

"Let's back up," she said. "Now, just to be clear, are we going with the fog or the hurricane?"

"The hurricane. I wouldn't need hip waders for fog."

"Right. So that's good. Now. Please plot for me the track of this hurricane. It started off down in the Caribbean as a tropical storm, and then . . ."

"I'm not really sure how it started," I said. "Well, I guess it started because Bethany went on a date and Delia picked me up from a party."

"Those things happened on the same day?"

"Yeah, they did."

She scribbled in her notebook.

"Tell me about Bethany's date. Did she ditch you to go out?"

"No," I said. "That wasn't it. It's just . . . it's complicated."

"I'm good at complicated. That's why they pay me the big bucks," she deadpanned.

I sighed. Then I explained to her, in very abbreviated terms, the whole Greg situation. I may have left out the part where I'd talked to him again last night.

She said, "Hmm."

"Big bucks, Doc," I said. "Big bucks."

"They aren't actually that big. So, that's an interesting series of choices you made."

"Really, that's your analysis?"

"You know, they told me you made Lisa Fagan cry, but I didn't actually believe it. Let's keep going. You said that was how your mood started. But then something else happened."

"Yeah, I also had a fight with Delia."

"This is all in one week? What happened?"

I explained about stopping by the party (without mentioning my Zora consumption) and that I'd danced with some guy and then gone home with Delia. "So we were driving home, and everything was fine, basically, and then she told me I have, like, an obsession with other people needing me. Or something."

"An obsession?"

"That wasn't the word she used. She said that I engineer my relationships with people so that they need to have me around, because I'm such an ugly loser I don't think they could actually want me around of their own free will."

She nodded and made a bunch of notes.

"You're writing this down?"

"Always. So I'm guessing that made you pretty mad."

"Well, yeah."

"Do I even want to know what you said to her?"

"Well, I was mad."

"Uh-oh."

"And I may have told her that letting people need me in order to want me around was a lot less horrible than mutilating my own face in order for people to want me around, and even after she did that all she could manage was her douchebag boyfriend who will probably dump her in a hot second as soon as he gets a look at her baby pictures."

She put down her pen. "Oy gevalt."

I wanted to explain that this was the kind of thing I would really like to be able to blame on my id. I'd been an asshole, and I knew it. At the time, I'd been so mad that the words had come out unfiltered. The problem was, I kind of meant it, and Delia knew that. "That's kind of what Delia said, only with less Yiddish and more f-bombs." I sighed. "She not speaking to me at the moment. But I am also not speaking to her, so that works out okay."

Dr. Pascal took off her glasses and rubbed her eyes. "There's a lot to unpack here."

"Are you sending me back to Lisa Fagan?"

"No," she said. "No. But we're not getting through it all today, either."

I moved on to my second Life Saver.

"So," she went on, "I know from our many, many conversations that you love your sister, even though you're mad at her."

"Right," I said. "I mean, of course." I resisted the urge to correct *love* to *storge,* because she seemed like she'd had about as much of me as she could take that day.

"And you know she loves you."

I nodded. "I know I shouldn't have said that to her. But she shouldn't have said what she did, either."

"That seems to have struck a nerve, huh?"

I looked out the window.

"I just want to clarify one thing. . . . Did she say no one could want you around, or that you *thought* that no one could want you around?"

"The second one."

"You do recognize those are not the same, and what you told me initially was the first thing?"

"I guess I misspoke."

"No, Aphra, I don't think you did."

"Oh, here goes," I said.

"I think Delia's known you a long time, and she's probably aware of more that's going on with you than you realize. I think she called you out on how much your self-esteem is driving the bus for you, and hearing that from her hurt like hell."

"I have very healthy self-esteem," I protested. "I'm pretty much 70% water and 30% ego. Delia's the one with the low self-esteem. She's the one who thinks her face is so damn important. I know mine is the least important thing about me."

"I think the fact that Delia has low self-esteem is what helps her to recognize the same issue in you."

I picked up the puppet from the table and said, in my highest falsetto, "Elmo says bullshit!"

"Aphra, you met a boy you liked. You developed a friendship

with him, and then you handed him over to your best friend. Why did you do that?"

"Because it was the right thing to do?"

"For whom?"

"I love that you say *whom*," I said. "So many people don't."

She glared at me. I said, "For them."

"For them. And what about for you?"

"For me, too!"

"Hmm. Now, that's interesting. How was it best for you?"

But then the little alarm she keeps on her desk went *ding*, meaning it was time for me to skedaddle because her next patient was waiting. For the first time, she actually looked annoyed that our time had run out.

"I want you to think about that," she said. "Maybe write something down. I want you to think about why you did it, and why you think it was the best thing for you, and that's what we'll start off with next time."

Chapter Seventeen

I put Dr. Pascal's words out of my mind after that. The thing was, I knew exactly why I'd done it, and that I was right. It was the best thing for everyone. Bethany was happy. Greg was happy. And I was happy because they were happy. Really, I was.

Greg was not at crew that day, not that I'd expected him to be. He seemed to show up when he had time for it, and I didn't know if that meant he was definitely going to be on the team next year or if he was still deciding. It was cold and drizzly, which is my second-least favorite rowing condition after snowing, which doesn't happen all that often in the spring around here. Usually I get so hot rowing that I actually enjoy the cooler temperatures, but today I couldn't seem to stop shivering, maybe because my hair was wet. I should have worn a hat, I realized, but that would have been wet, too, so I'm not sure it would have helped much. Afterward, the coach handed out hot cider from a big thermos, and I wrapped my hands around it and tried to get the feeling back in my fingers.

"Are we going to your house?" Bethany asked, breathing the steam from her drink. Her fingers were pink, and so was her nose. "I found this math website I think Kit would like."

I frowned a little, because I kind of didn't want to have Bethany over with Delia there, not right after what she'd said last night. "Can we do your house?" I asked. "Delia's there with her boyfriend."

She smirked. "You'd rather hang out with Colin?"

That was actually an easy question, because Colin was generally only awful to his own relatives, not to me, and whatever snide comments he lobbed in my direction were easily parried. I'd been insulted worse. Recently, in fact. "Yeah, actually, I would."

She whistled. "He's that bad?"

I bobbled my head side to side. "It's not him as much as the two of them together."

"Got it," she said, even though she didn't. But Bethany is very good at taking my word for things. I really appreciate that about her. Like, I don't have to bleed for her to convince her something's a problem.

We got to Bethany's house and dropped our backpacks in the kitchen, and I stopped short because the door to the basement was standing open, with Colin nowhere in sight.

I inclined my head toward the door. "Bethany," I hissed.

She'd been getting a banana from the fruit bowl, but when she turned around and saw me pointing to the open door, she stopped peeling and dropped it on the counter.

"Is he gone?" she mouthed.

I shrugged. I didn't hear anything down there. "Mom?" Bethany called. "Where's Colin?"

There was some splashing upstairs, like maybe she was in the tub. She called back, "Dentist. He just left."

Dentist. He'd be gone at least an hour. Bethany and I exchanged a wicked smile and bolted down the stairs, running shoulder to shoulder. "I'm picking the game!" I said.

"You picked last time!"

"That was six months ago!"

But since Bethany did have to live with the slug, I didn't complain when she ran over to Colin's very involved game filing system. "Do you think he still has that pony game?"

"God, I hope not."

"Ugh," she said, flipping through the games. "First-person shooter, first-person shooter, *Grand Theft Auto* . . . There's got to be at least, like, an adventure game or something. . . . Ah. *Zombie Air*," she read. "'Your plane crashes in the mountains, and you have to survive freezing temperatures, zombies, and even a yeti to get off the mountain and find rescue.' It has a two-player mode."

"Cool," I said. "Let's fight some zombies."

She stuck the cartridge in, and we watched the intro video, which involved a harrowing plane crash scene.

"Ugh," she said. "Maybe this is too graphic."

There was a sonic boom, because Colin has this whole setup hooked to a pair of surround-sound speakers, and we both jumped.

"Okay," I said. "Okay. Here goes."

"I'm stuck in my seat belt," Bethany said. "I can't get out."

"Use a piece of broken glass," I said, having already cut myself free. "We should see what we can salvage from the plane before we look for cover. . . . It's already getting dark."

"Should we check the cockpit?"

I followed her in there. The pilot was slumped over the controls.

"Is he dead?" Bethany asked.

I used my controller to poke him a few times, Pygmalion-style. "He's definitely dead."

Bethany scoured the cockpit and came up with a bottle of water, some wire, and a roll of duct tape. I said, "Do you think we should . . . eat him?"

"What? Ew, Aphra, oh, my God!"

"What? That's like the number one rule. Your plane crashes in the mountains, first thing you do is eat the pilot."

"That's not the number one rule of anything! Where did you even hear that?"

"I . . . I read it. In. In a book."

"What book?"

"Uh. A big book. Big, fat book."

"You did not read that in a book."

"Well, it's true!"

"It is not true."

"You do recall that he's just pixels, right?"

"It's the principle!"

"Pshhh," I scoffed. "I'm eating him. I'll just"—I clicked a few things on my controller—"put him in my food inventory . . . there."

The screen was filled with gore and crunching sounds. I screamed and threw my hands up in front of my face.

"I told you not to eat the pilot!" Bethany screamed.

"I didn't know it would do that! I just thought he'd end up in my food stores like a little steak or something!"

"He's not a steak!"

"I see that now, thanks. Oh, hey! I got 200 bonus HP."

"Oh, well, that's all okay, then,. you're a cannibal, but you got your bonus HP— Zombies!"

"Shit! Shit!"

We ran our little avatars down the mountain. Bethany was lagging significantly behind.

"Why am I running so slow?" she demanded, jabbing her thumbs into the controller.

I nodded toward her health indicator. "You're hungry. 'Cause you didn't—"

"Oh, shut up. Wait. Wait!"

But hungry e-Bethany was being consumed by zombies, with more gore and crunching and a flash on the screen that said PLAYER ONE HAS DIED.

"I can't believe you just left me behind!"

"Oh, they would have just eaten me, too."

"You suck." She tossed her controller down on the couch and stretched her arms over her head. "So I applied for a job last night."

"What?" I said, because my character, unlike Bethany's, wasn't dead and I was still running from the zombies. Was I supposed to have a weapon? What weapon do you even use on the undead? They're already dead, that's the whole point. "Did you want to start over? I don't really want to play this by myself."

But Bethany had gone extremely still. "Aphra," she hissed, jerking her head toward the back of the couch, and I thought,

Oh crap, now we're going to have to listen to Colin throwing a tantrum because we're sitting on his precious pleather couch. But I turned my head, and it was not Colin standing behind us, looking highly amused. It was Greg D'Agostino.

I dropped my controller.

Say something, I willed Bethany. *Talk to him. Say anything.*

"She ate the pilot," she said.

Ugh.

"I. I did. Do that."

"Your mom let me in," he explained. "Sorry. I didn't realize I'd be interrupting your . . . uh. What game is this?"

"*Zombie Air,*" I said, getting up. "It's okay, we didn't even get to the part with the yeti yet. I need to head home anyway."

"Did you still want to get a cupcake?" he asked.

"Oh," Bethany said. "Yeah, that's what we said, right? Cupcakes? And maybe sandwiches, because I kind of didn't eat dinner yet."

"We were fighting zombies," I explained.

"I hear it makes the time get away from you," Greg said.

"I hear the same thing." I started up the stairs. "See you guys later."

"You didn't have dinner, either!" Bethany blurted out, getting up from the couch. "Because of the zombies!"

I stopped on the bottom step. "Yeah, that's why I'm going ho—"

"You should come with us! And have a sandwich! With us!"

Greg looked a little discombobulated, though I wasn't sure if it was because Bethany was talking like she'd just taken a hit of meth or because she'd just invited me on their date.

"Oh," I said. "No, I really don't think—"

"If we go to Cake Baby, you can get one of those wraps you like! They have coffee, too, can we go there?"

Greg's forehead wrinkled; torn between not wanting me there and wanting—badly, I expect—to make the new girlfriend happy. The latter won out. "Y-yeah, let's go to Cake Baby."

"No," I said. "I really don't want to crash your date, I should—"

But Bethany had crossed the room and taken my wrist in her hand and was doing the best Bethany eyes I'd ever seen. "Please?" she said. And then, "I mean, I think it'd be fun for all of us to hang out."

I looked over at Greg, who had obviously given himself over to this turn of events. "You should come, Aphra. It's cool."

So we went out. I had a wrap, Bethany had a panini, and Greg had a cup of decaf and a devil's food cupcake.

At first, everything seemed pretty normal. I was trying to be inconspicuous because I didn't want to get in the way of Bethany talking to Greg herself and also because I was starting to have trouble remembering what I knew about Greg from real life and what I knew from the Deanna app.

The problem started after Bethany finished her sandwich and ran out of excuses to not say anything. She stared at the bean sprouts that had fallen out of my wrap and onto my plate. She stared at the table. She stared at the light fixture. Greg made one failed conversational attempt after another.

"So," he said. "How was crew today? I bet it was cold out there."

"It was freezing," she said, and then nothing.

"So," he said. "Did you finish the lab write-up in chemistry? I had to redo all my math. It took me forever."

"Yeah, I finished that last week," she said, and then nothing.

Finally, I couldn't take it anymore. "So what were you doing while we were rowing on a freezing river?" I asked.

He looked downright relieved. "Oh. Yeah. I had a meeting with a prof over at NVCC."

"Really? I thought you were done for the semester."

"I am, but I topped out of Russian classes there, so I'm doing an independent study over the summer."

"Can you take something over at Mason?" I asked. "The department's a lot bigger."

"I looked into it, but the classes cost like three times as much. Anyway, I thought an independent study would be kind of fun."

"So it's just you one-on-one with a professor? Who designs the curriculum?"

"Me, mainly. I wrote up a syllabus for myself and cleared it with the professor there."

"What's it about?"

"Russian poetry," he said.

I elbowed Bethany, hoping she'd make some reply to this. It wouldn't have even been that hard. All she had to do was say that sounded cool. Instead, she said, "I have to go to the bathroom," and then she did.

I sat staring at Greg, who said, "Is she okay?"

"Panini," I said, "in her teeth. Probably. I've got some dental floss in my bag. Let me just"—I got up—"make sure she's good."

I went into the bathroom, where Bethany was in front of the sinks with her face in her hands.

"What is with you?" I asked.

"I can't do this," she said. "I just can't."

"Can't do what? You already went out with him yesterday!"

"That was different! It was a movie!"

"You must have talked to him at some point."

"Not," she said. "Really."

"So what did you do after the movie?"

She went very red.

"Right, never mind. So you can wear a bikini in front of him, and you can sit next to him, and you can make out with him, but you can't talk to him? That doesn't make any sense."

"I can't do this!"

"Yes! You can! He already likes you. Just talk to him."

"I don't know what to say! It's like, I look at him and everything in my brain goes dead."

"It's just because you're not used to him," I said. "You'll get over it."

"Yeah, but by then he'll be gone. He's not going to wait around for me to, like, act like a normal person."

I frowned. She was probably right.

Bethany was beautiful. That was obvious and indisputable. Bethany was smart, too, but that was less obvious, because she was hiding it. And the kind of boy who wanted to spend his summer reading Russian poetry—and was cute enough to get the attention of any number of other girls—was not going to settle for a pretty face. She needed to level up or he was going to get bored. And the thing was, she *could* level up. All she had to do was open her mouth and talk like she always did with me. Any kind of verbiage from her would be better than this.

But she wasn't used to him, and the Russian poetry thing

was probably not helping, because now she'd be intimidated instead of just nervous.

"I don't even know how to go back out there," she said.

I felt, in that moment, really bad for her. She was so, so close to getting everything she wanted, and this one thing that was mostly out of her control, this fear, was snatching it away from her. I knew all about that. The worst part was she would probably get over her Greg-induced brain freeze eventually, but it was going to take too long. He wouldn't wait.

What Bethany needed was something to help her along. A crutch, so to speak. She'd been able to give an entire five-minute presentation in chemistry because she'd had cards to read. I would just have to be her cards, her temporary crutch. It was totally selfless, really. I was going to subsume my own ego and become Bethany's charm, just for half an hour.

"Here's what we're going to do," I said. "I'm going to help you."

"I can't just sit there and smile while you do all the talking," she said. "I look like an idiot."

"No. No, you're going to do the talking. I'm just going to . . . feed you some lines."

"Feed me lines?"

I waved my phone in front of her face a little. "Listen! This is perfect. I'm just going to give you something to say until you get over . . . whatever this is. I'll text you under the table. You'll read the messages out loud."

"Won't that be obvious?"

"Not if we do it right. Look, he already likes you, like, a lot. All we have to do is get him to keep liking you until your voice starts working again. Right? And let's admit it, between your face and my words, we're basically the perfect girl."

"But . . . in this scenario, is he falling for me or for you?"

"You," I said. "Obviously."

"But—"

"It's just temporary, right? We both know how great you are."

"Aphra."

"It's true! I'm just . . . getting you over the hump."

"Aphra!"

"Poor choice of words. The point is, it's just for today. Listen, he's sitting out there all by himself, and he probably thinks we're in here talking about him."

"Well, we are."

"Yeah, but that's bad. Let's go back out there and make conversation for 20 minutes, and then you guys can drop me off at my house and you can . . . Never mind."

"20 minutes."

"Yeah."

She took a deep breath. "Are you sure about this?"

"I'm sure," I said. "Let's go."

Chapter Eighteen

Bethany and I were in the same class in second grade, and again in third grade, and then in fourth grade we were split up.

This happened because it was decided by the powers that be at our elementary school that I was destined for greater things (in other words, the advanced academics track), while Bethany would stay in the general ed program.

We discovered this the week before school started, when we got our class placements. Bethany's response, when she found out, was to go silent. As in, she stopped speaking, not just to me, but to anyone. My response, not surprisingly, was to be very loud about the injustice of the situation to anyone who would listen.

"It doesn't make any sense," I told my mother. "Bethany's better at math than me by tons. And she reads as well as me, too. She's just . . ."

"I know," she said. "But there's nothing we can do about that. Her mom can appeal it if she wants, but it's not up to us."

"But it's not fair!"

"I know, honey. It's not."

And for most people, I guess, that would have been the end of it. But on the first day of school, I walked up to the teacher (Ms. Marks, if you're wondering) and said, "My name is Aphra Brown. I'm in this class. And my friend Bethany's in Ms. White's class, but she should be in here, too, because she's the best at math in the whole fourth grade."

She gave me this frozen smile and said, "Hi, Aphra. I've heard all about you." I didn't get the sense that that was a particularly good thing, but I was on a roll, so I just barreled ahead.

"So," I went on, "if you could just, like, go and get her, we'll be all set here."

"I'm afraid it doesn't work like that, but you'll still see your friend at recess. The whole fourth grade goes out at the same time."

"No, that's not it. She actually should be in this class. I don't know why she's not."

"Why don't you take your seat, Aphra?"

"Yeah, I will, as soon as I go get Bethany."

"Miss Brown," she said.

"Ms. Marks," I replied.

"Sit down."

"No."

"Sit down, or you can go see Ms. Baumgartner."

Ms. Baumgartner was the principal. I guess most fourth graders would have been cowed by that particular threat, but I'd been in her office enough times to know the worst I'd get for mouthing off was a call to my parents, whose response to her reports that I gave someone lip was, "Really? Again?" And then, to me, they'd say, "Could you just keep it under the phone-call level? I'm tired of that woman yanking me out of class."

So I said, "That's fine. I'll go talk to her."

I gave the same spiel to Ms. Baumgartner, who looked very tired and said, "I'm proud of you for advocating for your friend."

"Thank you."

"But it's not really appropriate. If there's a problem with Bethany, then Bethany's parents should come talk to me, or even Bethany herself. Not you."

"Yeah, but she won't come talk to you because she's scared. I just think you made a mistake, that's all."

She cleared some files off her desk. "You know, there are three things we look at when we're assembling that class."

"Okay."

"Standardized test scores, teacher recommendations, and the GBRS." Only she said the acronym like "gibbers."

"The what, now?"

"The Gifted Behavior Ratings Scale. It's a questionnaire the teachers fill out about how a student performs in class, like whether they ask incisive questions or demonstrate leadership skills, things like that."

I chewed on that a minute. "What about if you have someone who does badly on that because they don't speak much English? Or they're shy or something?"

"Well, we'd still have the test scores."

"Okay, but don't you still need to talk well to do well on the tests? I mean, if you speak mostly Chinese or you were really nervous that day, maybe you'd do bad."

"We do look at the whole package, Aphra."

"But Bethany—"

"Is not for you to worry about." She got up and patted me on the shoulder, which I hated so, so much. "You're a good friend. But I think you need to worry a little more about Aphra and let Bethany worry about Bethany."

I scowled, but I knew I'd lost. They weren't going to listen to me. So I went back to class. I didn't forget about it, though. I just needed to find a way to prove them wrong.

I waited about three days, until the class was being super rowdy and everyone was complaining that our math was all stuff we'd learned the year before.

Ms. Marks was getting super frustrated. "This is just a review," she said. "We'll be getting to the harder material next week."

One of the boys said, "I can do algebra. My dad got me this app that teaches you."

"That's not real algebra," somebody said.

"Yes it is!"

"Fine," Ms. Marks said. "I'll give you guys one real algebra problem to mull over, and then we'll go back to our review." She turned to the whiteboard and wrote a very long problem. I can't remember it now, but *x* was all mixed into some big fraction and there was an exponent, which we hadn't learned how to do yet. We stared at in in stunned silence, which I guess was the desired effect. After a few seconds, I put my hand up.

"Aphra?"

"I don't know how to do that," I said. "But I know somebody who does." I'd copied the problem down on a piece of paper, and before she could stop me I made a beeline out of the room. Ms. Marks was right behind me. I was lucky she had a bad knee.

Bethany's class was on the other side of the hall, and I burst in and slapped the paper down on her desk. She looked at me with wide eyes while her teacher sputtered at me. Then both Ms. White and Ms. Marks took turns screaming at me while discussing how I was out of control and which of them was going to haul me down to the principal's office. I heard the term "oppositional defiant," and I didn't know what it meant, but it sounded a good deal worse than "pain in the neck," which was what my teachers usually called me when they thought I was out of earshot. Ms. Marks had just grabbed ahold of my elbow to escort me down the hall to my certain doom when Bethany got up from her chair and handed me the piece of paper.

I pulled away from Mrs. Marks and looked down at it. She'd done a bunch of steps, and at the bottom of the page, she'd written $x = 4/7$. I handed it to Ms. Marks. I knew it was right as soon as her eyes scanned down the page.

After that it was decided, that Bethany would join my class for math only. We were never allowed to sit together, though. I was banished to the back of the room, while Bethany took a desk at the front.

I was in my dad's office when he got the call from Ms. Baumgartner that day after school. "Oppositional," he said. "Huh."

Upon hanging up, he looked at me for a good long minute.

Then he opened the top drawer of his desk and took something out. "I was saving this for myself," he said, handing it to me. "But I think I'll give it to you instead." I took it from him: it was a chocolate bar with little bits of toffee in it, the kind he likes to get at the airport, which is my favorite and his, too.

"Aren't you mad about the call?"

"Should I be?"

"She called me . . ."

"Oppositional, yeah. You opposed. What did you oppose?"

"They wouldn't let Bethany take the advanced class even though she's smart enough."

"Right. Something unfair. I'll never be angry to hear about you standing up for someone. That's always the right thing to do. And if that makes Ms. Baumgartner's job a little harder, well, that's just too bad."

I tore open the wrapper and snapped the candy bar down the middle, then handed half to my dad. "Yeah?" he asked, and then took it. He held out his part and tapped it against mine. "To opposition," he said.

"To opposition," I replied.

I wasn't sure what I was opposing in the middle of Cake Baby. The unfairness of the universe, maybe, which had made Bethany so wholly unable to communicate with the boy she liked. It was okay, though. I was fixing it. We were fixing it.

Greg had finished his cupcake while Bethany and I were in the bathroom and was checking something on his phone when we got back to the table.

I'd already fed Bethany a line, so she said, "Sorry. I had enough spinach in my teeth to make another panini."

She smiled at me. I smiled back. Greg looked slightly relieved.

She sat back down, looking a little less terrified now, and propped her phone on her knee. I texted her, *Which Russian poets are you looking at, specifically?*

"Uh. Alexander Pushkin, Vasily Zhukovsky, and Alexander Blok are the main ones."

She glanced down at her lap, and then gave me a look like *Are you sure?* I widened my eyes a little. She said, "That's a very masculine list."

He looked a little surprised. But he said, "I never thought about that."

Glancing down again, she said, "How'd you come up with it?"

"I guess . . . they're just the big names. You're right, though. It needs work. What about you? What are you doing this summer?"

I thought she should be able to answer this one on her own, but just to be sure, I typed, *Aphra and I are going to be counselors at a crew camp for middle school kids.* She was getting the hang of sounding less like she was reading. She was even starting to exude a small measure of confidence. Maybe I was rubbing off on her.

"That's cool. Where is that?"

"West Vagina," she said emphatically. Then, giving me the world's nastiest look, she said, "*Virginia.*"

I typed, *Sorry, autocorrect.* She said, "Sorry, auto—"

I kicked her. "Auto. Uh. Matic. The camp is supposed to help the rowers learn to operate as a team in a way that's automatic. Like, instinctual. You know."

Greg looked like he was trying really hard not to laugh, like he found her occasional inability to form coherent sentences utterly delightful. I typed, *Are you planning on rowing for real next year?*

"I'm still thinking about it," he said. To me (to me!) he said, "I've sort of given up swimming, so I'm looking for a new sport for next year."

Bethany's jaw dropped, because of course she wouldn't know this. I said, "Oh! No more swimming?"

"No more swimming." He took Bethany's hand from across the table and squeezed it. "It was time to try something new."

"That," I said. "Uh. That must have taken some hard thinking. To quit after so long."

"Well," he said, smiling fondly at Bethany, "you know. I'm bold like that."

I typed, *I always knew you had it in you.*

"Yeah," he said. "You did." He leaned in and kissed her on the cheek.

I said, "I just remembered, I promised my brother I'd read Harry Potter tonight. Do you guys mind dropping me off really quick?"

"I should go, too," Bethany said (on her own!). "I have. Uh. Homework. There's. Like. Spanish."

"That's right! Aphra said you're taking Spanish. Puedo ayudarte si quieres; he hablado Español con mi mamá durante toda mi vida," he said.

Bethany glanced at me. Why, I have no idea. I typed, *I DON'T SPEAK SPANISH, BETHANY.*

She said, "Uh—uh—uh—sí, me gusto mucha si me ayudar."

Greg's eye twitched just a hair, which probably meant that hadn't been a good answer. I texted, *Kiss him. KISS HIM!*

She shot me a desperate look and then pitched face-first over the table. Her mouth met his. He appeared to be surprised and pleased by this. But mostly pleased. As they broke apart, she stole a glance at her phone and said, "Sorry. Must've been the accent. I guess I was a little overcome."

He grinned at her. I was, if I'm honest, getting a little tired. And grateful when Greg pushed back from the table and said, "I'll take you guys home. I think we're scandalizing Aphra."

He dropped us off at Bethany's. After we walked inside, she pulled me into a tight hug. "Thank you," she said. "Thank you thank you thank you oh God."

"It's okay—wait, are you crying?"

She leaned away and wiped her nose on the back of her hand. "I don't even know."

"It was fine," I said. "There were a couple of little flubs, but he thought they were cute. That went really well. He's completely smitten."

"I know. It's not that. I don't think it's that."

"Don't you like him?"

"I do. I really do."

"Then what?"

She snuffled a little more and wiped her eyes. "I'm not sure, Aphra."

I put my arm around her. "Hey," I said. "Do you want to work on Spanish here, or you want to do it at my house?"

That was when I remembered who else was at my house. Well, Delia could bite me. If she said one nasty word to Bethany, I'd make sure she'd need a second nose job.

Bethany said, "Your house?"

"Cool," I said. I rubbed my hand up and down her arm. "Let's go get your stuff, okay?"

"Yeah, okay." And then she hugged me again.

Chapter Nineteen

When we got home, my parents were in the kitchen with Delia and Sebastian having a late dinner. Kit was using his chair as a table so he could sit on the floor with the cat.

"Hey there," Mom said. "I thought you two were having dinner at Bethany's."

"We did," I said, pulling up a chair. Bethany sat on the floor next to Kit and ruffled Walnut's fur between her fingers. "We came over here to do homework."

"It's a sucker's game," Sebastian said. Mom set out four glasses of water. She managed not to dump Sebastian's over his head, but I could tell she was thinking about it. Dad was taking a frozen pizza out of the oven while Delia and Sebastian picked the radishes out of a salad.

"Delia was just telling us how she and Sebastian met," Mom said. I crossed my fingers and hoped they hadn't met at a YouTube convention or something horrible like that.

"We were in the same biology class," he said, resting an arm on the back of her chair. "She spilled coffee on my lap during the midterm."

"Was it hot?" I asked, perhaps too hopefully.

Delia rolled her eyes. "It was cold by then. And mostly empty, there was only like an inch left in the cup."

Sebastian said, "So I picked up the coffee cup, wrote my number on it, and put it back on her desk."

I had to admit, that was kind of cute. If a little nauseating.

"So she called me up, and I asked her to come over and wash my pants."

Okay. A little less cute now.

"I didn't do it," Delia said. "We had lunch in the dining hall."

"Nothing says romance like spaghetti under a heat lamp," Dad said.

"And then what?" Kit said.

"Nothing," Delia said. "That was it."

"Oh," Kit said, a little disappointed, though really, it hadn't been a horrible meet-cute, except for the "wash my pants" bit. "Mom and Dad met in college, too," he said.

"It was graduate school," my father corrected him. He loved telling this story.

"We didn't have YouTube back then," my mother added. "It was a dark time."

"I'm amazed we got through it."

"I'm not sure we did, sometimes."

"So," Dad said, because now that Kit had mentioned the story, there was no way he was not going to tell it. "The Latin American Student Union was having a dance," he said. "I went with my roommate, and they had a salsa band, and there was the prettiest girl you ever saw, in her Lisa Loeb glasses—"

"Not the Lisa Loeb glasses again," Delia said.

"In her Lisa Loeb glasses, and my roommate and I were watching her salsa-ing by herself, and he said—this was Alex Castro—he said, 'That girl is the worst dancer I've ever seen.' "

"I wasn't that bad," Mom said.

"She was," I said. "We've all seen it."

"Hey," Mom said. "That's your gene pool you're maligning."

"Not mine," I said. "I got my rhythm from Dad. Delia, on the other hand . . ."

Delia threw a sprig of parsley at my face. I handed it to Bethany, who turned it into a makeshift cat toy, to Kit's delight.

"So we felt so bad for this girl," Dad went on, laughing now, "because everybody's looking at her, because she's dancing alone and what she's doing has nothing to do with the salsa, and we decided that no one that hopeless should have to dance alone, and the only gentlemanly thing would be to ask her to dance with one of us."

"You were too kind," Mom said flatly.

"We really were. So we played a round of rock-paper-scissors and I lost."

"And if you hadn't," I finished, "our father would have been Alex Castro, and we'd all be living in California because you got the girl and he got the job at Stanford."

"I got the better deal," he said, proudly taking a sip of his water.

"It was Stanford," Mom reminded him.

He tugged on a lock of Mom's hair and said, "Even so."

"How was your day, Aphra?" Mom asked.

My bizarro-world date didn't seem to match up with "adorable meet-up during a biology final" or "adorable meet-up at a dance." There was really nothing adorable about "I fed lines to my friend so she could talk to a boy she liked, who is also the boy I like, and she still managed to say the word *vagina* to him." So I said, "We played *Zombie Air* and then we got sandwiches."

"That's a good game," Sebastian said with a mouthful of lettuce. "It's hella hard, though. I missed class for like two weeks just to get past the first level." He pointed a finger at me. "You know the trick, right?"

"Yeah, you have to eat the pilot right after your plane crashes. We figured that out."

My mom said, "Excuse me?"

"Otherwise you aren't fast enough to run away from the zombies," Sebastian explained.

"What kind of game is this?"

"Come on," Dad told Mom. "You know that's the first rule of plane crash survival: you eat the pilot."

"*Thank* you," I said. I crossed my eyes at Bethany, who rolled hers back at me.

"That is not a rule," Mom said. "What are you even talking about?"

"It's like in *Lost*," Dad said. "The plane crashes on the island, and at the end of the first episode they eat the pilot."

"They did not eat the pilot!" Mom said.

"Sure they did! That's why he wasn't there for the rest of the season! It was that guy who played the roommate on *Felicity* and they ate him."

"They did not eat the pilot! The smoke monster got the pilot!"

"She's right," Delia said. Walnut had jumped up on the table, and she set him back down on the floor. "My suitemates and I watched that during finals last fall."

Dad said, "Ooooh." He took a bite of salad. "Then what show am I thinking of?"

"No one knows," Mom said, kissing him on the head as she took a piece of pizza from the middle of the table.

"*Battlestar Galactica*? No. It was that Tom Hanks movie where he talks to the volleyball."

"Tom Hanks did not eat the pilot in *Castaway*," Mom said.

"But he should have," I pointed out.

"*Thank* you," Dad said.

"That's it!" Sebastian said, smacking the table. "I haven't done *Castaway*." He mashed his pizza with his fork. "The scene where the volleyball floats away and Tom Hanks is crying. That's so fucking perfect."

Everyone stared at him. He said, "For 'Careless Whisper.'"

"Ah, yes," Mom said, murderously stabbing a cucumber.

"That actually would be pretty funny," Dad admitted.

Bethany had gone home and I was in the middle of studying for my Latin test when Greg messaged Deanna again.

I rolled over and grabbed my phone, knowing this was all kinds of wrong, but I was already in it up to my neck, so there wasn't a whole lot I could do about it now. He'd said, *It was great seeing you tonight. I didn't know you were into gaming.*

Yeah, well. I'm a woman of mystery.

That much was obvious from the very beginning. Hey.

Yeah?

I know you get nervous sometimes. I just want you to know, you don't have to be with me. I think you're amazing.

I rubbed my eye a little. *I think you're amazing, too.*

That night, I had a dream, one of those third-person things in which I get to watch myself as if I'm starring in a movie inside my own brain. These are not my favorite dreams. I prefer the ones where I am looking out through my own eyes.

It started with me in a wedding dress, a poufy white affair with lots of lace. I'm not sure how my subconscious came up with something so cliché, since it's not like I spend a lot of time reading bridal magazines. Anyway, I couldn't see my own face under the veil, but Delia and Bethany were my bridesmaids, and they both looked beautiful in their strapless white dresses. My brother was playing "You Are My Sunshine" on the harp, and I walked up the aisle to find Greg standing at the altar. I looked over at Bethany to see if this upset her, but she was all smiles, daintily wiping a tear from the corner of her eye. I turned to face Greg, and he reached out to lift my veil, and I was all breathless anticipation, waiting for the moment when he would kiss me, and the veil went up, and under the veil I was a duck.

I lay in my bed after I woke up, wondering how Dr. Pascal would parse this dream. I do this, sometimes, imagine conversations with her, which saves me the trouble of having to bring them up in therapy, since I already know what she'll say.

I imagined her asking, "Why a *duck*?"

I didn't have an answer to that one.

Chapter Twenty

I felt a little like I was going to die the next morning. On top of the weird dream, I'd been up too late studying for my Latin test, and then I'd been doing that thing where I am so stressed out for no reason that my inner monologue won't shut up and I just lie there for hours thinking *Stop talking, stop talking, stop talking.* Only I can't, and it's like my brain is having verbal diarrhea, which makes it almost as hard to sleep as when you are having the real thing.

I was asleep, though, when my alarm went off at 6:30, which was unfortunate because sleeping for half an hour right before your alarm goes off feels so much worse than not sleeping at all. I got up, jabbed my contacts into my eyes, and staggered into the kitchen, where my dad was downing a cup of coffee and Kit was putting his shoes on. Delia, on her way to some pre-internship orientation, was heading out the door in a pantsuit, leaving Sebastian on the couch in his boxers with a bowl of oatmeal.

"Remember," Dad told me. "It's your day to take Kit to the allergist."

"I remember," I said. "I put a reminder on my phone and everything."

"Are you sure you can manage? It's pretty tight for you, schedule-wise."

"Absolutely," I said. "Everything is in a three-mile triangle. It'll be cake." I patted Dad on the head. "Don't worry your pretty little head about anything, Dad-o."

He ruffled my unbrushed hair. "I'm taking him to school," he said. "Don't forget to eat breakfast."

"I never do." He went out the door with Kit, and I poured myself some cereal.

"Hey," Sebastian said. "Look at this."

I went into the living room and looked over his shoulder at his phone. On it was a video of Tom Hanks crying in *Castaway* while his volleyball floated away and "Careless Whisper" played in the background. I laughed with my mouth full and spat some of my Cheerios back into the bowl.

"Right?" he said, pointing at the number of hits in the corner of the screen. *"Right?"*

"Yeah, okay," I said, wishing it had been maybe 20% less funny.

I watched the clock all through third period, waiting for the bell to ring. I had exactly 30 minutes to leave, get Kit, drive to the allergist, drive back, drop Kit off, and be at my next class. For Kit, this was no problem; using lunch and recess time, he had an hour before he had to be back. But for me, despite what I'd told my parents, it was going to be tight. I ran slalom through the halls, dodging and weaving, until I came face to face with Officer Barry by the back door.

I really didn't have time to banter with him, and I certainly didn't have time to bring him a burger that day, so I just started babbling my explanation as rapidly as my larynx would allow. "I have to take my brother to the doctor I'll back as soon as I can and I'll bring you a donut tomorrow morning but I can't talk now okay sorry please thank you."

To my surprise, he continued to block the door.

"Uh," I said, trying to catch my breath. "I really do need to go."

He stared back down the hall. I followed his gaze to where Ms. Turner, the junior vice principal, was staring at us with her arms crossed.

"Damn it," I said.

"She's been standing there for 15 minutes," Barry said, grinding his teeth. "Please try to look like you're not expecting me to let you out of the building."

I glanced back to Ms. Turner, who looked like she'd just eaten a lemon. "HA HA HA," I said to Barry. "And then he said, 'YOUR MOM? I THOUGHT IT WAS AN ESPRESSO MACHINE!' "

He looked at me oddly, then slapped his thigh and let out a very obviously fake laugh.

"Seriously," I said through my own fake laughter. "I need to leave."

"There's a fire door at the end of the arts wing," he muttered. "I was smoking out there earlier and I forgot to lock it when I came back in."

This didn't make me feel too great about the security of the building, but I nodded and went back down the hall. As I passed Ms. Turner, I said, "He's so funny. You should ask him the one about the chicken and the milkshake." And then I ran like hell back down the arts wing.

I arrived at the front office of Kit's school five minutes late. I was on the list of people who were allowed to pick him up, but I'd never picked him up in the middle of the day before, so I hoped they wouldn't notice that my ID said I was still 17.

"I'll bring him right back," I said. "He's just getting allergy shots. Your blouse is gorgeous, by the way. Where did you get it?"

The secretary smoothed the floral print over her torso. "Oh," she said as she ran my ID through the scanner. "You know, I got it out the outlet mall in Leesburg last spring."

"*So* pretty," I said, taking my ID back while she smiled and preened a little.

Just then, Kit came into the office, scowling and saying, "You're late."

"Long story," I said. To the secretary, I added, "I will bring him right back."

"Nordstrom Rack," she said. "I think it came from Nordstrom Rack."

"Perfect!" I said, ushering Kit out of the office. "Thank you!"

Back in the car, I glanced at the clock and said, "Oh, crap."

"You were really late," he said. "I'm going to miss the movie about the lost colony."

I pulled out of the parking lot, "Yeah, well. Spoiler alert: the colony gets lost."

"Yeah, I know. They carved *CROATOAN* on a tree and no one knows why."

"Seems like you already know all the important parts." I pulled out of the lot as fast as I could. Kit's allergist is only two miles from his school, so I figured with any luck, I could make up some time on the drive over.

"Why are you driving so fast?"

"No reason," I said.

I sprinted with Kit into the doctor's office and was relieved to find there was no line for the shot clinic. Kit rolled up his sleeves and took the shots like a champ. I waved a grape Dum-Dum at him and held the door so we could leave.

"I'm supposed to stay 20 minutes," he said.

I stopped short. "What?"

"After the shots. I'm supposed to stay 20 minutes. To make sure I'm not having an allergic reaction or something."

"That's . . . What? Really? Mom didn't mention that. Is that really a thing?"

He pointed to a sign on the wall: PLEASE REMAIN FOR 20 MINUTES AFTER THE ADMINISTRATION OF ALLERGY SHOTS.

"Ugh," I said.

"Can I play on your phone?"

"Sure," I said, handing it over and descending into the nearest plastic chair.

I watched the minutes tick by on the big analog clock next to the door. After 15 minutes, I said, "Hey, let's go."

"It's only been 15 minutes."

"Yeah, well, I'm sure that last five minutes is kind of a grace period anyway, let's go."

"I'm supposed to show my arms to the nurse."

"What?"

"To make sure I'm not having an allergic reaction."

"Fine, fine, go do that." He flashed his triceps to the nurse, who was too busy to notice he was five minutes early, and then I hauled him out of the office.

"I'm hungry," he said.

"What?" I was, too, but I'd brought a PowerBar and a yogurt drink to have on the way back to school, since there was no time for me to have lunch. Kit was supposed to bring whatever Mom had packed so he could eat it while I drove. "Why didn't you eat on the way here?"

"I forgot my lunch. It's still in my cubby."

It was now 12:23. I was three minutes late to Latin. "Can't you just eat when you get back?"

"Lunch'll be over by then," he said.

"Ugggghhh," I said.

"I'm really hungry," he whined. He pointed across the parking lot. "There's a Potbelly's over there."

I reached into my bag and handed him my PowerBar.

"That isn't lunch," he said.

I growled a little, but I couldn't very well drop him off for four more hours of school without having eaten something, so I parked in front of the Potbelly's and said, "We have to be quick."

But there was a line, and by the time we'd gotten up to the front, I was 15 minutes late for class, and I realized I didn't have enough cash to get both of us lunch. I ordered Kit a grilled cheese and a bag of chips, and then it occurred to me that I'd forgotten to specify I wanted it to go.

At this point, I decided Latin was not happening. So I took Kit's lunch, along with two (free) cups of water, and went to sit down at one of the tables.

"Why didn't you get anything?" Kit asked.

"Wasn't hungry," I said.

"But they have those hummus wraps you like."

"I know. I ate before I left school."

Kit frowned at me. Then he tore off half of his sandwich and handed it over. I started to object, but then I just said, "Thanks, bud." I chewed for a while and then asked, "How're your arms?"

"Okay," he said. "Do you think Walnut can sleep in my room again soon?"

"I . . . don't think so. Sorry. I think that part's permanent."

"Oh," he said. "Okay."

Just then, I got a text from Mitzi, saying, *We are about to take the unit 21 test. Where are you?*

I felt a little faint. How had I managed to forget about that? How?

"What's wrong?" Kit asked.

"Nothing." I put my phone away. Kit was done, apart from his barbeque chips, so I said, "Mind if we head out now?" in my calmest voice.

He threw out his trash and I drove him back to school, pulling into the kiss 'n' ride and then putting the car in park.

"See you at home," I said, and then, when he didn't get out, I said, "What?"

"You have to sign me back in."

"Oh, for crying . . ." I turned off the car and put on the hazard lights. "Let's go."

When I got back to the car, there was a police officer there.

He said, "You're parked in a fire lane." He pulled out a pad of paper.

"I'm so sorry," I said. "I was bringing my brother back to school."

"Your brother. How old are you?"

I started to say 19 but realized that if he asked to see my driver's license, I was screwed. I said, "You know, time is kind of a relative thing, making age a sort of theoretical black hole."

He said, "Age?"

"17."

"Hm," he said. "Why aren't you at school?"

"I am going there right now, actually, as soon as I'm done talking to you."

"Really."

"Yeah,see, here's the thing: my brother is allergic to his cat, and he had to either get shots or give him away, but my parents can't take him to his shot appointment the first week of the month because they have meetings, so I said I'd do it, and I did think I could get there and back during my lunchtime, but I was running late because the junior vice principal chose today to narc on our narc, and then my brother hadn't eaten, so I had to feed him, and now I have missed the first half of a very significant Latin test, but if you call my parents they are going to make my very adorable little brother give up his cat and he'll probably have a breakdown and possibly even end up in the juvenile justice system, and do you really want that on your conscience?"

He frowned. "Do you always talk that fast?"

I said, "Yes."

Just then, I heard the officer's radio turn on with the dispatcher's report of a shoplifting at the local pet store, where someone had made off with a puppy in their purse.

"Damn," he muttered.

"Go!" I said. "Save the puppy!"

"Tell me you aren't going to do this again."

I said, "Um."

He waved me off and went back around to the driver's side of his car. "Just don't park in the fire lane next time."

"I won't! Thank you!" He turned on his ignition. "And that puppy thanks you!"

By the time I got back to school, I was 40 minutes late for Latin.

"Aphra," Ms. Wright said. "Do you have a late pass?"

I did not, and I was lucky I hadn't been caught coming back into the building by the still-unlocked art door. "Sorry. Long story."

"You've missed almost the entire test."

I swallowed.

"Where were you?"

There were a limited number of things I could tell her. If I told her I'd been at the doctor with Kit, she'd probably call my parents. If I told her I was smoking behind the dumpster, I'd get suspended. If I told her I was in the nurse's office, she'd want to know why I didn't have a pass. I said, "I fell asleep. In the cafeteria."

"And . . . none of your friends woke you up?'"

"No," I said, then added, "Dirtbags."

She handed me the test. "You have ten minutes left," she said. "You might want to write fast."

I was still writing furiously when the bell rang. I heard the rest of the class shuffling their way out of the room, and then Ms. Wright was standing in front of my desk, her hand hovering above my test, which I'd very nearly finished, except for the last page. "Aphra," she said. "Time's up."

"Time," I said, "is a relative thing."

"Yeah, no. Not in this case."

I was writing as fast as I could, translating a paragraph of Virgil. *Hic. Haec. Hoc.* "No, no, this is like a universal concept. Did you see the Neal DeGrasse Tyson special on *NOVA* last week? It was amazeballs." *Hic, haec.* "Almost makes me want to forgive him for that whole demoting Pluto business."

"Aphra."

"Ms. Wright," came Greg's voice. I hadn't realized he was still there. "I have a question about the homework."

"Hm?"

"Well, I noticed the *Aeneid* translation in our textbook didn't match the one from the Wheelock book, and I was wondering what was going on with that?"

"What? They match."

"No, they don't, actually, and I'm wondering about the cases—"

Bless Greg D'Agostino. Ms. Wright wouldn't be able to resist looking it up, especially since Greg was the one asking, I blazed through the rest of the paragraph. At this point, it hardly mattered if it was perfect; I just needed to finish it and I'd get at least half points.

"Aphra, your reprieve is over," she said just as I finished the last sentence.

"I'm done," I said.

"You should thank Greg," she said, taking my test off my desk. "You didn't deserve the extra time."

"Thank you, Greg."

Greg smiled his most perfect smile. I kind of wished he hadn't. After we exited the classroom, I said, "Seriously, though. Thanks. I owe you."

"Did you really fall asleep in the cafeteria?"

"That depends."

"On what?"

"On how you define words like *asleep.* And *cafeteria.*"

He chuckled. We were ten minutes out from the bell, so the halls were mostly emptied. I was supposed to ride with Sophie to practice, but a glance at my phone told me she'd given up on me and left five minutes ago. Greg said, "You need a ride to practice?"

"That depends."

"On how you define *practice*?"

"On whether you're offering."

"I am, actually. I got a text from Coach Allen that Samir Rice has strep, so I can try out one of the fours today."

"Oh, then yes."

The idea of rowing that afternoon kind of made me want to run away, but at least I wouldn't have to talk anymore, because my brain was exhausted..

"You okay?" he said on the way to his car.

"Yeah. Why?"

"I just don't think I've ever seen you this quiet."

I got into Greg's ancient silver Ford Focus on the passenger side, pushing his gym bag out of the way with my feet. The truth was, I was tired of talking, of running my mouth, of turning on the charm every second, of making sure everyone else was okay. I just wanted to say *Today sucked and I'm cranky and all I had for lunch was a third of a sandwich that wasn't even the kind I like.* I wanted someone else to do the talking. Somebody else to be in charge. Like, the image of the fairy-tale princess has never particularly appealed to me, but right then, it almost did. Let someone else slay the dragons. I just wanted a shoulder rub and maybe a nap.

Is it so terrible to occasionally want to be rescued?

I slumped a little sideways in Greg's direction. Maybe it was an unconscious move and maybe it wasn't. I remembered that I still hadn't eaten the PowerBar I'd brought for lunch, but I was so tired I couldn't even manage to get it out of my bag.

"Hey," Greg said. "Seriously, are you coming down with something?"

"I don't think so," I said.

He put an arm around my shoulder and gave me a little squeeze. It was friendly, not romantic—not at all—but I still went into semi-shock from the contact. "Don't worry about that Latin test," he said. "I'm sure you did fine."

"Yeah," I said. He'd withdrawn his arm, but I hadn't yet moved away from my squeezed position next to him. He smelled so good.I was so tired. His shoulder was so . . . there. I thought, *We are friends, and it would not be odd at all if I laid my head there for a hot second,* so I did. I put my head on Greg's shoulder. And he didn't flinch. In fact, for one second, he leaned his cheek against the top of my head. And then I did what I'd never thought I'd do with Greg . . . I fell asleep.

I woke up to the sound of Greg's voice saying, "Hey. Sleeping Beauty, we're here."

Sleeping Beauty indeed. I opened my eyes and saw, with mounting horror, that there was a filament of drool connecting my mouth to Greg's shoulder.

I sat up, saying, "I am so sorry," though whether I was apologizing for sleeping on him or drooling on him I wasn't sure, and I certainly wasn't going to mention the drooling if he hadn't noticed it. I rubbed a kink out of my neck.

"No worries," he said. "Hope you're rested, though, because this is not going to be fun."

He opened the door and got out, and it was only then that I realized it had started to rain.

"Oh," I said. "Joy."

"Carpe diem!" he said, running from the car while being pelted by fat raindrops.

I watched him get soaked as he ran off between the trees, and I set a hand to the middle of my chest. Maybe I wasn't awake yet, I don't know, but I felt kind of muddy, like whatever was going on inside my chest was more than just one thing; I couldn't name it, and it made me uncomfortable, but not in a bad way. It wasn't eros, exactly, and it wasn't philia, exactly. If it was equal parts both, then what was it? Love should be something specific, not something amorphous, like mashed potatoes. The word you use for your favorite song should not be the same one you use for how you feel about the person who lights up your whole life.

That was the word for how I felt about Greg, I realized. Not eros and not philia. Lux. Light.

I followed him through the rain toward the river and the rest of my team and our boats, where everyone was cranky and drenched, but I couldn't think of anything besides Greg's shoulder and how for 15 minutes it had felt so perfectly like home.

Chapter Twenty-One

Mom was in the living room with a cup of tea when I got home. She looked not exactly happy, but that was kind of her resting face since Delia had brought her boyfriend home, so I wasn't sure if it meant anything.

"So," she said. "How was Latin today?"

I started getting the idea that maybe this was more than a case of resting cranky face. "Oh," I said. "It was great You know, *hic, haec, hoc,* the usual. There was a test, I aced it, blah blah blah, but I have an essay for English tomorrow—"

"Your teacher sent me an email."

I swallowed. "Did she? Ms. Wright? Huh. That was, uh. Friendly. Of her."

"She said you missed most of your test. Because you fell asleep in the cafeteria."

"Ha ha! Yeah. I was up too late, can you believe it?"

"You're really going to go with that?"

I flopped down on the couch. "Yeah, no."

"What happened to the 'I triangulated the route and can be back in 30 minutes' story?"

"That didn't quite happen."

"You were 40 minutes late!"

"35! And you could have mentioned to me that you have to wait 20 minutes at the allergist!"

She blinked at me. "What?"

"They make you wait 20 minutes. Surely you read the sign."

She scowled at the carpet. "Your father always took him. Before today, that is."

"He never told you about the waiting?"

"Must've slipped his mind. Aphra . . ."

"Listen, I am trying!" I said. "I am trying to do the right thing here! And yes, I was very late today, but next time I'll remember to make sure Kit has his lunch, and I'll go out a different door, and I won't park in the fire lane. I'm sorry, okay? It's not like I was late because I was smoking weed in the parking lot."

"I know you weren't. Aphra, the thing is, you missed half a test."

"I finished that test! Look, what did you want me to do? I took him today because you asked me."

"I know. I shouldn't have asked you. And I didn't know about the 20-minute waiting thing."

"So if you'd known, you were just going to miss your meeting?"

She sighed. "I don't know. But your job is to go to school. Not to run your brother all over town in the middle of the day."

"So let me get this straight. Am I in trouble or not?"

"No. Of course not. It was my fault. There's just one thing I don't understand. Why did you tell me you could do this when you knew you couldn't? Even without the 20 minutes, you would have been late."

"Otherwise you were going to make Kit give up the cat."

She recoiled a little in her chair. If I hadn't been paying attention, I probably wouldn't have noticed.

"That's it?" she said.

"Yeah."

She stared out the window for a minute; then she said, "Dinner'll be ready in 20 minutes, if you want to take a shower first."

I picked at a snag in my crew uniform on my way up the stairs. Sometimes I feel overwhelmed by the number of things that happen to me in the space of a single day, like it's just more than 24 hours' worth of stuff. Maybe that's why I was so tired, and my throat was kind of scratchy, like I was fighting something off. All I wanted to do was crawl into bed and stay there.

After my shower, I decided to lie down for a minute before I got my clothes on and went down for dinner. I ended up falling asleep instead.

When I woke up the next morning, I felt a thousand times worse. Like, my throat wasn't worse, but whatever nasty little virus was inhabiting my epithelial cells had migrated to my head and was setting up shop in my sinuses. My head hurt. My face hurt. Most of all, this area behind my eyes that I was usually unaware of felt like it was full of molten lava.

I got up and took a decongestant. Mom and Kit were in the kitchen, and she took one look at me and said, "Yikes."

"I'll be fine," I said. "I'm sure the drugs will kick in in half an hour."

She put a hand to my forehead.

"I'm dying," I said.

"You're hot," she confirmed. She went looking through the drawers. "I can't find the thermometer. Are you stay-home sick or go-to-the doctor sick?"

"Stay-home sick, I think."

"How come you never ask me that?" Kit asked.

"Because *one* of you likes to fake it to get out of school."

That was not me. Not anymore, anyway. Staying home may be fun when you're nine, but by the time you're in high school it just means you have to make up all the work, and it tends to snowball on you until you wish you'd just gone in the first place. It's hardly ever worth staying home unless the alternative is, like, puking on your desk.

"I think I should go," I said.

But by then, Mom had found the thermometer and was jamming it in my ear. I said, "Ow."

"100.2," she said.

"Damn it," I muttered.

"Lucky," Kit said.

I spent the day on the couch watching cartoons and wishing someone else was home; Delia and Sebastian were downtown at some museum (which seemed shockingly unironic for Sebastian), and everyone else was at school. Kit'd left some books on the coffee table, so at one point I started thumbing through his library copy of *World Fairy Tales,* stopping on "The Ugly Duckling."

I hate "The Ugly Duckling" with a passion; it is, in fact, my least favorite fairy tale, because the moral of the story is that it's bad to be mean to ugly people because they might turn out to be hot later on. Like, how is that a good message for kids? Why couldn't the duck have stayed ugly and the other ducks have realized it's just wrong to treat people badly? Or to treat ducks badly. Or whatever. Anyway, it's a rotten fairy tale. The swan doesn't even *do* anything except grow up to be cute.

There are actually a lot of fairy tales I don't like. For example:

> "Beauty and the Beast": It's good to love someone despite their appearance, because your love might make them super hot eventually.
>
> "Cinderella": If you are super hot under your rags, a handsome price might see past your menial existence.
>
> "Snow White": More of same.
>
> "The Little Mermaid": Well, in the Disney version, it's that if you're hot enough, no one cares whether you can communicate. In the original, it's that if you are hot enough, you can steal some poor mermaid's man and then laugh like hell when she turns into flotsam.

It was really disheartening reading these as a homely child, let me tell you. I wanted just one fairy tale where the princess was ugly and stayed that way and got the prince anyway. But there are no stories like that. I slid the book to the other side of the coffee table and picked up the mug of mint tea I'd made myself. I was kind of in that twilight state where I was too sick to sleep and too tired to be awake, so I decided to split the difference and take a bath, which did actually make me feel a little better. Afterward, I texted Bethany so she'd know I was sick before she got to lunch, saying, *I am so sick OMG.*

She texted back. *OMG, me too.*

I may die from this, I said.

Sore throat?

No, head cold.

My throat hurts so bad I can't even talk.

Ugh.

Ugh.

I hate this.

I hate it more.

I wish I had soup. Colin ate all the ramen.

I also wish I had soup. But then I'd have to cook it, and I can't since I'm dying. Hey, if you told Colin you were dying, do you think he'd go out and buy soup?

HA HA HA no.

Seriously, though. You could try.

Hang on.

. . .

. . .

He said no.

Damn it.

Yeah, I really drew the short straw for brothers.

To be fair, Kit wouldn't get me any, either, if he were here.

Only because he can't drive yet.

That's probably true.

I glanced at the clock. Almost time for Latin. Oh, crap, Latin.

Hey, I said. *Gotta go text someone about Latin homework before I forget.*

Okay. I'd say talk to you later, but I'll be dead then.

Hey, so will I. If you go first, save me a seat, okay? Wherever you end up.

What makes you think we're going the same place?

Just what are you implying?

Nothing, she said. *I'll save you a seat between me and David Bowie.*

You're the sweetest.

I texted: *John, John. John. John.*

Where are you?

Sick. Can you text me the Latin homework?

Are you going to be back on Friday? I got stuck with Joel and he sucks.

Probably? It's just like a sinus thing.

Wow, he said, *a sinus thing. You sure that's not serious? That's like if Kim K broke her ass, right?*

I stared at my phone. I did not answer.

Aphra? Come on, it's a joke.

I still didn't answer, because there are very few things I do not joke about, but my nose is one of them. It was worse because John was my friend. We'd been in Latin together since I was a freshman and he was a sophomore, and we'd been on crew together just as long. We didn't really hang out socially, but I'd always thought we were cool. Sometimes it seems like whenever I start to feel like maybe I am overreacting about my nose, somebody says something like that and I realize I'm not. It's like the universe's way of instituting a course correction. *Don't go that way, Aphra. You know where you belong, and it's not on the path of "almost pretty in the right light."*

Never mind, I said. *I'll ask Mitzi.*

It was just a dumb joke. I'm sorry. Don't ask Mitzi.

I turned my phone off and went back to sleep.

When I woke up, it was three o'clock and someone was knocking on my front door. My throat was better but my head was worse, and I hoped it was just UPS or something, but after 30 seconds, the knocking came again. A voice said, "Aphra?"

A boy's voice. I knew that voice.

I got up and staggered toward the door.

It was Greg, carrying a takeout bag. "Uh, hi," I said. I was still in my pajamas, which consisted of a pair of leggings and an old Mason T-shirt that used to be my dad's. I hadn't actually found my way to a hairbrush yet. Or a toothbrush.

"Hey," he said. "Sorry for just, like, showing up, but I was at Bethany's and she said you were sick, too." He held up the bag. "I brought soup."

"You. Brought soup?"

"Well, the thing is I was going to get some for Bethany, and she kind of mentioned the hot and sour at Yen Cheng is her favorite and also your favorite, so I just got two containers." He paused. "I hope that's okay."

"No, it's . . . it's really nice. I actually forgot to have lunch."

"You might need to heat it up," he said. "I was at Bethany's first, so it's probably not that hot now."

"But still sour, I hope."

He smiled. "I'm sure it is."

I took the bag from him and extracted the container of lukewarm soup. He'd even remembered the crunchy noodles, which are the best part. I went into the kitchen to nuke it, and he followed me, which I guess made sense since I hadn't said goodbye or anything. I realized I might be a little more out of it than I'd thought.

"You didn't have to do that," I said. "But thank you. I mean, really. It's really nice."

He smiled. "Well, you know. My mom always said the way to a girl's heart is through her best friend."

I turned away to get a bowl out of the cabinet. I said, "Oh, right. Okay."

"Not that . . . Ugh. That sounded better in my head."

"It's okay. I'll make sure to tell Bethany you came over." I dumped half the soup into the bowl and put it in the microwave. I felt grungy and gross and sick, but on the other hand, at least there was soup. Also, Greg was in my kitchen. Talking to me. Talking to me, knowing who I was. I felt a little naked, and not in a good way.

"Well," he said, "I guess I'll just . . ."

"Can I get the Latin homework from you?"

"Oh, yeah, sure. It's written down in my notes, but I'll text you with it later."

"Thanks."

"Sure."

I wanted him to leave. I didn't want him to leave. I said, "Um, so Bethany said you took your Mandarin final last weekend."

"Oh. Yeah, at NVCC. I did."

The microwave beeped, and I got my soup out and sat down

with it, taking a second to breathe in the steam. "What about Latin? Are you going to take that at NVCC next year? Since you already did the AP?"

He sat down opposite me, like we were old friends. We kind of were old friends. He said, "No, I was thinking about letting that one go. I only took it in the first place because it's supposed to be a good gateway language."

"Right. And you already spoke Spanish."

"Yeah. What about you? You never wanted to speak to the living?"

I laughed a little and tested the temperature of the soup against my lower lip. "I mean, I guess so. I just grew up with a lot of Latin in the house, 'cause of my dad, so I wanted to learn it. I really like it, though."

"Yeah?"

"Yeah, there's something kind of . . . finite about it. I don't know. I guess I like the way I can draw boundaries around it."

He nodded. "I can see that. What are you going to do next year?"

"What, for Latin? I'm not sure. I've already got five years of it. I thought maybe I'd just do some other elective."

"What about NVCC?"

"I don't know. I guess I never really thought about it. Isn't the scheduling kind of hard?"

"Most of the classes are evenings or weekends, so it isn't too bad."

I slurped at my soup. "It'd be nice to sleep through first period."

"That part is very good." He got up. "Well, I hope you feel better."

"Yeah," I said. "This is the magic soup, so."

"Is it really?"

"It definitely is. Good for what ails you, my mom always said. When she was pregnant with my brother it was the only thing she could keep down for weeks."

"Huh. Well, I guess I'll have to try it next time I'm sick. Or pregnant."

I got up to let him out. "I'll bring you some. Or, um, Bethany will. I'm sure she will."

"I'll leave it to you to make sure that happens."

"Oh, absolutely. I will be your soup enforcer."

"See you," he said.

"Bye," I said, and then he was gone.

In the bottom of the soup bag was a fortune cookie. Now, I'm not really into astrology or fortune-telling on the whole, but I have found that occasionally you can get some really excellent advice from a cookie. Like the time I had one that told me a clean environment is best for learning, and then I found ten dollars when I was throwing crap out of my desk.

So I tore the cookie open. Maybe it would tell me what to do about the mess I was in. It said: A BIRD IN THE HAND MAKES EXCELLENT DIM SUM.

Perhaps not so useful this time.

I was finishing the last of my reheated soup that night when Greg messaged me.

Are you feeling better?

I am, thanks. I tried to remember my Russian fairy tales. Was there one about magic soup? *Baba Yaga would approve.*

You're getting into the Russian stuff. I told you you would.

I laughed. *With all the languages you know, you always lead with that one. Couldn't you occasionally say something in Italian or Spanish?*

I could, he said. *But for our purposes Russian is better.*

Oh really. And why is that?

It's more romantically evocative, of course.

I laughed out loud.

Right. Russian is known globally as the language of love. That whole business about it being French is just really good marketing by the Parisians.

I'll have you know that Russian is an extremely romantic language. Dr. Zhivago? Anna Karenina? War and Peace? They're all, like, giant romantic epics.

Fine, I said. *Tell me something romantic in Russian.*

He typed:

Я вас любил безмолвно, безнадежно,

То робостью, то ревностью томим.

I said, *Be still, my quivering heart.*

Oh please, you don't even know what it says!

Of course I don't!

. . .

So are you going to tell me what it says?

So now you want to know.

Fine, don't tell me.

I'll tell you.

. . .

It says: I loved you wordlessly, without a hope,

By shyness tortured, or by jealousy.

Some little noise came from my throat. I hated that noise. He didn't know. *He doesn't know. Those are just words to him.*

That they happened to be exactly the right words was another matter. I stared at the screen and then typed, *Oh.*

That's Pushkin, he said.

It's very romantic, I said. *You were right.*

...

...

Hey, he said. *Did I scare you off? Here. Here's another one: I was not born to amuse the tsar. That's Pushkin, too. Just ignore the other one.*

No, I said. *No, the other one was perfect. It's perfect.*

Oh. Good. That's good. It's just, I don't want to freak you out or anything.

You didn't. It's just, I've felt that. Those words, I've felt that.

About me?

Yes, about you. All the time.

You know you don't have to be wordless with me, right?

I know. It's just hard to say what I'm feeling.

Why?

I don't know.

Your words mean a lot to me. I want you to know that.

My words.

I mean, you must know how beautiful you are. And you are. You're probably the most beautiful girl I've ever seen. But you're so much more than that. It's like, when we're talking like this, I just feel this—

I typed, *Connection.*

Yes! Tell me you also feel that. Like, like there's this direct line between my brain and yours, like we just telegraph on the same frequency. I've never had that before. It's like you see past everything that isn't important right to the stuff that is.

I typed, *I feel that, too.*

Maybe it's because we can't see each other. There's nothing but thoughts.

We're both unseen and unseeing. There's nothing but the part of ourselves that's inside us.

YES

I put my hand over my mouth. Did he know? He had to know. He must know. He couldn't know.

He said, *Damn it, my phone's down to 3% and I left my charger in my car. I'll see you tomorrow, right? If you're better?*

Tomorrow. Of course you will.

I can't wait to see you for real.

For real. What was I doing? What had I done?

Everything suddenly snapped back to reality. I would see Greg tomorrow, but he wouldn't see me. For all he was talking about seeing down to the essentials, he had no idea who I was. I wanted to type, *How can you not know? How can you not know who I am? I'm right in front of your face every day!*

And I couldn't understand it, that was the thing. I legitimately didn't understand how Greg could not know that Bethany couldn't possibly be on the other end of this conversation. She just didn't use words the same way I did.

I suppose I could have forgiven him for not knowing that part, since he probably barely knew what Bethany *did* sound like. But the thing was, I was there, too. I was there talking to him, with my own words, in my own voice. And all I could think was if he didn't recognize that I was the same person IRL and online, it was only because he didn't want to. Someone who could speak six freaking languages should have been able to recognize my speech patterns, my language, my words.

I typed, *I can't wait so see you, either.*

Because it was true. I'd probably be with Bethany, and he'd come ambling up with his happy-go-lucky gait, and he'd kiss Bethany and not me. But I'd be there. And I'd be happy to see him. More than happy. It would be the best part of my day, watching him put his arm around my best friend and smile at me like we were buddies.

Chapter Twenty-Two

I actually did feel a little better the next day, and I like to think it was due to the magic soup, though it could have been the fact that I slept in until 11:30. My sinuses felt less like impacted golf balls, and after I took a couple of decongestants I felt almost normal. I texted Bethany, *Your boy brought me the magic soup, and now I am magically healed.*

She replied, *You must've gotten the only magic bowl. I'm still sick.*

Damn. Really?

Yeah, my throat is on fire. I'm going to get it swabbed in a little while to make sure it's not strep.

Oh. Sorry. Hope it's not strep.

While I was eating my cereal (and wishing I had more soup), I pulled up the course catalog for NVCC. They didn't have a huge Latin department, and it looked like I'd probably place out of most of their classes if I did well on the AP, but they did have one on Virgil that looked interesting. It was on the Annandale campus, which isn't too far away, on Mondays and Wednesdays from five to seven. I don't row in the fall, so logistically, it was possible. I went in search of my dad. He was sitting at his desk with a pad of paper on his lap and some computer program open on the monitor in front of him.

"It lives!" he exclaimed, without turning around. "I was beginning to wonder."

"I'm okay," I said. "Ish."

"What do you know about SAS?" he asked.

"Only that I'm full of it."

"Not sass," he said, smiling. "S-A-S. It's a statistical programming language. Supposed to be very easy to learn."

"I'm guessing it's not?"

He pushed away from the desk. "Maybe it's me."

"Isn't this the kind of thing you have grad students for?"

"I just need a simple program that'll make me a database."

"You could ask Sebastian."

He gave me a dark look. I said, "He does computer stuff!"

He made a face. Dad was analyzing medieval tax documents over the period of several hundred years to see how the money moved around. The pipe roll of 1130 was the first surviving English tax document, and then there were a bunch missing because of the civil war that happened right after that, when the English barons promised to support Henry's daughter Maude as the queen and then her cousin tried to take over anyway and the whole country spent 20 years eating itself alive in a civil war because the patriarchy sucks.

Anyway, that's what Dad was doing, and had been doing for the past couple of years, but it was not going well because he is not very good at math or computers.

"It took Einstein ten years to learn calculus," I reminded Dad.

"When you're Einstein, you can take ten years to learn calculus. Unfortunately, I'm not him."

"He was a crappy family man," I said. "So we're probably better off."

"Did you really come down here to talk about the pipe roll?"

"No, actually, I came to talk about my classes for next year."

"Yeah?"

"It's just,you know they do dual enrollment with the community college, right?"

"I remember Delia mentioned it a couple of years ago."

"Yeah, so I'm kind of topped out on Latin as of this year, and I was thinking maybe I could take a class over there so I don't have to give it up."

"At NVCC, huh? How would you get over there?"

"I'm not really sure about that part. I have this, uh, friend. And he's talking some classes over there, and he seems to like them. Otherwise I'll have to sit out Latin next year."

"Hm," he said. "We'd have to figure out the logistics with your mom. You ever been there, even?"

"No," I said. "I haven't."

"Well, when you're feeling better, why don't you head over? Check it out. See if you think it's workable to get there on your own." He smiled at his program. "I don't suppose dual enrollment means the classes are free?"

"No, I don't think so. But the credits transfer, so it's probably cheaper in the long run."

He nodded thoughtfully. I suspected what he really wanted was to get back to work. "Maybe I'll just go over there today."

"Aren't you still sick?"

"Barely," I said. "Can I use the car this afternoon?"

"I'll be doing this until I retire," he said. "So sure."

NVCC has like six different locations, not one contained campus like GMU. Annandale is the biggest one and also the closest to my house, so I decided to head over there that afternoon. I stopped at a bench on the quad and watched the students go by. It was kind of a mixed bunch in terms of age. There were people who looked like they were my age or younger, and then a couple of ladies in hijab walked by who looked like they were probably in their fifties.

I wasn't sure why I was there, except that I was curious. Middleridge was starting to feel kind of tight, like a shirt I'd outgrown, and this was the logical next size up. Plus, there was something undeniably appealing about the idea of telling people, "Sorry, I won't be here tomorrow. I'll be at college." I smiled thinking about it. I wandered around the main building, where most of the classes were held, and then went down to the basement to check out the bookstore.

There wasn't a lot in the language section, so I meandered down the aisle to see what they had for English. There was a huge tome of the giants of Russian literature on the shelf for a literature in translation class. I pulled it out and sat down on the floor with it on my lap.

The type was really small. I'm not normally one to be bothered by that, but it was like the publisher had tried to save money by using the least amount of paper possible. And on top of that, there didn't seem to be normal punctuation marks, like quotes or paragraph breaks.

"Good grief," I muttered, two pages in. I wasn't even sure what I was reading; a short story by Chekov, I knew that much, and there was a little boy and he seemed to be eating soup? With his nanny?

Someone walked up to me and, in a low voice like a movie announcer's, said "Aphra Brown."

I looked up into the face of Greg D'Agostino, who was grinning from ear to ear.

"Hey," I said. "I mean, hi. I mean." Of all the times to be channeling Bethany.

Geez, that was a mean thought.

He said, "Aren't you sick?"

"Not so much now. There was, you know, the soup, which you brought. That you brought. Which you brought. Ugh, they both sound right, I don't know."

"I think it's *which,*" he said.

"Are you sure?"

"Well, it's a nonrestrictive clause, right?"

Brilliantly, I said, "Um."

"Nonessential information," he explained.

"Well, then no, because the origin of the soup was important. So I've changed my mind. It's the soup *that* you brought."

I wished this felt less like flirting. I was pretty sure bantering about the rules of English grammar didn't count as flirting for Greg. I wondered if he and Bethany flirted, but I imagined they just skipped that part and went straight to the making out. "So," I said. "I didn't think you'd be here."

"I was meeting with the professor about my independent

study," he said. "I had to rework the syllabus since your girl Bethany reminded me I'd included no women."

That's right. She had said that.

"Are you signing up for next semester?" he asked.

"I—I'm not sure. I just wanted to look around, I guess."

"And you decided to do a little light reading?"

I looked down at my book. "Something like that."

"That translation isn't getting you anywhere," he said, putting the book back on the shelf. "Too archaic. I have the Robert Payne at home, if you want it."

"Don't you usually read this stuff in the original?"

"I go back and forth," he said. "Depends how ambitious I'm feeling."

I got up off the floor. The decongestant I'd taken seemed to have struck the edge off my wits, or maybe that was just Greg. "I guess I'm done, then," I said. "I was just looking around."

"I'm just picking this up," he said, flashing me a slim paperback with a title in Russian that I couldn't read and didn't feel like asking about just then. "I was going to get something to eat now, though." He inclined his head toward the door. "Did you want to something? I mean, the food's not great, but it's better than the stuff at Middleridge." He grimaced. "Barely."

"Are you sure? I was just going to go home, but . . ."

"Oh," he said. "No, of course. That's fine. I was just offering." And he looked . . . sad.

I said, "I . . . I guess I could get a sandwich or something first, though. I mean, I am kind of hungry."

• • •

I waited in line for my turkey club and then sat down across from Greg, who had a greasy-looking burger and a paper cup full of curly fries. The dining hall was pretty empty , and I mentioned this to Greg.

"Yeah, that's kind of the downside. Mostly everyone here's part-time, and they aren't exactly here to make friends. Don't come for the social life."

"I was just coming for the Latin, actually, if I can figure out how to get over here."

"Well, you could ride with me, if we have class at the same time."

I stared at him, my jaw popping a little. "What?"

He shoved a fry into his mouth. "Why not?"

My head spun a little. Damn decongestant.

"What else were you thinking of?"

"What else?" I repeated.

"If you want to miss first period, you have to take more than one class." He suddenly looked a little embarrassed. "I mean, I know it's kind of expensive."

"It's not that," I said, even though I honestly had no idea how much community college classes cost. "I just don't know what I'd take."

He opened the NVCC course catalog on his phone and slid it toward me. "Well, have at it. The world is your oyster, Aphra Brown."

Chapter Twenty-Three

I spent the rest of the evening ignoring my actual homework and looking at the course catalog, wondering if I really had to stop at two courses. Middleridge was feeling more and more like baby school to me, and there just weren't that many different things to choose from. I could do half my classes at NVCC and get real credit for them, and I then wouldn't even have to con someone into letting me out of the building if I had to take Kit for his shots or something. I'd be—for three courses out of seven—an adult. It certainly had its appeal. After an hour, I narrowed my choices down to the Virgil, Intro to English Lit, and Russian 101. That meant the only academic classes I'd have to take at Middleridge would be math and science. I also figured out that if I could get my counselor on board, I could miss the first two blocks of the day and come in at 11:45 on the days I didn't have Advisory, leaving me mornings to study.

It was just Delia and me for dinner; Mom had a department meeting, Dad had a dinner with some visiting Middle Ages professor from Vassar, Kit was with a friend, and Sebastian had been felled by the authentic gas station burrito he'd had for lunch.

Walnut seemed to be feeling my brother's absence rather keenly, so while Delia and I ate spaghetti and salad-from-a-bag, he curled up on my lap, his claws dug rather painfully into my pants.

"Is he okay?" I asked, to the sound of Sebastian slamming the bathroom door for the tenth time in the last 15 minutes.

"I told him not to eat that burrito," she said. "It was probably sitting in the case for the past week. But he was all like, *I can eat anything. I went backpacking in Thailand.*" She twirled some spaghetti on her fork and stuffed it in her mouth while the toilet flushed.

"Huh. Well, better out than in, I guess. How's your internship-orientation thing?"

"It's fine," she said. "They just want to make sure I know all the lab protocols before I start. I know where they keep the good pipettes."

"Are there bad pipettes?"

With a full mouth, she said, "That was a joke."

I wondered how much Delia was getting paid for pipetting this summer; I knew it was something, but I didn't know the details. I'd left my list of NVCC classes on the table next to my plate and wondered how much money I'd save taking a half a semester's worth of classes next fall. "How come you never did dual enrollment?" I asked.

She leaned over to look at my list. "At NVCC? I don't know. I guess I didn't see the point."

"Well, there's more classes you can take."

"Yeah, but I took two AP science classes senior year. I'm not sure how that would have worked. Why, are you thinking about it?"

I nodded. "Yeah. Just to try something different, I guess."

"You think you can you manage that with crew? College classes are a lot more work than high school. Like, *a lot* a lot."

"Yeah, I know. I think I can do it, though."

"Just make sure it's worth the trade-off."

"I really can't see how there's anything I'd be giving up."

Downstairs, the door slammed again. "Everything's a trade-off," she said, getting up and putting her plate in the sink. "You just have to figure out if you say yes to this what you're saying no to."

I wanted to ask her what she meant, but she was already heading downstairs to play Dr. Delia with Sebastian. There's something vaguely romantic, I suppose, about taking care of your sick boyfriend, not that I've ever done it. I wondered what it'd be like to take care of a sick Greg. He'd rest his feverish brow on my tender, symmetrical bosom, and I'd stroke his hair and offer him tiny sips of soup until he recovered his strength and sobbed into my lap in gratitude. "Aphra," he'd say. "I'd never have gotten through this without you." And then he'd say something romantic in Russian that I'd have to look up later.

From downstairs I heard Delia hollering my name. "What?" I called back.

"I said we're out of toilet paper, can you bring some down?"

I made a mental note to make sure Sick Fantasy Greg had something more romantic than a case of the runs.

• • •

On Sunday, I needed a cupcake, like, more than I had ever needed anything in my life. I texted Bethany *MUST HAVE CUPCAKE NOW WILL YOU COME?*

No answer. To a cupcake text.

Probably she was with Greg.

I borrowed my mother's car and went off to Cake Baby for a black midnight cupcake with mocha frosting, which is my particular favorite. The frosting isn't even too sweet, which is my usual cupcake complaint. I was going to have a black midnight cupcake with mocha frosting and a cup of Earl Grey tea, which I drink in honor of Captain Picard even though it is technically not my favorite. It makes me feel like a big nerd, though, which always satisfies.

When I got to Cupcake Baby, the first thing I saw was Bethany. Behind the counter. In a baby-blue Cupcake Baby hat and a baby-blue Cupcake Baby apron.

"Hi?" I said, approaching the register. "You're working here?"

Her eyes widened. "My interview was on Tuesday and I totally told you about it."

"You . . . you did?"

"You forgot?"

I couldn't even remember having had the conversation. I guess I'd been thinking about Greg and NVCC, imagining driving to campus with him twice a week and studying in the library together and flirting about grammar. I said, "I'm sorry. My head's still kind of wonky from that cold." Which was true. I was still taking decongestants twice a day, and those make me a little stupid.

Also, not really the issue at the moment. I said, "You got a job?"

"Technically I'm still in training," she said.

"But—"

"May I take your order, please?" she said.

"Bethany!"

She scowled at me and whispered, "I have a break in 20 minutes. Can you just order? There's a line behind you."

I glanced over my shoulder. "Uh. I just want a black midnight with mocha frosting and an Earl Grey tea," I said. She handed me a cup, a cupcake, and a tea bag; I paid her four dollars and 30 cents, filled my cup with hot water, and went to sit down, waiting for an explanation.

I watched her wait on the next three people with some curiosity, like I was seeing a rare ostrich trying to swim. She smiled. She recited the same line with each customer, took their order, and handed them their change. Then the fourth customer said, "Are there nuts in the carrot cake? I'm allergic."

She blinked rapidly a few times. "I—I—I—need to. Uh. Ask. I need to ask. I'm not sure. Sorry, I don't know."

The woman stood back with her arms crossed while Bethany panicked.

"Could you go ask *now*?" the woman said.

Bethany looked around helplessly. "I—I'll be right back," she stammered, and then disappeared. The whole interaction gave me a stomachache. The lady should have been nicer. But the thing is, that's how people are. They aren't very nice a lot of the time. What was Bethany thinking taking this job?

A few seconds later, a man with a beard appeared at the counter and said, "The carrot cake has walnuts, but the spice cake is pretty similar and it's nut free. Everything is stored separately so there's no cross-contamination." Bethany stood looking at the floor while he said this.

"That's fine. I'll take two of the spice cupcakes to go."

The woman took her cupcakes and left, and Bethany told the guy, "I'm sorry."

"It's fine," he said. "That's why you're training." He pulled out a stapled packet of paper from a drawer under the register. "This is a list of ingredients in everything we sell," he said.

"Should . . . should I memorize that?"

He laughed. "No, don't memorize it. But it's here the next time someone asks." He waved her off. "Go take a break. I'll handle things up here for a bit."

I'd already eaten the top half of my cupcake when Bethany came to sit down. "What," I said, "are you doing?"

"Working," she said. "Isn't that obvious?"

"You're working *here*? Isn't that kind of . . ."

Her eyes narrowed. "Kind of what?"

"It's just . . . a lot of interaction with strangers."

Her eyes cut to the window, where there was a picture of a stork carrying a sling with a cupcake inside. She said, "It's mostly scripted, though."

"Scripted?"

"Like, 99% of the time, I know exactly what to say to people. I thought . . ." She shrugged.

"You thought?"

"I wanted to make myself as uncomfortable as possible."

At the table next to us, two middle-aged women got up, said, "This was great!" and left.

"What?" I said. "Why?"

"Because I don't want to end up like Colin. Look, the manager was willing to take me on nine hours a week. So I get to feel super awkward for three hours at a time, and then I get to go home."

"I'm failing to see what this has to do with Colin."

"Colin's going to have to go from being a couch dweller to being out in the world in, like, one year. He has no idea how to have a job or deal with people or, like, *anything*. I'm trying to avoid having to do it that way."

"So you're trying to build up your tolerance? Wouldn't it make more sense to find something that plays to your strengths?"

"Which strengths, Aphra?" she said defensively.

I shrugged helplessly. "I mean, you're so good at tutoring Kit. What about that? You could go work at the Mathnasium or something."

"The Mathnasium won't hire anyone without a college degree."

"Bethany," I said. "You're going to hate this."

"That's the point."

"Making yourself miserable is the point?"

"Yes! I'm trying to . . . to . . ."

"Have a nervous breakdown?"

"Would you stop? Would it kill you to be supportive?"

"I am!"

"No, you're really not. How about you could say, *Congratulations, I am so proud of you.*"

"Congratulations, I am so proud of you," I repeated. "Um, there's—" I pointed to the counter, where there were now four people in line and the manager was motioning for Bethany to take over while he took a phone call.

"Oh, crap." She got up and went to the counter while the manager stepped into the back. "Sorry," she said. "May I take your order?"

"I have a coupon," the woman in front said.

Bethany looked at the slip of paper in her hand. "That's—that's—that's from last year."

"I know," she said. "I've been saving it."

"Okay," Bethany said. "Okay. Could you just—" And she disappeared into the back room again.

I put a dollar in the tip jar by the register and left before I said something else unsupportive.

Chapter Twenty-Four

In app design the next day, Bethany and I sat in the back while Mr. Positano handed back our projects. My green folder came to me with a Post-it on the front with a giant A, underlined three times.

"This was really excellent work, Aphra," he said.

"Uh," I said, because honestly it wasn't. "Thanks."

"I didn't think you'd be able to pull this off. This is college-level work. I showed it to some of the other teachers, and we were all highly impressed."

"You," I said. "Showed it to other teachers?"

"You know, this could have been a real crash-and-burn situation, but you took a risk and it paid off big-time. I think you should consider sending it to the CS department at Mason. They'd love to see an example of how someone used their source code."

"Yeah," I said weakly. "I'll think about that."

He nodded and tossed Bethany's project down on her desk. She got a B+ and made a little face at it. After he walked away, she said, "How did you—"

I cut her off before she could ask me how I'd fixed it by taking the dual enrollment form out of my backpack and putting it next to my keyboard. I'd been planning on talking to Bethany about NVCC over cupcakes, but since that hadn't happened, this seemed like a good a time as any. Bethany's eyes went over my list of proposed NVCC classes and my request that I get the first two blocks of the day as free periods.

"What is this?" she asked.

"My ticket to adult life," I said. "Greg was talking about his classes when he came by with my soup, so I just started thinking about it." I didn't mention that I'd seen him on campus.

Bethany took the paper and read it again. "So you're just not going to be here until *after lunch*?"

"That's the plan," I said.

"But," she said. "But."

"I'll still be here for the last two blocks of the day, but it'll really free me up to do other stuff."

"Other stuff? What other stuff?"

"Take class at NVCC? Or if some of my classes are at night, I can have time in the mornings to study so I don't have to stay up so late after crew. You should think about it, too; they have tons of math and science stuff. You could take physics and bio there instead of at Middleridge."

She frowned. "What would the point be? If I get a four or five on the AP, I'll get the same credits without having to pay for the classes."

"That's true, but . . ."

"But what? Isn't the point to get college credit?"

"I mean, yeah, that's part of it, but . . ." I sighed. "Don't you want more than this?"

"More than what?"

"More than high school! Like, to be in the world!"

She looked doubtful. "It's community college."

"I know that. It's just . . . more. Bigger, I don't know. Don't you want that?" On the other side of the room, Mr. Positano was arguing with the seniors about their crappy *Steak Ninja* game, which had earned them a C-minus. He kept saying, very slowly, "It doesn't even *run*," and they kept replying, "But we *tried*."

Bethany looked away from them and back to me, saying, "Aphra, I just started a job."

"I know."

"Where I have to deal with people, like, every two minutes. That's already as much *more* as I can handle right now."

"But—"

"Can you please not talk me in circles about this? Like, could you please just not?"

"What?"

"Just stop trying to talk me into it! I told you I don't want to do it!"

"I'm not trying to talk you into it. I'm just pointing out that there are some options you might want to—"

"Stop! Would you stop? God. Everything is so easy for you, you don't get it."

"Everything is not easy for me, Bethany."

"It is! You just . . . you just go so fast. You think fast. You talk fast. I'm just not that way."

"You're acting like you're stupid, and we both know you're not."

"I'm not. I know I'm not. But I'm not like you."

"Fine. You don't want to take classes there, then don't."

"I won't."

"Good. Fine."

But Bethany looked like she was holding her breath. "So what's the deal now?" I asked.

"You never even told me."

"Told you?"

"That you were planning this. You never even mentioned it."

"I really hadn't thought about it until this weekend. I still have to apply, I guess, but NVCC will take you in high school as long as your PSATs are high enough, so—"

"This is a big deal! And you never even told me!" Her face had gone from too pale to too flushed.

"It's a big deal for me, but I don't get why it's a big deal for you."

It occurred to me then that Bethany was actually upset. I couldn't figure out why; we'd barely had more than one or two classes together since freshman year, so it wasn't like she was really going to miss me. Except . . .

"You can still have lunch with the rest of the crew team," I said.

Bethany did not reply.

"I mean, you know I actually don't have to be there for you to sit with them."

"I know that," she snapped. At the front of the room, Mr. Positano had finished passing back the assignments and was trying to start class.

"Ladies," he said. "Am I interrupting something? What's the deal?"

"Nothing," Bethany muttered, more for me than for him. "The deal is nothing."

"Bethany," I said.

"No, you're right. It's not a big deal. I'm being dumb." She took a deep breath. "I'm sorry."

I was still thinking about Bethany's over-the-top reaction when I got to Latin that afternoon and was surprised to discover Greg sitting in John's chair while John stood in the doorway scowling at him. I breezed by him as if he didn't exist and dropped my books at my regular desk.

"Mitzi's out today," Greg said. "Can I sit with you instead?"

John stalked over and crossed his arms. "Did you seriously tell him to take my seat? Really?"

"No. I didn't."

"I love how you're all Miss Sense of Humor until the shoe's on the other foot," he said. Which actually made me start laughing, because of how ridiculous it was, because I have literally never made fun of somebody because of how they look. Well, except Delia, maybe, but that's a special case.

"Dude," Greg said. "What did you do?"

"I made a joke," he said. "And she's making a big-ass deal about it."

"Literally, you are the only one talking about it," I said.

"Not my fault you don't have a sense of humor."

"When have you ever been funny?" Greg said. "Sit down, John."

John made a nasty face and then went to sit in Greg's desk.

"Seriously," Greg said. "What'd he say?"

"I already forgot," I said.

"Good," he said. "Good. So I actually wanted to talk to you. See, I just found out something kind of significant."

I dropped my pencil on the floor. "Oh," I said. "Really?"

"Yeah. It kind of involves, you know. Me and Bethany."

At the front of the room, Ms. Wright told us to move to the next section of Ovid. We opened our books to the story of Adonis. I tried not to cry from the irony. I did my best to ignore the Adonis next to me and started working on the first few words.

My translation didn't look right. "Is this tree pregnant?" I asked.

"It's just, I kind of found out something by accident."

I froze in my seat a little. He couldn't know. Could he know? No, if he knew he'd be mad, and he didn't seem mad. He seemed nervous, or maybe a little excited. "Okay?" I said.

"Sophie Bell told me Bethany's birthday is Friday," he said.

"Oh. Yeah, I knew that."

Of course I knew. I'd had her present in my sock drawer for weeks: a charm bracelet with elemental symbols, to add to her collection. I found it on this website last summer and had to save up for the little enameled charms for three months.

"Right. So I was thinking . . ." He did spirit fingers at me. "Surprise party."

"Oh. No," I said. "No, no."

"What?"

"No surprise party. Not for Bethany. That won't go over, like, at all."

"Everybody loves surprise parties!"

"If by loving it, you mean Bethany will spend the whole party in the bathroom breathing into a paper bag, then sure. She'll love it."

"I wouldn't invite anyone she didn't know," he protested. "Just, like, the crew team and stuff. I thought you could help me make a list. I checked and Sophie said we could use her basement if we want."

"You ran this by Sophie? And she didn't tell you this was a bad idea?"

"Come on," he said. "She's turning 17! She should have a party."

"I feel like you are not hearing me. She doesn't want a party. Bethany hasn't had a birthday party since she was nine. Her mom hired some chick dressed as Princess Belle and she hid in her closet the entire time."

"Princess Belle hid in Bethany's closet?"

I smacked his arm. "Quit being obtuse."

"Come on," he said. "That was eight years ago."

"She hasn't had a personality transplant since then. Listen. Lis-ten to meeeee. She doesn't want a surprise party."

He let out a long-suffering sigh.

"Does that mean you get it?"

"But she was at prom," he said. "That was a party. She looked like she was having fun then."

"Well, yeah. But that's because it wasn't for her. She wasn't the center of attention."

"But you agree that she did have fun at that."

I thought about it. We'd gone together, and we'd had an amazing time. . . . We went out to dinner first with the crew girls, and then we danced for two hours until our feet hurt, and then we all spent the night at Sophie's house. It was great. "Yeah, she did."

He gave me a little half smile. I loved and hated that I could tell what he was thinking just by the look on his face. Or maybe our brains were wired for the same network. I don't know. "So you're suggesting," I said, "that we have a party for Bethany that is not actually for Bethany."

He smiled wider.

"But if we do that, it can't just be her friends, or she'll know," I said. "There needs to be a lot of people, and most of them can't know why they're really there."

"A stealth birthday party," he said. "We'll just happen to have a really big cake on hand. That does not say *Happy Birthday, Bethany* on it."

"That's perfect," I said. "She'll love that. She'll love the whole thing."

"So it's all settled, then," he said.

"Apart from any of the logistics, yeah." He raised his water bottle and I clinked mine against it.

I sat down on Dr. Pascal's couch and grabbed my usual three mints out of the bowl. Today, Abby Cadabby was on the table with her wand. She'd always been Bethany's favorite. Personally, I was more of a Grover-stan, but you know. Everybody's different.

"Do these guys help?" I asked as she finished shoving her intra-patient yogurt into her mouth.

"Sure, for some kids," she said.

"You never use them with me," I pointed out.

"I don't think they'd help you."

"Maybe you're selling the Muppets short," I said. "I mean, Jim Henson was a genius. Did you ever see *The Dark Crystal*?"

Rather than answer that, she said, "So what did you decide about why you handed Greg over to Bethany?"

"I'm amazed you can remember all these names from one week to the next."

"Copious notes," she said, holding up her pad. "Answer the question."

"Well," I said. "I did try to think about it. In psychological terms, I would say that my superego has overwritten my id."

"Just so you know, nobody currently practicing psychology still buys into any of that."

"What?"

"The Freudian stuff. It's about 100 years out of date."

"No kidding."

"Afraid so. As much as the 'monsters from the id' worked in *Forbidden Planet,* it doesn't really hold up to modern clinical scrutiny."

I'd never seen *Forbidden Planet,* but the phrase *monsters from the id* struck me. "Huh. Well, that's disappointing."

"You think?"

It was, because I'd liked the idea of these little compartmentalized units coexisting in my brain. Plus, when I was being an asshole, I got to blame it on the monsters from *my* id, which is sort of like saying *I didn't do it and it is therefore not my fault.* I felt like my id was not me in the same way my pancreas is not me. I liked the id. It was like having a dog around you could blame if you farted at the dinner table. *Sorry for my stinky behavior, it was just my id passing some gas, ha ha. I'll make it go in the other room now.* I said, "Yeah, I guess."

"But what you're saying is that your desire to do the right thing was more important than what you wanted. Which was the boy."

I shrugged.

"And you felt like the greater good was taking yourself out of the equation, because you don't deserve to be with him."

"It's not that I don't deserve it, it's that it wasn't going to happen," I said.

"Hm," she said. She handed me a giant book off the corner of her desk. "I thought maybe we could try something different today. Take a look at this."

I took it in my hands. The front cover had embossed eagles on it and read *Frontier High School 1992.* "This is a high school yearbook," I said. "This is your high school yearbook?"

"Indeed it is."

"Oh! So where are you?"

"Page 37. Be kind, please."

I glanced up from the book. "Does this mean you ran out of the tricks you learned in head-shrinking school?"

"Please. I ran out of head-shrinking tricks three months ago."

"Wait. Seriously?"

"Just look at the book."

I flipped to page 37 and scanned down until I got to *Pascal, Laila,* in that stupid off-the-shoulder drape they've been making girls wear in their senior pictures for the last 50 years. She looked surprisingly the same, with different glasses and pudgier cheeks. "You were cute," I said. "And you weren't even wearing that nasty plum lipstick, so bullet dodged there."

"Thank you. So here's what I want you to do with that book. I want you to go through it and tell me which girl in the senior class you think was the prettiest."

I looked up from the book to see if she was serious. She seemed to be. "If I say you, do I get a prize or something?"

"No. Go ahead."

"Do I have a time limit? Like, how long do I have to consider my options?"

"Let's try to keep it under five minutes, how about that."

I went back to the beginning of the senior class pictures. "Can I have some Post-its or something?"

She opened her desk drawer. "You're taking this very seriously."

"You're the one who asked me to do it," I said as she tossed me some little pink sticky flags.

So I started with Abadah, Renee, and kept going. It was a harder exercise that I would have thought, partly because reduced to a 2x2-inch square and wearing the same top, the girls all started to look kind of the same, and partly because I kept wondering if this was some kind of trick. Was she hoping I'd pick someone not obvious? Someone who looked just like Bethany? I couldn't figure out what the point was, and it made me uncomfortable. Finally, after I'd gone back through everyone I'd left a Post-it on, I settled on Garcia, Claudia.

"Claudia," she said thoughtfully.

"Was she nice?"

"It was a big class," she said. "I didn't really know her that well, but I think she was. Why'd you pick her?"

I shrugged and looked back at the picture. "She has a nice smile," I said. "And her hair looks good."

"Okay, that's valid." She took a piece of paper off the top of her desk. "So here's what I did before you showed up. . . . I wrote down the names of the four girls in my class everyone thought were the prettiest, the ones who kept getting elected to the homecoming court and things like that."

I reached forward and took it from her. "Is she on it?" I asked.

She wasn't. I went back and looked up the pictures of those four girls. I mean, they were pretty. I'd flagged three of the four. But they weren't any prettier than the girl I'd picked. Less, I thought. To be honest, they really weren't any prettier than, like, the top third of the class or so.

"What do you notice about those four girls?" she asked.

"Well, they're all skinny and white," I said. "So basically you're telling me you went to a crappy high school."

"It had its problems for sure," she said. "Now. Pick the ugliest."

I felt a little like I'd been punched in the gut. I hate that word, especially applied to people. Ugly sentiments I can live with. Ugly buildings, sure. Ugly people? I hated hearing it.

"What?" I said, like maybe I'd misheard what she was asking me to do.

"You heard me."

"I'm not doing that."

"Why not?"

"Because it's mean!" I handed her the book back. I was actually about ready to leave at that point. "Please tell me you did not write down the name of the ugliest girl in your class."

"No," she said. "I didn't."

"Then why ask me?"

"Because I knew you wouldn't do it."

I sat back on the couch. "I think maybe you should stick to Muppets," I said. "That was gross."

"You don't like to hear that word applied to other people."

"No."

"But you use it when you think about yourself. You said it in here the other day."

"I don't think so."

She held up her notepad. "I write stuff down, remember? So why do you think you're less deserving of your own kindness than other people?"

I didn't have a ready answer. "I just like to be honest," I finally said.

"What I'm trying to get you to see is that attractiveness—conventional attractiveness—is completely arbitrary. It's not real."

"That's not totally true," I said. "It has to do with facial symmetry and—"

"No. Aphra, no. And the other thing I'm trying to tell you is that the people who you think meet the definition for conventional attractiveness aren't empirically any more beautiful than the people who don't. Was it hard for you to look through that book and pick someone?"

"Yeah. It was."

"Mmm-hmm. You probably thought about half the class looked pretty good. Am I right?"

"Yeah. I guess."

"And the ones you didn't pick, it was probably because their glasses were out of style or they had weird makeup or too much hair spray."

"What is your point?"

"My point is that you are getting completely hung up on an illusion. You picked Claudia, but I can tell you that back in the day no one was beating down her door asking her out."

"So what you want me to say is that beauty is an illusion, I look just as good as Bethany, and I should have scooped up Greg for myself. Come on."

"What I want is for you to see that beauty is relative, you are not ugly, and you should have given the boy a chance to say *yes* before you put the *no* in his mouth for him."

I put a mint in my mouth. I was already up to my third, which meant I'd run out before the end of the session, and that annoyed me badly.

She said, "When you went to that college party, what was the first thing that happened to you?"

"Uh," I said, because I didn't think I should mention that the first thing that happened was that someone gave me a cocktail. "I talked to the guy who was working the bar."

"No. You got *hit on* by the guy who was working the bar."

"It was dark," I said.

She scoffed.

"It was. And he was not completely sober—are you going to tell my parents this?"

"No." She got up and went to the door and flicked off the light switch, leaving only the light that crept in around the edges of the closed blinds. "Was it this dark?" she asked.

"Maybe a little darker."

"But close."

"Sure," I said, rolling my eyes and hoping it was too dark for her to see. "It was close."

"Can you still see what I look like?"

"Yeah, mostly . . ."

"Uh-huh. But you think this boy couldn't see you. It was light enough that he didn't trip over your feet, but you think he has no idea what you looked like."

"He was—"

"Drunk boys still have eyeballs." She turned the lights back on. "I'm going to be straight with you right now."

"You mean you haven't been up until now?"

"I haven't used this word because I knew you'd just fight me on it, but what you have is called a dysmorphia."

I threw up my hands.

"Nope. Nope, nope, do not answer back to me, Aphra Brown. Here is the honest-to-goodness truth about you: You don't look like a Barbie doll. Guess what. Neither do I. Neither do most people." She held up a finger. "However, you are also not ugly. Not even close."

"My nose—"

"Is big. You have a big nose, Aphra. That doesn't mean you're ugly. It just means you have a big nose. That's it. That's all it means."

But it wasn't all it meant. Not really. Not at all. Because it wasn't just my nose. It was everything.

Chapter Twenty-Five

Greg and I had three days to plan a party for Bethany that was ostensibly not for Bethany.

This was no problem, I told Greg, because I had an idea.

It wasn't even a new idea. It was something the team had been talking about for the last month. The idea was that the girls' crew team wanted to have a fund-raiser to help offset the cost of next year's uniforms. We'd gone around and around about whether to go door-to-door or do a car wash or have a bake sale, and it occurred to me: we could use the fundraiser as a cover for Bethany's party; all we'd have to do was move it up to this week. And instead of selling brownies or whatever, we'd have a party at Sophie's—she's the only one with a house big enough—and charge five dollars at the door.

Which was all very good—we planned it for Thursday, to take advantage of the teacher workday on Friday—right until Sophie called me that night and told me her parents were having a dinner party on Thursday and we couldn't use her house after all.

So things were not off to a great start. After I left Dr. Pascal's, I'd spent the afternoon calling every county-owned facility I could think of—down to the horse barn at Frying Pan Park—but they were all booked solid, and anyplace else was going to be too expensive. It was beginning to look like the party was not going to happen

Greg called me later that night. It was a little disconcerting, because I hadn't realized he actually had my number.

"Hey," I said. I was on the couch with Sebastian, who was reading my father's dog-eared copy of *Dune*. I was doing a Latin translation on the coffee table next to some giant Lego structure that Kit had made that afternoon and left out for us to admire. "Hi. Greg."

"Good news," Greg said. "I called the community center."

"Which one? I already called Fairfax, Oak Mill, and McLean. They're all booked. I honestly don't know what we're going to do."

"You're right—they're booked. But I dug a little further and found out the Oak Mill one is booked for a birthday party for a six-year-old. The atrium's rented from five until 11:30 because that's how they rent it out, but they're only actually using it until seven."

"Until seven," I repeated. Walnut kept trying to sit on my Latin, and I scribbled out a second page of decoy homework for him to sit on, pushing him onto the fake. He gave me a grumpy look, as if only a real Ovid translation would do for being under his sanctified cat butt.

Greg said, "Right. So I talked to the mom, and she said we

could have the room from seven on as long as we agree to do all the cleanup afterward, and we don't even have to pay for it. The only downside is that we have to redecorate the room."

"But that'll take forever."

"Yeah, I know, but it's a free big room. I don't think we're going to do any better than that."

I exhaled loudly, popping the head on and off one of Kit's Lego people.

"Yesss?" Greg drawled.

"It's just . . . it's a weeknight party at the community center. It's not exactly what I was hoping for. I really wish we could have done it at Sophie's."

"Yeah, I know, but it's what we have."

"Nobody's going to show up."

"The crew team'll show up."

"Nobody *else* will show up."

"So we need a hook."

"A hook? They're not going to let us have alcohol, and we can't afford a band or anything." Walnut had abandoned the decoy homework for Ovid, and I put him down on the floor, where he batted at my ankle.

"What about a DJ?"

"That either," I said.

"Doesn't have to be a real one," he said.

Walnut jumped up on the table and knocked Kit's Lego house—I think it was a house—onto the floor, where it smashed.

"Damn," I said.

"What?"

"Nothing," I said, trying to get the pieces back on the table.

Sebastian, who had put his book down, picked up part of a roof and set it on top of my homework; Walnut had already batted the Lego head under the couch. "You want to get a fake DJ?"

"No, like, it can be a real person. We just have to embellish his credentials a little. You know anybody who can actually do it?"

I thought for a minute while I attempted to rebuild Kit's house. Sebastian shook his head at my effort and took the four-by-four piece out of my hand and replaced it with a one-by-eight, which I stacked around the periphery of the base. "Celia Cardon rows JV. She's always bragging about how she used to spin at parties when she lived in Annapolis, but I'm not sure it's true."

"Good enough," he said. "Text her and see if she'll do it."

I did, while Sebastian worked on a dormer window.

"She's in," I reported back after we'd talked. "I hope she actually knows how. She's the only senior who hasn't moved up to varsity."

A few minutes later, Greg texted me an e-flyer advertising the party. *FEATURING DJ CELIA*, it said. *Winner of this year's Montgomery Lights Mix festival!*

Does that even exist? I asked.

It does not! he replied.

I had no idea you were such an accomplished liar, I said.

I'm not averse to a bending the truth for the greater good, he said. *There's one problem. . . . I just talked to the mom who was throwing the party to find out if we can reuse her decorations, right?*

And?

It's a My Little Pony party.

I smiled at my phone. *That's actually perfect.*

Because nothing says DONATE TO CREW like dancing ponies?

Nope, I said. *Nothing does.* I tossed my phone down on the couch as Sebastian made a flourish at the Lego house.

"Well?" he asked.

It didn't look like Kit's house; it was actually a little better. He'd added a fence and something I think was meant to be a topiary. I set my headless minifigure in front. "There," I said. "A Dullahan."

He looked a little puzzled. "The headless horseman," I explained, "was a Dullahan."

"Ah," he said. He pulled the head off another minifigure and set it down next to mine. "There. Now he has a friend."

Delia walked in from the kitchen holding a glass of milk and a plate of cookies, with a towel wrapped around her hair. She looked at the two of us, a smirk spreading across her face. "Are you guys . . . playing Legos?"

"No!" I protested.

"Indeed not," Sebastian said. "This is serious." He held up another Lego person, which was all black with purple eyes. "The Dullahans are fighting off an invasion of Endermen."

"Actually," I said, "a Dullahan and an Enderman would probably get along. Since an Enderman can't stand to be looked at—"

"And a Dullahan has no face," Sebastian said. "Good point." He handed one of the minifigures to Delia. "Here. You can be Wilbur."

• • •

Thursday afternoon, Greg and I hit the Costco and bought half a dozen appetizer platters and way too many two-liter bottles of soda, along with a purple inflatable baby pool that we planned to fill with ice and use to serve the drinks. I just hoped people actually showed up; we'd put stuff up on Twitter and Instagram, but the notice was kind of short. On the other hand, it was five bucks to see an (allegedly) award-winning DJ. You could hardly beat the price.

"So," Greg said as we drove back from Costco. "You know Bethany pretty well, right?"

"Sure. We go way back."

"Yeah. Yeah. So, I mean, you know I kind of overheard you guys playing *Zombie Air* in Bethany's basement that time."

"Is she still mad because I let the zombies get her?"

"No. No, it's not that. It's . . . she talks to you."

I stared at him. "Of course she talks to me."

His eyes cut sideways toward the sunset. "She doesn't talk to me."

"What do you mean she doesn't talk to you?"

"I mean, in person, she just . . . she just doesn't talk. She barely says more than three words in a row."

"But you guys have been out like six times. What do you do if you're not . . . talking . . ."

Greg blushed and looked away.

I winced. "Never mind. Look, Bethany's kind of shy until she gets used to you. It's temporary."

"I feel like when we're not talking in person, when we're texting or whatever, it's like she knows me better than anyone. And then we get together, and I try talking to her about the same things, and she . . . shuts down. I don't get it. Am I scary?"

"No," I said. "You're not scary at all."

"Then what is it?"

"It's just how she is," I said.. "Give her a little time. Bethany's . . . she's worth it."

The light caught his eyes. "She's lucky to have you, you know."

I unfolded my legs; I'd been sitting on my foot and it was asleep. "It's really the other way around, trust me." I looked out the window. "She has the best heart of anyone I know."

"I know," he said. "It's like, I know there's this bold, brave, amazing person in her. I see it sometimes, and I wish she'd let that out. That's the girl I want to hang out with. She changed my life."

I felt my throat constrict. I said, "Oh."

"Everyone thinks she's just this pretty face, and she's not! She's . . . she's so funny. And she's . . . she sees things down to the essentials. It's like, when we start talking there's, like, a purity to it, I don't know."

"Nothing but thoughts," I said.

He glanced over at me. "What was that?"

"Nothing," I said, wondering if some part of me had said that on purpose. Damn id acting up again. I did my best to tamp it back down. "Nothing, I mean, I understand. That's all true, about Bethany. She gets people."

"So just be patient, huh?"

"Right. Just be patient."

He dropped me off at my house, "See you tonight," he said. "You think she'll like it?"

"Yeah," I said. "She totally will."

• • •

Bethany still had my red dress, and I stood in front of my closet in my underwear trying to figure out what to wear. Not that it mattered, especially, because this was Bethany's not-birthday, not mine, and no one was going to be looking at me, but the truth is I hate looking schlubby. Someone like Bethany can get away with going out in public looking like she just woke up. I can't. I pulled out a white dress with blue polka dots before deciding that I'm too old for polka dots and putting it back.

I settled on a different route. I pulled out a pair of skinny black pants, a button-down shirt, and a gray vest. Then I grabbed a tie from my father's closet.

I went down to the basement, where Delia was reading some science article on her laptop and Sebastian was sprawled on her bed watching videos on his phone.

"Hey," I said to Delia. "Can you tie this?"

"Is this like a costume thing? You should ditch the shirt and just wear the vest, if you're going for edge."

"Really?" I looked in the mirror. It did look a little costumey, so I went out in the hall and took the shirt off, then put the vest back on over my bra. "Better?" I asked.

"Much," Delia said.

"Okay. Can you do the tie?"

"No," she said. "Sorry, that's above my pay grade."

"Damn it," I said. "There's probably something online that shows you. Can you look it up?"

"I can tie a tie," Sebastian said, putting the phone down and sitting up.

"No," I said, "that's okay."

"You want a four-in-hand or a Windsor?" he said, getting up

and taking one end of the tie in each hand. "Or maybe a Trinity? That'll be sick."

When I stared at him, he said, "I didn't spend four years at Andover for nothing."

"You went to Andover?"

"Yep," he said, fumbling with my tie. "Apparently they even let in vacuous douchenozzles every now and then." From her desk, Delia smothered a laugh into her fist.

I felt myself go very hot. "Uh," I said.

"You have a voice that carries."

"Yeah, I seem to be afflicted with that."

He straightened the tie and spun me toward the mirror on the back of Delia's closet. "There," he said. "Very Marlene Dietrich. Pre-Code Hollywood."

I did not actually know who that was, but I said, "Thanks."

"Sebastian wanted to go to film school," Delia said.

"Don't tell her that," he groaned, flopping back onto the bed.

"Why? Why not?"

"Because it's not happening."

"How come?"

"Didn't get in."

"Oh," I said. "Sorry. Couldn't you apply again? Or apply somewhere else?"

"I don't know," he said. "I don't know. It's such a pipe dream, you know?"

"No more than making bank from a YouTube channel."

"Yeah, but that's different. If I fail nobody cares." He picked his phone back up and unpaused the video he'd been watching.

"What shoes are you wearing?" asked Delia.

"Not sure," I said, watching Sebastian fake-laugh at whatever he was watching. "Uh. Chucks?"

"If you're going Marlene Dietrich, you need heels," she said, sending me back upstairs with a gentle push. "And a bold lip."

On my dresser, where I keep the few pieces of makeup I own, was a tube of scarlet lipstick I bought at the MAC counter with Bethany last year when we decided to get free makeovers before homecoming. I'd had no date because no one had asked me, Bethany'd had no date because she'd said no to everyone who'd asked her, and we'd decided to go together, along with a group of girls from crew who were similarly dateless. The truth is, it's more fun to go to these things with a group anyway. Nobody's nervous. Everyone has fun. We sleep over at someone's house afterward, eat waffles, and don't have anybody to cut out of pictures after the inevitable breakup.

I hardly ever wear the lipstick— it always ends up all over my teeth, my water bottle, and the back of my right hand—but I keep it anyway, because of what happened the day I bought it.

At the store, there was a middle-aged woman with tarantula eyes who gave me a significant glance and then muttered to her friend, "You can't turn a sow's ear into a silk purse."

Bethany had wanted to leave the store then and there, but I'd turned to that woman and said "Ma'am, you can buy a silk purse for a dollar on eBay. And I'd rather be a pig's ear than a horse's ass."

I'd turned to the makeup counter girl and bought the lipstick, along with some amazing concealer I use all the time.

To this day, I will never understand what would make a grown woman compare a teenage girl to a pig's ear, but it doesn't matter. I showed her that day. The universe could play whack-a-mole with me all it wanted, but I wasn't going to stay down. I was fabulous. I was amazing. I owned the reddest lipstick on earth.

That was the lipstick I wore.

Chapter Twenty-Six

The parking lot at the community center was packed.

I'd volunteered to drive Bethany over. Greg was already there with most of the guys from crew, and I'd gotten a text from Claire about 15 minutes earlier telling me we were in trouble because we hadn't bought enough soda.

Greg and I had figured we might get both crew teams plus about two dozen other people, if we were really lucky. I'd texted back, *How many are there?*

She said, *Almost 100 so far.*

I'd stared at my phone. *How is that possible? We don't even have booze.*

I think Greg told the people on the swim team, since we have most of them, and then they brought friends, too, and Celia told all the seniors to come. I just sent Jenna out for more drinks.

Also, she added, *I think someone brought booze.*

Well, at least the fund-raiser part was going to be successful. We hadn't had to pay for the room, so besides the drinks and the snacks, everything we made was profit. Bethany, who had been reading my texts over my shoulder, looked a little nervous.

"That's a lot of people," she said.

"It's fine," I said. "It's smaller than prom."

She was wearing, finally, my red dress, looking like I only wish I looked in it. Everything about her was effortlessly perfect, like she never even had to try. I could try from now until the end of the world and I'd never look a tenth as good. I fiddled with my tie.

"You look amazing," she said.

"Nah," I said.

"I wish I could pull that off."

"Please. Are you ready?"

She checked her makeup one last time in the visor mirror. I'd done her eyes for her, with my favorite bronze liner. Mine were done in black, which Delia said I needed to go with the outfit and the red lip. "Okay," she said. "It's just a fund-raiser, right?"

"Yeah, of course. With dancing and stuff."

"Dancing?"

I got out of the car and Bethany followed me. "There will always be dancing, B."

I wasn't sure how My Little Pony would play with people our age, but with the room so full, the decorations were actually pretty inconspicuous. Claire and Sophie, who were collecting five-dollar bills at a table by the door, jumped up when they saw us. Bethany went to get her five dollars out, but Claire said, "You don't have to pay! It's your—" and then Sophie dug her fingernails into her elbow. "I don't have change," Claire amended. "Just pay me later."

"I have a five," Bethany said, handing over her money.

I handed mine over, too, and then we went inside, where DJ JV Celia was spinning with one arm in the air, and everybody—everybody—was dancing.

Maybe it was because there was almost no place to sit, or because it was nine o'clock on a Thursday before a three-day weekend, or because someone had snuck in some alcohol, but it was wild. John O'Malley was dancing on a table with a Pinkie Pie–shaped balloon while a handful of people took pictures that would probably haunt him for life.

I heard someone calling my name, and suddenly I was pulled into a dancing circle of the boys' crew team. I craned my neck. Bethany was still where I'd left her, only Greg had found her and was looking at her like he was having an experience of the divine. I watched him take her by the hand, lead her over to the drinks table, and crack her open a soda, and then she kissed him on the cheek and I decided not to watch anymore, because I was just going to dance.

I danced with the crew team, and with the swim team, and with Sophie and Claire, who had abandoned their posts since we'd already made way more money than we needed. Talia gave me a can of store-brand cola and I drank it, and then I found myself dancing on a table with John O'Malley and his balloon and forgot for a minute that I was mad at him.

After that, my feet really hurt.

When the song changed, I climbed down from the table (John and a bunch of other people actually booed me then) and found a place to lean against the wall for a minute. I scanned the room for Bethany and found her between Sophie and Claire, watching the party and eating chips, looking a little dreamy-eyed but happy. I'd seen her dancing, too, at least a little, and I wished I'd thought to make her dance with me, but she looked like she was having a good time. I'd just decided to make my way back to her when Greg stepped up to me.

"Hi!" he said happily. Whether he was buzzed from Bethany or some secret stash of liquor I couldn't say, though he didn't smell boozy. "Uh, so, you have some lipstick on your teeth."

Damn it. I turned away and rubbed my teeth with a tissue from my pocket. I turned back to him and smiled.

"You're good now," he said. "Seriously, I don't know how you guys don't have it on your teeth all the time. Like, what makes it stay on your mouth?"

"Sheer animal magnetism," I said.

He smiled and stood next to me to survey the crowd. "Look how many people came!"

"I know," I said. "It's great. We should do this every week."

"Yeah?"

"Well, it probably wouldn't be fun every week."

"No," he said. "No, I guess not. But nobody even minds the pony decorations. Like, I thought people would say stuff, but nobody did."

"It's a party," I said. "All anyone cares about is the music. And the booze, I guess. Do you know who brought it?"

"I'll never tell," he said, with a Mona Lisa smile, then pivoted. "I didn't know you liked to dance so much. I think I saw a little salsa action out there."

"Oh," I said. "Yeah, my dad taught me when I was little."

The song changed to something a little slower, and I thought about taking off my shoes, but with them on I was nearly as tall as Greg, and for some reason I liked that. He said, "I think you danced with every single person here. Did I see you with John?"

"Uh, mostly I was dancing with Pinkie Pie. John just kept getting in the way."

"Yeah, he does that."

I laughed. He said, "That tie looks awesome, by the way. You tie it better than I do."

I said, "Thanks," and decided I could stand to be a little nicer to Sebastian.

"You look very Marlene Dietrich."

"So I've heard."

"You don't know who that is."

"No, I don't."

"My parents watch a lot of old movies," he explained. "Look her up. She was something else. Come on."

"Come on what?"

"If you dance with everyone here but me, Bethany'll think something's up."

"What? She won't think that," I said, but I'd already given him my hand and then we were dancing. It was the second time I'd touched Greg. No, wait. The third. It felt shockingly familiar and wholly unreal.

Someone turned the lights down, just a little, or so it seemed to me. Greg was very close, and very warm, and very him. His eyes, in the low light, looked black. "You're very tall," he said. "In those shoes."

"I'm very tall in any shoes."

We swayed a little. "I'm not sure about this song," he said. It was a Latin pop song that was always on the radio. "Can't be a salsa."

I didn't answer because I was dancing.

"Could work as a tango," he said.

"I don't know the tango," I said.

"I could teach you," he said. "But we'd have to be closer."

"Like this?" I asked, and stepped a little closer.

"Yeah," he said. "It's like this: slow-slow-quick-quick-slow."

I moved to follow him.

"That's good," he said, and we did a little more, a promenade, and then we moved in a square. It was fun, and he was laughing, and I wanted to laugh but I was too busy concentrating on my feet, and then he was looking at me like he'd suddenly become aware that I was a girl, a person, an Aphra, not just an object that occupied space near him, but me, me, me. His hand was holding mine and his eyes were on mine and I felt hot and dizzy and alive.

He twirled me, my hair spinning behind me, and then pulled me back in. My cheek brushed his, and it was smooth, like he'd just shaved. The corner of my mouth grazed the corner of his mouth, just a little. Not a kiss, but maybe a kiss's distant relation. I felt him swallow next to my ear.

"This is . . . ," he said, and then he let go of me. I felt a rush of cold air where he'd been standing a second before.

What was I doing?

I looked anywhere but at him. "I was actually on my way to find B," I said a little too loudly. "We bought her some, some cupcakes."

"Good," he said. "Good. Good. She likes those a lot."

My brain reached for anything, anything, anything. "Well, I guess I can teach John the tango now, so thanks for that."

He exhaled; I could see it. "Yeah. Yeah, I think you're good. As long as you don't squash his balloon. I mean—"

I was still dizzy from twirling and his eyes on me. "Why, Greg," I managed to say, putting a hand to my chest. "I never."

He laughed, looking at the floor, and ruffled the back of his hair.

I made eye contact across the room with Sophie, who was looking at me a little oddly. I mouthed "CAKE" at her, and she nodded and went to dig something out from under one of the purple tablecloths. Greg and I made our way over to Bethany, who was standing between the wall and a fake potted plant festooned with a purple streamer.

"Hey!" Sophie said, elbowing her way to us. "So the mom of the birthday kid earlier accidentally double-ordered her cake, and she left the second one with us." She thrust a white bakery box in our direction.

"Cake Baby?" Bethany asked.

I winced a little, because I'd forgotten to tell Sophie not to use them since Bethany worked there now. "Let's see what they left us," I said, and opened the box, which was filled with two dozen assorted cupcakes in Bethany's favorite flavors. "You should have one, B. They're all the kinds you like."

She carefully selected a lemon meringue and lifted it out of the box with her fingertips, then looked at the rest of us, who were watching raptly. "Well?" she said. "Aren't . . . aren't you going to have one, too?" I took a spice cake and used my eyeballs to encourage everyone else to do the same.

Greg said, "Happy birthday. To the girl with the extra cupcakes." He had an almost imperceptible dot of my lipstick right at the corner of his mouth.

"Should we sing?" I asked.

"To . . . to . . . to the little girl who's not here?" Bethany asked.

"It seems polite," said Greg, who would not look directly at me. "She did leave us her cupcakes."

"What was her name?" Bethany asked.

Nobody knew. So we decided to just hum the happy birthday song, and at the end, Claire stuck a candle in Bethany's cupcake and we all blew it out together.

I drove Bethany home after, taking the long way, because I'd convinced Greg that I should be the one to execute the last step of the Bethany's Birthday Project.

"I'm soooo tired," she said as I pulled up in front of her house. "Like, I could sleep all of tomorrow and I think I'd still be tired."

"You had fun, though, right?"

"Yeah! It was great. Especially that cupcake part. I mean, it was almost like someone knew it was my birthday." She raised her eyebrows at me.

"What?" I said. "No, of course not. I told no one."

"Come on," she said. "I know you were behind the cupcakes."

"I may have been slightly behind the cupcakes."

"Well, thanks for that, anyway."

"You liked it, right? You can have another one; I brought home the leftovers."

"There were leftovers?"

I took the box out of the trunk. "Et voilà," I said.

"Ooh," she said, and took a second cupcake and started to work on the frosting. At her urging, I grabbed one, too, and then found out, upon biting into it, that it was coconut and had to spit it out on the lawn.

"Really?" she said.

"I'm fine," I said. "It's nothing."

We went into the house, stopping in the kitchen so I could wash my mouth out, and up the stairs, past the sound of Colin playing some shoot-'em-up game in the basement and her mom listening to a podcast in her bedroom with the door closed. "Oh, by the way," I said, "happy birthday." And then I opened her bedroom door.

Inside were enough pink and purple balloons to fill the room, plus one big balloon of Fluttershy the pony in the middle, and then, on her bed, were eight wrapped presents, from me and the rest of our boat, plus one from Greg. Her hand flew over her mouth and her eyes went sideways to mine. I bounced on my toes a little, because I was so very proud of myself.

"The fund-raiser—"

"Oh, it was a real fund-raiser. We made $427, by the way."

She lowered her hand. "Does Greg know?"

"That it's your birthday? Please, the whole thing was his idea." She looked at me skeptically. "It was!" I said. I had to bat some of the balloons out into the hallway so we could sit down. "Mostly. Here, open mine first."

She hesitated just a second before setting the rest of her cupcake down and enthusiastically ripping the paper off my gift. "It's perfect," she said, sliding the bracelet on over her hand. "And you even remembered the selenium."

"How could I ever forget the selenium?"

She pulled me into a hug and I patted her back. "Aphra," she said into my shoulder, "this is the best birthday I've ever had. Including the one where I was actually born."

She slid the rest of the presents out of the way and sat down on the bed. I said, "Since that one involved having your head squeezed through a vagina, I'm not surprised."

She slugged me on the shoulder. "I was a C-section. And you know that."

"I'm not sure that's better."

"Mm-mmm," she said. "Mom said the doctor cut her open like a salmon."

"You know, I'm not sure that analogy works. If she was a salmon, what were you?"

"Uh. I don't know. Salmon guts, I guess."

"Ah," I said. "I know. If we make it a sturgeon instead of a salmon, then *you* are caviar."

She smiled and ducked her head. "Caviar."

"Cavi-ar," I said, rolling the *r*.

She picked up Greg's present. "Should I open this one?"

"Of course you should!"

"Do you know what's in it?"

"Nope," I said. "But I told him absolutely no dick pics, so you should be safe there."

"Thank God for you, Aphra." She tore open the wrapping of the tiny box, which I'd assumed held earrings or some other kind of jewelry, but inside was a key. She picked it up and looked at it, like it might turn into something else on closer inspection. "Huh," she said.

I took the box from her and ran my fingers inside. Stuck in the bottom was a little card, and I handed it over. It said, *You'll find out what this opens tomorrow. Happy birthday to the most beautiful girl in the world.*

"Well, that's adorable," I said.

She flopped sideways, landing her head in my lap. "I think I might be falling in love with him," she said. "Maybe I should tell him. Do you think I should tell him?"

I tried to laugh. "Don't you want to see what the key opens first?"

"Today was perfect. The whole key thing is perfect." She yawned. "*He's* perfect."

I started to think of a comeback to that, but honestly? He kind of was.

Chapter Twenty-Seven

I hope you had a great birthday, Greg wrote that night.

For some reason, this seemed to be crossing a bigger line than usual—like if I answered, I was pretending to be Bethany in a way I had somehow convinced myself I wouldn't. I was stuck, though, again, because if I didn't answer, he'd want to know why. I said, *Thanks, I did,* because I knew she had.

Then, because I couldn't help it, I typed, *What is the key for?*

Tsk. You'll have to wait until tomorrow.

What happens tomorrow?

Brunch, remember, after you get done at Cake Baby? Or did you forget?

Bethany hadn't mentioned she was having brunch with Greg. I wondered if that was deliberate or not. Probably not. Why wouldn't she tell me?

Right, I said. *I meant, what happens with the key?*

Well, you'll be presented with the lock, obviously.

Obviously. I hope it doesn't open something horrible. Like a big box of spiders.

Would a small box of spiders be better?

No, you're right. The size of the box is irrelevant. Like an non-restrictive clause.

. . .

. . .

What did you say?

Sorry, I typed quickly. *Antiquated grammarian terms are kind of my jam.*

I thought you hated English.

This was not good. *Ha,* I said. *See, I have a very specific sense of humor. You need to work on your sarcasm meter.*

I guess so. You weren't being sarcastic about loving pancakes, were you?

No, no, I said. *That was all sincerity.*

Good. I'll see you tomorrow, мое истинное сердце.

Are you really going to leave me hanging with that?

Indeed I am.

And he disconnected. I ran it through Google Translate. He'd written *my truest heart.*

This was becoming less than ideal, which is a very nice way of saying things were heading south, which is a slightly less nice way of saying things were becoming a shit show. While I was trying to pretend to be Bethany without acting like I was trying to pretend to be Bethany, I was getting increasingly bad at pretending to be Bethany, and that train of logic was so twisted even I couldn't follow it. I needed to delete the app. But I couldn't delete the app. It was a classic catch-22. I know this because we read that book in English last fall. I wrote a paper on it and got an A. I am very good at English papers.

I needed a way to get rid of the app that wouldn't result in Greg's asking Bethany about it. I suppose I could just preemptively tell him I was going to do it. I could tell him I needed the space on my phone. Or I could tell him the app got corrupted and he should just text me like a normal person, and that whatever silly sentimental attachment he had to the app as our personal meet-cute needed to be thrown by the wayside because I never, ever wanted to talk about it again. Ever.

Things were simpler, I think, before people had cell phones.

I got up early the next morning because I'd promised to take Kit for mini-golfing and lunch. Of course, mini-golfing with an uncoordinated nine-year-old takes twice as long as mini-golfing with a normal person, so by the time we were done we only had time for a dollar hamburger at the drive-through. When we got home, Mom was in the kitchen on the phone, talking very fast. When we kicked off our shoes, she said, "He's here now," and then hung up.

"Kit," she said. "Go to your room for a minute."

"Am I in trouble?"

"No, I just need to talk to Aphra."

"Is *she* in trouble?"

"Just go," she said.

Looking a little uncertain, he went upstairs.

"Where were you?"

I was kind of surprised she was mad. Why was she mad? All I'd done was have fun with my little brother, and I hadn't even asked her to pay for the round of mini-golf. "What's the problem? I told Kit I'd take him to play mini-golf since he got a four on his Mali project."

"I've been calling you for two hours."

I pulled out my phone. "My battery's dead," I said. "I guess I didn't notice. Sorry. Why were you calling?"

"Because I didn't know where my nine-year-old was? I called all his friends! You never told me you were taking him out."

"I thought he told you."

"He's nine. You can't count on him to tell anybody anything."

"Well, I'm sorry. Next time I'll tell you myself. Look, he's fine, I'm fine, we're both fine, except it took him ten shots to get through the windmill and I had to threaten the people behind us with my club because they kept doing that loud sighing thing."

Mom did her own loud sigh. She said, "I like how invested you are in Kit. I think it's wonderful. But you do realize that in a year, you're going to be gone? Just like Delia?"

"I'm not going to be anything just like Delia," I said hotly.

"Aphra, my point is you're creating a very confusing situation for him."

"So what you're saying is you want me to do less with him?"

"I want you to remember that he needs his main caregivers to be the people who aren't about to move out of the house!"

"Oh. Great. Well, might I suggest, then, that you and Dad actually step up a little?"

"That's not fair."

"It is fair. You've always let Delia and me take point with Kit because you're too busy. And now you're complaining about it?"

She took a deep breath. "Your dad and I have probably relied too much on you and your sister. I'll admit that. But in the past year, you've gone a little too far. I don't know if it's because Delia's gone or because you're mad at her, but you need to realize that it'll be easier on Kit if you start pulling back now, instead of just disappearing next August."

"If Kit likes me better than you, maybe that's because I'm the one who actually cares about his feelings."

"Are you talking about the cat again? I can't put his feelings before his health, Aphra!" This, I suspect, was because Kit's face was still rashy, but it was weird. . . . It would get better for a day or two and then get worse again, but the cat was there the whole time. It didn't make sense.

"Mental health *is* health! Isn't that why you're spending all this money to send me to Dr. Pascal?"

"Ugh!" she exclaimed. "You're impossible!"

"You're just mad because I'm right."

"No. I'm frustrated because this is what you do. You can talk your way out of anything, so you never have to confront the idea that you might be wrong. Because in your mind, you never are! Why consider the thought that someone else might have a point when you can win any argument?"

"I don't win every argument."

"You do. The truth is, Aphra, you're too smart for your own good."

"That is not a thing," I said. "That's not a thing that exists. So what you're saying is that you want me to stop taking care of Kit now, because you think having me ignore him while I'm living here is going to be less confusing for him. What am I supposed to tell him? *Sorry, bud, I'd like to help you with your home-*

work, but it might have psychological consequences for you later, so get out."

"I'm not saying that."

"Well, what are you saying?"

"I'm saying . . . I don't know what I'm saying."

"There's your problem right there."

She huffed. "Kit needs you to be his sister. Not . . . not a third parent."

"If Kit thinks I'm his third parent, that's on you. Not on me." I went out the front door and slammed it behind me, only to realize that I was outside with no shoes. "Shoot," I muttered. But there's nothing worse than spoiling a dramatic exit, so I walked off to Bethany's house barefoot.

I remembered, once I was about halfway there, that Bethany was having brunch with Greg and might not be back yet. It hit me when Colin opened the door.

"She's not here," he said, scratching his head.

"Uh," I said. "Can I wait for her?"

"What, they don't like you at your house, either?"

"Not at the moment," I said.

"Huh. Sure, come in," he said. He went back into the kitchen and sat at the table with a copy of *Otaku* magazine.

"I didn't know you liked manga," I said.

"Huh? Yeah," he said.

"My sister used to get that," I said.

"Okay." He went back to reading. I went back to really wishing my phone weren't dead.

"So," I said, trying again. "What're you going to do when you have to move out next year?"

"I'm going to move out," he said, without looking up.

"But specifically."

"I specifically don't know."

"I'm going to take a couple of classes at NVCC next year," I said.

"Okay," he said. "Am I supposed to be impressed with that?"

"I just meant, I could show you the catalog. If you want to see it."

"I don't want to see it."

He stared at his magazine. I stared out the window. Finally, I said, "Do you have any gum?"

He got up and went back to the basement, leaving the magazine, which I happily commandeered. I proceeded to read the included bonus chapter of *My Hero Academia*.

Bethany came home about half an hour later, after I'd made liberal use of the Newmans' Keurig. There's something so obliquely wonderful about coffee any idiot can make, like, you don't even have to wait for it. You just plug the thing in and away you go. And go. And go.

It does make it a little too easy, perhaps, to overdo the caffeine thing..

Bethany came in and saw me sitting at her table and pulled up short.

"Hi!" I said.

"Hi," she said. She had her Cake Baby apron folded over her arm, which was when I remembered that she'd had an early shift at work and must have gone straight to brunch from there. She put the apron on the back of Colin's vacated chair. "Am I late? For something?"

"No, I just kind of stopped by. I was hanging out with Colin. You know. He's cool." I held up the copy of *Otaku*. "He lent me his magazine and everything. I think he just stepped out for a minute." Down the stairs I called, "Are you coming back up?"

He roared back, "Jesus Christ, what is wrong with you?"

Bethany sat down next to me. "How was brunch?" I asked. "Did you get pancakes?"

I realized, belatedly, that I wasn't supposed to know about the pancakes. She said, "Yeah, they were good. They were good pancakes."

"So did you tell him?" I asked a little more forcefully than I meant to. "Did you say *I love you*? Did he say it? Did you both say it?" I sounded, I knew, a little manic. More than a little manic. I needed to care about 1000% less.

"No," she said. "I didn't say it."

"You didn't?" I scooted closer. "So what was the key for? A diary? Al Capone's vault?"

"What?"

"Oh, it was this whole thing in the eighties. They found the key to Al Capone's secret vault and opened it on live TV, and guess what was in it?"

"What was in it?"

"Nothing. It was empty, and 30 million people watched them open it." When she gave me a look, I added, "It was a better story when my dad told it."

"Are you okay?"

"I'm fine. So what was the key for?"

"It was a box."

"And in the box was . . ."

She pulled a silver pendant out of her shirt. It was a compass rose, pointing north toward Bethany's face. "It's engraved," she said.

"I see that," I said, flipping it over. It was engraved. With Cyrillic letters. "He had it engraved in Russian? Did he tell you what it said?"

"I was too embarrassed to ask."

"What?"

"I kind of . . . told him I loved it, and then I kissed him and then I bailed. I don't know."

"What? Why?"

"I thought I'd look stupid."

"That literally makes no sense."

"I just. I don't know."

"Ugh. So what does it say? Did you figure it out?"

She looked at me darkly. "I don't speak Russian."

"Google Translate," I said. "Is your friend."

"I tried that. What it spat out didn't make any sense."

I pulled out my phone and opened Google Translate.

"I already told you," she said. "That doesn't work. It's just gobbledygook."

She sat and watched me enter the letters one at a time. "How do you have a Russian keyboard app on your phone?" she asked.

"Uh," I said. "School. Thing. School thing. We were, uh, comparing Russian declensions. With Latin." I have no idea whether she believed that. It made no sense. But neither did accepting a gift and then running away because you don't know how to read the inscription, so Bethany seemed like an expert in things that make no sense. I finished typing and hit enter.

I lost you silently.

"I lost you?" I said. "That's weird."

"I told you," she said. "But you got closer than I did—I didn't even get the *I* part. I got '*R* lost you.'"

"You must have typed an *R* instead of an *Я*," I said, and then realized I'd typed a character wrong, too—there was an *o* instead of a *ю*. I recopied the inscription and tried again. This time, the words did make sense, kind of. They were just in the wrong order. "You loved silence?" I muttered. "No, it's . . ." And I didn't finish because I suddenly saw what the inscription was.

I loved you wordlessly, without a hope.

She was right. It was perfect. It was the perfect gift for *me.*

That night, I was going through Sophie's Instagram, looking at pictures of the party, while the sounds of Kit and Sebastian watching videos of other people playing Minecraft wafted up the stairs. There was Bethany, in my red dress, looking flawless and shiny and beautiful. There we were together, smiling, her with her colorless lip gloss, me with my matte red mouth. And then there was one of her and Greg together. They looked so perfect next to each other. He wasn't looking at the camera; he was looking at Bethany, like he couldn't quite believe this girl was tucked up against him. Bethany, on the other hand, was looking off to the side and laughing at someone else. That someone else, I'm sure, was me.

Delia, who'd somehow snuck up on me, snatched my phone

out of my hands and flipped it around to look at the screen. "So that's him, huh?" she asked. "Wow."

I grabbed for my phone, but she held it out of my reach. "Looks like he's really into her."

"Yeah," I said. "He is."

She handed me my phone and I turned it off. "Looks like you're really into him."

"Shut up," I said.

"Come on, you were mooning over that picture so hard you didn't even hear me come in."

"I was thinking about something," I protested.

"Yeah, like how much you'd like to make out with him."

"Whatever," I said.

She raised her eyebrows. "If that's your best retort, I must've hit closer to the mark than I thought."

"I'm tired," I said. "Some of us had to do something besides hang around and watch videos all day. I thought you had an internship."

"It's half days until next week," she said. "Which you know."

"Whatever," I said.

"Geez, you really are off your game. How long you been crushing on this guy?"

"Shut up, Delia. And feel free to go back downstairs and get your creepy boyfriend away from my brother."

"*Our* brother. What is with you?"

"I'm sick of you," I said. "That's all."

"You know," Delia said, "there's no reason you have to go on like this. There's nothing . . . honorable in keeping a face you hate. You'd meet someone in five minutes if you fixed it."

"Oh!" I said. "Gee, you're right! I, too, could turn myself into

Frankenstein's monster just so some guy will follow me home and do me in my parents' basement!"

"You're disgusting!"

"You're a complete fake! Does he even know what you really look like? You think I didn't notice you put away all your old pictures down in your room?"

"Those were high school pictures. I'm in college now."

"Bull. Shit. You put them away because you didn't want him to see them. You want to pretend you were born like this, because you know what'll happen if he ever finds out the truth."

"What? What do you think is going to happen?"

"He's going to dump you!"

"No he's not! Why would he?"

"Because you're a fake! Because . . . because you look like me!" I waved at her face. "This is . . . it's false representation!"

"Of what? This is what I actually look like now!"

"Yeah, now. But what are you going to do if you have a daughter who looks like you? I mean, how you really look. Are you going to start a trust fund to pay for her plastic surgery? How old will she be when you tell her she's too ugly to exist the way she is?"

"I never said that. You're being completely unfair because you know 100% that if you were prettier, that guy wouldn't be out with Bethany right now instead of you."

"I hate you," I said.

"Hate me all you want, but you know it's the truth. I was never going to get what I wanted from the world looking the way I looked, so I changed it. And you can act holier-than-thou all you want, but deep down, the reason you're mad is that you know I'm right. Your face is *always* going to be the thing that holds you back."

"Get out," I said. "Get out get out get OUT!" And I grabbed Delia by the shoulders and shoved her out of my room, slamming the door once she was on the other side. Then I flopped backward against the door and slid all the way down to the floor.

It wasn't true. It wasn't true.

It was totally true.

Chapter Twenty-Eight

I was kind of not in the mood for therapy on Monday afternoon.

Things were weird with my mother. I was not speaking to Delia, perhaps ever again. Greg, in Latin, looked toward me and then away so fast he might have given himself whiplash. He'd texted me right after I'd thrown Delia out of my room, and I'd said *I can't talk, I'm in the middle of the twelfth round with my sister,* and by the time I'd typed *I mean, brother* he'd already typed, *OK see you tomorrow* and logged off, and that was bothering me, too.

Then I ended up five minutes late to therapy because I got stuck behind a garbage truck for three blocks. Every time I tried to pull around to pass him, he moved to the left, so I couldn't. I hate when that happens. Hate it.

I flopped down on Dr. Pascal's couch and took my mints. Four this time, because I felt like I deserved an extra after the day I'd been having. The week, I guess, would be more accurate. Or longer. I don't know.

"So," said Dr. Pascal. "That mood hurricane looks like it's back."

"I think it's a typhoon now. Wait. Which is worse, a hurricane or a typhoon?"

"Same thing, different ocean."

"Really? I thought a typhoon was stronger."

"You're extra cranky today, in other words."

"Yeah," I said, chomping my first mint. "Pretty much."

She waited for me to elaborate. When I did not, she said, "Are you really going to make me work for this?"

"Fine. I had a fight with Delia. And my mom. And, uh, I think I kind of made a move on Bethany's boyfriend, but it was an accident because he was teaching me the tango."

"That sounds like a lot to deal with all at once."

"Yeah, and I'm pretty tired now, to be honest."

"All right. Tell me about it."

I told her how my mother had accused me of overstepping my sisterly role with Kit, which was totally not my fault. And how I'd had a fight with Delia because she'd pushed and pushed on that Greg button until I'd blown up on her, which was mostly not my fault. And how I was annoyed at Bethany for not even being able to ask about her stupid birthday present, which was 100% her fault. And how I was frustrated with Greg for not figuring out that I'd been the one with the Deanna app. I wasn't sure whose fault that was. I mean, I guess it was mostly mine for not telling him. But maybe not completely.

"Hm," she said.

"That about sums it up. So I assume you're going to tell me I need to work on my anger issues."

"I actually don't think you have issues with anger. I think you're feeling very hurt."

I frowned. "I don't hurt. Why are you saying I hurt? I'm not hurting."

She tsked at me. "All that anger you're feeling? You're mad at Delia. You're mad at Bethany. You're mad at your mother. You're mad at Greg. What do you think that is?"

"Anger is anger," I said. "That's why they call it *anger.* Because it's *anger.* Did you ever think maybe I *should* be angry at the way things are?"

"If your anger was getting you to do something constructive, I might say yes. But it's not. It's just keeping you from dealing with the root of your problems."

I ate another mint.

"Think of your emotions as a band. Right now, anger's your front man. But your drummer? That's hurt."

I sure hoped she wasn't feeding this bullshit to little kids. I picked up Cookie Monster, but she grabbed him out of my hand and said, "Leave Cookie out of this."

"I'm not hurting. I would know if I was, and I'm not."

"I think you do know. I also think you're terrified to admit it, because your hurt is something you can't control, so you like to pretend it doesn't exist. But as long as you keep pretending, I cannot help you, Aphra."

"Maybe I don't need help," I said. "Maybe you're trying to plumb the depths of something that's not there, did that ever occur to you?"

She sighed.

Well, great. Now in addition to being mad at everyone else, I was also mad at Dr. Pascal.

"Look," I said. "This was not my idea. It was not my idea for me to come here."

"No, but you've kept coming for all these months, and we both know you wouldn't be here if you didn't want to be, Aphra. You want to get to the bottom of this. That's why you're still in that chair."

"Or maybe it's because I like getting out of school early. I mean, who knows, really?"

I ate a mint. Then I ate another.

"Aphra," she said.

"Maybe I don't need to be here anymore," I said. "Maybe we're done now, right?"

She sat back. "Tell me," she said, "why you think you started coming in the first place."

"I'm here because of Delia!"

She shook her head. "You aren't here because of Delia. You really think that's why we're here?"

"Uh, yes?"

"No. The issue with your sister is a symptom. It was the catalyst that blew your cover. You're so good at hiding your real feelings that nobody knew what was going on with you."

"Oh," I said. "Really. And what is going on with me?"

"Aphra, your self-esteem stinks."

"Uh, no, actually, my self-esteem is great. I'm just very honest and realistic about my shortcomings."

"Aphra, you fell in love with a boy and handed him to your best friend because you think you don't deserve to be loved back."

I recoiled into the back of the couch. Outside, a couple of

crows were making a bunch of noise like they'd just gotten a dumpster open.

"It's not that I don't deserve it!" I said. "It's just that it's not realistic."

"It is *not realistic* to think that nobody could ever love you."

"It's not that I think that! It's . . . it's . . ."

"It's what?"

"Here's the thing. Do I think I could get a guy to like me through sheer force of personality? Of course I could. I'm smart. I'm funny. Pretty much everyone likes me."

"So you don't want a guy to like you because of your personality?"

"That's not what I'm saying. I'm saying I don't want to have to convince him to overlook"—I gestured at my face—"this."

"In other words, you want someone who thinks you're pretty."

Yes. No. I wanted that. I wanted more than that.

"Is that what you want?" she asked.

"I don't know. I don't know."

"I think you do know. I think you know exactly what you want, and I think you are so scared of what you want that it's making you lash out at everybody in your life right now."

I rubbed my forehead until it hurt. Everything hurt. Why did everything hurt? I hated this. Hated it.

"Aphra," said Dr. Pascal. "What do you want?"

I wanted to go home. I wanted to play checkers with Kit. I wanted to eat a cupcake with Bethany and not feel guilty because I was talking to her boyfriend behind her back. I wanted to talk to Greg and have him know who I was and decide to be *my* boyfriend instead of hers. I wanted him to look at me the way he looked at her.

I said, "I want someone who loves me *because* of the way I am. Not in spite of it."

I felt something inside of me crumple at the horror of my own admission.

I felt sick.

Dr. Pascal made a few notes before looking up at me again. She pushed her glasses up on top of her head, revealing a matching set of dark circles. I wondered how many patients she'd had before me that day, and how many she'd have after. Probably lots of them had real problems, like abuse or their mom died or they had an eating disorder. What was I even doing there? It occurred to me that I should probably feel guilty for taking up this woman's time, when she had people who really needed her, not just somebody like me with no actual problems.

Finally, she said, "And you think that's impossible."

"Yes. It is."

"I'm telling you it isn't."

"Oh, come on!"

She tossed her notebook on the table. "Here's the truth, Aphra Brown. You've bought into the notion of conventional beauty more than almost anyone I've ever met." When I balked, she put up a hand. "You think you haven't, because you don't read the magazines or buy the clothes, but you have. Not only that, but you're overemphasizing how important it is. You sit here every week and tell me your face is the least important thing about you, but you act like it's the most important."

"It's not that it's the most important thing. It just happens to be . . . the thing that gets in the way. But that's fine! It's fine. It's not a big deal. It just is what it is."

She shook her head. "When was the last time you really let yourself be vulnerable?"

"Vulnerable," I repeated. The word felt weird in my mouth. Another Latin-derived word, from *vulnerare,* meaning "to wound," or, if conjugated correctly, "to be wounded." It made me think of some Roman centurion skewering me so that my insides were no longer inside, which was generally where I liked to keep them. "That sounds like a terrible thing to be."

"It sounds scary, doesn't it?"

I made no reply.

"Aphra Brown, I believe you are worthy of being loved. So here's my question: Why don't you?"

I blinked a bunch of times. Then I said, "It's not that I don't think I'm worthy, it's that it's not—"

"Don't give me that 'not realistic' line again. Why don't you think it's realistic?"

"Because," I said. "Because I am ugly."

I was surprised that word had come out of my mouth. I hate that word. *Homely, plain, below average* I can deal with. But I hate the word *ugly.* It sounds so unredeemable, like *ogre.*

"I don't think that's true," she said. "But even barring that, okay. Ugly people are loved every day."

"I don't want to be loved like an ugly girl," I said. "I want to be loved like a beautiful one." Stupid id. Stupid, stupid id.

I started to cry, a little and then more and then kind of a lot.

Dr. Pascal got up and handed me a box of tissues. "That," she said, "is the truest thing you've ever said in here."

"Doesn't matter," I said. "Since what's wrong with me isn't fixable, except maybe if I do like Delia."

"Nothing's unfixable," she said. "You've just found your cri de coeur. Now let's get to work on getting you to believe what the rest of the world already knows."

I snuffled and wiped my eyes. "What is that?"

"That you deserve to be loved because of who you are, not in spite of it. And if you put yourself out there, you're going to see it happen. Probably over and over again."

"But that's not—"

"Mmm!" she said. "Mmm-mm." She held up the Muppet closest at hand. "Elmo says *bullshit.*"

Chapter Twenty-Nine

On Tuesday, the varsity eight girls had our annual spring sleepover.

This was actually only our second annual spring sleepover. The last one had been the night before day one of the final regatta of the season, and we had decided that was a Really Bad Idea, because we were all exhausted the next morning. So this year, we decided to go midweek. We'd eat spaghetti, we'd watch the 1934 classic *Eight Girls in a Boat,* and then we'd get up for a breakfast buffet before we left for school.

All this was to go down at Sophie's house, since her basement's huge, with a giant flat-screen. So after practice on Wednesday, we piled into two cars (Sophie's and Claire's) and stopped by the grocery store to get the stuff for the spaghetti, snacks for the movie, and things for breakfast, splitting the list nine ways and meeting up at the cars afterward.

My list consisted of Pop-Tarts (chocolate and one other) and Hershey's Kisses, one large bag. I paid for my part and made my way back to the car, where Sophie was impatiently tapping on the steering wheel while Claire and Talia sat in the backseat.

"Where's Bethany?" I asked, since everyone else was already there. I hadn't meant to take so long, but the bathroom was near the candy aisle and I'd had to pee.

"Not back yet."

"What did you ask her to get?"

Sophie, who'd made the list, said, "Cereal."

I said, "I'll be right back," and went back into the store. Bethany, as I'd expected, was standing in the cereal aisle. Her face was glued to her phone, and she was frowning rather hard. "Hey," I said.

When she didn't answer right away, I said, "Having trouble picking something?"

"What? Oh. Yeah, there's like 100 different kinds. Hey, Aphra—"

"Don't worry about it. Let's get one healthy, one sugary, and one in the middle. I grabbed Shredded Wheat, Froot Loops, and some kind of granola. "There, let's check out."

"Hey, Aphra . . . ," she said again as we walked to the front of the store.

"I'm not sure why we're getting these anyway. Everybody just ends up eating Pop-Tarts or toaster waffles. What?"

She took a deep breath, let it out, and then said, "I was supposed to get Twizzlers, too."

We grabbed two big packages and I dumped everything at the checkout counter. Bethany was unusually quiet for someone with multiple bags of candy.

"You okay? You loved the sleepover last year. Is it Cake Baby?"

"Oh, no, that's good. I got a raise this week."

"What? You've only been there like a week and a half."

The man in front of us was arguing about the sale price on four bags of coleslaw mix and asking for a manager. I'm not sure why I always pick the wrong checkout line, but I do it every time. Bethany said, "Yeah, I figured out that the supplier was shorting us on our flour." Her face brightened a little. "I brought my bathroom scale to work because I was wondering if a bag was really exactly 20 pounds, and when it came up a pound short I took one to the FedEx down the street and asked them to weigh it for me."

I stepped out of the way of coleslaw man, who seemed to have decided to return his salad to the produce section rather than pay 30 extra cents. I said, "You dragged a 20-pound bag of flour all the way to the FedEx?"

"Yeah, so then I checked the cubic volume of the bag and realized there was no way to fit 20 pounds of flour in it at all. They'd been cheating us since, like, always, I guess."

"Wow," I said. "Well, that's pretty cool. So work's good."

"Yeah. Doug put me in charge of checking all the deliveries now. Anyway, that's fine. I guess I'm just kind of thinking about Greg."

I paused while she handed her cash to the checker and grabbed her bag. "What's wrong?"

"It's . . . I don't know. Like, he's great. He's amazing. I don't know. It just seems like half the time I don't know what he's talking about. Like, yesterday he asked me about how much maple syrup they make in Canada. I was like, I have no idea how much maple syrup they make in Canada! Why would you expect me to know this?"

"Is that, uh. Is that what you said?" I asked, pausing in front of the gumball machine.

"No, of course not. I told him I couldn't remember and then I made out with him."

"Right. Okay."

"And then when I try to talk to him about science stuff, he kind of glazes over. All he wants to talk about is, like, Russian literature. All the time. And he does this thing where he says something in Russian and . . . waits for me to ask him what it means. And then just now he asked me—"

We waited while some lady coming through the door wrangled her toddler into the front of her cart. "Are you breaking up with him?" I asked.

"What? No! I'm . . . I don't know. Venting. I guess. I just, I've never gone out with anybody. I don't really get how it's supposed to work."

"I mean, you guys are still getting to know each other, right?"

"Yeah. I guess that's probably it. I'm just used to . . ."

Ten feet away, Sophie lay on her horn. Leaning out the window, she shouted, "Let's GO! We are BURNING DAYLIGHT, ladies." So Bethany and I got in and rode to Sophie's house. I wanted to ask her what she was used to, but I never did get around to it.

Bethany and I were texting during *Eight Girls on a Boat,* because if you talk during a movie Sophie will sit on you.

Bethany said, *Don't tell anyone, but I really hate this movie.* We'd already eaten our spaghetti, and the inside of my mouth tasted like garlic and Twizzlers. Which sounds gross and is.

Yeah, I said, *it's not my favorite, either. But there are girls and a boat, so.*

Maybe next year we can vote instead of watching this again?

Maybe, I typed. *I'm just happy to be out of the house. I'm so sick of Delia I could scream.*

Her eyes cut to mine above the glow of our phones. *Wait, what?*

She's just awful.

You guys are STILL fighting?

I hadn't actually mentioned our last fight to Bethany because of the fact that it was kind of about Bethany. Well, about Bethany and Greg. I said, *Yeah, we've moved on to round 12.*

Bethany's mouth popped open and she stared at me for a good 30 seconds. Then she started poking me in the shoulder. Repeatedly, and hard.

"Ow," I said. *WHAT???* I typed.

I need to talk to you. NOW.

What is it?

She poked me a few more times. I typed, *I am listening to you what is it?*

Come upstairs. Bring your phone.

We were just getting to the part of the movie where Christa's crew coach—not knowing she's pregnant—works her until she falls over, but I followed her up the stairs to Sophie's darkened living room.

"What do you need my phone for?"

"Have you been texting Greg?" she asked.

I felt my muscles freeze up. I said, "What?"

"You heard me. Have you been texting him and telling him that you're me?"

I stared at her in the dark. She waved her phone around and said, "He's always saying this random crap, like about the maple syrup and his classes at NVCC and Russian poetry, and I thought he was just trying to be funny or . . . or ironic or something, but we were texting when I was in the grocery store before and he asked if my sister and I had moved on to *round 13* or called a truce."

Oh, God.

I felt the blood drain out of my brain and pool somewhere around my ankles. I whispered, "What did you say?"

"Nothing," I said. "I didn't know what to say. Seeing as I don't have a sister. So I want to know, Aphra, why Greg thinks I have a sister, and why he keeps calling out all these inside jokes I don't get, and what the hell is going on."

I wanted to die.

"Whatever you say next," she said, "it better be the truth."

"Bethany," I said. I was going to cry now, big-time. It was stupid. I was in the wrong, I was so in the wrong, but I was going to cry, and not in the pretty, delicate way, either.

"Aphra, what did you do?"

I took a couple of deep breaths. "You remember the Deanna app?" I asked.

"Yeah. It didn't work, but you fixed it, right? You got an A on that."

"No. I couldn't fix it. But I didn't want to tell Mr. Positano that, so I kind of . . . fudged my data."

"What does this have to do with me and Greg?"

"Greg was using the app," I said. "I was typing the answers myself to hide the fact that the app didn't work, and he figured it out." I swallowed. "And then he saw you with the code, that day at school."

"The code?"

"The Deanna code. The day he kissed you, didn't you ever wonder why?"

"Because he likes me!"

"Yeah, he does, but he also thought he'd been talking to you. He thought it was your app."

Bethany sat back, her hand coming up to cover her mouth. The worst thing was, she hadn't even gotten to the bad part yet.

"Why didn't you say something?" she said. "Why didn't you tell me *literally* any of this?"

"You were so happy," I said. "And it would have been a big mess for nothing. I knew how much you liked him. I thought I was being a good friend."

"God, Aphra." She shook her head. "I can't believe you didn't tell me."

I waited for the moment she'd realize. There it came. "Wait. That was like three weeks ago."

I lowered my head onto my knees.

"Delia wasn't even here then."

I said nothing.

"You're *still talking to him*?" she asked incredulously.

"I'm sorry," I told the carpet. "I didn't mean to."

"You didn't mean to?"

"He . . . he logged in to the app. And I wasn't going to talk to him, but he was going through all this stuff with his parents, and I felt like maybe I should just help him get through it, you know? And then it kind of. Snowballed."

"It snowballed."

I opened the Deanna app and handed her the phone so she

could read through my messages, which she scrolled through without actually reading, her eyes huge. Finally, she stopped and looked up at me. "You've been talking to him *this whole time*?"

I looked away. "Yeah."

"And he thinks this is me?"

"That's pretty accurate."

"And you didn't think you should tell me he thought I was you?"

"What would the point have been? You're the one he wants. Look, I know I shouldn't have kept talking to him after you guys got together. I know that. But I just . . . did."

"You just did. You just kept pretending to be me while talking to my boyfriend late at night." She threw the phone down and stood up. "Exactly how do you expect me to feel about this? This is all kinds of messed up."

"I know. I know it is, that's why I told you."

"You told me because I found out!"

"Well, technically—"

"Ah! Shut up! Don't *Aphra* me right now. I don't need to hear the technical reason why you're right and I'm wrong. This is seriously screwed up. I can't believe you did this."

"I know! I know, and I'm sorry. I should have told you. I should have told you the first day."

"So why didn't you?"

"You were so *happy.*"

"I was happy. That's it."

"Not. Not just you."

"You mean Greg and me?"

"Yeah. You were together and you were so happy, and all I was going to do was mess it up. I thought . . . I thought it wasn't hurting anything." I handed her back my phone. "You can read it. Read all of it. You'll see, I never tried to get him to like me instead of you, I promise."

"I don't want to read it!"

I tried to push the phone into her hand. "Just look."

"No, Aphra, no. I don't want to read what you wrote! I can't—I can't believe you. I can't believe you did this to me."

"I know. I know! I'm sorry."

She stared at my phone, which had fallen between the couch cushions. After half a minute, she said, "We have to tell him."

"No. No, Bethany, we can't do that."

"We have to!"

"He won't understand! He'll hate both of us!"

"But—"

"Listen, I know how much you like him. And he likes you, too, I know he does, but if you tell him, it's over. I don't want you guys to break up over this. It wasn't even your fault."

"We can't keep lying to him!"

"*You* never lied to him," I said. "I did."

"Not yet, but I'll be lying if I don't tell him."

"Bethany," I begged. "Please don't tell him. Please. I'll . . . I'll stop talking to him. Right now, I promise. I'll tell him . . . I'll tell him something, I don't know. I'll wait until the next time he logs on and tell him I can't chat with him anymore. I'll figure out something. I'm sorry." I turned away and wiped my nose on my sleeve to give myself a second to put my face back in order. I didn't want Bethany to know what it was costing me to say I'd never talk to him again. He wouldn't be the last person I talked to at night anymore. I wouldn't be his secret keeper. He'd just be my best friend's boyfriend.

She got up off the couch. "Where are you going?" I asked.

"I just can't with you right now," she said. "I just can't." And she went downstairs to watch the rest of the movie while I sat in the dark and stared at the phone in my hands and wondered what I could possibly do to fix the enormous mess made I'd made.

Half an hour later, Greg logged in to talk to me. To Bethany. He logged in to talk to Bethany.

The movie'd ended and people were lining up to brush their teeth and stuff. Bethany had just finished washing her face and was laying her sleeping bag out on the floor. "Hey," I said.

"Hey," she said, smoothing out the wrinkles in her bag and carefully turning back one corner.

"I . . . I wanted you to know that I'm ending it. With the app. Right now. If you want to, like, be there to make sure I actually do it."

"So I can't trust you to do it unless I'm watching?" she asked.

"That's not what I meant," I said. "I just thought—"

"No," she said. "Just do it. I don't need to see."

I slipped out to the backyard and sat down on the edge of Sophie's closed-up hot tub.

Greg had typed, *You must be at that sleepover. Sorry if I'm interrupting.*

You're not, I said. *Everyone's getting ready for bed.*

Yeah? So are you in your pajamas right now?

I glanced to the door to see if Bethany had changed her mind and followed me outside. So far, she hadn't.

I typed, *I'm always in my pajamas when I talk to you at night.*

I guess that never occurred to me before now. I've been missing out on a lot of fantasizing.

My chest began to ache with what I had to say next. *I need to tell you something.*

Uh-oh. Should I be worried?

No. No, it's just, I think the reason I'm having trouble talking to you in person is because I'm using the app as a crutch. Like, maybe at first it was a good thing. But I don't think so anymore. I think as long as we keep talking this way there's going to be this distance between us. I think we should both delete it.

There was a long pause. Then: *Are you sure?*

I'm sure.

Okay, if that's really what you think. Does that mean no more texting, either?

I exhaled. *I think texting is probably okay.*

All right, if you think so. I'll miss this, though. Talking to you like this. I know this sounds cheesy, but it just always felt like magic. Even when you were pretending to be a computer.

I typed, *I'll miss it, too.*

I deleted the app.

Chapter Thirty

I felt awful, like there was this bright spot in my life that'd just been snuffed. There wouldn't be any more heart-to-heart talks with Greg online. And there probably wouldn't be any more in real life, either. It was like that whole part of my life was just gone. Not that it wasn't entirely my fault, because it was.

I didn't know how I could make things right with Bethany, either, and it didn't help that some part of me kept saying that I'd only done what she'd asked. I'd helped her get Greg. I'd made her sound clever and charming. That kiss in the hall? I'd *given* her that.

I wasn't stupid enough to point that out, though.

Two days later, during our advisory period, was the underclass end-of-year awards ceremony.

They used to have one big ceremony for everyone, but there got to be so many awards that it started to run over two hours. So starting last year, they'd decided to do the seniors (who got most of the awards) during graduation and have a separate assembly for the rest of us, who have to suffer through 90 minutes of the distribution of varsity letters, awards for the kids who got into District Band and whatnot, and the announcement of the winners of the student government elections. It was super boring, always, and I would have skipped it and gone out for a McFlurry except that by the time I remembered we were having it, there was an entire army of teachers manning the back doors to keep us from escaping the building. Thwarted, I filed into the gym and found Bethany sitting in the front of the bleachers, her eyes fixed on a crack in the linoleum.

"Hey," I said. I would have picked somewhere farther back so I could play on my phone undetected, but Bethany doesn't like to sit where she can't get out, so I went with it. When she didn't respond, I said, "Hey, B."

"Hey," she said flatly.

I'm sure I deserved that. "So I wanted to tell you," I said, but then Greg sat down on Bethany's other side and slung an arm around her shoulders. She went a little stiff, and then, noticing that I was watching, shot me a look. I glanced at the podium, where Ms. Turner was asking people to hurry up and sit down so we could get started.

Greg was murmuring something in Bethany's ear to cover the fact that he was kissing the space below her earlobe, and I was pretending like hell not to notice. Finally, he came up for air and said, to me, "Hey, did you pick your classes for NVCC yet?"

"Uh," I said.

"If you want, we should see if we can get sections at the same time so we can carpool or whatever."

Bethany glared darkly at me. "Uh," I said. "I . . . didn't do that yet, sorry."

By then Ms. Turner was going rather purple up at the podium, and the rest of the teachers were begging us to quiet down before she had a stroke. She gave us a lecture about the three *rs—readiness, respect,* and *responsibility*—announced the winners of the student government election, and read the list of kids with perfect attendance, despite the fact that they still had a month of school left to screw that up. I pulled out my phone and texted Bethany, *I'm still sorry.*

NOT NOW, she replied. She glanced at me and then typed, *WE HAVE TO TELL HIM THE TRUTH.*

No, Bethany, we can't.

I don't want to lie!

It's not lying if you just never bring something up!

That's ridiculous!

I started to type *technically,* but then out loud, she shouted, "Would you not?" with enough volume that Ms. Turner paused in handing out varsity letters to a bunch of sophomore basketball players and scowled in our direction. Bethany turned very red and slouched into herself. I put my phone away. Greg, looking confused, whispered, "What's up?" to Bethany, who replied, "Nothing."

The last of the athletes sat down, and Ms. Turner said, "It's my great pleasure to announce a new series of awards devoted to honoring the excellence of our junior class. Each academic department has met over the last two weeks and nominated several students who they feel have pushed the boundaries of excellence in their respective disciplines. I would like to start by asking the following students to come up on the stage," she said. "Sophie Bell, Aphra Brown, Greg D'Agostino, Neil Froderman, Bethany Newman,, Sam Nyugen, and Annette Park."

We all made our way awkwardly up to the stage and sat in the row of chairs designated for us. I wished I'd worn something else, like a T-shirt that didn't say *Rowers Stroke It Better.* I glanced over at Bethany, who was sliding her hand out of Greg's and looking a little pained. She pulled her shirt away from her body a little, like she wanted to use it to create some insulation between her and the stares of the rest of the student body. I heard Greg whisper, "It's okay. They all know you're awesome."

Ms. Turner was replaced at the podium by Dr. Rishi, the head of the math department, who said, "We'd like to start by honoring a math student who has really hit the mark of excellence this year."

I wondered how many times they would use the word *excellence.* I'd counted three so far, and they'd only just started. This was going to take forever, and I was sure the only reason they'd decided to hand out awards to the juniors was so we could list them on college applications. I was so ready to be done with this place.

He went on: "One of only three juniors in BC Calculus, this student maintained a 98% average this year, and every day brings a terrific energy to her classroom, where she asks thoughtful questions, patiently helps her peers, and has been a real bright spot for our entire class. On a personal note, I can't wait to have this student in my Linear Algebra class next year." He turned and smiled at Bethany. "Congratulations, Bethany Newman."

We all applauded. Bethany stood up, Dr. Rishi put a medal

around her neck, and she came back and sat down between me and Greg. I whispered "Congratulations, smart-ass." She fiddled with her medal and smiled.

The World Languages award went to Greg, of course, and then I was a little surprised when the English award went to Sam Nyugen, since I'd assumed that was why I was there. Well, I guess I must have been there for History. Ms. Young said my paper on Wounded Knee was the best one she'd read that year.

Then Mr. Positano took the podium for the tech department award.

"This year," he said, "the technology department was blessed with a student whose work in computer science was so remarkably creative that we felt an award was mandatory." I glanced at Bethany, but she was looking at Greg's profile. This whole thing was so boring; I wished Mr. P would give his award to whatever kid aced the AP CS class so we could get out of there. I wanted to text Bethany again, but you can't really do that kind of thing when you're sitting on a stage in front of 2,000 people.

"I'll admit," Mr. P went on, "that when she submitted her project proposal to me, I thought it was so ambitious it was impossible to pull off. She ended up proving me wrong, and created an AI so sophisticated that it pushes the boundaries of what we can do with a smartphone app."

Bethany stopped looking at Greg and turned to me, her eyebrows shooting up.

He went on: "On top of that, she made a point of using her work to help other students in distress by creating an app designed to give anonymous advice on everything from STIs to family troubles, all using an interface based on everyone's favorite counselor from *Star Trek*."

Greg smiled at Bethany and mouthed, "You're getting *two*!"

Bethany looked sick.

I felt the stage slide a little sideways, like someone had tilted it up on one end and I was about to tumble off, and everything inside my head was suddenly very loud.

I tried to make eye contact with Mr. Positano and shook my head furiously. Next to me, I could hear Bethany's breath coming in short little bursts.

"Aphra, come on up."

When I failed to move, he said, "Aphra *Brown.*" He chuckled a little. "As opposed to the five other Aphras we don't have at this school."

I failed to move.

Next to me, I heard Greg murmur to Bethany, "Wait, he mixed it up. That was your app. You should tell him they mixed it up."

Bethany looked nothing short of terrified. "Bethany," he said. "Go tell him, don't let him give your credit away." To me, he said, "Aphra, come on."

She sat frozen, like she was wishing the world would somehow fold in on her and she would disappear into the depths of a black hole. I know this because it was exactly how I felt.

"Come on!" Greg urged her. "Go be the girl I know you are!"

Bethany said, "I'm not." Her face crumpled. "I'm not."

From the other side of Sam Nyugen, Sophie whispered, "The counselor Troi app was Aphra's. Bethany's was about the weather."

Greg said, "What?" He didn't understand, I realized. His brain was still fixed on the idea that Bethany was this . . . this perfect angel, and he couldn't accept that the person whispering in his ear had been me.

"Greg," Bethany begged.

At the podium, Mr. Positano was watching this exchange, too far away to hear what was being said. Greg grabbed Bethany's shoulders and said, "Я вас любил безмолвно, безнадежно. What does it mean?"

Sophie hissed, "You need to chill the hell out."

Greg ignored her and repeated, "What does it mean, Bethany?"

Bethany said, "I don't know."

Mr. Positano coughed, like he was just realizing that giving me this award was probably a mistake, and said, "Aphra, let's move this along."

Figuring the only way out was through, I got up and grabbed the medal from him.

"Congratulations?" he said, like he wasn't sure that was the right word.

I did not put the medal around my neck. I hovered halfway between the podium and the rest of the junior awards winners, because I was supposed to go back and sit down, but that meant sitting down next to Bethany, who was still crying.

I heard one of the teachers mutter the word *brittle,* like they thought Bethany was crying because she hadn't won the tech award in addition to math.

Greg took out his phone and opened the app. He'd been talking softly before, but his voice was getting progressively louder, to the point where he was getting picked up by the microphone. "You told me to delete this, remember? But I didn't. I didn't delete it. Because I didn't want to lose all those chats. I go back and read them sometimes. Did you know that? Did you? I told you stuff I never told anyone. Not my friends."

His voice cracked. "Not my parents. Are you saying the *whole time . . . ?*"

"I didn't know," Bethany said. "I didn't know she was doing it."

"Who?" he roared.

Everything went silent.

Except for one person who shouted, "What the fuck is going on?" and someone else who shouted, "Bethany Newman's getting her sweet ass dumped!"

I couldn't understand how he wasn't getting it. Mr. Positano had called my name, Sophie had confirmed it, and he still didn't see the truth.

I walked the rest of the way across the stage and said, "Me. You were talking to me."

Mr. Positano muttered, into the microphone, "Oh, Jesus Christ."

"Is this some kind of sick joke?" Greg shouted. "Was I some kind of . . . like a toy for you guys to pass back and forth?"

"No," I said, because Bethany was way beyond the power of speech. "No, of course not—"

"Why are you the one talking?" he said, rounding on me. "She's the one I'm with! She's the one I . . ."

The one he actually wanted.

I said, "None of this is her fault. It was always me. She didn't know."

"Aphra," Bethany choked out. "Stop."

"Just answer me this," he said to Bethany. He was shaking. He was actually shaking, and I realized that he wasn't just mad. He was hurt. "Did you ever ask her to talk to me? To get me to . . . to get me? For you?"

Bethany turned away, and because she, unlike me, is not a liar, said, "Yes. I did."

Several people in the audience went "Ooooooo." I glanced over and saw that a bunch of people were recording this on their phones, smiling with unmitigated glee over the humiliation of the prettiest girl in the school.

I thought, *I hate everyone.*

Greg swore under his breath with one hand over his mouth. After a second, he said, "I never want to talk to you again." Looking at me, he added, "Either of you." He flung his World Languages medal down on the stage and stormed out of the gym.

The gym erupted into shouting and loud exclamations while Bethany doubled over into Sophie's arms.

"It's okay," Sophie whispered. "It's gonna be okay." At me, she mouthed, "What the *fuck*, Aphra?"

Ms. Turner muttered, "I do not get paid enough for this shit," unaware that she was still close enough to the microphone to be picked up.

I felt a hand on my shoulder; it was Mr. Positano, who said, "Just to clear something up, was Mr. D'Agostino chatting with your AI or with you?"

I winced and said, "Yeah, it was me."

His mouth was very, very flat. He said, "We need to have a conversation."

Five minutes later, after admitting I'd faked my data, I had a zero on my app for academic dishonesty, and as Mr. Positano reminded me, I was damn lucky not to be suspended or worse.

The zero was bad enough. That project was 35% of my grade, so I was staring down the barrel of a flat-out F in the class.

Needless to say, I was not given the tech award. I rather suspected the Junior Academic Awards would be quickly consigned to Middleridge's list of failed experiments best never repeated, like the unfortunate year the student government had two presidents because of an electoral tie, and they ended up having a fistfight over the homecoming theme. I imagined that Ms. Turner was getting drunk in her office right now, crying into a potted plant and slurring, "Let's never do this again."

I texted Bethany after school, *Are you okay?* Which seemed like the stupidest thing ever to say to someone who was just dumped by the boy of her dreams in front of 2,000 people.

I don't want to talk to you, she replied. *Ever.*

Chapter Thirty-One

Friday was the last crew practice of the season. I'd never wanted to attend practice less in my life.

Bethany wouldn't look at me, and when I passed Claire doing sit-ups she shook her head and said, "Damn, Aphra." No one else really wanted to talk to me, either. Even the people who didn't go to Middleridge.

I just wanted to get through it. I'd committed to finishing the season, which meant this practice and the regatta over the weekend, and then I'd just have to figure out how to get up in the morning and deal with my life. For once, I was actually grateful I'd be seeing Dr. Pascal on Monday, though I didn't know what she could possibly say to me apart from "You did *what*, now?"

I was out on *Dullahan* when, from the launch, Coach Kim hollered at us across the water.

I have no idea why she does that. We can never hear her. Sophie cupped her hand around her ear and shook her head, and Coach switched on her megaphone. "I just got a message for Aphra."

We'd stopped to catch our breaths before doing a second 1,500. I couldn't imagine who might have been trying to reach me via Coach Kim.

"It's from your dad, Aphra. He says your brother's in the ER."

I recoiled hard enough to rock the boat, and everyone else made sounds of dismay.

"I have to go!" I said. "I have to get out of this fucking boat right now!"

"Okay," Sophie said. She was so calm. How was she so calm? "We're heading back to the dock. Ladies, we're coming around to port. Let's go."

Three seats in front of me, Bethany craned her neck to glance back at me. Sophie said, "Ladies, get ready to spin the boat. Ready all, row."

We did a turn and rowed back to the dock. Unfortunately, I realized once I got out of the boat that I had no way to leave on my own.

"I'll drive you, Aphra," Sophie said. "Can you guys put the boat away?"

"Sure," Claire said.

Bethany said, "Is he okay?"

I didn't answer, or actually register that she'd spoken to me. I just got in the car with Sophie and left.

Sophie dropped me off at the hospital 20 minutes later. I didn't ask her to come in, and she didn't offer, which was kind of a relief.

The admin person at the front desk buzzed me back, and I found Kit and my parents in one of those little curtained-off booths. He was covered in raised red blisters. "Holy shit," I said.

"Aphra," Dad said. "What are you doing here?"

"You texted that Kit was in the ER!"

"Yeah, but . . ."

"What's wrong with him?"

"Did you not get the message I sent your coach?"

"She just said he was here. . . ." I fished my buzzing phone out of my pocket. It was a text from Coach Kim, who said, *Your dad says he's fine, had an allergic reaction and has to stay a few hours because they gave him an EpiPen.*

"Maybe next time you should lead with the 'he's fine' part," I said.

"Sorry," Dad said. "I just wanted to make sure you got the message. I tried calling, but your phone was off."

"Yeah." I took a couple of deep breaths. Kit was okay. He was fine. He just looked like he'd gone headfirst into some poison ivy. "It's no big deal, though. What's up, Kit-Kat?"

At this, he snuffled. Mom said, "I think I need a soda. Will you come with me to the vending machine?"

"What? No."

"Aphra," she said. "Come with me to the vending machine."

We went back to the waiting room and she pulled me onto a couch next to the Coke machine. "What's going on?" I asked.

"I came home and found him like that," she said.

"He was home by himself?"

"Oh. No, Delia was in the shower. I walked in and he had his whole face buried in that damn cat, and when he looked up he was wheezing and his lips were swollen, and—well, you saw."

"The cat? But that never happened before."

"The doctor said these things can get worse over time."

"But . . . but before he was just itchy. And sneezing sometimes."

"Aphra, you have to listen to me. Walnut has to go, and you have to stop fighting me on this."

"But you don't know it was the cat!"

"Aphra! He is allergic to the cat! His mouth swelled up—he could have died if I hadn't come home in time!"

"But you don't know it was the cat!" I repeated. "That doesn't make any sense!"

Her voice dropped. "We discussed this. You are his sister. I am his mother. You are going to have to accept that I'm the one with the authority here."

"This isn't about your authority!"

"It's exactly about that. We cannot keep that cat. We will find him a very good home, I promise, but we can't keep him."

"But Kit—"

"Stop! Aphra. Stop."

I got up and walked out of the waiting room. I wasn't sure where I was going, but I went down the hall and then stopped and pressed my forehead against the wall, because this whole thing was my fault. I tried so hard, *I tried so hard*, and I just managed to make everything worse. Everything I touched turned to crap. I let out one sob, and then another, and I felt a little like I might be having a heart attack. I'd screwed everything up. Everything. I didn't know what to do. I thought I might be having a panic attack. I couldn't breathe. I couldn't breathe.

I couldn't breathe because I was holding my breath. I let it out on a ten count, because I'd read somewhere to do that. I didn't really feel any better, though. My chest hurt. My hands felt all tingly. I'd messed up everything and I didn't even have anybody to talk to, because I'd made literally everyone in my life mad at me. There was no one I could call.

Well, except one person.

I took out my phone and called Dr. Pascal's emergency number.

I expected to get her answering service or something, but instead, I heard her voice saying, "Hello?"

"You gave me your actual cell number?" I said incredulously, wiping my eyes and pretending I hadn't been just crying.

"Aphra?"

"Yeah," I said. "Hi. It's me."

"Are you all right?"

"No. I mean, yeah. I mean, I'm sorry I called. I didn't know this was your cell. I'm sorry. It's just, my mom's going to make my brother give up his cat."

Why that seemed like the worst of what I was dealing with right then, I don't know, but it did. There was the clinking of glasses in the background. "Are you," I said. "Where are you?"

"I'm on a date, Aphra."

"Oh," I said. "Wow. Sorry. I, uh. I thought you were married."

"I'm on a date with my husband. So you called me about your brother's cat?"

"Yeah, it's just . . . it's not fair. It's not fair."

"To the cat?"

"To my brother! He loves that cat, he loves him so much, and he shouldn't have to . . . I mean, if you love someone so much, you should be together." I was crying again. "Shouldn't you? You should be able to be with the person you love!"

"Are we still talking about the cat?"

"Yes! We are talking about the cat."

"I don't think we are," she said. She was chewing.

"Are you eating?"

"I am eating my dinner, Aphra. I don't think this is about the cat. I think this is about the boy. The cat is the boy."

"The cat is not the boy!"

"The cat is the boy. This is called projecting. Why does he have to give up the cat?"

"He's. He's allergic. To the cat."

"That sounds like a pretty good reason."

"But it isn't fair! He's . . . Kit's . . . It's going to break his heart." I sobbed once and then twice.

"Aphra," she said. "Honey."

"Why does everything hurt so much? Why does it have to hurt *so much*?"

"Because," she said. "You lost your anger. But you're going to be okay. You're going to figure this out."

"How? How will I figure it out? Everyone found out I was talking to Greg with the app. And now Bethany hates me, and Greg, and Delia, and my mom, and now probably Kit, too. . . . I just, I just don't even know what to do!"

"I don't think they hate you."

"Yes. They do."

"They're angry, and you're going to have to make that right, but first, Aphra, it's time for you to learn to let go."

"Of the cat?"

"Of more than the cat. You need to let go of this boy. You need to let go of the idea that things should be fair, and the idea that you know what's best for people. You are 17 years old, and you're still figuring out how the world works. Give yourself permission to learn. And just accept that your brother is allergic to the cat."

I sighed. I heard ambulance sirens outside—people with real problems, car accident victims or gunshot wounds, maybe.

"Here's what I think," said Dr. Pascal. "I think you know how much it hurts not to get the love you want, and you've made it your mission to make sure no one else in your life hurts like that, because you have a beautiful, kind heart. But that can't be your job. You have to let it go."

"Okay," I said. "Okay."

There was a pause. She said, "Wait, that's it?"

"Did you want me to argue with you?"

"No, I was just expecting it."

I laughed a little. "Thanks," I said. "I'm sorry for calling."

"That's why I gave you the number. I'll see you on Monday. Okay?"

"Okay," I said. "Bye." I hung up.

Let go. Let go. I didn't know how to do that. But right now, I had no choice. I was letting go of a lot of things that were already out of my reach. I guess what I had to do, really, was just accept that they were already gone.

I went back to my mother, who was still in the waiting room pressing a cold can of soda against her forehead. "Hey," I said. "I'm . . . I'm sorry for yelling."

"Yeah," she said. "So am I. But the cat has to go."

Delia had just skidded past, her hair leaving a wet mark on her shirt, and was talking rapidly to the lady at the desk. "Brown," she was saying. "Christopher. He's nine."

"Delia!" Mom called, and Delia jogged over.

"Next time could you bang on the bathroom door instead of

leaving a text? I got out of the shower and everyone was gone. Is he okay?"

"He's fine," Mom said.

To Mom, because I was still only 98% ready to let go, I said, "Is it . . . is it possible it was something he ate?"

"He didn't eat anything!"

Delia said, "Wait."

"We have all the same stuff in the house that we always do," Mom said.

"Maybe he ate something on the bus, though."

"Kit didn't come home on the bus today," Mom said. "Delia picked him up."

"Maybe someone gave him something at school! Like, like a cupcake or something. Maybe it was someone's birthday."

"There was no birthday!" Mom said. "Aphra, it wasn't something he ate."

Delia said, "I think it might have been something he ate."

Mom said, "Don't you start, too."

"No, listen—"

"You guys have to understand that I am the parent! You are the children! And you need to—"

"We stopped at CVS on the way home," Delia said.

"What?" Mom said.

"I needed tampons. So I got Kit a candy bar, and one for me, too."

"What did he have?" I asked.

"A plain Hershey bar," she said. "But I had a Mounds bar and he ate half of it."

"A Mounds bar?" I asked. "You gave him the white death?"

"Aphra," Mom said. "Honestly."

"But Kit hates coconut."

"No, that's you," Delia said. "You're the one always saying it's disgusting."

"Coconut *is* disgusting. Anyway, he always throws the coconut candy out at Halloween. I've seen him do it."

"Right, because you told him it's gross. But today he wanted to try it, so I let him."

Delia and I stared at each other, then at Mom. "Did they check him for coconut? At the allergist?" I asked.

"I'm not . . . I don't think so. It's not one of the things they usually look for, is it?"

But Mom had already leapt ahead and was touching her hair. "Oh my God," she said.

"That damn shampoo," I said.

"So are we saying," Delia said, "that Kit was never allergic to the cat?"

"No, he is," Mom said. "We know he is, they tested that."

"But those tests aren't always accurate," Delia said. "There are false positives. And even if he is allergic to the cat, it seems like he's way *more* allergic to coconut, so it's possible that's what was causing most of his symptoms."

"Mom," I said. "Kit's not allergic to Walnut. He's allergic to *you.*"

"That's why it's been coming and going," Delia said. "It flares up on the days you wash your hair. Is he still doing that thing where he mashes his face into your neck when you read to him at night?"

Mom put her head in her hands and whispered, "I am a terrible parent."

"No," Delia said. "No, you're not." She looked at me, but I

was still kind of upset, so I did a so-so gesture with my hand and Delia smacked it down. "But this is good. Right?"

"Well, so far as we know, he is still allergic to the cat," Mom said. "Just not in the anaphylactic sense."

"We'll have to go back to the doctor," Delia said. "See what he says."

"This is not a decision to be made by committee," Mom said.

We both stared at her. She said. "We'll have to go back to the doctor."

"I will defer to your authority," I said.

"Thank you," she replied.

The three of us sat in a row, watching the TV on the wall, which was turned to the weather channel. Sunny tomorrow, with a high of 72. To my mom, I said, "Can I have your Coke if you don't want it?"

She handed it to me and I cracked it open.

Chapter Thirty-Two

The team bus to the regatta left at 5:30 the next morning. I was the first one there, mostly because that meant I'd be the first one to pick a seat and I wouldn't be stuck trying to figure out whether to sit next to Bethany or not. She would have to decide what she wanted to do, and I'd have to let it go. Or whatever.

Bethany, as it turned out, was five minutes late. By the time she got there, there was only one seat left. Without looking directly at me, she sat down next to me.

After a minute, still facing directly ahead, she asked, "How's Kit?"

I wanted to explain about my mother's stupid shampoo, but it seemed like a lot to get into just then. I said, "He's fine. He's allergic to coconut."

"Oh." Then, "Did we know that?"

"No, we didn't."

"Oh."

I wanted to ask her if she'd heard from Greg. I said, "Did you . . . did you talk to him?"

"No, I didn't talk to him!"

"But maybe if you—"

"Shut up! God, would you shut up!"

"I was just trying to—"

"UGH. Would you QUIT?"

I stopped talking and turned toward the window.

But apparently Bethany wasn't done, and I had to turn back. She said, "You talk and talk and talk and you never actually listen. I told you I wanted to tell Greg. And you wouldn't listen to me."

"But that was because—"

"No! Don't you get it? You always have some . . . explanation. Some reason. And you make it all sound so fucking logical, but you won't just listen to me. But I'm a person. I'm not like you, but I'm still a person, and what I want matters."

"Of course you're a person!"

"You don't act like it!"

"What?"

"You act like I should be grateful that you're around to tell me what to do. Because I'm such a fuck-up I could never figure it out on my own. Well, I'm not grateful. I'm not grateful that you lied to Greg and then talked me into going along with it. I'm not grateful that you went behind my back to try to get Greg interested in me, because you think I'm so much *less* than you that he could never want me for myself."

"I never said that! I don't think you're less than me!"

"You sure act like it. You know what? Greg liked me before

you ever got involved. And if you'd just kept your mouth to yourself, everything would have been fine. But you just couldn't keep your hands off it. It's like you had to feel like my relationship had your fucking fingerprints all over it."

"That's not why . . ."

"Not why what?"

"Why I was talking to him." I pressed my hand over my eyes. "Bethany . . ."

"What."

This was the part I didn't like to admit even to myself. Because as much as I'd tried to convince myself I was doing this for Bethany, I hadn't been noble or selfless. Not at all. "I wasn't talking to Greg because I was trying to get him to like you. Or like you more than he already did."

"So why were you doing it?"

"Because I liked him." I let out a long breath. "Because I love him."

She stopped short. "What?"

"I'm sorry," I said.

"You are *not* in love with him."

I said nothing.

"You're not, Aphra. I know you're not."

"I never tried to get him to like me instead," I said. "I showed you the messages. You know that's the truth. I just wanted . . . I wanted to feel like . . . like there was some universe where he could want me back. I wanted to feel that."

"You wanted to feel . . ."

"Eros, I don't know."

"You wanted to feel eros."

"Yeah."

"With my boyfriend."

"Well, he wasn't your boyfriend when it started—"

"Do you not realize how gross that is?"

"I'm sorry!"

"That's disgusting, Aphra! Like, Greg and I are people. We're not just . . . like . . . psychological experiments for you to mess around with because you want to feel something."

"I know that. Obviously I know that."

She huffed out a breath. I felt . . . angry again, like my hurt had looped back around. Mostly I was mad at myself. But not entirely. "But, you know," I said, "you could have done some things different, too."

"Really, you're going to act like *any* of this was my fault?"

"You know, you could . . . you could have set your sights on someone who wasn't the only guy I've liked since eighth grade and then asked me to help you get him to fall for you. To rub sunscreen on you and type your texts for you and sit in fucking Cake Baby and have your conversation for you. How did you think that was going to make me feel?"

She blinked a few times. "When did you ever tell me that?"

"Tell you what?"

"That you were in love with him!"

"I told you."

"Yeah, you told me you liked him in middle school. You didn't tell me you still liked him!"

"Well, I didn't realize it was incumbent on me to tell you I never stopped liking him!"

"But—"

"When did I ever talk about anyone else?"

"That was three years ago!"

"Yeah. It was."

"So why didn't you tell me back when I told you I was into him? Why not say something then?"

"What would the point have been? You obviously knew Greg and I were never going to happen."

"Oh, right. Yeah. That's why I did it. I deliberately stole the guy you liked because I'm such a bitch." She scoffed. "You *always* underestimate me."

"That isn't fair."

"It's the truth. No matter how much you say you know I'm not some stupid airhead, whenever the chips are down you act like that's exactly what you think. You act like I can't get a guy on my own. Like I'd deliberately go after a guy you liked. You treat me like I'm the stupid princess and it's on you to save me all the time because I can't possibly function in this world without you."

"Well, did you ever consider that's how you act? You freaked when you found out about NVCC because you'd have to eat lunch by yourself! Like, I shouldn't have to feel guilty about you having to find someone else to eat a sandwich with! You won't do *anything* unless I'm there."

"I got a job without you," she said.

"Yeah, but apart from that. You only joined crew because I did. You wouldn't even go trick-or-treating without me. That one year I got the flu? You just didn't go out! It's exhausting. Like, I have to be there for you *all the time.* Did you ever think that I'm tired of feeling guilty for wanting to do things on my own?"

"I never said you had to feel guilty! There's no reason for you not to do things on your own!"

"Really."

"Really. I am perfectly fine by myself. I don't need you. At all. For anything."

"Is that so? Well, then. I'm glad we figured that out."

She turned sideways. "Sophie," she said. "Switch sweats with me."

Sophie said, "Bethany . . ."

"Now. Please."

They switched seats. My face was pressed against the window because I wished I were not on that bus. I hated everything. I hated Bethany for making me feel like crap. I hated being on a tiny bus that smelled like old socks. I hated the world.

Sophie said, "I thought the cheerleaders pushed the drama. Did you guys really have to do this now?"

I didn't answer.

"Oh, now you're quiet."

"Please just leave me alone."

"Well, that's a problem because you *aren't* alone. There are eight other girls on our boat depending on you to get it together. So get it together."

"I know," I said. "I will."

I was not getting it together.

We set up our team tent, and the parents, who had carpooled in together, fired up the grill and set up a table for pasta salad and bananas and chips. My parents were home with Kit, and I was actually kind of glad. No one was expecting me to smile or act excited. I checked the time; in six hours, I could go home. Then there was only one more day of the regatta, and then I could breathe.

The boys' team had come on a separate bus, and it was only after the tent was set up that I saw Greg was with them;. either they'd made him an alternate or he was just there to watch. He glanced at me and then away. I went and got a banana and ate it sitting in a lawn chair by myself.

The thing about regattas is they consist of about 10% racing and 90% waiting. In the past this hasn't bothered me, because during the 90% downtime I get to hang out with my friends and cheer on other boats. But today, that wasn't happening. Everybody'd heard the fight on the bus—which meant nobody wanted to be within five feet of me.

It seemed like nobody wanted to be within five feet of Bethany, either, so at least they weren't picking sides.

After a while, I went to throw out my slimy banana peel. Of course this happened to be at the exact second that Greg decided to throw out the wrapper from his breakfast burrito.

I decided the best course of action would be to look at my feet and go the other way, but Greg had other ideas. "Aphra," he said.

"Hello," I told my feet.

"Really?"

I looked up. He looked bad. Like maybe he hadn't slept all that well. "I'm sorry," I said. "I'm so sorry, I just, I don't know what else to say."

"Really. You don't know what to say."

"Is there . . . is there something you want me to say?"

"I want you to tell me the truth!"

"The truth?"

"I think you owe me that. Were you guys just messing with me? Was this just fun for you, jerking me around?"

"No," I said. "It was never that. I'm sorry, but it wasn't that."

"Then what was it?"

I huffed out my breath and closed my eyes. "The Deanna app was busted and I didn't want to flunk, so I took over and started writing the responses myself. I didn't know who you were. At first."

"But you figured it out."

"Yeah. Eventually."

"And when I asked who you were . . ."

"I . . . I freaked out. I thought . . . it would be awkward."

"Awkward why?"

"Because . . . because I liked you so much. Because . . . because I didn't think you could like me back."

He stared at me for a good long second, his face all contorted with whatever he was feeling. "So you lied to me? Jesus Christ, do you really think I'm that shallow?"

"No," I said. "No. I don't think you're shallow at all. I actually . . . don't think it's shallow to want to be attracted to the person you're with."

"Oh, I get it," he said. "So it's not that you think I'm shallow. It's that *you're* shallow."

There was some cheering from down by the river, which meant that the race had ended. It was one of the fours, I think. I wasn't paying that much attention.

"I was going to tell you," I said. "The next day, after you asked, I decided to tell you anyway, but then you saw Bethany with my code, and . . . and you were so happy." I screwed my eyes shut. "You were so happy it was her. She didn't know. She didn't know we'd been talking."

"You didn't tell her?"

"Not then. You guys were both so happy, and I . . . I know this doesn't make sense to you, but I thought I was doing the right thing, I swear."

"Because we were happy. Bethany and me."

"Yeah, because of that."

"And what about you?"

"I . . . was happy that you guys were happy."

"That's bullshit, Aphra."

"That's the truth." I drew in a shaky breath. "I knew you weren't going to like me. Not that way."

He said nothing for a while. Then: "But you were still talking to me online. And you knew I thought you were Bethany."

"Yeah."

"Why?"

"I . . . It was a mistake."

"You thought . . . what? You could pretend to be with me?"

"Something like that. I'm sorry."

"And Bethany found out?"

"Yeah, and she wanted to tell you, but I wouldn't let her, because none of this was her fault. It was all mine."

He shoved his hands in his pockets; unlike me, he wasn't wearing a uniform. Why was he even there? He wasn't going to be rowing that day. He exhaled loud enough that I could hear it over the hundreds of people around us. "You're right," he said. "It was. It was sick and awful and your fault."

I nodded. I couldn't quite look at him. Then, because I was already being more honest than I'd ever been, I said, "Я вас любил безмолвно, безнадежно."

I loved you wordlessly, without a hope.

I said it quietly enough that I wasn't even sure he heard,

and when he didn't answer, I raised my eyes just a little to see if he was still there. He was. I watched his throat bob as he swallowed. Then he turned around and walked away without saying anything at all.

"APHRA!"

I turned. Sophie and the others were waving at me from our tent. "WE HAVE TO CHECK IN NOW!"

I rubbed the tears out of my eyes and rejoined the group, because, if nothing else, I am always a team player.

Chapter Thirty-Three

"Okay," Sophie said. "Let's have eight hands on the eight."

It was time to move our boat out of the boathouse, and we were about to move it off the rack. I got into position with my hands on the gunwale. Sophie said, "Ready to lift." We'd just started to lift it when Bethany, who was standing way too close behind me, bobbled and lost her grip.

In that instant my hand ended up smashed between the hull and the bar.

I shrieked. And then I did it again, because the damn boat was still on my hand. "Get it up!" Sophie shouted. "Get it up!"

They pulled *Dullahan* up an inch and I slipped my hand out and cradled it against my chest.

Coach Kim reached for my hand, which I did not want anyone to touch. "Let me see it," she was saying while Bethany kept repeating, "I'm so sorry. I'm so sorry."

I showed Kim my hand, which was already starting to swell. She held out my hands side by side to compare them.

"Make a fist," she said. I did, saying the f-word about 20

times in a row. Finally, in as cheerful a voice as I could muster, I said, “Could I get some ice, maybe?”

“I think it’s sprained,” she said. “It doesn’t look broken, but you might need an X-ray.”

“Nah,” I said. “I’m good. It’s just . . . HA HA HA, that’s fine, it barely hurts.”

Claire said, “We’re due at check-in.”

Talia said, “Shut up, Claire.”

Sophie said, “Can you still row?”

“Ha,” I said. “Ha ha, sure. It’s nothing. I mean. I’ve got two hands, right?”

To Sophie, Kim was saying, “Go get Melina.” Melina was one of the better rowers on our JV eight.

“No,” I said. “No, I am totally fine.” I attempted to make a fist again, which didn’t go so well. “I can still row. I just need to ice it for a second.”

“Aphra,” Coach Kim said. “You are not rowing.”

“It’ll be fine in a minute!”

She was pulling me away from the rest of the group by my shoulder. “There’s next season,” she said. “You’ll row next year.”

Sophie came running back with Melina, who looked pretty damn delighted to take my seat. “Four-seat, right?” she chirped.

“Yeah,” I muttered.

Sophie said, “Let’s get to check-in.” Then, maybe because her cheerleader roots were showing, she cried, “LET’S DO IT FOR APHRA!”

Please, I thought, *you guys dropped the boat on my hand.*

“FOR APHRA!” they echoed, as if they hadn’t been ignoring me all morning. Bethany, at least, met my gaze and gave me an eye roll. Whether it was directed at me or at them, I couldn’t tell.

And so I was left to watch my team row their last race of the season with a freshman in my seat. I sat down by the edge of the water. After a minute John O'Malley sat down next to me.

"What," I said flatly.

He wordlessly handed me a baggie of ice.

"Did they really drop the boat on you?"

"Shut up, John."

"Hey, *I* didn't drop the boat on you."

I looked down at my hand, which was already going black-and-blue. It would be ugly tomorrow. At least it wasn't my right hand. Which meant I could still punch John if I wanted.

Together, we watched the boats row to the start line. John handed me his binoculars.

"Are you sure?" I asked.

"It's your boat," he said. And then, just in case I might have forgotten, he added, "Which they dropped on you."

"*That* they dropped on me," I said automatically.

"What?"

"It's a restrictive clause."

The starting beeper went off.

It was a 1,500-meter race. Those typically last about four minutes. Four minutes of putting your heart into your arms and legs, listening to Sophie shouting her orders, and loving her, and loving the girls in front of you and behind you, because for those four minutes you are one person, one organism with 16 arms moving in unison. There's a term in crew, *finding your swing*, which is the best possible thing that can happen. Everyone is in total sync. You can feel it like expertly rhymed poetry; you can even hear it in the whoosh of the oars moving together.

It's what we all pursue, that perfect synchronicity. It's better than winning a race, once you find it.

From the shore, I saw the second my boat found their swing. I could see it in their faces. They flew through the water, shooting between the other boats; they were in fourth place, and then third, and then second.

"Whoa," John said. "Are they going to win?"

I held my breath. I wanted them to win.

They were bow to bow with the boat from Great Falls, the best girls' eight in the county for the last three years. They were so close together I couldn't see who was ahead. I could hear Sophie calling over the crowd, which had gone furious with excitement. I felt the screams all around me in my bones.

I wished, so badly, that I was on the boat, that I could hear and see and feel what my friends were feeling. *Dullahan* under them and Sophie in front of them and boats on either side.

I couldn't tell who won. Then I heard it over the loudspeaker. "Occoquan Club takes it!"

John and I leapt to our feet. He hugged me, and I hugged him back, and we jumped up and down for a good long minute.

When the noise from the crowd started to subside, I could hear shouting from the boats by the finish line. John said, "They're calling you."

They were. My girls were calling my name. I jogged down to the dock, where they were pulling the boat out of the water. John, who was still with me, held me back. "You've only got one hand left," he said. But once the boat was put away, I went to be with my friends. Sophie jumped on my back and howled like a wolf, and Claire was so happy she kissed me on the mouth, which was a little weird but I went with it. Bethany alone hung back. I didn't want to ruin her buzz, so I said, "I need some Gatorade—that shit was exhausting," and went back to our tent while the rest of the team posed for victory selfies.

I drank my Gatorade by myself, and after a few minutes the team filtered in, still talking way too loud, like they were all a little drunk. Bethany wasn't with them.

"Where's B?" I asked Sophie, when it was clear she wasn't coming.

"I think she went to the bathroom," she said, then went to talk to Coach Kim.

I knew Bethany didn't love the big regattas. They're super crowded and very loud, and usually she doesn't like to walk off by herself because she's got this irrational fear she won't be able to find her way back to the tent. I scanned the area where they keep the porta jons until I found her, talking to some guy in a Great Falls uniform I'd never seen before. He was standing way too close to her, and she kept trying to back up, but there were so many people she couldn't really get away from him. He was smiling, and she was not. He was talking, and she was not. She shook her head. He leaned in and touched her shoulder.

From where I stood, I could see the shape of her mouth say, "Stop."

I bolted toward them. Or tried to. I weaved through the crowd, throwing my elbows to make a path. "Hey!" I shouted. "HEY!"

By now, I could hear what he was saying. "Come on, just come sit with us. You can ride back on our bus after."

I grabbed Bethany by the hand and said, "Let's go."

She blinked at me in surprise. The boy said, "Hey, we're talking, here."

"Coach Kim is looking for you," I said to her. "Come on."

Bethany looked relieved. The guy said, "Give me your number, okay? We'll hang out later."

He was, I realized, bigger than us. Usually I'm not all that aware of the size of the guys I talk to; like, I know Greg is bigger than me, but I never thought about the relationship between our sizes that much, because Greg doesn't make a big deal about it. He doesn't loom. This guy was looming. In this very quiet voice, he said, "Just give me your phone so I can put my number in it, okay?" He tried to take Bethany's phone out of her hand, but she pulled her arm back.

"She wants you to leave her alone," I said.

"I think she wants *you* to leave her alone," he said. "We were doing just fine before you busted into the middle of this."

I said, "Let's go, B," and started to leave, which was when I heard Bethany shout, "HEY!" and turned to see that he'd grabbed her butt.

I didn't even wait to see what she would do. I screamed, "I don't think so!" and stiff-armed him in the gut with my good hand.

He doubled over, grunting, and I thought, *We should probably run away now,* and then something hit me in the chest and there was an almost simultaneous explosion in my face.

My feet lost contact with the ground, and for a second everything went numb. It had been his fist, I realized. He'd punched me in the face. I hadn't even seen it coming.

What I did see, though, was Bethany, screaming. "You

fucking asshole. YOU FUCKING ASSHOLE!" And she kicked him in the groin. He went down silently, which was how I knew she'd gotten him good.

Beyond the pain in my face, I could see Bethany absolutely whaling on this guy, and I thought, *She is actually going to kill him,* which seemed perfectly okay to me, until I realized that you generally go to jail for that kind of thing. I watched her fist connect with his kidney as he curled around his crotch once, and then twice, and then two great big guys I didn't know were pulling her off him and she was screaming more bad words than I realized she even knew, like somewhere inside my Fluttershy-loving friend was a rage demon and it had just woken up.

There was a lot of blood running out of my face.

"Shit," Bethany said, having wrestled herself free of the boys pinning her arms back. "Shit. Shit. Let me see, Aphra, let me see."

But both my hands were over my face now. I was shaking. Suddenly, everything seemed very, very funny, and I said, "It's fine. You should see the other guy."

The other guy was still doubled over in the grass whimpering. A bunch of adults were sprinting toward us.

"I could have handled that," she said, but she was crying.

"Of course you could," I said. "Obviously."

Someone handed me a wadded-up T-shirt, and I used it to sop up the blood coming out of my nose. Blood was running down both my arms, and my bruised hand was covered with nose blood. "Thanks," I said to the owner of the shirt I was bleeding on. Then I realized it was the shirt he'd actually been wearing, because he was pressed up behind me and I could feel his bare chest against my back, and I thought, *This world is full of creepers.*

"Ten feet," said the male voice in my ear. "I was ten feet behind you. If you'd just turned around."

Of course it was Greg. I found myself leaning back against him, because I was really, really tired. "It's just as well," I said into his shirt. "Your face would have been a bigger loss."

Greg sighed. His hand was on my shoulder, and he said what we both knew: "He wouldn't have punched *me*."

I closed my eyes. Bethany kept saying my name over and over, and then, "Are you okay?"

"He . . . he hit me twice. How did he hit me twice?"

"What?"

I touched the place on my chest. "It hurts," I said.

"He didn't hit you there," Greg said. "Bethany pushed you."

"I was too slow," she said.

I managed to open my eyes long enough to say, "I think my nose is broken," and then I really didn't feel like saying anything else at all.

Chapter Thirty-Four

In the ER, I lay on a gurney with my parents on one side and Delia on the other.

"We'll need an CT scan," the doctor—the same one who'd seen Kit the day before, incidentally—said, "once that stops bleeding."

"You think he broke my nose?"

"Oh, he definitely broke your nose. I'm more concerned with your orbital sockets."

"Her eyes?" Delia said. "Oh, God."

"They're pretty fragile," the doctor went on. "A blow to the face can damage them pretty easily."

"And how would you fix that?" Delia asked.

"Best case, we wait and they heal on their own. Worse case, surgery, which you may need for the nose, anyway."

"Surgery?" I said.

"We'll do our best to make sure it heals straight," he said.

He said a few other things, and my parents answered, but I didn't really hear because I was thinking: *Surgery.*

On my nose.

Wonderful.

The doctor stepped out. To my parents, I said, "If you guys are all here, who's with Kit?"

"Sebastian," Delia said. "They're like best friends now. I can't believe that guy hit you."

"I can," I said.

"You're lucky your friend shoved you," the doctor said. "It could have been a lot worse if you'd gotten the full force of that punch."

"My nose would be worse than broken?"

"He means you could have died," Delia said. "People die from getting punched in the face in real life. It's not like the movies."

My mother put her hand over her mouth and my father looked distinctly sick. I said, "Is she here? She must be here somewhere."

"I think she's giving a statement," Delia said.

"To the cops?"

"Yeah. They'll probably want you to do that, too."

I lay my head back against my pillow. "Would it be okay if I was alone, just for like five minutes?"

"Yeah," Dad said. "Of course it would. Come on, guys." And everyone got up and left.

I rolled to my side and looked at the poster next to me, which had little frowny faces describing the ten levels of pain. I'd given mine about a seven, but now I thought it was down to a six. It didn't help that my hand still hurt like hell, but at least it didn't seem to be broken. Unlike my nose.

It occurred to me that if they were putting me under and

going in and messing around anyway, I could let them go ahead and fix me the way they'd fixed Delia. I could look just like her if I wanted to.

Hell, the insurance would probably even cover it.

I imagined my face looking like Delia's, and a boy like Sebastian following me home from college and begging to sleep in my bed.

Well, maybe not like Sebastian. Maybe a linguistic wunderkind with nut-brown eyes and a cleft chin.

If I looked like someone else, would Greg have wanted me?

If I looked like someone else, could I have admit that I wanted him?

I closed my eyes and dreamed of a world where I was so pretty Greg D'Agostino couldn't take his eyes off me.

When I woke up, it was dark, and Delia was touching my shoulder. "Hey," she said. "Time for your CT scan."

I sat up a little. "How long was I asleep?"

"Half an hour. Probably stress and the pain meds."

"Oh. God. They didn't give me opiates, did they?"

She laughed. "No, I think it was just Advil."

"Oh."

"Delia," I said. "I'm sorry."

"For getting punched in the face?"

"For being horrible. To you. About the nose thing. I get it. I get wanting to be pretty."

She stared at my vital signs blinking on the monitor for a while. Finally, she said, "It wasn't that I wanted my nose to be pretty." I gave her the best incredulous look I could muster with my face all mangled. She said, "I just wanted it to be something I never thought about. I thought about it *all the time.* Every time I looked in a mirror, or saw a picture of myself, or walked by a reflective surface, I was thinking about it. I just wanted it to be like . . . like my chin or something."

"Your chin? What's going on with your chin?"

"Nothing! That's my point. I never think about it, like, ever. It's just there. I wanted my nose to be like that."

"Yeah," I said. "Okay. I get that, too."

She smiled grimly. "Does that mean you're thinking about getting yours fixed? I saw your face when the doctor said you might need surgery."

"No. No, I don't need it fixed. It's not broken. I mean, I know it's literally broken, but not . . . No." I adjusted the too-tight wristband on my left arm. "I'm not getting it changed."

"But you thought about it."

"Yeah. I thought about it."

"But why not—"

"It's just like you said. I need it to be something I don't think about. If I had it changed, I would always be thinking about it. I'd always be wondering when a guy was flirting with me if he'd still be doing it if my face looked like it used to. I'd just be focusing on it all the time."

"But aren't you focusing on it now?"

I sighed. "Yeah. But honestly, that's kind of your fault, no offense."

"My fault? Because I got a nose job?"

"Well. Yeah. I mean, I forgive you. I get it." I patted her hand, which was resting on my blanket. "The world's hard to live in, isn't it?"

"Yeah. It is." She looked at me and said, "I'm sorry for not thinking about how that would make you feel."

I touched the bandage over my nose. "Maybe I could just leave it like this? It's got a certain je ne sais quoi, right?"

She laughed. "You know the difference between you and me? You can pull that nose off. Because all anyone can see"—she poked me in the chest with two fingers—"is this."

"My stupendous cleavage?"

"Don't do that," she said. "Not everything is a joke."

"You poked me in the boob!"

"I did not. . . . Gah. Aphra."

"I'm sorry," I said. "I get it. And thank you."

When the scans came back, they showed a clean, nondisplaced break of my nose and no breaks whatsoever of my eye sockets. I also appeared not to have a concussion, though sometimes those don't show up for a while.

"Thank God for your ridiculously thick skull," my father said. Delia, by then, had gone home to make sure Sebastian and Kit had not fallen down a YouTube hole.

"She got it from you," Mom said.

"Thanks for that," I said. "So can I go home now?"

"They're going to splint your nose, and then we can go."

Bethany came in through the curtain. Like me, she was still in her uniform. She had a splint on the index finger of her right hand.

"What happened to you?" I asked.

She held up her hand. "Broke my finger."

"Punching the dirtbag?"

"Yeah."

My mother said, "I think we should go find out what happened to your checkout papers," and pulled my father out into the hallway.

Bethany sat down next to me. "You look like shit."

"Yeah. I've heard that."

"Is your chest okay? I think I might have hit you kind of hard. I didn't mean to."

"No, I know you didn't mean to. Thank you for trying to get me out of the way. The doctor said you probably saved my brain."

"Move over."

"What?" I said, but I was already scooting over to one side of the bed. She lay down next to me and took out her phone.

"Please don't take a selfie of us," I said. She looked at me like I was stupid. Then she turned on an episode of *My Little Pony*, holding the phone so we could both see it.

She reached out and held my unhurt hand with her unhurt hand, my right and her left, and we stayed like that until my mother came back with the discharge papers and it was time to leave.

Chapter Thirty-Five

On Monday, I went back to school.

After I shut off my alarm, I went downstairs to see if Delia could help me do something with concealer that would help cover up my black eyes. Instead, I found Sebastian sitting on the bed looking at the photo of me and Delia in our Sailor Moon costumes. The rest of the bed was covered with badly folded clothes, and his suitcase was half full on the floor. I couldn't remember whether his flight left that day or the next, because I'd been kind of distracted.

"Oh," I said. "Hey. Uh. Is Delia here?"

"She already left for her internship."

"Oh. Right."

"Yeah." He turned the picture toward me so I could see it. "Who is this?"

I fiddled with my ponytail. "Where'd you find that?"

"It was on her dresser this morning. Do you guys have another sister?"

"Um," I said. "That's, uh . . ."

He put his hand over his mouth. "Oh my God. Did she die? I'm sorry. Wow."

"No," I said. "No."

"Seriously, though. This explains a lot."

"No," I said. "We don't have a dead sister. That's Delia."

He looked at it again.

"Before her nose job," I explained.

I could see the scales lift from his eyes as he understood. He said. "Oh." And then he looked at the picture for a really long time.

"Well?" I said.

"Well what?"

"You don't . . . you don't have something to say about that?"

He set the picture on the dresser and went back to putting his stuff in his suitcase. "Look," he said. "I get that you're, like, the alpha around here or whatever, but my opinion on your sister's nose job is none of your business." He stuffed the last of his clothes into the suitcase before zipping it up.

It was . . . not an unrespectable thing to say, even though I really wanted to know what he was thinking, if he was disgusted by her earlier face or her current one or the plastic surgery itself. I wanted to know so many things. His face gave nothing away, like the whole subject was just a passing curiosity.

I said, "Okay."

I waited to see if he might change his mind, or ask me when she'd had the surgery, or why, or what I thought about it, or if I felt bad about it, or if I wanted to do it, too.

He did not say any of those things.

I said, "Are you really not going back to UVA?"

"I'm really not."

"So you're just going to make YouTube videos in Denver?"

"I actually don't want to go back to Denver. I'd rather be here."

"In my basement?"

He rolled his eyes. "In the DC area. I like it here. Plus, I could still see Delia on the weekends. It's just, I need a day job and a roommate, and I don't have either of those, so I need to go home and figure shit out."

"You need a roommate?"

"That's what I said. It's too expensive to live around here by myself."

I said, "I might actually know someone."

At lunch, I met Bethany in front of the cafeteria. People were staring at us; me because of my face (ha), Bethany because she now had a rep as an industrial-grade badass, which seemed to have overwritten her rep as the girl who got dumped in front of the entire school.

"Hey," she said.

"Hey," I said. "I really don't want to be here."

"Me either."

"You want to go off campus?"

"We can't," she said.

"Oh yes. We can. I mean, if you want."

I took her by the hand and walked to the back door, where Officer Barry was standing with his hands behind his back. "Hi," I said.

"Holy shit," he said.

"Yeah, right?"

"Does it hurt?"

"More to look at, I think." I smiled. "A seven-layer burrito might help with that."

He nodded and moved sideways to allow Bethany and me to go through. "Wait," she said, once we were on the other side. "That's it?"

"Yep."

"Seriously? You just tell him you want a burrito and he lets you out?"

"Yep. Come on, I'm hungry."

We walked the three blocks to Taco Bell in companionable silence. Finally, I said, "I'm sorry, by the way. Again. About the thing with Greg. You were right. I should have told him. I should have let you tell him. I don't know."

"I wish you'd just told me you'd been talking to him. You really should have."

I said, "Yeah. I know."

She kicked a rock along the sidewalk. I wondered how she was taking notes with her broken finger. I said, "You broke your hand for me."

She said, "You broke your face for me."

"To be fair, I actually didn't mean to."

"Yeah, well. Me either."

We walked some more. I wanted to make an excuse, because at the time, everything I'd done had seemed so reasonable. I'd made sure Bethany and Greg were happy, and I was just trying to subsist on Bethany's romantic bread crumbs, because I thought I could get away with that. I thought maybe it was the best I could do. I thought I could do that and still be a good person.

But the fact was, I wasn't a good person with a crappy face. I was a bad person with a crappy face. I'd told so many lies. I'd become such a shitty friend just so I could get some tiny scrap of what I wanted. Because what other way was there for me to be loved than from deep inside Bethany's shadow?

That didn't make it right, though.

"It's just," I said. "You don't know what it's like. You don't know what it's like when you know—*you know*—nobody's ever going to love you."

Bethany's face crumpled a little. "You think I don't know what that's like? Are you . . . ?" She snuffled and let out a sob or a laugh or both.

"What are you—"

"Aphra, Nobody wanted me around. Nobody *ever* wanted me around."

"That isn't true!"

"It *is* true. Do you know what it's like to be eight years old and have nobody want you? My dad left. My mom and my brother barely talked to me. The kids at school called me a weirdo. I had no one, Aphra, *no one*."

She pushed the button for the *walk* sign at the crosswalk. "I used to, like, hover on the edge of people's conversations. And then they'd give me this look like *What do you want?* So I'd leave, because you have to leave, you know? Nobody wanted me around! Do you know what that's like?"

"Bethany—"

"And then there you were! And you were so obnoxious, and you just started talking and talking and talking, and you didn't even care if I said anything back! You just kept going, like we were best friends. I thought you'd be gone the next day, but you weren't. You saved me a seat at lunch."

"Nobody wanted to sit by me anyway."

"Stop. You saved me a seat. You wanted me there. You wanted me around. Don't you get it? Nobody wanted me around before you. So don't tell me I don't understand what it's like when no one loves you. You feel like . . . like everything inside you is hollow. Like the place where you're supposed to feel loved or wanted, it's just *empty* and it *hurts like hell.*" She wiped her face on her arm. "I can't believe we're talking about this in the Taco Bell parking lot. I'm sorry, too."

"What are you sorry for? You didn't do anything!"

"Yeah, but maybe I did. What you said on the bus, you were right. I think I lean on you too hard. It's just, you're so . . ."

"Sturdy?"

"Well. Yeah, that's what I thought."

We moved out of the way of a mom getting lunch for her four little kids. Bethany said, "Did you really want that burrito?"

"I kind of did," I said. "Actually."

"Okay. Except I just remembered I didn't bring any money."

"It's okay," I said. "I've got you."

We went inside and through the line, and I got burritos for me and Officer Barry, and Bethany got three chalupas because apparently beating the shit out of someone burns a lot of calories and she was *starving.* At our table, I watched her eat the first one and then the second one. My face hurt, which made eating my burrito hard, so I had to cut it with my fork.

"I can't believe it's only Monday," she said.

Monday. That was right, it was. At least there wasn't practice after school. After therapy, I could go home and lie down for the rest of the night.

"Hey," I said. "Do you want to, like, come to therapy with me today?"

"What? What do you mean?"

"I don't know. Do you want to come?"

"To see Dr. Pascal? What would we talk about?"

"I don't know. Maybe about how we could, like. I don't know. Be better friends?"

"You're my *best* friend."

"Not better friends like that. But maybe how we could both, I don't know. Need each other less. A little less. Or . . . or we could talk about something else. If you want."

"Is that even allowed? If I just show up?"

"Sure. I'm the one paying her. Well . . . I'm not, but it's my session, so."

"Okay."

"Really?"

"Yeah, I'll go today."

Back at school, I slid into the back of my app design class and did my best not to make eye contact with anyone. We spent the class talking about how to convert apps between platforms, and then when the bell rang Mr. Positano said, "Aphra, stay a minute, please."

I reluctantly hung back.

"So," he said once everyone was gone. "I had another look at your Deanna app."

I nodded. I was tired and my face hurt and I wanted to go home.

"What I concluded was that you did the work, or you tried to. It was just too ambitious a project."

"Story of my life," I said.

"The fact is, if you'd turned it in and told me what was wrong with it, I would have given you at least a B. Why didn't you come to me in the first place?"

"Because . . . because it should have worked. If nobody had messed with it, it would have been fine. And I thought . . . I thought if you saw how it was giving out porn links and stuff, you'd flunk me. So I just . . . faked it. I didn't know what else to do. I guess I panicked."

"You know that was cheating?"

"Yeah," I said. "I know."

He flipped through the pages. "I read through these responses a little more carefully after our talk the other day," he said. "I probably should have guessed that these couldn't have been written by a real AI. They were pretty personal. And from what Greg was saying, it sounded like this went on for a while after you turned in the project."

I said, "Yeah."

For a second, he actually looked sympathetic. "For what it's worth," he said, "I do actually remember what it's like to be 17 and screw up."

I closed my eyes. "I pretended to be my best friend so I could talk online to her boyfriend."

"That is pretty bad. Why did you do that?"

"My superego overwrote my id," I said. I shook my head,

"Actually, I'm already in therapy once a week talking about this, so if you don't mind, I'd rather not rehash the whole thing."

"Fair enough," he said. "But I also remember what it's like to be 17 and screw up and have that screwup turn into an avalanche." He bent down to catch my eye and smiled. "I believe you're more than this mistake. As for your project," he went on, "it just so happens that I'm teaching this class again over the summer, and I may have made an inquiry into whether someone could take this class for credit recovery, and the answer may have been yes."

"Credit recovery?"

"It means you take the class over, and your F gets wiped out and replaced with whatever grade you earn over the summer."

But I was supposed to be working this summer. At crew camp. I'd been looking forward to it, especially now that Bethany wasn't mad at me anymore. We stay in these cabins near this beautiful river and it's really fun and there are s'mores. "But," I said.

"Does that not seem fair to you?"

"No, it's extremely fair. I just . . . I'll have to figure out how to do it."

"Well, you're going to have to think about that." He smiled. "Let me know what you decide."

"Right," I said. "Okay. Thanks, Mr. P."

When Bethany and I got to Dr. Pascal's office, I realized she hadn't heard the story about me getting punched, because she'd been eating her yogurt and she dropped her spoon. "Hey," I said. "So this is Bethany, she came today."

I saw Dr. Pascal's eyes go from my face to Bethany's messed-up hand and knew immediately what she was thinking.

"She's not the one who hit me," I said. "She's the one who saved me."

I sat down on the couch, took six mints out of the bowl, and handed three to Bethany, who said to Dr. Pascal, "It's nice to meet you."

"It's nice to meet you too," Dr. Pascal said. "I hear you're a really great friend."

Chapter Thirty-Six

The summer seemed long without Bethany there for six weeks.

While she was off rowing, I spent my mornings in summer school and most of my afternoons watching Kit while my dad worked on his medieval tax documents, Mom worked on some article about early English novels, and Delia went to her internship.

I hadn't ultimately needed surgery on my nose, so once my black eyes faded, I was left looking the way I've always looked, no better and no worse.

I did, however, move my Russian 101 class up to the summer session, so on Monday and Wednesday evenings, I went off to NVCC to be in a class with about 30 other people who wanted to learn Russian. It was weird being the youngest one there; lots of the students were the same age as my parents or even older. And it turns out that Russian is actually a lot harder than Latin, which had always been pretty easy for me. On my first test, I got a C and thought about dropping the class, but my parents talked me out of it.

I saw Greg when I was at the pool with Kit a couple of times. When Kit skinned his knee one day, Greg was the one who put a Band-Aid on it while I stood awkwardly off to one side. My bikini had been relegated to the dustbin of history (which is to say, I threw it out and hoped everyone else forgot it existed), and I was back in the comfort of my red one-piece.

"Hey," he said after, when Kit had run off to play Uno with his friends because it was break. "You don't have to be like that. Like, you don't have to pretend you don't know me."

I made a circle on the concrete with my toe. "I was trying to give you some space," I said.

He smiled at me as if to say, *And yet, here you are.*

I said, "Yeah, I know, sorry, I know it's weird that I keep coming here, but my brother's friends all go to this pool, and—"

"It's fine," he said. "You can go wherever you want."

"Oh. Okay, yeah. So are you . . . are you done with that poetry project you were working on?"

"The independent study? Not yet. I think maybe three more weeks. It's taking longer than I thought it would."

"Yeah," I said. "I've actually been taking Russian this summer."

"At NVCC?"

"Yeah, just the 101 class."

"With Pavlova or Rodin?"

"Rodin. It's kind of harder than I thought it'd be."

"Yeah, there's a big learning curve in the beginning." He picked up the first-aid kit and stood. "See you."

"Bye."

I went back to sit on my chair and work on my Russian conjugations.

Люблo

Любишь

любит

I looked up and Greg was at the foot of my deck chair. "Hi," I said. "Again."

He looked over my shoulder and pulled the pencil out of my hand, changing Люблo to Люблю. "There," he said. "'I love.'"

"Oh. What did I write?"

"Nothing, it wasn't a word."

I shouldn't say this. I shouldn't say this. "I miss talking to you."

"Yeah. Me too." He shaded his eyes with his hand. "A lot. Actually. I kind of hate you for that." He rubbed his temple like he was thinking of what to say next. "Why didn't you just tell me?"

The answer was so hard. I didn't have a good one. "I . . . I guess I was being selfish and selfless at the same time, and it just kind of turned into a mess. I don't have an excuse." I closed my eyes. "I've made so many mistakes."

Some kids were doing cannonballs off the diving board, and the girl in the chair was yelling at them to go one at a time.

Greg said, "You said 'Я вас любил.'"

I loved you. I closed my eyes and nodded. "Yeah, I did."

"любил. You loved. Past tense. So not anymore."

I didn't answer. He said, "Aphra."

"I'm trying to decide what answer doesn't make things worse."

"The truth," he said, "wouldn't make things worse."

I opened my eyes. "It isn't любил." I sighed. "Not I loved. I love. I'd give you the future tense, too, but we haven't learned it yet."

"любить," he said. *I will love.*

I swallowed and said, "I should probably write that down, thanks."

Greg said, "You were wearing this red shirt."

"What?"

"That day, in health class. It said *This shirt normalizes menstruation.*" He laughed. "I thought it was so gross."

I remembered the shirt. Mostly I wore it to annoy Delia. "What day are we talking about?"

His face colored a little. "The day I gave you the Heimlich. You probably don't even remember."

"No," I said. "No, I remember."

He looked away. "I never put my arms around a girl before that."

I stared at him, not speaking. He said, "You were wearing that stupid shirt, and you told off that guy, what was his name?"

"Kieran." Only I actually hadn't told him off. Greg had.

"Kieran, right. I thought you were going to put him through a wall, but then I thought, *This is what a girl feels like.*"

My own arms were wrapped around myself. "Sorry if I traumatized you," I said.

"Would you shut up?"

I pressed my lips together and looked away.

"Anyway, I guess I had a crush on you after that. For a while."

"A. A while."

His eyes met mine. "A while," he repeated. He got up and said, "If I don't go up in the stand, Shannon's going to kill me."

"Okay," I said. "Bye."

"I don't forgive you."

"Okay," I said. "I deserve that."

"I'm still really, really mad."

"Yeah."

"I probably won't ever forgive you."

I nodded.

"Fuck it," he said, and he stepped forward and put a hand on either side of my face and leaned down and kissed me.

It wasn't slow or soft. It was so unanticipated that I hadn't even been able to prepare myself for it. I just thought, *Greg D'Agostino is on my mouth,* and kind of froze up, and then I thought *Greg D'Agostino is on my mouth,* and then I realized I was missing out on my chance to kiss him back, and then I stopped thinking at all.

It didn't matter that I'd barely ever kissed anyone. It turned out I did know how to kiss him back, and I did.

With all the times I'd fantasized about this moment, I realized that kissing him was nothing like I thought it'd be.

It was so much realer. And so much better.

It was also a little shorter. He pulled back and stood up.

"Sorry," he said. "Won't happen again."

I touched my mouth and nodded. He sounded like he meant it, which meant he probably did.

"I'm going," he said.

I nodded again, and he turned to go. Finally finding my voice, I called out, "Greg!"

He turned around, like he'd been hoping I'd call him back. I smiled and said, "До свидания." See you later.

He said, "До свидания."

• • •

Bethany came home from camp the next week, tanned and looking like she could crack walnuts with her biceps.

"Wow," I said when I saw her. "Your arms are bigger than mine now."

"I know, right? I'm a beast."

"So how was West Vagina?"

"Good," she said. "Really good, actually." She grinned wickedly. "Surprisingly humid, though."

I laughed pretty hard.

We were sitting on the front steps of Bethany's house enjoying a random August cold snap. The pool where Greg worked was probably empty, but I hadn't seen him since the kiss. I kind of didn't want to, at least not yet. This way, I just got to remember that it happened, and I didn't have to worry about what came next. He kissed me, *me,* Aphra, my own self, knowing who I was and what I'd done and that I didn't deserve for him to kiss me. That seemed like enough for right now.

I couldn't quite understand why he'd done it. I felt like love was something you had to earn, and I hadn't earned it, not at all. I'd unearned it. And I mean, it wasn't love, it was just a kiss, I got that. But still, I wondered about it. There was probably a name for something like that.

"I can't believe I have to go back to work on Monday," she said. "I told Doug I'd work the lunch rush. I don't know what I was thinking."

I laid my head on Bethany's shoulder, and she rested her head against mine. "You're amazing," I said. "You know that, right?"

She shrugged.

"No, really. You just . . . you deserve to be happy more than anybody else I know. And you're a hell of a lot braver than I am."

"Ha ha," she said.

"No, that's the truth. You do the things you're scared of. You put yourself in front of the guy you like. You get the hardest job you can think of. Me, I . . . I couldn't even admit that I had a conversation with someone."

"That was kind of cowardly."

"You don't have to rub it in."

"You know what, though?"

"Hm?"

"I am happy. I'm happy about pretty much everything in my life right now."

"Well, yeah, except for me getting you dumped."

"No, I'm over that. I mean, yeah, I got dumped, but you know, it's okay. I liked him. But I don't think he was the one or anything. I just think there's someone out there who's really going to get me, you know? Like you do. And that was never going to be him." She laughed. "He doesn't even get the difference between chain and positional isometry."

"To be fair," I said, "I don't exactly get that, either."

On the lawn, some robins were hopping around, making eyes at each other, two flashy red males and one plain brown female, because that's how birds work—the men have to do all the sexual labor, and the women just kind of show up and pick somebody.

"Hey," she said. "I have something for you."

We went inside to her bedroom, and Bethany opened the box she keeps on her desk with all her little sentimental treasures: a necklace from her great-grandmother, a few blue ribbons from summer swim team in middle school, a handful of bracelets with charms of ponies and cupcakes and mathematical symbols. Her dangling radish earrings, which she'd gotten special for our joint Halloween costumes—we'd been Hermione Granger and Luna Lovegood, and it had gone over so well that we'd worn them for three years until our cloaks had gotten too short, and by then we'd been too old to go out anymore anyway.

In the bottom was a folded piece of paper, and she took it out, saying, "I made this the first day I met you," and she handed it to me.

I unfolded it; it was a drawing, in crayon, of two ponies with human faces with a rainbow stretching between them. One was blue and the other was pink, and underneath she'd written *Me and Aphra*. We were standing on little clouds, and we were both smiling.

I looked for some clue in the picture that she was pretty and I was not, but there was nothing. We both had two eyes, a watermelon slice of a mouth, and no nose at all.

I said, "What do you see? When you look at me?"

She tucked a stray piece of hair behind my ear. "I see my friend."

"No," I said. "No, come on. Just say it."

"What do you want me to say? That I think you're ugly? I don't think that. I don't see that."

I sighed a breath of unhappiness from the bottom of my lungs. I tried to believe what Dr. Pascal kept saying—that I was afflicted not with ugliness but with a broken mirror. But it was hard. It was very hard. And the mirror that was broken, I didn't think it was only mine. I whispered, "Please," but whether it was a sarcastic *please* or a genuine plea—*Please, make me stop feeling this way*—I couldn't say.

I imagined a different kind of fairy tale from the ones I'd read, no ugly duckling or beauty and the beast, a story where the princess gets a choice: to *be* beautiful or to *feel* beautiful. I think if I could choose, I would rather feel it.

Bethany said, "I love the way you look. Because you look just like my friend." She kissed the crown of my head.

I put my arms around her and mashed my face into her shoulder. "I love you," I said, and in that moment, I *felt* it—it was so much more than just words. If it weren't for eight-year-old Bethany, with her silly sense of humor and her giant soul, loving me exactly the way I was, I would have turned into someone else. I wondered who I would even be now, if I'd still have my big mouth and my panache, or if I would have shrunk down into some smaller, lesser version of myself.

I didn't know what kind of love that was. I didn't deserve it. I hadn't earned it. It was so big and so much and so many things, like it was too big for just one word. I couldn't define it or label it or draw a circle around it; it just *was*, this big, beautiful feeling. All I knew for sure was that I was so, so lucky that the universe had created Bethany Newman and put us in the same place at the same time.

"You philia me," she corrected.

"No," I said. "I love you."

About the Author TK